TRUE BLUE

THE IMPERIUM COAST SERIES
BOOK 1

ALACIA HALE

Cover Design by Insta-love Graphic Design

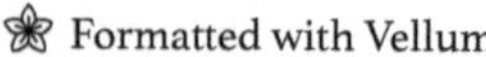 Formatted with Vellum

For the little girl who thought we would be writing the next great American novel...

we write smut now 😈

TROPES, TAGS, &
CONTENT WARNINGS

Tropes

Multi-POV, 'why choose', university romance, best friend's brother, roommates, enemies to lovers, forced proximity

Tags

MM, MF, MMF, MFM, golden retriever x black cat x doberman vibes, biting means I love you, instalust, instalove, you can take it, plant daddy, obsessed MMC, anxious FMC, let her win, rock paper scissors decides, trying to find him a nickname, eyes on me, baby, sweetheart, blue, sunshine

Content Warnings

This book deals with themes that may be distressing to some readers including grief, neglect, non physical abuse from a parent, homophobia, and characters dealing with anxiety and panic attacks.

True Blue also contains open door sex scenes between two and three characters at a time and include mentions of impact play, choking, dominance, snowballing, biting, and voyeurism. The main characters are all 18+ but still only freshman in college.

If any of these elements are distressing to you, *please protect your mental health.*

1

Janette

Dread returns to the pit of my stomach as I round the corner. The seven-foot white brick wall surrounding our house looms several hundred feet ahead, making me slow my feet even further as I start to cool down from the run I just finished.

I can't stay here.

That was my only thought an hour ago when Christopher dropped me off. My last high school final just had to be at eight a.m. The only saving grace was it being history, the subject I pass in my sleep. Always remembering dates and timelines comes as both a blessing and a curse, but for school, it weighs more on the blessing side. Still, my nerves felt like they were foaming up under my skin as I walked into the gym with the other 358 Northridge seniors at five minutes to eight.

Finally walking out two hours later gave me a rush of euphoria. I did it. I finished high school. One of the things I had been counting down to for years was finally over.

Of course, Christopher had to burst my joyous bubble as quickly as possible.

He called me over to his ugly green mustang idling next to the gym and I suppressed my sigh as I walked over. My mom probably sent him. Pushing the passenger side door open from the inside, Christopher bopped to the blaring stereo, flashing me a quick smile as I sank into the cracked leather bucket seat. I tried not to grimace as I attempted to get comfortable. The second my door closed, Christopher took off, the tires squealing a bit as they slid away from the school.

Huffing, I shake my head at the irony of my last exam feeling like a breeze, while a fifteen-minute drive with my boyfriend felt more like a patience test.

One more thing to thank the Senator's crafty little mind for. Any opportunity to get another foot in the door is worth it, even if her daughter pays the price.

I wanted to run the second I realized she wasn't home. I haven't seen her in three days. Today was my last high school final and she probably has no idea. Sandra Davidson 2.0 remembering her own daughter's schedule? Unheard of.

Cold beads of sweat crawl down my face as I stop outside the dark metal gate set into my mother's beloved wall and start to input the code. My fingers shake and my blood rushes with the fading adrenaline of my run. It compounds as the anxiety my runs are meant to dispel settles back in. Trimmed magnolia trees create an arched canopy over the street and shield me from the sun, but the moist humidity of the Georgian summer clings to my skin, soaking a few black curls to the back of my neck.

Maine never got this hot in June.

The thought brings all others to an abrupt halt as my heart jolts with the reminder. I close my eyes and just listen to the mechanical sounds of the gate slowly swinging open.

Sixty-eight days. I only need to make it sixty-eight more days.

Another deep breath.

Opening my eyes, I immediately focus on the perfect cream siding and glass paneled double doors of my mom's dream house. My eyes burn as I remember walls made of big, mismatched stones and a worn cornflower blue door a thousand miles away. The sound of Dad's voice calling me in from across the street echoes in my ears and I swallow the ball of spikes sitting in my throat.

Jogging up to the white monstrosity, I glower at the mansion and its clean facade mocks me. I stop to stretch more, using my cool down routine as an excuse to spend a few more minutes outside. Tall shrubs line the front lawn, trying to block the view of the brick wall and make the enclosed space seem less like a cage.

Entering the sterile battleground, I get blasted by the chilly air conditioning in the foyer. White walls with abstract black and grey art greet me as I slip my sneakers and sweaty socks off, ripping my hair tie out and letting my mashed curls out of the sloppy bun I threw them in. I lean down and right my shoes, lining them up with the perfect row of the Senator's pumps and wedges. Standing, I stare down, feeling the absence of the muddy green polyester rug with mismatched work boots and different sized sneakers flung across it in our haste to get inside. Focusing back on the bleached oak panels below my feet, I kick my running shoes out of line, smiling at the small sign of disarray.

Heading past the stairs, I toss my socks into the laundry room on my way to the kitchen.

I startle a bit as I enter, finding Mom sitting on a bar stool at the island, documents and papers scattered around her as she writes something on her iPad with a stylus. Glancing at the clock, I realize it must be one of her randomly free lunch hours. Got to make it seem like you check in on your daughter every now and then when you live in the public eye.

"Went for a run?" she says, pushing her glasses up her alabaster nose without looking at me. She wears her usual black pantsuit and pumps, resting them on the bottom rung of the bar stool she rigidly perches on. Flashes of her old, stained overalls, wide grins, and messy buns hit me like they always do during the random times I've found myself alone with her in our mausoleum the last five years.

"Yes, but it's hot out there," I say, as I pass her and head for the cabinet beside the fridge, grabbing a glass. I hold it under the spout in the refrigerator's stainless-steel door, waiting for the glass to fill with cold water and repeating my countdown mantra internally so that the words on my tongue stay in place. She doesn't say anything more. Doesn't ask about my finals or celebrate me finishing high school. Anger bubbles in the back of my throat, but as mad as I am, there's no point in starting a fight when she's letting me leave in two months.

Mom shuffles some papers behind me, and I sip my water, turning to face her and stepping back toward the island. "Hopefully, it's not as humid on Friday," I say, unable to hold myself back. I place my glass down and grip the edge of the smooth granite.

Mom glances at a document on her right, her pin straight hair slicked back into a tight bun at the top of her head. It doesn't move a millimeter out of place as she stares down at the packet of paper. She picks up the stapled pages, starting to flip through as she murmurs, "Friday?"

I frown, taking another sip of water before I answer, needing to douse the mounting fury in my veins. She forgot. Of course, she forgot. "Graduation," I say once I've swallowed. "It's at one."

Mom's head swivels from the document to me, unfocused eyes slowly clearing as she gapes across the island at me. "Fuck, Janette." She slaps the papers down on a pile in front of her. "And you're just telling me this now?" She picks up the iPad, angrily swiping and typing across the screen. "I have a charity appearance scheduled. Guess I'll have to get Pietro to rearrange things."

I drink more water, watching her type before the sound of an email sending goes off. "The reminder went out a few weeks ago," I say, gripping the island edge again to stop myself from clinking my nails across the top. The words seem to get lost before reaching her. Stepping back, I add, "You don't have to cancel, Mom. Christopher will be there, so I won't be on my own." The sentiment sours my stomach and I dump the rest of my water out in the sink.

"And miss your graduation?" she says. I turn back, but her head is still bent over the iPad. "What would the press say if they found out?" Her head pops up to give me an incredulous look. She starts typing again on her screen and her phone starts ringing under the piles of papers surrounding her.

I head back out to the hall as she picks up the call. "Pietro? Yeah, Janette just told me about her graduation on Friday, so we need to reschedule..."

Rounding the corner, her voice fades as I climb the dark wood stairs. More modern art passes me as I climb, and then clean white walls lead to my bedroom door at the other end of the floor from Mom's. Like every time I make this trek, my mind fills with the ocher walls lined in mismatched frames and beaming faces from a different life. My stomach churns as I continue walking and flex my fingers.

I push my door open, immediately closing it and leaning back against the wood. Taking a deep breath, I look around at my different sized cork boards covering the sky-blue walls, each covered with pinned photos of my life back in Maine. Pictures of me smiling, of Mom smiling, of Aunt Tati, of Dad. Pictures of the before era.

"Hi, Dad," I say, touching the framed photo of him on my dresser as I pass. He's smiling, brown eyes rolled upward as he watches a small, toothless me ugly laugh atop his shoulders. His dark hands hold me by my calves, and I feel the ghost of that comfort waft over my skin.

The black and white Imperium Coast University logo on his sweatshirt makes me smile as I walk into my bathroom, pulling my sports bra off and starting the shower. Only sixty-eight more days till I'm there. Till I'm there with Layla.

Waiting for the water to heat up, I drag my leggings off and study my reflection for a moment, smiling at my disheveled state and sweat covered umber skin. My phone buzzes on the sink.

Grabbing it to read the notification, I smile, finding a text from Layla reminding me to read the letter she just emailed. Excitement zips through my chest, tickling my nose like champagne, as I rush through my shower and quickly towel off, running some cream over my wet curls.

Donning one of Dad's baggy old t-shirts and some pajama shorts, I grab my laptop and plop down on my giant beanbag. Taking a second to look at the photos of Layla, Axel, Gwen, and I spread out around my room, I wait for my emails to load, tapping my nails against the keys. The ping of a notification finally sounds, and I click on Layla's latest email, sitting back to read.

From: Lay_Cliff_96@gmail.com
To: BlueJay_DSon77@gmail.com
Subject: RE: WRITE BACK ASAP

Hi babes!

Sorry I haven't been able to write lately. Packing up Gwen and my dorms and shoving them into Dad's car, then unpacking everything at home and getting settled back in here has been a whole thing. I think I slept for a full week after I got home. I'm already thinking about two months from now when school starts again though. At least this time I'll have you there! Don't get me wrong, I love our email tradition, but I cannot wait to actually talk in person!! Five years overdue, babes.

Can't believe it's been that long since we've seen each other. Since Mom and Uncle Levi died...

Sorry, that was a downer turn. Back to happier thoughts. I passed all my classes! None of them were that hard, but I still got nervous for some reason? Filled my gym requirement with that juggling class I was telling you about. I had to record myself juggling my practice clubs for the final, so I attached the video. Figured you would love the laugh.

Are you done with finals yet? Axel still has two more this week and then his graduation is next Friday. He's still annoyed that I skipped seventh grade, but I think he liked being an only child at home with Dad last year. Plus, we each have separate graduation parties now, so it'll be all about him at this one. I'll get him back next year and beg Dad for a combined twin birthday party for old time's sake. Remember when he threw a fit over the half Spider-man, half Bratz birthday cake? He always sucked at sharing.

Gwen's going to RA again this year so you might get her if you end up in the West Tower. I still wish we could room together. Stupid freshmen floor rules. Although, those same rules do make it so that I don't have to room with Axel. That would be a nightmare. Maybe second semester we can figure something out. I convinced Dad to let me get a single this year after the disaster that was Amber. Thank God she dropped out at the beginning of this semester. Let me know when you get your orientation packet so we can Facebook stalk your new roommate and try to figure out if she's going to be a psycho or not.

How's Christopher? I'm rolling my eyes as I type that, because I know you know I don't care, but I feel like I have to ask since you won't just BREAK UP WITH HIM ALREADY. And before you start typing, I know your mom would freak, but you're leaving for school soon anyways so who really cares?

Write back ASAP. I'm so freaking bored here in Maine. Can't wait to see you!

Love you,
Lay

I smile, rereading the email and feeling the ever-present ache of the distance between us. Reminding myself of my countdown, I open the attached video file at the bottom. Lay pops up on my screen, standing a few feet away from the camera and holding three different colored clubs in her hands.

"Hi, I'm Layla Clifford, and this is my final presentation for PED 161: Juggling." Lay takes a step back, looking up and taking a deep breath before tossing one of the clubs into the air. She throws the other two up afterward, concentrating and biting her tongue as she catches and throws the clubs for three minutes straight. I smile as she catches them all at the end, chuckling as she shouts excitedly and dances around for a second before facing the camera again. "Thank you," she says and the video cuts on the last frame. Layla smiling at the camera stares at me.

I stare back for a moment. We've sent pictures over text and with emails before and follow each other on all our social media, but not having seen my best friend in person in five years always makes me savor a new look into her life back home. She started dyeing her hair a few years ago and the colors change rapidly, so I always like seeing what new one she's chosen next. It's blue in the video, her dark roots visible in her part. She'll change the color soon, if she hasn't already, since the grow out has gotten an inch long and the dye looks faded. She wears a hoodie in the video, her mom's bakery logo printed across the chest, and I wonder if she raided one of the storage boxes in her garage to pull it out.

Clifford Cupcakes has been closed ever since the accident; Uncle Jack unable to run it after Aunt Tati and Dad died. I thumb the logo on the screen, hearing the greeting bell that rang every time someone walked into the shop.

"Janette!" Mom's voice startles me from the memory, and I close my laptop.

"Yeah?" I call back, standing. Mom stands at the threshold, staring down at the phone in her hand while her other one rests on her hip.

"Are you doing anything today?" she asks, not looking up. She never looks in my room.

I toss my laptop onto my desk. "No, I was just going to relax since finals are done."

I wait for her to say something about finishing school, but Mom just nods, typing something out. Her French manicured nails tap across the screen as her eyes rove the keyboard. "Get dressed. Pietro thinks he found you a summer job that can get us some good media exposure for the campaign."

I close my eyes, counting down in my head before opening them again. I read online that's supposed to help when you're stressed. So far, I've seen minimal results. "What is it?" I ask as I walk back over to my closet.

"Something with Habitat for Humanity. Chris is going to do it too. Casual clothes will be fine for today, but if Pietro gets you the interview he's working on, we'll need to get Dotty to get you and Chris coordinated campaign approved outfits." I turn to complain, but she's already walking away, heels clicking against the hallway's hardwood floor. Fighting Mom on this would only lead to her sending her whole team in to convince me how good of an opportunity this is and how it will look on my resume in the future. I already know that when Sandra Davidson 2.0 wants something, she'll have someone else fight dirty for her.

Changing into some jean shorts and a less baggy tee, I grab my laptop and type out a quick response to Layla.

From: BlueJay_DSon77@gmail.com
To: Lay_Cliff_96@gmail.com
Subject: RE: WRITE BACK ASAP

Hey Lay,

Glad you made it back home in one piece! I remember the camping trips when Uncle Jack would pack every square inch of the car around us so that he didn't have to rent the U-Haul trailer Aunt Tati always tried to sell him on. I'm imagining getting your and Gwen's stuff back from college being a similar experience.

I'm done with finals, but Mom is roping me into some summer job thing at Habitat for Humanity with Christopher. Probably some optics thing that she's trying to leverage for a fundraiser or something. I might not be able to write a lot if I'm working there and at the Humane Society. Mom probably forgot I volunteer there in the summer, so we'll see how packed my schedule gets.

I'm dying to see you too! Your juggling video made me miss you more. Keep sending me updates on the school countdown. I'll let you know about the roommate thing when I get my packet.

What classes are you taking this year? I got to change the prepicked one's last week, but I'm still in mostly gen-eds. HIST-156: Medieval History is the only one that counts toward my major. Dr. Howards is teaching it. Did you ever have him? Any insights you can share?

I'll write back when I can. Send me pics of Gwen and Axe in your next email.

Miss and love you,

J

I send off the email and close my laptop. My heart

squeezes for a sec and I bite my cheek, putting on the game face I've perfected to hide in front of Mom.

Walking down to the front door, I find her standing next to it and talking on the phone. "She just came down. We're leaving now." She nods toward the shoes lined up on the mat, my sneakers mysteriously back in the perfect row beside her. I slip them on, grabbing my shoulder bag while she continues her conversation.

Tuning her out, I follow as she walks out into the sweltering heat, repeating my countdown. *Sixty-eight days, sixty-eight days, sixty-eight days.*

2

BENTLEY

"**C**ongratulations graduates. Your next adventure awaits!"

My smile tries to crack my face in two as the stillness of the sea of robe clad graduates explodes into a flurry of motion. The cacophony of cheers and whistles pierce my ears as Principal Desmond steps away from the podium and walks off stage. I stand, throwing my cap into the air, and watch it disappear amongst the hundreds of other emerald green airborne squares. Placing my fingers in my mouth, I whistle, and the sound melts into the other cheers and whistles going off around me as the applause from the bleachers surrounding the football field creates a dull thrum in the background.

Camera flashes go off and for a second, my smile dims. Most of the flashes probably emanate from proud parents wanting to capture the excitement of the day. But I also know some belong to telephoto lenses, zoomed in, trying to get a shot of Heather and Michael Marshall's son for the tabloids. Shaking off the ever-present itch of being watched, my chest heaves, and my smile returns. I glance around and just let the excited energy of the atmosphere invade my body, mingling with my own ecstasy. All around me, people hug and squeal and try to move through the crowd to find their loved ones.

Focusing on the bleachers, I attempt to find familiar faces as the caps rain back down upon us. Most of the crowd is either looking down as they shuffle out of their seats toward the field, or they're stopping to wave at the people around me, having found their person in the green sea. Giving up, I search the crowd level with me and easily find my target, having seen her face nearly every day since I was five.

Mira stands near the stage, dark brown waves blowing around her face as she tries to push it back over her shoulders without the graduation cap to hold it in place. Her honey brown eyes search the throng of green clad seniors, not spotting me as her head swivels around. Having sat in the front row throughout our graduation thanks to her alphabetically superior surname, Adams, she has the luxury of standing in front of the stage to survey the crowd, all directly in front of her. Meanwhile, I was stuck in the middle with the other M's waiting forever for them to call Marshall.

I weave through people, smiling and nodding to those that recognize me and those that don't. Mira stares up at the bleachers, probably hoping for a glimpse of her own parents in the melding crowds that are now mostly on even ground. It makes it nearly impossible to find anyone just by sight.

A clear path forms from me to her when I get about three feet away. I zoom through it, grabbing Mira by the waist, and spinning us around.

She squeals and starts swatting my shoulders. "Bent! Put me down!"

I grant her wish and beam. "We did it. High school is officially over."

She smiles up at me and shakes her head, eyes returning to the crowd around us. "And yet you're still acting like a child."

"I don't think a child would have been able to pick you up."

She rolls her eyes and sticks her tongue out at me, reaching up to poke the dimple in my left cheek.

I laugh, swatting her hand away. "Who's being childish now, Mir?"

She slaps my chest before gasping and waving at someone over my shoulder. "Autumn! Over here!" I turn and open a space for our grim-faced friend to quickly slide in next to me. Her dark blue eyes flash, jaw set, and arms folded tightly over her chest.

"Shhhhh!" She grabs Mira's hand and pushes it down. "I'm trying to avoid my parents finding me so quick." Heat colors the skin beneath her freckles, shading her fair complexion.

"Pretty sure they're going to find us eventually," I point out, gesturing to the stage behind us. "We're kind of the whole reason they're here."

"Yeah, but the longer I avoid them, the less time I have to spend at my grandmother's with them fawning over Sage." She rubs her forearm, and I throw my arm around her shoulders, squishing her into my side.

Autumn's parents doting on her little sister on the day of her high school graduation doesn't surprise me, but the usual spark of anger I feel toward the Greens kicks in anyway. "Don't worry, we'll come kidnap you in an hour or two. No way we'd leave you with your family all day."

Autumn smiles up at me and Mira nods at her before

going back to searching the shifting throng of people surrounding us.

I poke her side. "Settle down, Mir. April will find us eventually." Mira's mom probably already has eyes on the three of us and is just finding the politest way to push through the crowd.

"Harley came," Mira whispers. Autumn glances up at me while Mira is distracted and raises an eyebrow. I shrug.

"He usually goes where Ramsey does," I comment. Autumn nods. Mira always gets jumpy around her older brother's best friend, ever since he started avoiding her like the plague a few years ago. Autumn and I usually try to soften the blow whenever we know Mira is going to be around him.

Mira glances back at us and takes a deep breath. "Yeah, that's probably why he's here. I didn't even know Ramsey was going to show." She laces her fingers together, but the tension in her shoulders remains.

"At least none of us fell off the stage." I jostle Autumn's shoulder with my arm, and she gives me a small smile, but glances over her shoulder, probably realizing her parents will find her sooner now that we aren't moving.

"I thought you were going to do a backflip," Mira says, poking me in the stomach and grinning.

I shrug. "Guess stage fright set in."

Autumn rolls her eyes and Mira audibly scoffs. "When have you ever gotten stage fright?"

I shrug, looking away from them. I didn't remember to do anything flashy when I was walking across the stage. The second I got to the top of the stairs, shouts and flashes from the edge had stolen my attention. A couple school security officers tried to usher them off, but the half dozen paparazzi that managed to stick around kept trying to get me to look over at them or stop and pose. When I shook Principal Desmond's hand, she apologized and patted me on the shoulder, posing for the school photographer as the people at the stage edge went wild. The only thing I could focus on was not falling in front of all of them after that.

"There you all are!" April Adams bursts through a hole in the crowd and walks over to us with a huge smile eating up half of her face. Wearing a blue sundress and sandals and sticking out amongst the other ultra-wealthy Emerald Grove Preparatory parents, her presence banishes all the frustration previously foaming up inside me. "Congratulations!" She grabs Mira in a fierce hug as Ramsey, Harley, and Conrad walk up behind her and fill out our little circle.

"Thanks, Mom," Mira mumbles against her shoulder.

Pulling back, April holds Mira at arm's length with tears in her eyes. "I can't believe you're done with school!"

"Smothering, Mom," Ramsey says in a low voice over her shoulder.

"Hush," April responds, but releases Mira who smiles at her brother. April turns toward me and Autumn, as Mira's eyes quickly flick to Harley who pointedly stares to the left of everything.

"Congratulations you two!" April holds her arms open, and I release Autumn just in time for her to wrap an arm around each of our necks as well. I bend down to help her out and return the hug with a smile. Her familiar warmth makes me close my eyes for a moment. Ever since I met Mira, April has treated me like I'm one of her kids, sliding into my life as a second mother without complaint or judgement.

"Thanks, April." I hug her a little tighter.

"Thanks, Mrs. Adams," Autumn replies and smiles up at April. I catch Ramsey rolling his eyes.

"I can't believe you guys are all grown up." April sighs as she releases us and steps back, placing a hand on either of our cheeks. Mira shakes her head over her mom's shoulder.

"I can't believe you're all following me to the Coast," Ramsey mutters, then looks up surprised. He smiles, eyes darting between Mira and me and openly avoiding the third graduate in our midst. "Just missed me so much the last few years, huh?" He throws his arm around Mira's shoulders and squeezes her as she tries to shove him off.

"I'm just following this one," I point at Mira with my thumb who rolls her eyes. "Figured we've gone to the same schools our whole lives, why change a good thing?"

"Oh please. You're the one with alumni in your family. I'm the one following you, Mr. Instant Admission." Mira rolls her eyes at my grin. "And of course, Autumn had to come along. No way we'd leave her here to fend for herself." Mira finally breaks free of Ramsey's hold when he freezes up at the mention of Autumn. She reaches forward, gripping Autumn's hand as she smiles. Ramsey scowls and looks over at Harley who glances at Mira with narrowed eyes before looking away again.

Conrad stands off to the side in a dark blue three-piece suit, watching everything mutely. April gives him a pointed look and he steps forward, reaching out and gripping Mira's shoulder. "Congratulations, Amiria," he whispers when she looks over at him.

Mira beams. "Thanks, Dad."

I smile. Someone taps my shoulder and I turn, nerves jumping only to find my grandfather behind me, alone. He opens his arms, and I lean in. "Congratulations, dear boy," he says softly in my ear as I return the hug.

"Thanks, Grandpa." We lean out of the hug, and I glance around. "Mom and Dad couldn't get out of filming?"

Grandpa's eyes crease a little further as he shakes his head slightly. "Afraid not. But they sent Ryan to capture the whole thing." He nods over his shoulder, and I glance back, seeing my parent's go-to stateside videographer wearing a chest mounted camera rig and watching a monitor in front of him as he films us from a few feet away.

I bark a laugh, giving the camera a wave.

"And they gave me this to pass on." I look back at my grandfather and he hands me an envelope.

I take it from him, and he puts his hand on my shoulder. Inside, I find a letter in Mom's curly handwriting. Scanning the words, I smile at the congratulations and well wishes as well as the comments on how fast I grew up. Near the end they apologize for not being able to make it and how much they miss me. My heart aches for a moment, but stutters at the last line.

But we will both see you soon. Love, Mom and Dad.

My mouth pops open and I look up at Grandpa who has a smirk on his face. He hands me a second envelope and I tear it open faster than the first and find plane tickets to Croatia then another to Spain. The first one leaves in two days.

"They're flying you out to their film locations?" Autumn asks, on her tiptoes so she can try to read the tickets over my shoulder.

"Yeah!" I exclaim, tipping the tickets so that she could

see them. "I fly out in a couple days. Looks like I'm traveling Europe for the summer!"

"You're going away for the summer?" Mira asks, overhearing me telling Autumn.

I turn back toward the Adams family and nod, showing Mira the tickets. "Mom and Dad are having me meet them on location and spend the summer with them!" Mira smiles and I feel my stomach twist. "Fuck! This ruins our plans." I read the tickets again, frowning. "I won't get back till the week before school starts."

Mira shakes her head and Autumn follows. "It's fine, Bent," Autumn says.

"Yeah, go see your parents," Mira adds. She nudges my shoulder. "I doubt you'll miss us much while you're lounging on beaches in Europe."

I grab them both around the waist and drag them into a tight hug. "I'm still going to miss you guys," I say, pulling back. "Even from the nude beaches." Mira slaps my shoulder and I laugh. "Don't worry, I'll send pics." Autumn shoves me away.

"One more gift for you," Grandpa calls, making me turn back toward him. He wears the indulgent look he sometimes has when he is around me and my friends. I smile at the sight of it. It usually meant he was going to sneak us cookies before dinner or let us take a ride in Dad's mustang while he was out of town.

He hands me a third envelope, this one bulging in one spot and I open it slowly, feeling the weight of the item inside. The card I pull out sings Pomp and Circumstance as I open it and read the quick message scrawled in my grandfather's chicken scratch. *Don't take the turns too fast* is written at the end of the message and I turn the envelope over. A key fob falls into my palm. The Mercedes logo shines at the top. My jaw goes slack, and I whip my head up to meet my grandfather's eyes.

"No way," I whisper.

"She's parked in the lot," Grandpa says as his smile widens. He steps forward and grips my shoulder to turn me back to the bigger group. "In your name and everything."

I've been begging my parents to let me get a car for the last two years, but they kept telling me it was unnecessary since they had several cars at the house that I could use whenever. But I wanted one that was mine. More specifically I wanted a Mercedes that was mine. Just mine.

I beam as Autumn and Mira laugh.

"Still can't believe you didn't notice when I stole your license," Autumn says.

"You guys knew?" I look between them. I didn't think they were good at keeping secrets, but now I'm not so sure.

"We helped him with the registration," Mira says, pride playing in the tone of her voice. She's a terrible liar so keeping this secret for however long has probably been killing her.

"Autumn Dahlia Green! We have been looking all over for you!" Autumn's mother breaks through the people around us and pushes her way into our little circle as Autumn cringes slightly into my side. Mrs. Green wears a pinstripe pants suit and austere expression, blonde hair pulled perfectly back in a tight ballerina bun at the back of her head.

"Hello, Tina," April says, smiling and forcing Autumn's mom to look away from her daughter. Autumn's father stands directly behind his wife, placing a hand on her shoulder.

Mrs. Green seems to realize the rest of us are here suddenly. "Hello, April," she says with a strained smile and nods to Conrad, Ramsey, and Harley before turning to Mira and me. "Congratulations, Amiria and Bentley."

"Thank you, Mrs. Green," we both mumble.

She turns back to her daughter. "Let's go, Autumn. Your sister is already at your grandmother's practicing for her summer recital, and I want to make sure she's nailing her fouetté." Mrs. Green reaches forward and grabs Autumn's arm. Autumn gives us all a half smile as she follows in her mother's wake.

"Oh, Tina!" The trio stops and turns toward April. "We're having a little graduation party at our house right after this. You're all welcome to join!" Autumn smiles at April, but Mrs. Green frowns.

"We have a small family party to attend, but we might be able to send Autumn over after," Mrs. Green says, looking to her husband who nods.

"Perfect! Congratulations again, sweetie." April steps forward and hugs Autumn despite her mother's grip on her arm. Autumn glances at us over her shoulder, and I mouth *Jailbreak. One hour.* She smiles and releases April, letting her mother pull her away.

Ramsey glares at the trio as they disappear, but I can't tell which member has offended him most.

April watches them go, before turning back to the rest of us. "You're welcome as well, Tyson."

"Thank you, April. We would be delighted," Grandpa answers with a smile. He always raves about the cooking at April's parties.

"Well then, let's get going," Mira says, looking around and realizing we're still standing on our high school football field with the majority of the senior class and their families around. "The sooner I'm away from Emerald Grove the better."

I nudge her with my shoulder as we all start to walk around the stage and toward the parking lot. "It wasn't so bad."

"That's only because you didn't have to constantly fend off questions about how the 'Regal Ravens' pack are doing in college," Mira says, using air quotes and rolling her eyes as she references Ramsey and his group of friends. Ramsey jogs up beside her and chuckles.

"I'm sure our admirers were glad you were there to give a full report," he says.

I laugh. "I'm pretty sure they stopped asking after the second time she told them you were all probably jacking off together in your dorms."

Harley chuckles quietly behind us, and Ramsey touches his chest in mock outrage. "Saboteur!"

Mira shoves him. "Like you lot don't do fine on your own. I doubt me telling a few cheerleaders you guys were gay really had any effect on your game." She smiles but her eyes flick back at Harley for a second and I see the look slip.

Ramsey shrugs, facing forward and missing the moment. "It'd be weird to try to get with anyone in your grade anyways." He shakes his head as we stop at the crosswalk and wait with another group of graduates to cross the road to the student lot. "Way too young."

April and Conrad catch up to us as we wait and I glance over at them, just catching April scowl and whisper something that makes Conrad's jaw clench. I turn back to the group, angling myself between Mira and her parents.

"Think you guys will finally let me into your clubhouse when we get to the Coast?" I ask, seeing Mira glance back at Harley again. He stands with his hands in his pockets and stares at the ground with a frown.

Ramsey rolls his eyes. "I'm sure you and Mira will make

your own clubhouse when you get there, like you always do."

I laugh and we start walking across the street. I twirl the silver ring on my new key fob around my finger. "Wanna find my new baby?" Mira's eyes light up and she nods, jumping to grab the key as I hold it higher, out of reach.

The brownish-red brick facade of Emerald Grove looms ahead. We all walk through the opening in the chain-link fence surrounding the school's student parking lot. I double click the lock button on the fob and a couple beeps go off to our left. I share a smile with Mira and Ramsey laughs behind us. Mira takes off toward the sound and Harley rolls his eyes as Ramsey and him walk after her. I go to follow, but my green graduation gown swishes around my legs and starts to trip me up in the wind. I stop to take it off and ball it up before jogging to catch up.

A shout carries on the wind and stops me. I glance back to find Conrad and April among the people making their way into the lot. They stand off to the side, by the entrance still, a good ten feet away. April is gesturing and her mouth is set in a hard line when she stops. Conrad stands over her, jaw tense and arms crossed.

I look back over the lot to find Mira. She's two rows over, still running with Ramsey and Harley walking after her. I catch up to them and elbow Ramsey before nodding my head over his shoulder at his parents. He looks back and sees them before turning to find Mira, Harley doing the same. Mira stops a little bit ahead of us and looks around at the cars near her. I beep the Mercedes' horn again and she shoots off to the next row over, where the sound came from.

"Come on Bentley!" she yells, and I throw my gown at Ramsey before following her. We reach the car, and I stop right in front of the hood, fingering the little silver logo in the middle.

Mira jumps up and down beside me. "Unlock it!" I click the button, and she runs to the passenger side.

Green covers my eyes and I push the fabric away, my graduation gown falling to the ground.

"Not your pack mule, Marshall," Ramsey says to me and crosses his arms.

"They still arguing?" I whisper, watching Mira climb into my new car. She starts pushing buttons on the dashboard before looking through the windshield at me and waving me in.

"Probably," Ramsey whispers back. He nods toward the driver's side of the car. "Go on. We'll make sure she doesn't see." Harley nods behind Ramsey, looking back toward the entrance.

I walk over to the driver's side door, letting my hand glide along the shiny black paint as I do. Getting in, I put my hands on the steering wheel and smile, taking in the smell of the leather interior.

Mira shakes my arm. "Start it, Bentley!" I laugh and press down the brake while pushing the start button to my right. The engine purrs and Mira claps. "This is so cool. You have a car!"

"Most people we know have cars, Mir." I roll my shoulders, studying the lights and controls on the dash. "I've driven you to school every day for the last year and a half."

She looks over at me. "Yeah, but this is *your* car, Bent." I smile and she follows suit.

A knock on the window startles the two of us and I huff out a breath when I see Ramsey standing next to my door. I roll down the window.

"We're going to head back to the house with Mom and

Dad." He leans down to look across me. "You riding with him, Mir?" She nods and he pats my shoulder. "Nice car, Marshall," he says before walking off with Harley.

I roll the window back up as Mira puts her seat belt on. I adjust the mirrors and buckle my own belt. "Ready to go celebrate our academic freedom?"

She giggles. "It'll be a short-lived freedom. Freshman year starts in less than 3 months."

I shrug and put the car into drive. "A window of freedom then." I pull out of the spot and marvel at the smoothness of the ride. Looking back in the rearview mirror, I watch my forgotten graduation gown float back to the ground and Emerald Grove disappear as we drive out of the lot.

AXEL

I pet the split leaves of my monstera deliciosa, tipping the glass of water and pouring around her pot until the soil starts to drain. "There you go, Delilah. Now, Dad's going to water you while I'm away, but I promise I'll remind him to check your soil every week and facetime at least twice a month." I check the soil of my golden pothos, Zeke, on the shelf next to Delilah and add some water to him as well.

"Aren't you supposed to be packing?" Layla says, appearing in my doorway, face stern. Her baggy grey hoodie and sweats do nothing to dull the intensity of her posture, arms crossed with one hip stuck out touching the doorframe.

I ignore her, grabbing my mister and spritzing my arrowhead vine, Miles, who sits on top of the cluttered bookshelf.

Layla's foot starts tapping so I turn back to her. She raises an eyebrow at me through her thick, black-framed glasses. My sister can be intimidating when she wants to be.

"Probably, but what's the point?" I say, plopping down on

my unmade bed and leaning back against the wall it's pushed up against. "We don't leave till Sunday, and I can't take my plant babies." I pick up a lacrosse ball laying in the crumpled mass of grey comforter and start throwing it in the air and catching it. "Why bother with the rest?"

Layla rolls her eyes at my dramatics. "Maybe because you only have forty-eight hours till you move out of state, dumbass. Kind of hard to do so, if all your clothes are still strewn about like the after photos of a tornado disaster." She walks into my room, looking around at the mess I've left it in and eyeing the half-filled boxes scattered around. Groaning, she grabs a converse off the floor and tosses it into a box. "You're not even halfway there."

I shrug, watching her go around and pick up random things off the floor in an attempt to organize. Her shoulders are tense, and she tugs on the end of her firetruck red-dyed hair every time her hands are free. I continue to study her, watching for the twitch, as I say, "I'll just wear the same outfit every day. It'll make it really easy for people to remember me quickly."

Lay snorts, but the sound feels forced. "Yeah, I'm sure that'll make you super popular on campus. A six-four dork walking around in the same green and blue Hawaiian shirt and ratty old converse, slowly smelling more and more putrid." She stands up, facing me again. "You're going to make so many friends."

I chuckle, glancing over her face to see if anything tics. "I'm six-one, Lay."

She shrugs. "Whatever." We may be twins, but I got all the growth genes, coming in at almost half a foot taller than her.

Leaning over to pick up a discarded lime green button

up, her shoulder twitches and I lean forward, stomach knotting.

"What's wrong, Lay?"

Layla startles, standing up quickly and turning away from me to start folding the shirt. "Nothing's wrong," she murmurs, draping it over the back of my desk chair.

I roll my eyes, holding the lacrosse ball in my lap. "You're a shitty liar, sis. You hate packing. Plus, I can feel your nerves from here." Wiggling my fingers at her, I say, "My twin senses are tingling."

Layla rolls her eyes back, grabbing my favorite purple cardigan off the floor.

I get comfortable on the bed again and wait in silence for a bit, before asking, "What's up, Layla?"

She huffs, tossing the now folded shirt into a box and plopping down on the empty chair. I lob the lacrosse ball at her, and she catches it. "J is going to be at Imperium Coast."

The back of my neck prickles at the mention of Janette. Layla isn't the only one who hasn't seen her in five years. Tamping down my reaction, I catch the ball when she tosses it back and raise an eyebrow. "Okay," I lead, but she stays silent. I send the little white sphere back to her hands, but she just throws it back, not saying a word.

Sighing, I throw it back at her. "And that's got you nervous because?"

She catches the ball in front of her face, dragging it down to her lap and picking at a spot peeling in the seam. "What if we don't get along anymore?"

I shake my head, but she keeps staring down at the ball in her hands.

"What if it's been too long and we've grown into different people, or seeing me brings up all the feelings of losing her dad again, or seeing her reminds me too much of Mom?"

Her voice gets softer as her words speed up. The knot in my stomach loosens a bit but clenches at the mention of Mom. "What if she's just been writing back to me to be nice and I've been thinking she's still my best friend this whole time?"

"Layla," I say, making her look up at me. "You two have been emailing back and forth for five years. No one keeps a tradition like that up for *that* long if they aren't best friends. And Janette has known us since we were all in diapers on the same playmat. I doubt she's going to see you and immediately write you off. She's not her mom." My voice hardens at the end.

Lay nods but starts gnawing on her bottom lip as she glances around the room again.

I lean closer to her. "She loves you, Lay. Besides, didn't you say she doesn't really have many friends in Georgia?"

"Yeah, she had a tough time after Aunt Sandy moved them down there, so she didn't really make any close friends. I think she thought her mom would move them back here eventually." She gets up, leaving my ball on the desk behind her, and starts folding more colorful clothes as she picks them up off the floor. "She's said a couple times that she's lonely there and can't wait to see us all again when we get to the Coast."

I nod, watching her pick up and pack my stuff. Her posture is less tense, and I relax a little further. "And she's said hearing from you makes her feel less alone there, right?"

"Yeah," she says, dropping a pair of pants into a box. "But, what if—wait how did you know she said that?" She turns to face me, forehead scrunched as her eyes light up. Guilt twists in my gut. "Have you read our emails?"

I shrug, threading some of my comforter through my fingers. "You left your laptop open, and I was curious how she was doing." Layla scoffs and I pick my head up to look her in the eye. "You weren't the only one Aunt Sandy took her away from," I say, voice harsher than I intended. Aunt Sandy may have been Mom's best friend, but I will never forgive her for abandoning Dad and taking Janette away from Layla when we all already lost enough.

Layla's eyes soften and she walks over, climbing onto my bed and sliding over till her shoulder touches mine. "I miss Mom," Layla whispers.

I stare at the wall across from me, finding the picture of Mom in front of her bakery. Dad, Aunt Sandy, and Uncle Levi surround her as they all smile in front of the *Grand Opening* sign. It's tucked into the pin board Gwen made for me, concert tickets and random pins surrounding it. Mom's reddish-brown hair is long and frizzy, her belly round with Gwen, as she beams at the camera and Dad stares down at her with a similar smile. "Me too," I say and turn toward Layla. "Seeing Janette is going to bring up old feelings again. For both of you." I wrap my arm around her shoulder as she nods. "But Gwen and I will be there too." Picturing Janette, smiling at her mom's campaign event on Instagram, I repeat, "For both of you."

Layla nods again, leaning her head on my shoulder. We sit together for a little bit, the silence comfortable since we've sat in these feelings before. We'd been in a similar position right after Mom's funeral, Layla sticking to my side through the whole thing and barely talking the entire day. A week later, she had barely left the house, only moving from her bedroom to the living room couch when Dad poked his head in and tried to rally her to get up. I knew I couldn't do anything about losing Mom, drowning in my own feelings around that, but Janette was still out there. Layla came down to breakfast for the first time on her own the day after

I suggested emailing Janette since we didn't have her new number yet.

"I'll be there for you too, Axe," Layla says suddenly, lifting her head up to look at me. "Perks of having the nerdier twin go to college first, I already know the whole campus and which bars will serve us underage." I chuckle.

"Neither of you should be drinking yet," Gwen says, standing in my doorway with her hands on her hips. Our goody-two-shoes older sister always keeps her nose clean, even when she's sticking it where it doesn't belong.

I roll my eyes at her. "Yeah, 'cause you've never had a drop of alcohol, right sis?"

"I'm almost legal," she says, walking into my room and eyeing the mess similar to how Layla did when she showed up. "You two are not."

"Almost is still not legal, G," Lay says, scooting off the bed. Standing near each other, I note the jarring differences in my sisters, Lay in loungewear and fuzzy socks and Gwen in a patterned dress, black hair curled and pinned up on either side of her head. Still, I see why people initially think they're the twins out of the three of us. Minus their hair colors and Gwen's heterochromia, they share all of Mom's features, including her average stature.

"How do you live in this?" Gwen asks, pointing to the mountain of dirty clothes next to my scattered pile of shoes on the floor by my closet.

I stay on the bed, raising an eyebrow again. "Did Dad send you guys to harass me?"

Gwen picks up a loafer I don't remember the last time I wore, searching for the match through the scattered pile. "We leave for the Coast in two days, Axel. You need to get packing."

I slouch down, huffing out a breath, and eyeing my

plants across the room. "I can throw all my clothes into some bags in under an hour. What more do I need to pack?"

Layla hands Gwen the matching shoe, turning back to the box she had been slowly filling with clothes and sitting down to fold more of my stuff.

"Shower stuff, laptop and charging cords, bedside lamp, sheets, towels, laundry basket, pictures for your walls." Gwen ticks off each item on her fingers as she spouts her list.

"Spare contacts, extra solution, back up glasses," Layla adds, not looking up from the shirt she's folding to push her own glasses up her nose. Gwen points at her but looks at me with a nod.

I cross my arms over my chest. "I have time."

"You really don't," Gwen says, turning toward my closet and pulling open the door against the clutter stacked in front of it. "Go down to the garage and grab another box, please."

I scoot off the bed, knowing they won't leave if I try to stop them. Layla stands with the box she just filled with random clothes, handing it to me as I head toward the door. "Put this by the stairs on your way."

I glare down at her as I take it and head out of my room, passing the floor to ceiling patchwork of framed photos as I walk down the hall toward the living room. Mom's smiles make me grin and my eyes snag on a picture of Layla, Janette, and me covered in mud and laughing in Aunt Sandy and Uncle Levi's backyard. Remembering how Janette started that mud fight after I pulled her hair, I shake my head, continuing past.

Dad sits on the couch, typing on his laptop as a soccer game plays on the TV across from him.

"You had to send the troops in after me?" I walk past

him, dropping the box next to the stairs beside the pile of packed crates and suitcases my sisters have already filled.

Dad chuckles, glancing up at me with his glasses balanced on the tip of his nose. "They volunteered when I asked how far along you were. I take it things are moving faster now?"

"They've taken over the packing. I've been relegated to box retrieval." I pout for a moment, walking into the kitchen and passing the breakfast nook. I open the garage door right next to it, shivering as the chill of the dark room permeates my tee shirt. I don't think a car has entered this garage for the entirety of my life, two rows of storage shelves taking up the middle of the cement floor. I weave through them, going to the mountain of boxes in the corner my family tends to hoard whenever we get a decent sized one. Picking one at random, I turn to leave, my eyes automatically trailing over to the pile of bakery equipment sitting in the opposite corner of the room.

An industrial spiral mixer, rolling sheet pan rack, and dough sheeter sit together collecting dust, Mom's bakery stickers stuck to the side of them. I can't help but glance over at them every time I come in here, a stabbing ache striking me between the ribs each time I see them. A warm feeling hits me every time I see her photos in the halls or smell the bottle of perfume Dad keeps on his dresser. But the equipment always makes me feel like we failed her. Clifford's Cupcakes was Mom's dream, and we couldn't keep it alive after she died.

I pull my eyes away from the pile and take the box into the kitchen, shutting the garage door behind me.

"You going out tonight?" Dad asks as I walk past.

I stop in the threshold of the hallway to turn back.

"Mason's having a party, but I've been trying to find an excuse not to go, so no."

"I thought you broke up with him!" Layla's voice shouts from the open door of my room down the hall.

"I did! Hence the need for an excuse!" I shout back, shaking my head at Dad.

Dad nods, pushing his glasses up his nose. "Tell him your dad is requiring your presence at a final family dinner and game night before his children leave him all alone in an empty house." I roll my eyes as my sisters come rushing out of my room, flying past me to stand in front of our dad.

"You'll be fine," Layla says, at the same time as Gwen assures, "You can call us anytime, Dad," her mother hen tendencies on full display.

"I'm not picking up if I'm in class," I say, leaning against the edge of the wall on my left. Dad chuckles and Layla glares over her shoulder at me.

"I'll be fine girls, but I will probably check in every now and then." They each nod. "On each of you," he adds, leaning around them to pointedly look at me with a smirk. "And I do want to have one last family night before you all leave. If you're all free?"

"Of course," Gwen says, taking out her phone and typing quickly on the screen. Cancelling whatever plans she had probably.

"Can we play Scrabble?" Layla asks, glancing over at me as I groan. "What? Scrabble's fun!"

"For you, maybe. You always win." I fold my arms over my chest, the box in my hands brushing against my side as it ends up behind me.

Layla walks over, grabbing my forearm with both of her hands. "Please, Axe. We can play Uno after!"

I look skyward, avoiding the pleading eyes she's aiming at me. "Fine," I sigh as she starts shaking my arm.

Dad laughs again, turning back to his laptop. "Go finish packing," he says, Gwen already heading past us down the hall, face still bent over her phone. "I'll order sushi and we can go get ice cream at Scoops after dinner, before the games begin." He waggles his eyebrows over his wire framed glasses, some white and grey hair sprinkled amongst his naturally black strands. I smile.

Layla nods, dragging me by the arm down the hall and back into my room. Tossing the box onto my bed, I sit down on my desk chair, swiveling back and forth a bit.

"Why is Mason inviting you to parties?" Lay asks, grabbing the box I just brought in and walking over to my dresser. Gwen sits on the floor, still organizing my shoes and placing them into another box.

I roll my neck, hearing a satisfying pop as my spine cracks. "I don't know. He can't take a hint?"

"Did you hint at a breakup or actually break up with him?" Layla starts pulling things off the top of the dresser and dropping them into the box, now balanced on her hip.

I let my head fall back, staring up at my ceiling. "I broke up with him. Very direct. 'We are over' wording." I close my eyes, focusing on breathing through my nose and out through my mouth.

"That why you made out with Sofia in front of everyone next to the fire at Tyler's last week?" Layla asks. Gwen's head shoots up in my periphery, but she stays silent.

I tip my chin back down, narrowing my eyes at Layla. "How'd you hear about that?"

"I ran into Kiera at Weston's yesterday," she says, glancing over at me. I mutter a curse under my breath, knowing Kiera was probably all too happy to gossip about me to my own twin sister. "She filled me in when she realized I skipped the bonfire."

Silence stretches as they wait for me to say something, but I don't.

"It's probably good you guys broke up. Long distance starting college never works," Gwen says, standing up to start pulling clothes off hangers and folding them on the end of my bed.

Layla nods. "Plus, he's a dick."

I shake my head, smiling and getting up from the chair. Taking the box from Layla's hands, I open my top dresser drawer and start pulling out the random shaving accessories and contact cases I've thrown in there. Layla smiles at me, sitting down on my bed and organizing the clothes Gwen has folded. As we work on packing up my room, they each chime in with different things we'll have to do when we get to the Coast, and my excitement to leave starts to grow.

4

BENTLEY

My foot taps impatiently against the carpeted floor as I lean against the elevator wall emblazoned with the Imperium Coast University logo. Pressing the button for the eighth floor, I wave to Autumn and her new roommate, Aria, as they head for the stairs, only needing to go up two floors from the lobby of West Tower dorms. Mira, April, and I stand in the elevator in silence, each leaning against a different wall, the two of them feeling docile from all the pasta we ate at lunch. I feel energized though, finally able to go see my room.

Pulling up to the Coast this morning, I practically bounded from the car the second April put it in park outside the West Tower dorms. Mira had been quick to follow, the two of us taking a moment to just stare up at the massive building, half covered in crawling ivy with bare brown brick on the other side. Rounded turrets lined the two front corners of the ten-story structure, making the facade look like a skinny greenish castle with two massive black doors set in the center. One sat propped open, glass sections in the other revealing the cozy looking lobby on the other side. A massive stone fireplace took up over half the wall across from the entrance with plush looking chairs and a couch, an industrial elevator sitting beside the set up. Other new students waltzed in and out, some carrying bags and boxes while others passed them empty handed.

Grinning at Mira, I started bouncing on the heels of my feet, up until Ramsey knocked into me, carrying one of Mira's overstuffed boxes and telling us to get out of the way and start helping.

Six rounds of carrying Mira's stuff up to her room later and the initial excitement had died down a bit. My room was being set up by movers Mom and Dad hired and the longer it took for them to finish, the more antsy I got.

Now, coming back from the lunch April bought all of us, that initial excitement was back tenfold. Mom texted me while we'd been out at Romero's.

MOM

The movers are all set with your dorm.
We're so proud of you!! Let us know if you
need anything.

I quickly texted back a thanks and let Grandpa know I was all set. He texted back a similar message to Mom's.

The elevator door opens, and we step out. I lead the way to suite 815, turning left down the hall and walking a couple of feet, finding my dorm basically right next to the elevator. A pile of furniture lines the side of the hall next to my suite's door, a couple of chairs and side tables stacked on top of each other in a way to try to leave room for people to pass by.

"It's not that big of a deal, Gwen," a bored voice drifts through the open door as I stop dead in the entryway of the suite. The voice belongs to a caramel-haired guy, leaning against the wall across from the door. His smooth, golden skin stretches over angular cheekbones and a straight edge jawline. Dark brown strands with red and gold highlights stick out around his head and over his ears, giving him a bit of a frazzled, just woke up look. Rich mahogany eyes flick over to the three of us, stuck in the doorway since I froze when I saw him. His arms stay loosely folded over his torso, the curve of his biceps on display under the sleeves of his loud yellow cutoff tee shirt. It shows off his flat midriff, more olive skin on display. The elastic band of his athletic shorts grip his hips, and I drag my eyes back up to his, startling when I realize I'm caught checking him out. The corner of his lips twitch as our eyes lock across the room, before he examines Mira and April, poking their heads in around me.

Heart pounding, I step out of the way, entering the suite and looking around. A soft leather couch takes up the living room area, L-shaped and completely different from the two green cloth couches that were the center of the common room in Mira's dorm. A black barrel chair finishes the set, framing a dark wood center table with random décor pieces and two remotes on top. Matching side tables sat on either side of the setup, potted plants taking up a quarter of the surfaces. A large TV hangs, mounted on the wall opposite the couch and my switch and Xbox sit in a new shelving unit underneath it, probably already hooked up and ready to go. The room looks completely different from the provided set up Mira has in the dorm two floors below mine and I don't need to look at the pictures adorning the bookshelf to know my parents are the reason for the upgrades. Still, their smiling faces bracket mine in each photo, the collection a tradition we have in each new country I visit them in.

Amongst the furniture stands Gwen, Mira's new RA who

we met this morning, and a man wearing dark framed glasses, but resembling both Gwen and the guy across from us in different ways. Gwen's hair is a less grey version of the black on the older man's head, but his skin tone is an almost exact match, save for some light wrinkles dusting the corners of his eyes and forehead, for the guy I'm assuming is Axel Clifford. My new roommate.

Gwen gestures around, saying, "It's like six building violations, Axel. And where did all the furniture go?" before noticing the three of us and quickly lowering her hands, eyes wide and cheeks reddening.

"Hello," the man beside her says, stepping toward us, eyes locked on April next to me. "I'm Jack, Axel's father. And this is my daughter, Gwen." April steps forward to take his hand when he offers it, smiling up at him. I can see Axel in my periphery, feel his eyes rove over me, and I stand totally still until I feel them slide away. With a glance, I see him check out Mira in a similar fashion.

"I'm April Adams," April says, letting go of Jack's hand and sliding her arm over Mira's shoulders. "This is my daughter Amiria and her best friend Bentley." She nods over to me, and I put my hands in my pockets, keeping my eyes on Jack and Gwen even though I feel Axel looking at me again like an itch under my skin.

"Mira is one of my freshmen, Dad." Gwen steps forward, her giant smile from when we first met back in place. "I met her and Bentley this morning. I didn't realize you were Axel's roommate." She looks at me and I smile before glancing over at my new roommate again. He unfolds an arm and gives a curt wave before tucking it back in against his chest. A smirk paints his lips, but the direction goes toward Mira, and I take a small step forward, standing between them. The move surprises me for a moment, unsure if I actually did it to protect her or just to get his attention back on me.

Ignoring the moment, I ask Gwen, "Are you my RA too?" already knowing she isn't but needing to refocus on the other people in the room. My pulse is racing, and I can feel sweat start to slick my palms. I've never been shy about my sexuality, having dated men and women, but I tend to be more cautious with guys I'm attracted to. I'll wait till they show their hand first before I do anything. No need to make my new roommate uncomfortable if he's not into guys or just me in general. I've also never been this struck by someone and now I just have to casually live with him.

Gwen shakes her head with a tiny giggle. "No, you have Sean. He was here earlier. I just came to see Axel and Dad before he left." She glances around at the living room setup again, the corners of her mouth falling a bit. "Did you do all this?"

I recoil a bit, knowing my parents mean well, but how it looks to other people when they do things like this. "No, my parents sent people. I can text them to figure out where the other furniture went." I turn to Axel, rubbing the back of my neck to keep myself grounded. "Sorry, they somehow managed to be overly hands on while not actually being here."

Axel shrugs, grinning. The view of his beaming smile nearly bowls me over. "It's fine with me. I couldn't bring my plants down with me so thank your parents for all these new ones." He glances at a couple on the table near him with a smile. "Gwen's just a bit of a goody two shoes." He looks to his sister, another smirk at play.

"Axel," Jack says sternly to him.

Gwen shoots him a glare before turning back to us.

"That'd be great. I'm sure Sean will want to know so their disappearance doesn't fall back on him."

I nod, not wanting to get anyone in trouble, but Axel responds to her before I can say so. "I doubt he cares. Didn't seem like it earlier." His eyes meet mine as he pushes off the wall. "I took the left bedroom; hope you don't mind."

I shake my head, not trusting my voice at the moment and grab Mira's hand. I tug her toward the door of the right bedroom, the excitement from down in the parking lot back in full force. Turning the knob, I lead us into my new room, grinning as I meet a complete replica of my bedroom back home. Posters from my favorite bands line the walls above the queen-sized bed taking up half the room and clearly a replacement of the standard twin Mira has downstairs. It's covered in a black comforter and several red and blue plush pillows. A soft checkered rug lays beneath it, covering the center of the floor. My shoes sink into the shag as we move further into the room.

"Oh my god, they're monsters," Mira teases.

I try for a look of disdain, but the warm feeling in my chest forces the grin on my lips to remain. "They're insane, that's for sure," I say. Sometimes having Hollywood stars for parents isn't the worst. We may not be all together as often as I wish, but they tend to overcompensate for that in extravagant ways.

Mira bumps my shoulder. "You love it though," she whispers, eyes sparkling when she looks up at me. I shrug, glancing around again before we walk back out into the living room. Axel now sits, sprawled out on the barrel chair and swiveling on it lightly with one foot on the floor. He watches his dad and April as April laughs at something Jack says. Gwen stands over Axel, quietly saying something down to him before they all turn toward us.

"Everything in place?" April asks. I nod, waving her to come see my room.

She touches Jack's arm as she walks toward us, and my eyebrows shoot up, peeking over at Mira and seeing her notice the same thing with a frown. April follows me back into my room and I try to ignore the fact that she's missing her wedding rings as I show her around.

"This looks amazing, Bentley. Heather and Michael outdid themselves." She smiles at me, eyes showing the sincerity of her words. I can hear the others talking in the living room, but the sound is muffled standing next to the window beside my bed.

The view from this floor shows the entire campus, a continuous road looping around the walled off stone edge with four entrances marked by iron gateways running perpendicular to each other. The gravel walking paths weave throughout the different cropping's of more brick and ivy-covered buildings and open grassy areas. Trees frame the roads, branches arching over in some places and dotting the campus in greenery. New mixes with old as the modern science building and domed athletic center sit off on the east side of campus, covered in shiny windows and clean cream walls. The East Tower dorm spire looms straight on in the distance, identical to this one and marking the other side of campus.

And dead in the center sits the looming cathedral that started it all. Campus was supposedly built around it after the church sold the building to the founders of Imperium Coast who modeled the rest of campus around the Gothic style. Spires and blue-grey brick mark every part of the building, with intricate marble carvings and heavy stone stairs. The cathedral was gutted, repurposed into the library, which Grandpa always told me felt like a sacred space when he went here.

April pats my shoulder as we look outside and I wrap an arm around her shoulders, squeezing lightly. "Thank you," I say quietly, remembering all the times she was there when my parents couldn't be.

She beams up at me, arm squeezing me back around my waist. "Of course, sweetie."

We stand together for a couple more moments before I let go of her shoulders and offer her my elbow. She drops her arm from around me, linking it with mine and we turn around. Walking back into the living room, we find tension in the air as Axel now stands, closer to Mira than before, but Gwen stands in front of him, seemingly between Axel and Mira.

Jack has his hands in his pockets and head tucked downward. "I should probably say goodbye to Layla before I go."

"Are you walking out?" April says beside me.

Jack looks up at her, his eyes pinched slightly as he nods.

"I should probably get back as well." She unlocks her arm from mine and hugs me again, wrapping both around me this time. I hug her back, closing my eyes for a moment.

After we release, she walks over to Mira, putting a hand on her cheek. "Have a great week, baby. I'll see you on Friday." They hug and my eyes drift over to my new roommate, who watches the exchange with envy burning in his eyes. Ignoring the urge to find out what's wrong, I look back at Mira and April as they separate.

April turns toward Jack. "I'll walk out with you."

He nods, stepping forward to clap Axel on the back in a quick hug. "See you in a few weeks, son." Axel tips his chin once and Jack drops his hand. I watch the exchange, suddenly feeling the absence in the room and understanding the earlier look in Axel's eyes.

Gwen turns and squeezes Axel's shoulder before facing their dad again. "I'll go with you to see Lay, Dad." Jack nods and gestures for April and Gwen to lead the way. April turns back and waves at Mira and I before they all walk out, leaving the door open in their wake.

Mira immediately turns to Axel once we hear the elevator doors close in the hallway. "I really am so sorry. I shouldn't have asked about your mom like that."

I raise an eyebrow, but the two disregard me as Axel shrugs.

"It's fine. Dad wasn't exactly being subtle with *your* mom."

I agree with him, but Mira bristles at his implication. He follows it up with a smirk. I feel my guard start to rise.

Axel doesn't seem to notice, barreling on. "Guess it's fair for me to ask where your dad is now?"

I cross my arms over my chest, stepping in front of Mira and knowing exactly why this time. "Back off, dude," I warn. His smile seems to dim for a second.

Mira's hand touches my arm as she steps out from behind me. "No, he's right. I asked about his mom so it's only fair."

I keep my eyes on Axel, but he looks away, running a hand through his hair.

"He's in Helsinki. He has businesses all over the world, so he travels a lot." She shrugs but dry swallows before continuing. "He'd be here with Mom if he could, he just couldn't make it today."

"So, they're still together?" His eyes fly back to Mira's. "Didn't seem like it a few minutes ago," he murmurs.

Mira tenses and I feel myself follow suit. Attractive or

not, this guy is pushing his luck. Mira has always put her parent's happiness above her own. He might not know the exact buttons he's pushing for her, but I do, and I'll always put myself between my best friend and people that might hurt her.

Axel puts his hands up though, eyes darting between the two of us. "I just mean, she didn't warn dad off and she wasn't wearing a ring."

I look down at Mira, trying to read her expression. "She probably just forgot it at home," I placate, noting the worry lines on her forehead. She nods, but her eyes stay a bit unfocused.

Changing the subject, I nudge her. "Wanna go see if your roommate showed up?"

We spent a few hours this morning unloading all of Mira's stuff and putting most of it away, but her roommate never turned up in all that time. I know she's more nervous about meeting Janette, having sent her a couple messages over the summer, but Janette never responded. They probably got her number wrong by a digit or something, but the lack of response made Mira nervous, worried it was intentional.

I hear Axel flop down on the couch behind us and turn back to him. "You want to come?" My stomach twists when he smiles and flashes his bright white teeth.

With a shake of his head, he looks over toward his room. "I got more stuff to unpack so I'll pass." His eyes land back on me again. "Sean mentioned a floor meeting at seven by the way."

I nod and he gets up, heading into his room. I turn back to Mira, walking out of the suite and closing the door behind me. "He seems chill," I say, watching her reaction. But her mind must be somewhere else. She starts wringing her hands together after pressing the elevator button.

Realizing I don't have a key to get back into my suite, I clench my jaw and shake my head before releasing the tension. "I should probably go find Sean to get my keys," I say, glancing down the hall to see which way 801 is. Mira doesn't respond, still staring ahead when I turn back, so I add, "Meet you there?"

She nods and I pause for a minute, debating getting the keys later, but then the elevator dings and I walk off toward Sean's room, quickening my pace so that she won't be alone for too long.

5

Janette

Annoyance heats my blood as I walk back out to my suite's living room area to grab another box off the pile beside my bedroom door. Christopher lays across one of the green couches, feet hanging off the edge and hands folded behind his head. He's been lounging there since we arrived, after he asked for my login to the Wi-Fi and started streaming a baseball game on the TV across from him. Even made himself a coffee in the Keurig during a commercial break.

Amiria texted me a month ago that she got one, so I knew not to bring another, but I never got the chance to thank her for that info. I bite my lip, looking over at the other bedroom door. She wasn't here when we arrived, Christopher following me as I heaved the rolling cart with all my stuff piled on into the suite. "I loaded some of the boxes onto it. I've done my part," he said when I asked if he could help me get it all into my room.

I texted Mom after that, letting her know we made it to campus, the blue bubble joining the one above it telling her our flight landed a couple hours ago. She still hasn't responded, but I figure she can't use her phone while she's at the fundraising event she has today.

Placing the box onto my bed, I open the flaps, revealing my shower stuff packed into the little caddy I got at Target last week. My summer was jam packed, with most days spent in the morning sun hammering nails and lifting frame pieces into place and then afternoons walking dogs at the shelter or feeding and cuddling the litter of kittens someone brought in after finding them on the side of the road. Weekends had also been scheduled by Mom with photo opportunities and public events so she could cash in on the last of the mother-daughter opportunities she could before I moved out of state. I spent the spare hours of free time I had shopping and packing for school on my own, forgetting to answer Amiria's texts and not even being able to email Layla more than twice before it was suddenly moving day.

Arms wrap around my torso, making me jump and Christopher chuckle. His lips touch the side of my neck and I feel the usual nothing I get from his affection. "Take a break, babe. You have all week to get settled in."

"I'll have classes," I say, pulling out of his hold and taking the caddy over to my desk. Straightening the bottles and then turning back, I walk past him to pull the folded cobalt towels from the box on my bed.

"Well, you don't have to go to school, babe." He catches me around the middle again, looking down at me once we're chest to chest. "You know I'd take care of you."

I hold back the urge to roll my eyes. "We've talked about this, Christopher," I say, trying not to sound like I'm chastising a kid. I pull away, heading back toward my closet to put the towels away. "I don't want to be a trophy wife. I want to go to school."

"I still don't get why you have to go so far away though.

GSU is only an hour away from home and would probably cost your mom half as much in tuition." He walks to the door, checking the TV to make sure his game is still on commercial.

I sigh. We've had this argument at least three times since I told him I got into the Coast. And every time it feels like he's barely listening. *Most* of the time it feels like he's barely listening.

"Mom went to Imperium. It's where she met my dad." And Aunt Tati, but I leave that part out.

I've never told Christopher anything about my life before Georgia and he's never asked. But I know he talks with Mom sometimes and I don't need him mentioning any of that to her and setting her off. She already drinks her weight in rosé every year on Dad's birthday. Christopher would ask too many questions if she broke down in front of him because he didn't know not to say something.

"And Mom is fine paying the out of state tuition. She's already setting up an event to meet up with Alums in a couple weeks when she comes to visit, so me attending will pay off for her." An off-campus event and only as a sanctioned campaign event. I doubt I'll see my mother set foot inside Ring Road. She might have been excited for me to attend her alma mater, but only because it was not in Maine, and she could probably push aside the memories of Dad and Aunt Tati. It wasn't the Coast she ran away from.

Christopher mumbles a *mmhmm* in response, drifting back to the living room and laying down again to watch more baseball. I finish with the box on my bed, breaking down the empty cardboard and sliding it into the pile in the back of my closet. Christopher shouts as something happens in his game and I head back for another box, my annoyance peaking yet again. I just want to go find Layla, but I can't until he leaves, or he might rat me out to Mom and I do not want to deal with the headache of having that conversation over the phone.

"Why did you take that room?" Christopher asks, watching me as his head hangs over the side of the couch. Commercials play on the TV again which must be why I've caught his attention.

"Other one was taken," I say, lifting another box. I opened the door to Amiria's room when we first got here, finding her stuff mostly set up and some boxes stored inside. Not really caring which room I got, I just shut the door again and started unpacking my stuff into the other one.

"Wait, your roommate picked her room before you even got here?" He speaks in an affronted tone, but I know it's not on my honor's behalf. He grew up in wealth, never wanting for anything and getting his pick of whatever choices arose in his life. He'd never had a door closed to him before and probably couldn't fathom the idea of someone choosing something for him. And seeing me as an extension of him, he feels I should always get the same treatment. I'd thought it was endearing when we first started dating, but now the arrogance and possessiveness of it rubs me the wrong way.

"It's fine Christopher. I don't care which room I'm in." I count the boxes left, finding six still piled on the cart and debate just bringing them all into my room or continuing to unpack each one. Christopher will have to leave to catch his flight back soon and the moment he is gone, I plan on leaving to find Lay.

"She should have waited for you to pick rooms together. It's just rude," Christopher prattles on.

A knock on the open door calls both of our attention to the chestnut-haired girl standing just inside the suite. She's taller than me. I can already tell from across the room. It's not surprising since most people are taller than me, but it's always the first thing I notice. She's wearing heeled boots too which adds to her height.

"Hi," she says, taking another step into the suite. Her voice is soft, and she glances from me to Christopher. "I'm Mira." A few more steps toward me. "You must be Janette." Her posture is tense, and she wrings her hands as she stands in front of me.

I start to nod, but Christopher cuts me off, jolting upright. "I thought your roommate's name was Amy or something?"

His voice scrapes my nerves at this point. "Amiria," I correct him, walking back into my room to put the box down. I hoped she wouldn't show up until Christopher left. Now he's going to want to talk and interact with her, stake his claim in everything the way he always does with new people. And he'll probably come on too strong. The less they interact the better, so I'll need to make this interaction short if I want to go find Layla any time before dinner.

"Do you shower in the morning?" I ask, walking back into the living room. Christopher still sits up, the TV now off, and watches Mira who peeks over at him before answering.

"Um, usually," she says. Already uncomfortable. I need to finish up and get him out of here.

I grab another box, saying, "Perfect. I usually shower at night, and I really didn't want to have to change up my routine." I bring the next one to my closet, setting it on the floor.

"You could always just come back home with me, J. Keep your routine exactly how it's always been." My spine snaps straight and I grind my teeth, dropping the box onto my bed in a rush. I hear something bang inside the box and curse under my breath. I need him gone.

Poking my head out the door, I plaster a faux smile on my face. "Nice try, Chris." My voice comes out harsher than I want. "Mom already paid the tuition so there's no backing out now." I head back over to the box, ripping the flaps open and pulling stuff out. A mug broke near the bottom, the chunks scattered around the other random things packed in the box. I start pulling the pieces out and tossing them in the trash.

"Do you want some help?" Mira's voice drifts into the room and I drop the pieces in my hand back into the box to run back out to the living room. She reaches for my bedside lamp sitting on top of one of my boxes, but I slide in between her and the pile. If she gets involved, Christopher's interest will peak. He always flirted with any of the girls who tried to befriend me in high school, and I didn't want him making Mira uncomfortable or overstaying his welcome.

"No, it's okay," I say hurriedly. "It looked like you had plenty to unpack yourself."

Mira takes a step back and I realize how rude I sound. She starts wringing her hands again. "Okay. Um, about that Keurig. I texted you to make sure—"

"Don't worry about it," I say, remembering the text. I grab my lamp, needing to finish moving the boxes so I can kick Christopher out. "I don't drink coffee. The caffeine is really bad for you." I try to think of something to say to make up for my abruptness but can't and just end up walking back into my room. Taking a moment, I stand by my bed, lamp in hand and breathe. I'm fucking this up. Panic starts to bubble up in my throat and I try the breaths I read about. In through my nose, out through my mouth.

The sound of keys jangling interrupts my breathing. "All

set. This your new roommate?" a new voice says. A new male voice. My eyes fly open. The only thing that could make this worse is Christopher getting into a pissing match with Mira's boyfriend.

I rush to the doorway, saying, "No, that'd be me." The last word dies on my tongue as I put my hands on my hips and take in the guy standing beside Mira in the living room. His hazel eyes find mine as I openly gape at him. He's massive, taller than Mira, and probably taller than Christopher. Broader too. His baseball shirt clings to his chest, the black sleeves cutting across his shoulders to show off his build. Christopher always wears crisp button downs, trying to look more like his father, but they always make him look stiff. This guy looks comfortable in his clothes, right down to the worn-out converse on his feet.

I realize I'm openly checking him out in front of my boyfriend. And Mira. I change my expression to disdain, not wanting her to think I'm interested in her guy and blatantly making it obvious. Pulling my eyes back up to Mira's, I say, "This your boyfriend?" trying to sound unimpressed.

Mira shakes her head. "No, Bentley's just a friend."

Christopher sits up on the couch. A flutter goes through my gut and the panic returns. If Bentley was Mira's boyfriend, Christopher might not be too bad. But now he'll be unbearable. Even if he leaves right now, he'll be texting every few days asking if Bentley's around, what I think of him, making comments about not liking him. It's how he was with every unattached guy I've ever interacted with in front of him before, no matter how innocuous.

Bentley's voice pulls me out of the panic swirling inside me. "You wound me," he says and clutches his chest, looking down at Mira. She frowns up at him.

Christopher suddenly stands. "You gay or something?"

He steps closer to Bentley and Mira and the panic climbs higher in my stomach, matching the growing tension in the room. I dig my hands further into my hips, trying to ground myself.

Bentley glares at Christopher as his eyes switch over to him. Christopher tries to stand taller, but Bentley has a few inches on him, even in his relaxed posture. "You have a problem with it if I was?"

Christopher's shoulders fall as he backs down a bit. "No, just want to make sure you're not sniffing around my girl."

I tighten my grip again, pinching myself so I don't scream. Ignoring the urge, I snort, forcing myself to say, "Babe, come on. This guy is so not my type." I grab a box and rush into my room to hide my face as heat rises on my neck and chest from the lie. Having more of my father's darker complexion probably saves me a bit, but feeling the flush always makes me think people can see it all over my face.

"Don't worry," Bentley calls as I hide in my room. "Snob isn't mine." The words stab into me, and I hug the box tighter against my abdomen. My mom's face flashes in my mind, the fake laughter she uses for investors, practiced smiles and perfectly honed expressions of shock or outrage that she can pull out perfectly when needed. I always thought I wasn't like her. Not the her she is now. Senator Mom and Maine Mom are very separate in my mind, and I held onto the memories of Maine Mom every time she would cancel on me or schedule me for an appearance somewhere so I wouldn't be in her hair. But maybe being around the Senator the last five years has affected me more than I thought. My first reaction to Mira and Bentley had been being a bitch and I'm not even really sure why.

I hear Christopher grind out, "Stay away from Janette."

His footsteps draw closer, and a door closes in the living room. I put the box on the floor next to the other I dropped earlier, going back over to the one on my bed and picking up the pieces of the broken mug again.

Christopher sits next to the box, looking up at me. "Want me to stay the night, babe?"

I grip the shard of ceramic a little too tight, a piece slicing into my palm. Wincing, I pull my hand back from the box. "No, it's fine." I walk over to my desk, getting a Band-Aid out of my purse. "You have work tomorrow and already bought the ticket home." I walk out to the kitchen, running the faucet and holding my hand under the water. Mira's door is closed, and I hear faint music coming from the other side.

Christopher comes out of my room and leans against the doorframe. "I could call in sick."

Shaking my head, I turn off the faucet and grab a paper towel off the roll I left on the counter earlier. "Your dad will be mad at me if you call in sick just to stay here. And then my mom will hear about it and chastise me for distracting you and not supporting you. She'd never forgive me if I distracted the son of her biggest backer and caused a rift between her and your dad." I roll my eyes, and Christopher pushes off the wall, coming over to me.

"Okay, babe. But I already got dad to promise me the company jet to come see you next week. And you better be distracting me while I'm here." He kisses the side of my head as I peel the paper off the Band-Aid, ignoring his words.

"You should probably get going," I say, nodding toward the clock on the microwave. "You still have to give back the car and your flight leaves at four fifteen."

He glances at the time. "Shit. Yeah, I better get going."

He ducks back into my room, grabbing his keys and wallet off my desk and tucking them into his pockets. I walk to the door, meeting him as he walks out. "I'll see you on Friday, babe." He leans down, wrapping an arm around my waist and kissing me. "Try not to miss me too much," he says with a wink before walking out of the suite. I lean back against the doorframe, closing my eyes.

"Cute." Bentley's voice forces my eyes open, and I watch him as he walks past me and into the kitchen. Opening the fridge, he grabs a water bottle and closes it quickly. "You two seem good for each other," he adds with a smirk. Something hot rages in my blood and I clench my fists. "Try not to miss him too much," he mocks before going back into Mira's room with a chuckle. I step fully into my room, slamming the door closed behind me.

Standing in my new dorm, finally alone, I try to erase the image of Bentley's condescending face from my mind. My cell buzzes on the desk and I walk over to the perfectly timed distraction.

MOM

Glad to hear it. See you in a few weeks.

I stare at Mom's text, reading it a couple of times before clearing the notification. The heat simmers to a low boil, as I look at the framed picture of Dad sitting next to my purse. It was the first thing I unpacked, keeping it in my bag to make sure it got here unscathed.

"Back at your old stomping grounds, Dad." Tears blur the edge of my vision.

Another text makes my phone shake in my hand, and I look down, seeing Layla's name pop up.

LAYLA C.

Are you done unpacking yet? Dad finally left
and I kicked Gwen out with him, so you
better be free.

I smile and wipe my eyes, replying that I'm coming down.

Excitement and nerves crash against each other as I grab my room keys and walk out of the suite, abandoning the rest of my boxes. Walking down to the elevator, I tap my foot while I wait.

What if we don't click? What if too much has changed, too much time has passed? What if I say stupid shit like I did with Mira?

The doors open and I step inside, feeling my stomach lurch as it descends to the first floor. My phone vibrates again.

LAYLA C.

Can't wait!!

I squeeze the keys in my other hand, feeling the new wound throb in my palm.

The elevator dings as the doors open again and I step off, walking slowly down the hall toward 126. A few people still have their doors open, but I keep my eyes ahead as I pass, checking the numbers of each room to double and triple check I'm heading in the right direction while my heart pounds in my ears.

125 appears ahead and I look to the other side, seeing the black numbers painted on the wall next to the open door of Layla's room. With one more deep breath, I step into view, seeing Layla for the first time since Mom moved us to Georgia. She sits on her bed, reading something on her

phone, but only a second passes before she looks up, muddy brown eyes locking with mine.

Layla screams, jumping up from the bed and rushing me. Her arms wrap around my shoulders and mine automatically encircle her waist, relief momentarily paralyzing my brain as I try to catch up with seeing her again. And then we're jumping and laughing, and I can feel the tears from earlier spilling down my face.

"Janette," she says, squeezing me tighter. I can hear the tears in her voice, and it makes me sniffle.

"Hi, Layla." I close my eyes and we just keep hugging.

6

BENTLEY

Axel raps his knuckles on my door, leaning against the opposite side of the door frame. "You ready yet?"

I nod, saying, "Yeah, one sec," and go back to putting on my socks and shoes.

Gen-eds make up most of my schedule this semester, with one business communication course that counts toward my degree. The first night, Axel and I compared schedules and found out we have three classes together. On Monday we headed to MATH-144: Elements of Statistics together and sat next to each other in the back, not really speaking much while the prof went over the syllabus and handed out a general assessment quiz. Afterward, we hung out on the patio near the coffee shop and it just kind of became a silent agreement that we would go to our mutual classes together.

I slip on my shoes and grab my bag, following Axel as he pushes off my doorframe and heads out of the suite. We walk over to the elevator, and I sling my backpack over my left shoulder. Axel stands beside me, rocking back and forth on his heels, backpack on his back and hands resting on the straps under his arms. The posture makes his chest look defined against the black undershirt underneath his open pink and green short sleeve Hawaiian shirt. The pattern should be too loud, but for some reason it works for him.

"Think King Arthur will be on the syllabus?" Axel asks, stepping into the elevator and pushing the lobby button. I follow after, leaning against the back of the metal box to try to add some distance between us so I don't brush up against him.

"Pretty sure King Arthur is fictional." I pull out my phone and load up my schedule, double checking the room we need to find for HIST-156.

"For real?" Axel's face scrunches up, looking like he just bit into a lemon. "That was like 75% of the reason I picked this class. I was hoping we'd get to dress up as knights or something."

I laugh, stepping off the elevator when the doors open. People cover the sidewalk outside, moving between the buildings to get to their next class. We push open the heavy glass paneled doors, entering the fray and moving around Ring Road toward the seminar building we need.

"Probably going to be more about the Magna Carta and the Black Plague." I sidestep some people stopped in the middle of the sidewalk, all bunched around one person's phone looking at the campus map and arguing about where Siegal Hall is.

"Bubonic Plague," Axel says when we step back together, his shoulder hitting mine and making my feet falter for a moment.

"What?" I turn right, checking the sign on the corner to make sure we're still heading toward Riggs Hall.

"It was the Bubonic Plague or Black Death, not the Black

Plague." Axel chuckles, strolling down the sidewalk like he knows exactly where he's going. I raise an eyebrow when he glances over at me, probably feeling me staring. "My sister Layla is really into true crime podcasts. Her room is right across from mine at home and we both left our doors open most of the summer." He shrugs. "Guess I picked up some shit. Want to hear about how BTK was caught?" He grins when I shake my head, not even sure what that means.

We walk up to Riggs, heading up the stone steps to the front door. Axel reaches the door first, grabbing the handle and waving me ahead as he holds it open. I walk in, holding the second set of doors open for him. Air conditioning greets us as we make our way to the stairwell in the center of the building. "Charlamagne was a knight. I'm pretty sure he was in the Medieval Age."

Axel grins as we start climbing the stairs. "Maybe I'll get to rent a suit of armor after all."

I shake my head, gripping my bag strap tighter. His grin always makes me want to do something stupid, like reach out and touch him when I shouldn't.

We make our way to the third floor. Room 331 sits right across from the stairwell, and we pass it, heading down the hall and around the corner, looking for 353. When we walk into the open double doors, we find ourselves at the top of a stadium-style seating arrangement with at least a hundred seats across five tiered levels all leading down to a large desk and whiteboard area at the bottom. Twenty or so students already sit in patches around the room, some people quietly chatting while others stare at their phones or look around nervously.

Axel double taps the back of his hand against my chest, pulling my attention from surveying the room to nod at some seats to the right of him in the back of the room. I nod, unable to speak, and follow him into the row, tossing my bag in the seat next to me after we sit and pulling out a notebook and pen. Throwing my bag onto the floor at my feet, I lean back, going back to surveying the room as more people walk in and grab seats.

A ponytail of light brown, tight curls sitting in the front row snags my attention. Smooth amber shoulders sit tensely underneath the hair, a mechanical pencil gripped tightly in the hand attached to the end of her arm. Janette turns her head to the right, her profile on display and showcasing her angular bone structure. She'd been cute with the tight space buns and little wispy curls around the back of her neck when we'd met in Mira's dorm. Her pretty green eyes had been wide and rimmed with thick black lashes when she'd appeared in the door, looking up at me with her lips slightly parted. It was when they opened further and unleashed the dismissive attitude toward not only me, but Mira as well, that had turned me off.

She chews the inside of her cheek, eyes glancing around at people as they settle into seats, only two others in the front row, but on the other side of the center aisle. Janette cranes her neck back further, eyes finding mine and widening before sliding over to Axel on my left. He wears a smirk, waving at her when she sees him. She glances back over at me before waving back, turning around quickly once the interaction ends.

"You know her?" I whisper. An older looking Asian man walks into the room, kicking the door jamb out and walking down the center aisle to the desk at the bottom while the doors swing closed behind him.

"She's Layla's best friend," Axel whispers back. The prof pulls some papers out of his messenger bag on the table and hands them to Janette, telling her to take one and pass them around. "We should sit with her next time."

I stay silent, not sure what to say.

He looks over at me, bumping my shoulder with his. "She doesn't bite."

I roll my eyes and take the stack of papers from the girl passing them back from the row in front of us. She smiles, hand lingering on the stack longer than she needs to. I smile back, whispering, "Thank you," as I take them. I pass a syllabus over to Axel and take one for myself, getting up and walking the stack over to the guy sitting at the end of our row.

The prof pulls down the overhead projector screen, plugging in his laptop and starting a PowerPoint going through the syllabus and introducing himself. I sit back, jotting down notes on the different papers and deadlines we have throughout the year.

"You'll have a semester long research project that will account for thirty percent of your grade for the year." I underline the project twice on my copy of the syllabus. "I'll break you up into groups next week and your research topics will be due by next Friday. There is a list of possible topic choices on the last page of your syllabus, but you can choose any historical event that falls between the 5th and 15th century."

Axel looks over at me and points a bullet point on the last page. *The reign of King Charles the Great (Charlemagne).* Axel winks and mouths "suit of armor" and my stomach knots at the gesture. I force a grin back, turning to face forward again and immediately finding Janette in the front row. She hunches over her notebook and syllabus, writing hastily over the top of both. Her hand flies over the paper like she can't get the words out fast enough. I watch her, unable to look away as Dr. Howards continues going over the class schedule and midterm expectations.

Axel shifts next to me, his thigh pressing against mine once he settles. I grip my pen a little tighter, the contact and warmth making my dick twitch as I stare at the back of Janette's head. Her ponytail fell to the side when she started scribbling and I suddenly picture kissing the back of her neck. The thought makes me jolt and I try to play it off, shuffling in my seat. Axel glances over at me and I move my leg over so that it no longer touches his.

Breathing through my nose, I force my eyes to stay on Dr. Howard for the rest of the class, only half hearing the end of his introduction to the medieval period. When he finally wraps up, everyone starts packing up, throwing their stuff into bags, and rushing out of the room.

The girl who passed back the stack of syllabi turns around again before I have the chance to toss my stuff into my bag.

"Hi, I'm Cassie." She shoves her hand out toward me, and I look at it for a second before shaking it, glancing over at Axel who smirks at me.

"Bentley," I say, smiling at her politely.

"Axel," he says beside me, making her turn her wide eyes toward him and off of me for a moment. "Nice to meet you." Axel flashes her his white teeth and she swallows, looking kind of owlish with light blonde, pixie cut hair and big dark eyes.

"Are you guys history majors too?" She shoves her stuff in her side bag, slinging it over her head and standing rapidly as we pack up at a more normal rate.

Axel shakes his head. "Business," he says, tapping his chest. "Big guy over here is on the pre-law track." Axel points toward me, already standing with his hands on both backpack straps again. "This just seemed like the most interesting history class to satisfy the gen-ed requirement."

Cassie nods, walking out her row at the same pace as us and rushing up the center aisle to walk beside me. "I love the Middle Ages. Such an interesting time period. I don't know what I'm going to pick for the research paper. There's too much to choose from." She shakes her head like the decision is already weighing on her. Then her eyes are on me again as we pause outside the classroom door. "We should volunteer to be the three-person group next week when Howards makes the group assignments." She stares up at me with a hopeful smile and Axel starts to snicker, covering it with a cough beside me.

"Yeah, maybe," I say, rubbing the back of my neck. Janette emerges from the double doors, looking between the three of us as she passes.

"Hey, J. Long time no see," Axel calls, nodding to her as his eyes light up. She pauses, looking over at me and Cassie quick before looking at him again. Cassie stares at her, eyes roving her short frame with a worried look.

Janette walks over, stopping close to Axel, but angling her body away from Cassie and me. "Hi, Axe. I've got another class, but we should get together with Lay this weekend." The top of her head can't come to more than my shoulder height and she's wearing an off the shoulder blue blouse with black denim shorts. My eyes slide down her legs unwarrantedly, stopping at the curl of ink around her ankle, half hidden under her black sock. I can't make out what the tattoo is, but I have the urge to reach out and run my fingers over the spot.

Axel nods, reaching out and pulling her in for a quick hug. He whispers something to her and she beams, a shot of white-hot lust running south through my body at the sight of her smile in his arms. I continue watching, unable to look away as she lets go of him, nodding, and walks off, not even glancing back at Cassie or me again.

What the fuck was that?

Axel watches her go as well, turning back and looking directly at me before his eyes slide down to Cassie. She's stepped closer to me since Janette walked up and I want to take a step back.

"See you on Friday?" she says a little too softly.

I just nod in return, and she hesitates, waiting for me to say more before giving me a tight smile and heading down the hall.

Axel laughs lightly once she turns the corner, looking up at me with his eyes open wide and batting his eyelashes mockingly. "Looks like you've made a new friend." He bumps my shoulder and chuckles again.

"Shut up." I shoulder him back, feeling a jolt of the lust from earlier, before we walk in the opposite direction down the hall toward the stairwell again.

He shrugs. "She's cute, if not a little over-enthusiastic. Probably be a really good partner for the research project."

I nod, remembering Janette rapidly writing notes during the beginning of class. "You'll have to convince her to let you dress up as a knight though and that might be a tough sell if she's taking the class seriously."

"Hey, I'm taking the class seriously!" Axel argues, slapping a hand against my chest again. My heart thumps from the touch. "I just think it'd be more fun to present in costume." His sly smile makes me roll my eyes, but my stomach flips at the look. Maybe having Cassie as a distracting buffer will help me get through spending even more time with Axel outside of just living together.

7

Janette

ayla knocks on the door to my suite and Christopher groans. "Why are we hanging out with them again?"

I breathe through my nose, trying to release the pent-up anger and irritation that has been sizzling inside me since he showed up yesterday afternoon. It started when he immediately complained about the cafeteria food at dinner and kept growing each time he tried to convince me to drop out and move back home with him. I had to keep reminding myself that Mom would have a cow if I randomly broke up with her biggest backer's son. She basically doted on Christopher whenever he was around, practically frothing at the mouth when I told her he asked me out at the governor's Easter party over a year ago.

I stand from the couch, Christopher's arm falling off my shoulders. "Because they're my friends and I haven't seen them in years." I feel like I've explained this a thousand times in the last twenty-four hours. Thank God Mira went home for the weekend. I needed to go to the bathroom and just sit on the side of the tub and breathe several times already.

Opening the door, my annoyance dissipates, Layla already beaming at me with Axel standing behind her, hands in his pockets. They look like total opposites, Layla in a baggy grey sweatshirt and leggings while Axel wears a baby blue button down with little pineapples speckled across it, open over a white tank and khaki shorts. Her hair is flaming red, having redyed it in the bathroom of her dorm yesterday after class while I sat on her bed and did homework. Meanwhile, Axel has the natural wavy brown I remember Lay having when we all lived in Maine.

"Hi babes!" Layla squeals, grabbing me in a hug. I grin, squeezing her back and wave at Axel over her shoulder. He has a small, warm smile on his face as he watches us hug.

"Hi, Lay, Axel. Come on in, guys." I release Layla, holding the door open for them to walk in. Christopher stays on the couch, eyeing Axel up and down immediately. "This is Chris, my boyfriend," I say, closing the door and turning around to stand next to Layla by the couches. "Chris, this is Layla, my best friend, and her brother Axel. We grew up together in Maine."

Surprise flashes in Christopher's eyes and I clench a fist behind my back. I've already told him this at least twice in the last two days, but clearly information retention still isn't something he's picked up around me. He waves at them, still lounging on the couch and only glancing at Layla before turning his narrowed gaze back on Axel.

Axel looks around the room, not even paying attention to Christopher on the couch. He surveys the space, and I follow his eyes, realizing how little personal touches Mira and I have added to the generally provided furniture. The walls are bare and other than a fuzzy red blanket Mira left thrown over the back of one of the unoccupied couches, there isn't any extra décor on the side or coffee tables. Nerves bubble in my stomach, wondering what Axel thinks of the space as his eyes come around to meet mine.

"Nice place. I haven't seen one of the normal suite set-ups since Gwen and Lay each have singles so there's no common room area." He rocks on the balls of his feet as he speaks. Layla sits down on one of the couches and he takes a seat next to her, taking his hands out of his pockets and setting them on his knees as he fidgets a little. My eyes track the movement, noting how big his hands seem. My stomach clenches at the thought and I shake my head, looking away.

"Aren't you rooming with that guy Bentley?" I walk over to the kitchen and open the fridge, needing something to do with my hands so I can distract my thoughts. Christopher looks over at me, eyes still narrowed as I mention Bentley's name.

"Yeah, but his parents had all their furniture replaced with nicer stuff. Their TV even got mounted to the fucking wall." Layla laughs and accepts the water bottle I hand her, Axel also taking one from my hand.

"Damn, they must really be loaded if they got away with that." I plop down next to Christopher again, offering him the last bottle, but he shakes his head, arm coming down around my back and hand gripping my upper arm to pull me a little closer to him. Axel eyes the move over the edge of his water as he guzzles from it. I force myself not to watch his Adams apple bob against his bronze skin as he swallows several times.

"He's Heather and Michael Marshall's son," Axel says once he's downed half the bottle. "So, they're pretty well off." I had seen the acting couple in a few films, both separately and together, over the years, but had no idea Bentley was their son. I wonder how growing up with parents at that level of fame affected him. I've only been in the spotlight for the last few years and the constant façade for cameras grew stale real quick.

"Not that surprising," Layla says, twisting the cap on her water bottle. "The Coast is the college for every echelon of the world's elite. Most people here have parents with -aire at the end of their net worth." She shrugs. "Pretty sure Dad's status as an alumnus who became a professor helped swing us in."

We all sit for a minute, the conversation petering out. "Do you guys want to watch a movie?" I glance over at Christopher, but he's gone back to watching Axel. "Or we could play a game? I think I have a deck of cards, maybe even Uno."

Layla's face lights up. "Oh, Axel loves Uno," she says, drawing out the o in loves and then grinning.

Axel rolls his eyes. "I do not love Uno. Layla cheats, though not as bad as Gwen."

Layla punches Axel's shoulder. "I do not cheat! Gwen cheats, but I play fair."

I laugh, shrugging out of Christopher's hold to go find the cards. "Uno it is." I grab the box from my desk drawer and open it to shake the cards out into my other hand as I walk back to the living room.

"Hiding draw fours is not playing fair, Lay," Axel says, leaning over to put his water bottle down on the side table closest to him.

Layla starts moving the coffee table, making room for all of us to sit on the floor and Christopher grumbles about it as he gets off the couch, sitting down next to me. Layla raises her eyebrows at me when he isn't looking and I roll mine back, noticing Axel watching us.

"No twin telepathy," I say, pointing between the two of them. Axel holds up his hands, smirking at me.

"Oh please, we haven't been on the same side for a game since we were seven," Layla says, taking the cards from him and shuffling them easily.

Christopher, still silently staring down Axel, places his hand on my knee under the table. I flinch a little and Axel narrows his eyes.

"So, where do you go to school, Chris?" Layla starts dealing the cards and Axel immediately picks them up and organizes his hand, not looking at Chris as he speaks.

"I don't," Christopher sneers. "I work full time for my father, Paul Tonkins. He's the CEO of SMC Fund Management."

Axel grunts in response, still looking at his cards. I chew the inside of my cheek, feeling Christopher's hand tighten on my knee. I focus on my cards, organizing them by color and ignoring the mounting tension between the men.

"Who wants to go first?" Layla asks quickly, looking between her brother and my boyfriend.

"You go, Lay," I say when no one speaks for a beat.

"Okay, we'll start clockwise." She throws a green skip down over the six she flips from the top of the deck. Axel rolls his eyes at her while she smiles behind her cards.

The game goes quickly, Layla attacking Axel every chance she gets, then playing her number cards when the order reverses since I'm sitting on her other side. Christopher attacks pretty much no matter what, even frowning when he only has a number card to play on me or Axel.

Taking it from both sides, Axel ends up with a hand of at least twenty cards, not even so much as grumbling as he grabs more when Layla plays another draw two on him and laughs maniacally. I laugh too and his eyes flash to mine.

"You're lucky I'm between these two, Blue. You'd be the one with twenty-six cards if we were sitting next to each other." My breath catches at the old nickname, remembering when he used to call me that as a kid. Dad always called me his Bluejay and hearing Axel use his modified version again makes my chest pang.

"That a threat?" Christopher says, eyeing Axel over the top of his hand.

Layla raises an eyebrow at me.

I jump in quickly. "Of course not, Chris. He's just trash talking. Calm down, it's just a game." I pat his thigh, but my eyes are glued to the little smirk on Axel's face.

"Yeah, Chris. I think she knows what I mean," Axel says lazily, shuffling his cards in his hand and not looking up. Layla slaps his knee under the table, but the noise reaches us above it. My heart rate picks up, but I can't tell if my blood is pounding from panic or the tone of Axel's voice.

Axel glances at the floor beside him, picking up a draw four and holding it up. "Told you she cheats." He faux glares at Layla, the earlier tension seemingly pushed aside. "Cough up the rest, sis."

Layla blushes, pulling another card out of her sweatshirt sleeve and slapping it down on the table. I laugh as she sulks. "How are you cheating and not closer to winning?"

"Don't rub it in," Layla grumbles.

I smile, laying down a red seven. "Uno."

Layla glances at her cards, then stares at the one in my hand. "You have a blue, don't you?"

I shrug my shoulders. "I don't know, do I?"

"She has blue," Christopher says, leaning back over after

checking my card from behind me while I'm looking at Layla.

"Hey, everybody stop cheating!" I glare at Christopher, betrayal twinging in my chest.

Layla frowns, looking at her cards again. She plays a blue seven, looking at Axel and Christopher in turn. "One of you needs to change the color, it's the only card I can play."

"I can change it," Christopher says, picking a card out of his hand and holding it, ready to play.

Axel looks through his cards, expression never changing as he picks out and lays down a blue skip. Layla smirks and Christopher's head whips up toward him.

"Sorry, man. Only card I can play," Axel says, staring Christopher down.

"Bullshit," Christopher hisses. "You have a million cards!"

Axel shrugs and I throw down my blue three. "I win," I say, grinning at Layla and trying to ignore the little smile that Axel throws my way.

Layla groans, throwing her hand down. "I want a rematch!"

Christopher's phone rings and I see his dad's face on the screen when he pulls it out and checks who's calling. "I have to take this," he grumbles, getting up and going into my bedroom. The door shuts behind him.

"I have snacks. You guys hungry?" I get up, going to the kitchen while Layla starts gathering the cards and shuffling again.

I pull a container of French onion dip out of the fridge and open the cabinet to grab the chips I bought for tonight.

"Want some help?" Axel's voice startles me, and I jump, whipping around to face him while my heart tries to beat out of my chest. "Sorry," he says, holding his hands up and biting back a grin. "Didn't mean to scare you."

"You're good," I say, rubbing my hand over my chest as I try to soothe my nervous system. "Just didn't hear you come up behind me."

"Did you want some help?" he repeats, smile peeking through this time. I stare at his mouth for a minute, heart stuttering again.

"Um, can you grab the cookies at the top of that cupboard?" I nod toward the area Mira and I store our dry food. I had to get a little step stool to reach the top shelves in the upper cabinets, but at his height, Axel can probably grab it without assistance. He steps toward me, chest practically touching mine as he slides past in the small space. He reaches up, opening the cabinet and stretching to reach the cookies. My eyes stray to the flash of skin that shows between his tank and low-slung shorts.

"You let me win," I accuse, dragging my eyes back up to his face.

He grins conspiratorially. "I just played the only card I had, Blue." He squeezes past me again, our eyes locked as he passes, and heat licks up my skin.

I stand in the kitchen for a second after he heads back to the living room, practicing my breathing. "Hurry up, J," Layla calls. "I want to kick your ass this time."

I release a big breath, grabbing the chips and dip and heading back out to play another game.

8

AXEL

I pluck my favorite plum tee shirt out of the second drawer in my dresser and pull it over my head. It feels like I should wear it today, like there's something coming that I need good luck for. Lacing up my grey sneakers, I grab my bag and walk out to the living room. Bentley stands near the door, typing something on his phone and I watch his fingers glide over the screen and his soft green and brown eyes track their movement. His dimples show as he smiles down at the device. The veins on the backs of his hands strain as he types, and my mouth dries a little. Being attracted to my roommate would have been a lot easier if he was more of a dick. But I've yet to find something not to like about Bentley.

"Ready?" Bentley asks, looking up from his phone. His hair catches the light, revealing strands of gold intermingling in the coffee-colored waves. "No pattern today?" he jokes, nodding toward my shirt.

"Nope, it's a purple kind of day," I say, falling back into my practiced jovial demeanor.

We head out for our Wednesday history class, walking

side by side along the familiar route. People fill the sidewalk, as per usual at this time in the morning, but I notice one in particular, weaving her way through the throng ahead of us.

I watch Janette walk, straightened hair spilling down around her shoulders and back, much longer than her usual curls. Blonde highlights catch in the sun, the color not quite as golden as the ones I noticed in Bentley's earlier, but more like caramel dripping down from her crown.

"I don't think she likes me much," Bentley says, eyes watching Janette move ahead of us as well.

"Oh, come on," I say. "I'm sure she'd like you fine if she got to know you." Bentley squints a bit, thinking about it. "Maybe not as much as Cassie likes you..." Bentley shakes his head, side eyeing me as I chuckle. "But J is easy to get along with."

Bentley adjusts his bag on his shoulder, right hand swinging in time with his gait in between us. "She's my best friend's roommate."

"Mira?" Layla asked where she was while we were playing our fourth round of Uno, much to Christopher's disdain, and Janette had said something about a birthday party in her hometown.

"Mmhmm." Bentley watches Janette disappear into Riggs. "They're butting heads a bit. Or, well," he pauses, looking over at me with furrowed brows. "I guess they're not butting heads so much as not really communicating at all. Mira tends to be nonconfrontational with strangers and I sort of stepped in on her behalf on move in day when she and her boyfriend were being rude."

I snort. "Yeah, Chris is an ass. What'd you do?" I try to imagine Bentley yelling at Christopher or even Janette and can't picture him starting a fight, though given his muscle mass, he could probably take Christopher if he needed to.

"I called her a snob," he says, as we walk through the doors of the building Janette entered a few moments before.

My eyebrows raise, chest puffing a bit as I prepare Janette's defense.

"They were both dismissive of Mira and then Janette made a comment about me not being her type." His fist clenches at his side and all the air leaves my lungs. "She seemed relieved when her boyfriend left though."

Taking a quick breath, I shake my head. "I don't know why they're together," I mutter. "Lay and I hung out with them this weekend and he was the worst. She could do way better." Bentley and I climb the stairs in silence but when we reach the top, I see a frown on his face. "Come on," I say, leading the way down the hall and toward the seminar room. "You'll like her once she puts down her defenses."

Bentley follows me into the room, not really agreeing or disagreeing. Janette sits in the same spot she occupied in the two classes last week. I walk down the center aisle, hearing Bentley's footsteps continuing behind me.

"Hey guys," Cassie calls from her seat in the upper level as we pass. She waves us over to the empty seats around her.

"Hey, Cass. We're gonna sit down here today." I keep walking, feeling a little bit of guilt when her face falls at my words.

Bentley whispers, "Sorry," but keeps walking behind me.

We get to the bottom of the steps, and I turn toward Janette. She has her head bent over her phone, a swathe of hair blocking her face from view as we walk up. I drop into the seat directly beside her, causing her to jump and blink rapidly as she looks around. Bentley slides into the seat next to me, pulling his stuff out of his bag.

"What are you doing?" Janette asks, looking between the two of us with panic in her eyes.

"Figured we'd sit with you today, Blue." I pull out my notebook, clicking my multicolor pen to green for today. "You've already met Bentley, from what I've heard." I nod toward my roommate, and he glances over at her and nods awkwardly.

"Janette," he says.

"Bentley," she responds icily. Looks like the snob comment stuck with her. "You don't have to sit with me, Axe." Her tone softens when she looks to me. "I'm fine on my own."

"Of course, you are," I say, leaning back and stretching out my legs in front of me. "But maybe I didn't want to get left alone with this one in the back again." I tap Bentley's chest as I say it and he looks very unamused.

Janette snorts. "Fine, whatever. You'll have to actually pay attention though. Howards can see you down here." She goes back to scrolling through her phone and I smile at the side of her face.

I can feel Bentley staring and look over to see him glancing between the two of us before facing forward again. The noise of the doors closing comes from behind us and Dr. Howard passes to set up at the front of the room. Janette puts her phone away, uncapping a navy-blue pen and I smirk at the neat rows of notes already at the top of the page when she opens her notebook.

"Group assignment day!" Howards says with a clap of his hands. He looks over the room, and I sit up when his eyes rove over the three of us. Bentley tenses next to me. "Let's get started. You three up front can be our group of three and then the rest will be groups of four." He waves over to us then starts splitting the rest of the room into teams of four.

I smile, looking at first Bentley then Janette, practically jumping up and down in my seat. But both of their wary expressions temper my excitement. Janette glances over at Bentley, who side eyes her across me.

"It'll be fine," I whisper while Howards continues directing the room. "You can both play nice for one semester."

Janette sighs, pulling her hair up and fastening a high ponytail with a periwinkle scrunchie from her wrist. Bentley taps his pen against his notebook, leaning his chin in the palm of his hand.

"Okay, the rest of class can be used to pick your topics and start planning or researching. Use your time wisely. This will be the only class until December that you can use the time toward the research project. Topics are due by class on Friday, but no group can repeat topics. It'll be first come first serve." Dr. Howards sits down at the desk, pulling his laptop toward him and ignoring the room.

"I'm thinking something about the knights," I say, getting out of my seat and sitting crisscross on the floor facing the two of them. The rest of the room regroups behind them, the noise of chatter ringing around us.

"Which knights?" Janette asks, flipping to a clean page in her notebook.

"Move closer, Bent," I say, waving him to the seat I just vacated. "The knights in the shiny armor with the big swords."

Janette's face scrunches up. "What?"

"He wants to rent a suit of armor for the final presentation," Bentley says, settling into the seat next to Janette, but leaning away from her to use the opposite arm as a rest for his notebook. Janette looks at him with furrowed brows before turning the look on me.

"I think we'd get points for style." I shrug.

Janette closes her eyes and Bentley chuckles. "We could

do The Crusades," he says, sliding the syllabus out of the back of his notebook and pointing to the example list of topics. A few of them are circled and underlined and I watch Janette lean over and read the ones he's marked.

"That'd be really broad, and another group will definitely try to take it," she comments. I lean back, extending my arms out behind me and watching them. "Something like The Class Structure of the Middle Ages or Fashion of the Middle Class would be easier, but again, another group might choose it first."

"We could do The Impact of Gutenberg's Printing Press," Bentley suggests, pointing to the one on the list he's underlined twice and starred.

Janette pauses, looking over his shoulder at the list one more time, checking all the other topics. "Yeah, that would be a good one."

They stare at each other for a moment, and I feel my blood heat before they both turn toward me, and the simmer ratchets up to a boil.

"That work for you?" Bentley asks with a quirked eyebrow.

"No suit of armor?" I ask, pouting.

"No suit of armor," Janette replies sternly.

I sigh dramatically. "Fine, but you both have to make it up to me." I grab Bentley's syllabus and get to my feet, walking over to Howards.

"Do we just tell you the topic we've chosen?" I ask, scratching the back of my neck. He nods, grabbing a pen and looking up at me. "We want to do The Impact of Gutenberg's Printing Press. Is that one still available?"

"Sure is," Howards says, jotting down the topic and our names on a scrap piece of paper. "Good choice." He smiles up at me and I walk back over to Janette and Bentley.

"Are you a history major?" Janette asks Bentley quietly.

"No, English. Pre-law track."

She nods, chewing the inside of her cheek.

"But I don't like getting bad grades, so I'll take this project seriously," he adds.

"We both will," I say, plopping back down in front of them. "We got the Gutenberg one."

"Okay," Janette says, writing it down at the top of her page. "Do we want to make a loose schedule for researching, writing, and making the PowerPoint? I don't mind presenting at the end if either of you are crowd shy?"

She looks up at each of us, and I lift an eyebrow at her. "Do you really think I get stage fright?"

"Yeah, I'm fine presenting as well, so we can all take turns talking when we get to that stage." Bentley pulls up the calendar app on his phone. "We have twelve weeks till presentation time, not including the half week for Thanksgiving. So, we could do research for the first six, then start developing our paper after midterms."

Janette nods, jotting down the timeframe he's describing. "Making the PowerPoint and talking points should be easy after that so we could leave the last two weeks for that, giving us four weeks to finish the paper." Bentley nods and they both look over at me again.

"Works for me," I say, shrugging and continuing to enjoy watching the two of them nerd off in front of me.

We spend the rest of the class time talking about different thesis ideas, the two of them mostly going back and forth while I listen.

"So, we'll meet up at the library on Friday?" Janette says, packing her stuff up and standing with us. We both tower over her, forcing her to have to tip her head back a bit to look up at us.

"Yup," I say, placing my hands on the straps of my backpack to stop myself from reaching out to touch her. "We'll see you there, Blue."

Janette rolls her eyes. "That nickname doesn't make sense anymore, Axel."

"You're still Bluejay, Janette." I lean forward when she freezes, eyes starting to mist. "So, you'll always be Blue to me." She shakes her head, mouth twisting into a frown before she moves around us to start heading out.

"I'll see you guys on Friday," she says, looking over at Bentley before rushing away.

"Told you you'd like her," I say as we both watch her climb the steps of the center aisle and walk out the open doors at the top.

"She's not that bad," Bentley says. "Don't tell Mira I said that."

I cross my finger over my heart. "I'll take your secret to the grave."

Bentley rolls his eyes, heading toward the stairs. I follow behind him, suddenly wondering if Bentley checked out my ass when we came into the room the way I'm checking out his as we leave.

9

Janette

I lean forward and press my forehead against the laminated wooden table as the sounds of coffee being made, and orders being placed surrounds me.

"Class was that bad? It's only week two," Layla says across from me, taking a sip of her smoothie through a giant straw.

"I'm attracted to your brother," I say into the tabletop, unable to look up as the words leave my mouth.

"Yeah, no shit." Layla snorts. "You two were basically eye fucking all night last weekend."

I groan. "And I think I'm attracted to his roommate." I wait for the ground to open up beneath us and swallow me whole. Instead, the world just keeps bustling along, barista's rushing between machines to make the coffee orders of every sleep deprived student on campus.

Layla starts laughing. I pick my head up and glare at her. "Stellar taste, babes. Bentley Marshall is hot as hell." I pull my iced peach tea toward me, chewing on the indigo straw for a minute as I stare out the window next to me and watch people walk through the center of campus.

"They're both in my Medieval History class and as of this morning, we're all partnered up for the semester long research project so I can't even avoid them in class for the rest of the year."

"Why avoid them? Axel's definitely interested and I'm sure Bentley isn't blind." Layla shrugs, flipping her fading cherry red hair over her shoulder. "Just get rid of Chris and you're home free to take your pick. Or try them both out."

I turn back toward her. "Your advice is to break up with my boyfriend and start dating your brother and his roommate at the same time?"

"Yes," Layla says with another sip of her smoothie.

I shake my head. "I can't break up with Christopher." I suck down some more tea.

"You don't even like him." I try to swallow the gulp I just took to argue the point, but she continues before I can. "You complained about him countless times in your emails over the last year, not to mention you would flinch when he touched you the other night, and there's the fact that your boyfriend came up to see you for the first time when your roommate was gone for the weekend and you invited people over rather than spend time alone with him on a Saturday night. You don't like him, babes."

"My mom likes him." I stir my tea with the straw, watching the ice swirl and clink in the cup. "She's ecstatic we're dating since it basically solidifies her business relationship with his dad. She'd be pissed if I broke up with him."

"Then she should date him." Layla grips her smoothie tighter, the plastic cup crinkling a bit in her hand. "She's basically pimping you out for campaign funds."

I shake my head. "It's not like that. She just doesn't see

anything past her job. She hasn't since we moved to Georgia." *Since Dad died*, I add in my head.

Layla reaches across the table, taking my hand in hers and squeezing. "I'm so glad I can finally comfort you in person. I always wanted to jump through my screen and hug you. Or shake some sense into Aunt Sandy."

I laugh, my chest twinging when I hear her call Mom that again. "Yeah, I think you've said that a few times in the last few years. Either that or telling me I should just run away and move in with you and Uncle Jack."

"That would have been a flawless plan if you had just bought the tickets." She rolls her eyes then squeezes my hand. "But you should be able to date who you want. *Whoever* you want," she waggles her eyebrows at me, a sly smile slowly forming on her face. "Even if it is my dumbass brother."

I chuckle again, squeezing her hand back before letting go. "You do realize you're suggesting I make a mess of your brother's life? They're roommates. No matter which way I lean, I'll cause a rift. It's too messy. Especially with us all being in this group project for the whole semester. I'm just not going to do anything to rock the boat." I lean back from the table, crossing my arms over my chest.

"Yeah, that's probably smart," Layla says with another sip of her smoothie. "I'm sure it will be super easy to keep your hands to yourself with Bentley Marshall looking like a god and my brother practically drooling over you beside him." She chuckles when I grimace.

"Stop saying Bentley's name like that." I point at her and try to look stern, but she just puts her hands up, still smiling. "I don't think he'll be a problem. Pretty sure he dislikes me from our first encounter. And your brother will probably annoy me after a few weeks."

"No, he won't. You always laughed at him when he was pissing me off. You're going to fall way too hard for him if he actually tries for you." My stomach clenches, realizing she's probably right. "And just because he called you a snob doesn't mean he dislikes you." I roll my eyes at her, going back to my iced tea. She pulls her straw out mid-stir and points it at me. "You said you were acting weird because Chris was around. I'm sure Bentley will figure out how amazing you are now that you guys have to spend quality time together all semester." She waggles her eyebrows again, knowing smirk back in place.

"Ugh," I say, putting my forehead down on the table again. I thought going to the Coast would solve all my problems, having space from Mom and Chris while also getting Layla back, but I'm two weeks in and things feel more complicated than they ever were in Georgia.

Layla pats my shoulder. "It'll be fine, J. You just need a distraction to get your mind off the two six-foot Adonis's vying for your affections."

I lift my head up an inch to glare at her. She smiles back, teeth on display. I study the look, not sure why it sets the hairs on the back of my neck off. "What are you up to?"

"I'm not up to anything. I just think you should take a night to get out of your head. Have some fun." She shrugs, eyes quickly glancing away from me to look around the coffee shop.

"Lay," I say, drawing out the vowel. "Just spit it out."

"Okay, okay." She slams her smoothie down and I pick myself up, facing her fully. "There's a party tonight at the Raven's mansion and I need you to come along. Gwen is dragging me with her, probably thinks if she shows up with me, they won't kick her out. But she's going to run off and snoop the second she gets inside, and I'll be all on my own!"

She grabs my hand again and bats her eyelashes. "If you come with us, then we can have a little fun while we're there, get your mind off things, destress." She smiles wide at the end, eyes pleading with me to go.

I furrow my brows. "The Ravens?" Our mascot is a fox, and we don't even really have any good sports teams. The only one that ever wins is our hockey team and they're called the Arctic Foxes. I don't even know if they have a house together and there aren't any other schools nearby so it can't be a rival team's house either.

Layla waves her hand. "Gwen always calls them that because they were all high school athletes together and their high school's mascot was a raven. She acts like they're some secret society or something." She rolls her eyes. "They're just a group of guys who live together off campus. Mira's brother, Ramsey, is one of them and I've heard they throw killer parties."

I bite the inside of my cheek. "I have an eight a.m. tomorrow, Lay."

She leans forward, grabbing both of my hands this time. "I know, but we don't have to drink a lot or stay late. Just go in, have a drink and a look around, maybe talk to some cute boys." I glare at her. "Or not," she says, pulling her hands free to hold them up in surrender. "Please, J! I really don't want to have to sit in the corner by myself and wait for Gwen to get bored or kicked out."

I sigh. "Fine, I'll go." Layla claps, grabbing her smoothie again and taking a big sip. "But I want to be back home by midnight, Lay. And I'm only having one drink. Maybe just a soda."

She nods, trying to keep her face serious. "Of course, of course." I lean back and she smiles. "But we're still going to have a good time."

I roll my eyes, grabbing my bag from the floor next to me. "Then, I better head back to my room and figure out what I'm going to wear tonight."

Layla grabs her stuff and jumps up as well. "I'll come help," she says, locking our arms together. We head out of the coffee shop and turn toward West Tower while the knots in the pit of my stomach writhe.

10

Janette

I glare at Layla standing in the doorway of my bathroom. She smiles sheepishly, trying to apologize with her eyes, but I know Axel is here because she invited him. He stands behind her, Gwen at his side, and grins at me over Layla's head.

"Hey, guys," I say to Axel and Gwen. "I'll be ready in a minute." Gwen nods, going over to the couch and sitting down. She pulls out her phone, thumbs swiping over the surface immediately.

"No problem. Mind if I steal a water?" I shake my head at Axel, and he walks off to the kitchen to go hunt one down.

"Sorry, sorry, sorry," Layla says, walking into the bathroom and standing next to me facing the mirror while I brush mascara over my lashes. I glare at her again before switching to the other side. "I know you were supposed to be getting him out of your head, but he asked what I was up to tonight and I knew he'd bug Gwen next if I didn't tell him. He probably won't even stick with us once we get there. He's just bored since Bentley's hanging out with Mira tonight."

I grunt, finishing my makeup and fluffing my hair a bit.

"It's fine, Lay." I pull the edge of my crop top down a bit and do one last check in the mirror. It's a party, but I mostly want to be comfortable, so I paired the white crop top with a pair of frayed jean shorts and topped the whole thing off with an oversized turquoise cardigan. Dressing it up with some silver necklaces and makeup, I left my natural curls down around my shoulders.

"You look hot." Layla stands beside me in an off the shoulder long sleeve grey shirt that zips up the middle with a silver hoop adorning the black zipper at the center of her chest. It's tucked into high waisted black leather pants, and she wears a cute pair of open toed sandals on her feet. Her brassy red hair swings behind her head in a high ponytail, long brown shadow roots slicked back, so that it provides a colorful accent to her look.

"I was going for comfortably cute but thank you." I follow her out of the bathroom, walking over to the shoe rack by the door and pulling a pair of black suede ankle boots on. Gwen stands from the couch, eyes still on her phone screen and Axel comes over to the door, chugging a water.

"Ready?" I ask, opening the door and setting the lock as everyone nods and head out into the hall. I walk to the elevator, following Gwen and side by side with Layla. I feel Axel's eyes on me and glance back, catching his smirk at being caught staring at my ass.

Layla hooks her arm in mine as we get off the elevator, heading through the lobby and out onto the dark sidewalk.

"How far is the walk?" I ask.

"Not long. About ten minutes," Gwen says, looking back at us. "We'll probably hear the music once we get off campus since it's just down the road." We walk down the side of Ring Road, heading toward the tree shrouded section that splits the campus between academic buildings and the shiny sports complex and fields. Most of them are empty most days, but I've seen the lacrosse team practicing from the window in my room a few times.

We turn left, walking through an open iron gate and off campus onto a street lined with nice looking houses. The cool air makes me wrap my cardigan around my midsection.

"Layla said you're obsessed with the guys living at this house," I say, and watch Gwen whip around and glare at her sister, who shrugs. Axel snorts from behind us. "What's the deal with them?"

"I'm not obsessed with them," Gwen says, falling back to walk in line with Layla and me. She takes a minute to continue, an owl hooting in the distance. "I'm just curious, that's all."

Layla rolls her eyes at me. "Curious about what?" I ask. Gwen frowns, glancing between her sister and me.

"Gwen thinks they're part of the mafia," Axel says from behind us.

"No," she yells, looking back at him with narrowed eyes. "I think a couple of them might be part of the Bratva." Shock must register on my face because she continues. "The Russian mafia. There are some articles online about how Smith's parents and sister died that seem weird and his cousin is never alone, always seen with either Smith or this other burly man who doesn't ever speak a word, just stands next to him or in the back of his classes when Smith isn't around."

"She thinks she can write an expose about them in the school paper and not get her head chopped off in the middle of the night," Layla says.

Gwen rolls her eyes. "Of course, I can't do that, but the journalist side of me is curious. Don't you think it's weird that there might be two mafia princes going to the Coast?" Layla's words from the other day about everyone at the Coast having parents in every echelon of the world's elite drift through my mind. "I want to know what happens in that house. And how are the other three guys involved?"

"There's no story there, sis. You should probably give it up. You've already pissed them off enough," Axel says, and I look back at him, finding him shaking his head. The thump of a baseline invades the silence around us as we continue down the road.

"They caught you snooping?" I ask, looking back at Gwen.

"No." She bites her lip. "I sort of wrote an article about Tanner Hill our freshman year that blew up more than I thought it would." She starts wringing her hands.

"She eviscerated him. It was his first year playing for the hockey team and she basically ridiculed the school for letting him on the team." Layla looks around me at Gwen, daring her to disagree.

"It wasn't that bad," she says quietly, cheeks heating. "I didn't think it would get published. I was a freshman just starting out on the paper. I figured another article would get chosen and was just using the assignment as an outlet."

"She's on the Ravens' shit list now, hence the need for backup when entering their lair." Layla giggles, pointing at me and Axel.

Gwen crosses her arms over her chest and eyes me. "Well, hopefully coming with the birthday girl's roommate will win me some brownie points," she says, chewing her lip again.

I furrow my brows. "Wait, it's Mira's birthday? And this party is for her?" My stomach drops, panic blooming in the empty space and making my blood race.

We turn down a gravel driveway, the opening tucked between two rows of tall cypress plants that hide the house behind them from view. The wall reminds me of a softer version of the brick one we have in Georgia, and I wonder if the residents feel as trapped inside as I did. The music suddenly sounds much louder as we walk toward the three-story black and grey Victorian house. A large, covered porch wraps around the right side of the house, a circular turret sitting above it at the second and third floors. Multi-colored lights flash through the open windows of the bottom floor and shine out the glass beveled door, lighting the porch up as well. Cars line the circular driveway, a red truck the largest and parked closest to the door.

"You didn't know?" Gwen asks as we get closer to the house.

I swallow to try to soothe my now dry throat. "We don't really talk much." Gwen's forehead worries and Layla squeezes my shoulder. "I should have known," I whisper.

"It'll be fine," Layla says, letting go of my shoulder to walk up the porch steps. They creak under our feet, but the noise is almost completely drowned out by the loud music now pouring out the open areas of the house.

A large staircase welcomes us as we walk into the house, people mingling on the sides of it and spilling into the open living room to the left of the front door. The dark wood stairs are the only piece that matches the Victorian façade outside. Everything else is light and modern, cream walls framed by dark wood accent borders and an open floor plan where the kitchen can be seen beyond the living room. Another room opens on our right, decorated in green with a large bay window looking out on the driveway. It's filled with people leaning against the walls and on furniture facing the two folding tables in the center where people play beer pong, someone yelling as they miss one of the three cups left on the other side.

"Axel!" a girl yells from the beer pong room, waving at him from the couch on the other side of the room. Her friend looks over, eyes lighting up when they see him.

Axel waves back, an easy smile on his face. He puts his hand on my back as he slides out from behind us, heading toward the girls and I watch, something spikey and hard rattling around in my chest.

"Let's find Mira and wish her a happy birthday," Gwen shouts over the music, pulling on Layla's hand. Layla grabs mine and we shoulder our way through people, heading into the living room area opposite the room Axel just went into. My eyes immediately find Bentley, standing next to a curvy girl sitting on the arm of a leather couch. The girl throws her head back and laughs as Bentley pouts down at Mira sitting in an oversized armchair on the other side of him. A petite girl in all black giggles on the couch beside the curvy one and I recognize her from my Algebra class on Tuesdays and Thursdays.

Gwen sees them and starts dragging us over, tapping Mira on the shoulder once we're close enough. Mira turns around, smiling when she sees her then looking back at Layla who surveys the room and me. I fidget, ashamed I didn't know this was her birthday party.

"Hey, great party! And happy birthday! Figured I'd stop by. I've never been to one of the guy's parties," Gwen rambles and Mira nods, murmuring thank you. She looks over at Layla whose eyes track over the group before stopping on her.

"Leave her alone, Gwenivere," a large, white-haired guy says, walking up from seemingly nowhere and standing behind the couch that the girl from Algebra and her friend sit on. He's our age, with a barrel chest and tree trunk waist. His snow-white hair falls to his shoulders, the top half held back in a small bun at the back of his head. Stubble lines the edge of his sharp jawline, dark despite his fair hair. His eyes flash in the moving strobe lights that seem pitch black with his brows pulled over them but lighten to an icy blue when the light hits his face.

Gwen steps back toward us, and Layla whispers, "Tanner," under her breath to me.

Mira leans back to look up at him, and loses her balance, tipping toward the floor. Bentley flinches toward her, but the girl from my Algebra class beats him to it, grabbing her arm and holding her up for a second before she sits back up, facing the three of us. Gwen puts her hands on Mira's shoulders as she sways a bit, keeping her steady.

"You need water," she says, helping Mira up off the chair and toward the kitchen. We all follow, Bentley ending up beside me in the space between the cabinets and kitchen island. He watches Mira, eyes not even glancing my way while Gwen pours water into a solo cup. I lean on the island and away from him, folding my arms to avoid the urge to touch his next to me. Gwen hands Mira the water, looking over at Layla and avoiding the glare Tanner is trying to drill through her head.

"This is my sister Layla." Gwen grabs Layla's arm, pulling her closer while she frowns. Bentley folds his arms over his chest next to me.

"Mira," she yells. "Nice to meet you."

"Okay," Tanner cuts in, crowding in closer to Gwen and clenching his fists at his sides. "She got her water. Time to go, Gwenivere."

Mira side-steps between them, leaning back against Tanner. "It's okay, Tan. She's not bothering me."

He looks down at her, raising one eyebrow. "Don't let Ramsey see you get any more drunk." He walks away after that, not even sparing a glance at Gwen who practically shakes with nerves. We all watch Mira take a few more gulps of water, leaning against the island for support.

Noticing all our eyes on her, she glances over at the two girls from the couch, who now stand off to the side behind her where Tanner just left from. "This is Autumn and Aria," she says to Gwen, pointing to the curvy girl before reminding me of the girl from Algebra's name. "They're freshman on the third floor at West Tower." Gwen turns toward them, immediately starting a conversation about how they're liking their RA Keith.

I glance over at Bentley, whose eyes are still firmly fixed on Mira before deciding to keep my eyes solely on Gwen to stop myself from doing so again.

"Nicely done," Layla whispers to Mira. "She's a bloodhound." Mira looks confused so Layla leans in. "Hard to distract when she's got the scent." She smirks, and Mira smiles. I feel a pang of guilt, happy that Layla is good at meeting new people, but sad that I don't have the same talent.

"You go to the Coast?" Mira asks. Bentley shifts his weight beside me and I step closer to Layla to stop myself from noticing his every move.

Layla nods. "Liberal arts for right now. I'm trying to figure out what I want to do, and dear old dad didn't want me just lazing around the house while my brother and sister got degrees." She shrugs. "At least now I have J here to keep me company." She sneers over at me, and I flip her off.

Bentley steps forward and knocks his shoulder against mine, jostling me. "Ease up, Little Miss Sunshine. Try having fun."

The jab stings, reminding me of our first encounter in the dorm. I glare up at him. "I'm fun."

Mira snorts and even Layla snickers a bit. I turn my glare onto her.

She shrugs, only half attempting to stop smiling. "Come on, J. You haven't even had a drink since we got here."

I attempt to stave off my outrage, but the sting lingers. I give in, looking around the kitchen for something alcoholic. Unfolding my arms, I reach out across Bentley to grab a half empty bottle of expensive looking vodka. Looking at Bentley, who raises an eyebrow, then Layla and Mira, I uncap the bottle, take a long drag, and force myself to swallow against the burn in my throat. My face screws up once I finish, my tastebuds protesting the aftertaste. "Fun enough for you?" I ask, sneering at Bentley.

He laughs, moving between the group and toward the fridge. I glance around again, grabbing a solo cup from the plastic wrapped stack sitting on the counter. Pouring two or three shots into the glass, I feel a jolt of heat when Bentley's hand covers mine, taking the cup from me.

"Why don't we try mixing it with something?" he says, pouring orange juice in over the vodka. I cap the bottle, setting it back on the counter before taking the drink from his hand and staring him down over the rim of the cup while I drink a huge gulp. He smirks, watching me. The sweetness of the juice masks the burn of the alcohol and I hold my composure this time.

Lay chuckles, grabbing her own cup and pushing it toward Bentley who pours in half the amount of vodka I did and then covers it with juice as well. Layla takes it, sipping slower than I did as well.

"I need to pee," Mira says. "I'll be back."

Bentley nods, leaning back against the counter. "I'll be here. You're not back in ten, I'm coming to look for you."

Mira nods, wandering off into the crowd of people around us.

I drink more of my screwdriver, warmth sliding down my throat and nestling in my belly. It loosens my limbs and I feel myself relaxing. Layla winks at me, glancing at Bentley before turning to join Gwen, Autumn, and Aria in their conversation. I grit my teeth, thinking of ways to get her back for this later as I pour the rest of the drink down my throat. Slamming the cup on the counter, I pull the alcohol over and prepare another vodka heavy screwdriver.

"Whoa, slugger. Slow down," Bentley says, reaching over and taking the vodka bottle from my hand after I fill almost half the solo cup with it.

"Thought you wanted me to have fun?" I reach past him for the orange juice, pouring it into my cup.

"You just need to loosen up, not blackout tonight." He turns around, putting the vodka away in the top of a tall cabinet.

I glare up at him when he turns back. "I'm not going to blackout."

"Janette!" Layla calls, my eyes flitting over to her excited face. "It's your song!" I pause, tuning into the music pulsing around us and realizing I recognize the song. Layla and I made a dance routine to the throwback when we were twelve, posting it to YouTube before our moms found out and made us take it down. "Come on!" She reaches past Bentley, grabbing my wrist and pulling me away as he smiles down at me in passing.

We end up in the living room with Autumn and Aria, Gwen disappearing on the way over to the group of people dancing between the couches. I laugh, shaking my hips to the beat as Layla bobs her head and mimics some of the moves we made up over six years ago. She grabs my hand, twirling me under her arm and I tuck my other arm in, protecting my drink as I let her. The room spins around me, but Bentley's face sticks out, having moved to the area between the kitchen and living room to watch us. He leans against a support beam, eyes burning as he watches me.

I turn away, taking another swig from my cup and downing half of it in one go. Time to put on a show.

11

BENTLEY

My eyes stay glued to Janette as she shakes her hips and rolls her body to the music. Her curls bounce around her, alive and electric in the pulsing lights. Her cardigan falls off one shoulder as she brings her cup to her lips, her other arm high in the air, drinking more. My eyes wander the newly exposed skin, mouth drying as she bends her knees and sways her ass, lowering closer to the ground before springing back up, right on beat. I grip my biceps, rock hard in my jeans and fight off the visions of her over top of me, similarly moving her hips in far less than those shorts.

She holds the empty cup up, yelling something to Layla and Autumn before leaving the group and heading back to the kitchen. Glancing at the cabinet I stored the vodka in earlier, she glares over at me, before opening the fridge and looking around. I watch her pull a beer from the crisper drawer and crack the tab, chugging with her eyes locked on mine over the edge. I shake my head, regretting my jab from earlier. The girl is tiny, clearly already feeling the effects of the first two heavy drinks she's already downed. If I hadn't challenged her to lighten up, she probably wouldn't be this deep right now, trying to prove she can have a good time.

Layla appears at my side, watching her friend finish the beer and bow for the light cheers some of the people lingering in the kitchen give her. "This is your fault you realize?"

"Yeah, I already put that together." I watch Janette start dancing with some girls in the kitchen, neither even close to sober either.

"She rises to challenges. Keep that in mind." I glance down at Layla, eyebrows pulling together. "For next time." She smirks before gasping, eyes wide as she mutters, "Janette, no." My head whips back toward the kitchen, finding Janette standing on one of the stools by the island, climbing onto the granite next. The other two drunk girls follow suit, all three taking a moment to laugh before they start to dance.

Mira walks up to Layla and me, looking much more sober than when she left for the bathroom. "Is she okay?"

"She's proving she can be fun," I mutter, watching her tip her head back and mouth the words to the song. I glance down at Mira, double taking when I notice her red rimmed eyes. "What's wrong?"

She waves her hand with a little chuckle, trying to placate me. "I'm fine, just getting a little tired."

I nod. "Lemme grab Janette and we can all head back." Mira looks over at her roommate then around the room, noting each of our friends spread out and having a good time.

"Nah, it's fine. You should probably keep an eye on Miss Fun over there." She points her thumb over her shoulder at Janette who teeters a little before righting herself by grabbing onto the girl next to her. My stomach drops, but I look back down at Mira once I know Janette's okay. "I can make it back on my own."

I push off the post, standing up fully and opening my mouth to protest.

Mira waves me off. "It's fine, Bent. It's not even a ten-minute walk. I'll have my cell on me the whole time." She takes it out and makes a show of holding it firmly at her side.

I try again to get my argument out, but a collective gasp goes up around us and we all look over in time to see Janette lose her balance and start to topple off the island. Layla gasps and I rush forward, wrapping my arms around Janette as she falls clumsily, laughing her head off. I frown, looking to Mira who holds up her phone. Janette starts pushing against my chest, trying to get out of my hold.

"I'll text you when I get back to West Tower," Mira shouts over the music and I reluctantly nod, looking down at the girl in my arms.

"Put me down," she protests while Layla wishes Mira a happy birthday before she disappears. "Wanna dance."

I lower her legs to the ground, keeping my arms around her torso while she finds her balance. Her body leans against mine, reawakening my hard-on from earlier. "No more table dancing," I say, before gritting my teeth.

She tips her head back to look at me and my hand shoots out, catching the back of her head before she snaps her neck. My fingers tangle with her soft curls and I force myself not to focus on the feel of them against my skin. "You worry too mucccchhhhh," she slurs, tapping my nose once with the tip of her index finger.

Her warning's too late. I'm already going grey worrying about this girl tonight.

I narrow my eyes at her. "Janette," I warn.

She laughs, shaking her head out of my hold and sliding away from me. I try to stop her, but she quickly maneuvers away from me, her laugh lingering in my ears, despite the music. She weaves through people sloppily, going into one of the side rooms while I try to follow without running over those she's left in her wake. Layla follows right on my heels.

"You're never going to be able to wrangle her before she wants to be wrangled," she yells beside me. We make it into the room she disappeared into, finding her waiting for a guy to pour her a beer from the keg tapped in the corner. "She's stubborn like that."

I growl as we walk up to her, the guy holding the tap taking a step back. Janette whirls around, smiling at us as she sips her beer. "Hey, guys! Want to play beer pong?"

Layla laughs, shrugging in my direction when Janette grabs her hand, pulling her toward the beer pong table nearest us.

"Axel!" Janette shouts, throwing her hands up and spilling half the beer she just got. She abandons Layla, running over to him at one end of the beer pong table. My heart squelches when I see them come together. Axel grins as Janette comes to a stop before him, putting a hand on her waist when the abrupt halt makes her sway a little.

"Hey, Blue. You look like you're having fun."

She looks over her shoulder at me with a pointed look.

I tamp down a grin, settling against the wall behind me and once again crossing my arms.

Turning back to Axel, Janette shouts, "I am! We want to play." She gestures to the table and Axel nods, leaning over to the guy he was playing with and telling him Layla and Janette have winner.

The girls stand to the side, watching the end of the

current game as Axel and his partner easily finish the other team who only sinks the ball twice before it's over.

"Ladies," Axel says, gesturing to the side of the table they stand on and Janette bounces over, starting to move the cups back into the pyramid formation. Layla follows slower, taking one of the balls from her brother as he crosses to the other side. His eyes meet mine over the girl's heads once he and his partner face them.

Smirking, Axel winks at me and my dick twitches. I shift my weight, digging my fingers into my biceps once more and hoping no one can see the outline in my jeans. Still, I watch Axel as he helps his partner set up their cups, eyes lingering on the way his fingers flex and following the veins up his exposed forearms.

Janette and Layla laugh, drawing my attention to them momentarily.

The game starts, Layla and Axel facing off for the starter toss and I stay still through most of the game, smiling when Janette finally sinks one on her fourth try. A bead of sweat rolls down her neck, sliding in between the valley of her breasts. My tongue flicks out to lick my bottom lip before I raise my eyes and lock onto Axel's fiery gaze. We stare for a few beats, only breaking eye contact to snap our eyes back to Janette who stumbles a bit on her feet. I come off the wall, steadying her with a hand on her back. Axel nods to me, eyes narrowing on her when she giggles and takes another sip of beer, before he takes his next shot, missing for the first time.

They play for a while, Layla holding her own against Axel, each of their partners clearly the weaker players. I toggle between watching out for Janette and sliding my gaze over Axel, spending the entire game dizzy due to all my blood rushing south.

The game comes down to one cup in front of the girls and two in front of the guys. Layla throws and misses, leaving the chance to tie it up to Janette. I readjust my stance, unsure who I want to win at this point. Every time Axel makes a shot or meets my gaze, my stomach flips. But each time Janette sinks one, she jumps up and down and looks back at me with a haughty expression that makes my blood sizzle.

Janette mimes her shot a few times before letting the ball fly, the little white blur soaring across the table and sliding into the cup on the left without even touching the rim. Janette squeals, jumping up and down and spinning around while Layla laughs. Our eyes meet and Janette smirks once again. This time I return the look, letting the heat in my gut show on my face. She freezes, swallowing hard and staring at me with wide eyes. I chuckle, nodding toward the game still playing out in the other direction.

Axel takes the ball out of the cup, sliding it over to the side and centering the one left on their end. Then he stands, pulling his shoulders back and just flicking the ball across the table with his wrist. It hits the edge of the cup on the girl's side, Layla's hand swiping out to stop it but missing a second too late as the ball slides past to the water at the bottom.

Axel merely steps back, staring Janette down as a closed-mouth smile slides into place. I can't see her face, but I'm betting she looks pretty shocked at the moment. Layla groans, folding her arms over her chest beside Janette. The other guy across from them jumps up and down, hollering in excitement and grabbing Axel's shoulder roughly. My eyes narrow on the contact until Axel shrugs him off, glancing over at me before looking back at Janette.

"Don't pout, Blue. It was a close game," he calls to her.

"We want a rematch," Janette says.

"You have class in the morning, J," Layla says to her, touching her shoulder. "Maybe we should head back to West Tower."

Janette shakes her head. "Don't want to," she says, going to sip her forgotten beer on the side of the table and finding the cup empty. She looks over at the guy still standing by the keg and starts to head over.

I push off the wall, putting my arm out and catching her around the middle. "You've had enough tonight, sunshine."

"I'm not Little Miss Sunshine," she mumbles, sagging against me.

I chuckle, keeping my arm around her as she leans the side of her face against my chest and closes her eyes. "No, I guess you're not." I lean down to whisper in her ear, "But the name still fits, sunshine."

Axel comes around the table, letting some more guys step up to play. "You got her?" he asks me. I nod and he pats my shoulder before brushing a curl off her face. "Get home safe, Blue."

She murmurs something unintelligible back and he chuckles. "I'll be back to the suite in a bit," he says to me, then winks. "Don't wait up." Once again, the move makes me tense up and I hope Janette can't feel my response against her hip.

Layla snorts as he turns and walks out of the room, seeming to look around for someone. I look over at her and she smiles knowingly at me.

"Come on," I say. "Let's get her out of here."

Layla nods, following me as I shuffle her toward the front door. Making it without much problem, she starts grumbling as we help her down the porch steps and I sigh, crouching down and putting my arm under her knees to scoop her up. The move jostles her enough that she opens her eyes and looks around, confused before finding my face. I tighten my grip on her, and she snuggles into me, laying her cheek against my chest and closing her eyes again. The feel of her weight and warmth seeping into me has me fighting a grin I know Layla would call me out on. Nothing I can do about the raging boner I've had for the last hour, but the discomfort of walking back with it pressing against my fly is lessened by the sound of Janette's deep breathing as her mouth falls open and little snores escape her throat.

"I'm on the ground floor," Layla says, making me stop in the dorm lobby as she looks between me and her friend. "Can I trust you to get her to her room safely?"

I nod. "I won't hurt her. Her roommate's my best friend. She'll let me in and help me put her to bed. Then it's back to my suite. Swear on my life."

Layla studies me, looking at Janette a few times before nodding her head. "Axel trusts you. So does she, it seems. I will too." She starts walking toward the entrance to the hall for the rooms on this floor and I step up to the elevators, squatting a bit to push the button without letting go of Janette.

"I'll hold you to that, just so you know," Layla calls from behind me and I turn to the side to quirk an eyebrow at her, my head tipping a bit. "You said you won't hurt her. That's a binding agreement now and I'll hold you to it. Goodnight, Bentley Marshall."

She disappears around the corner and the door to the elevators slides open. I walk in, turning around and then looking down at the girl curled up in my arms. She sleeps against me, and I study her relaxed face as the elevator climbs up to the sixth floor. Her lips are parted, face completely slack in sleep, but I find myself mesmerized by the slope of her nose and curve of her chin.

Walking with her to Mira's door, I stop and consider how to do this. I look down at Janette and decide to try to wake her so I can knock on the door. Letting her legs down slowly, I call her name softly. Her eyes blink open a couple of times, and she picks her head up looking around.

"Bentley?" Her voice comes out breathy and I swallow.

"Hey, we're at your suite," I say softly. "I need you to stand up for a sec so I can knock, and Mira can let us in."

She closes her eyes, saying, "Don't wake her," and digging her hand into the back pocket of her shorts. She pulls out her key and holds it up, leaning her head back against me. I take the key, unlocking her door and helping her walk in.

The suite door shuts behind us and I help her into her room. "Do you want some water?" I ask but she shakes her head, letting go of me and stumbling over to her bed. Dropping onto the mattress, she buries her face in one of the pillows and curls up on top of the comforter. Her hand roots around in the front pocket of her shorts, and I damn near have a heart attack before she pulls out her phone, so it doesn't press into her hip, and slams it down on the bedside table.

I walk over, picking up one of her feet and pulling off the boot and sock before repeating the same thing to the other one. Tugging the blanket out from under her, I pull it up over her body, tucking it in around her shoulders. She murmurs something I don't understand, and I stand up, looking down at her as she falls asleep. I walk out to the kitchen and open the fridge, pulling out a water bottle and heading back into her room. Setting it on the bedside table, I watch her shuffle around for a moment, getting comfortable, but never opening her eyes and ending up on her back, arms raised above her head. I push the curls that fall over her face out of the way, heat lingering in my fingertips as they brush her face. She smiles in her sleep, and I pull back, stopping myself from touching her cheek again.

Her phone buzzes on the bedside table and my eyes automatically fly to the source of the noise, seeing an incoming text notification. The name Christopher glares back at me, and I step away from the bed, stomach souring. Looking at Janette's face one more time, I turn around and walk out, closing the door to the suite softly behind me.

My mind races, going over the events of the night as they all swirl together.

Watching Janette dance.

The look in Axel's eye across the beer pong table.

The feel of Janette asleep in my arms.

I walk into my suite, kicking off my shoes and letting the door bang closed behind me as I head straight for my room, flicking the light on and flopping down on top of my bed. I rub my hands over my face, trying to remind myself that Janette has a boyfriend and Axel's my roommate, as my mind recalls every moment of the night that made my dick swell. My jeans grow tight, the feeling way too familiar for the night. I groan, hands already at my zipper before I make the conscious decision to release the tight confines. Lifting my hips, I shuffle my jeans and boxers down in one go, leaving them on, but down my thighs enough to release my cock. Gripping it in a tight fist, I start to pump myself, closing my eyes and picturing Janette's body as she danced in the dim lighting, the colored strobe falling over her in haphazard increments. My fist picks up speed, remembering her face as she tipped her head back and laughed. Axel's wink as he touched my shoulder plays next, my mind's eye lingering on the curve of his lips and angle of his jaw. I reach down with my other hand, cupping my sac as my hips thrust up into my fist, eyes screwed shut tight. Janette's little smile as she played beer pong flits through my brain, the swell of her chest bouncing each time she sunk a ball. I feel myself climbing, twisting my hand at the top of my cock as I furiously jerk off.

Janette's phone appears in my head, the text from Christopher catching in my brain and the tightness in my chest changes, my body relaxing against the bed as it backs away from the edge of release.

"Fuck." I pop my eyes open, staring at the ceiling as my grip loosens and my fist slows down.

"You want some help with that?"

My head flies off the pillow, eyes finding Axel as he leans in the doorway of my room, staring at my dick in my hand.

12

AXEL

entley sits up so fast, I worry for a second that he's going to fall off the side of his bed. His feet land on the floor though, hand still around the base of his cock as his face goes red. He looks around, purposely avoiding my presence and probably trying to figure out what to say. His mouth opens and closes a couple of times and my gut twists.

I push off the doorframe, standing up and holding my hands up. "Calm down, man," I try, hoping if I play up some nonchalance, he won't beat the shit out of me for walking in on him jacking off. His eyes fly to mine, and I read the confusion mingled in with the embarrassment there. My stomach settles a little, and I glance down, noticing he hasn't gone soft in the slightest. "I'm bi and you're hot." I shrug, meeting his eyes again. "I'm willing to help out and given your reaction," I gesture toward his still hard cock. "I thought you might be interested." A long pregnant pause plays out between us as he seems to completely freeze. I can't tell if this guy gets turned on by being pissed off or if he really has no idea what to do right now. I take a step back toward the common room, holding up my hands. "No harm, no foul. We can just pretend this never happened."

He glances down at his dick, letting go of it and grabbing a pillow to cover his crotch. The movement makes me pause, holding my breath to see what he does next. His eyes slide toward me, not looking directly at my face before flitting away.

"I'm, um, not uninterested," he stutters.

My heart starts to pound in my chest at his words. I had practically been salivating, walking in to immediately see him working himself over so frantically with all the lights on like he couldn't wait another second after getting back to come. I head told me to walk past and just go to my room, but my feet carried me to his open door, gaze glued on this gorgeous man. Despite my cheekiness, his flustered response killed my reaction almost immediately.

"It's just," he glances over at me. "We're roommates. I don't want things to be weird between us."

I swallow, eyes widening at his words, as my brain explodes. Blood leaves my brain, rushing down to the head in my shorts as I stare into Bentley's eyes. I try to maintain an even voice as I roughly respond, "It won't be weird." Clearing my throat, I try again. "If we're both interested, no harm in exploring it."

Bentley looks around, whispering to himself. "What's a blowjob between friends? No big deal," before looking me in the eye again and nodding slightly. His words send a pang through my chest, warning me that I don't want to stay just friends after this, but I ignore it, not wanting to freak him out.

He slowly slides the pillow off his lap, his still hard dick coming back into view. I smile, stepping forward and he leans back on his hands. I fall to my knees between his legs, placing my hands in the sides of his jeans and shimmying them the rest of the way down his legs.

"Shirt off," I say, and he glares for a moment at the order but tugs it over his head as I wrap my hand around the base of his dick, holding it up in his lap. His chest come into view; sun-kissed skin speckled with a light smattering of hair that I trail my eyes down before looking back up at his face. He stares down at me with an intense look, holding his breath. I smile, knowing I'm good at this, and lean forward, slowly trailing the flat of my tongue up the back of his cock before swirling it around the tip and over his slit already weeping with a few beads of precum. I groan at the musky taste, closing my eyes and sucking his mushroom head into my mouth. My fist moves underneath, covering the lower half of his dick as I pull back and then suck more of him in, letting my lips drag across the skin without touching him with my teeth. He groans and my dick hardens with every hitch of his breath as I work him to the back of my throat, gagging for a moment before I breathe through my nose and push him a little bit deeper, hollowing my cheeks and suctioning. The weight of his cock on my tongue as I work him over makes the base of my spine start to tingle, sparks shooting through my veins.

"Fuck, Axel." His hand falls onto my shoulder, gripping into my skin as he starts to lose control. His hips stutter below me, and I open my eyes, looking up into his half lidded hazel gaze. I pull back to the tip of his cock, holding his eyes as I deep throat him again in one fast go. His eyes fall closed, chest heaving as he grips the bedding beneath him, and his fingers dig into the muscles of my shoulder. "So good."

The warmth from his hand urges me to go faster, wanting to see him come undone beneath me. For me. I quicken my pace and reach up to squeeze his balls, running my thumbnail lightly over the faint seam down the center.

"I'm going to come," Bentley says, voice rough as he gasps. I pull back, letting the tip of my tongue slide over the veins bulging under his skin before sliding back down and sucking, creating a slurping noise. "Fuck," he warns right before the tangy warmth of his cum hits the back of my tongue and I swallow around the tip of his dick, feeling him shudder beneath me as more cum floods my mouth. He lets go of my shoulder, falling back on the bed and letting his arm flop down to cover his eyes.

I pop off his dick, blood still sizzling, and sit back on my heels, swallowing the last of his cum as I stare at him heaving in breaths on his bed. My heart stutters painfully in my ribcage, my own breath coming in short pants, as I stare at the bottom of Bentley's face, waiting for him to look at me again. Needing him to.

He peeks out from under his arm, eyes meeting mine and we stare, everything seeming to stop as energy crackles through the room. Without a word, he sits up as I scramble toward him at the same time, ending up straddling his lap as our mouths collide. His hands grip my hips and I settle down over him. His teeth snag my bottom lip and I shudder, eyes rolling back behind my lids as he bites just enough to spread pleasurable veins of pain out beneath my skin. Our tongues meet and the kiss deepens as one of his hands snakes in between us, finding the button on my shorts and making quick work of the zipper. He grips my rock-hard dick in his wide hand, moving it quickly over me as I gasp into his mouth, letting my head fall back and my eyes close. Lightning lights through my bones at the feel of him roughly tugging at me without lube. It borders on too much, but he just moves his lips to my throat, kissing and sucking along to leave flickers of pleasure across my skin. I grip the back of his neck, pulling him closer.

"Pants off," he murmurs against my neck, and I scramble off his lap, pushing my shorts and boxers straight to the ground in one go. He slides off the bed, now on his knees before me, placing his hands on my hips to steady himself. My heart stutters almost painfully at the view as I tug my button down off my shoulders and pull the tee shirt from underneath up over my head. Bentley grabs my dick with both hands, warm tongue flicking teasingly at my tip. He starts to rotate his hands in different directions and my hips stutter, the feeling robbing all the breath from my lungs.

He groans, leaning in and encasing my head in his mouth, sucking hard on the just the first inch or so. My balls draw up at the sensation, already right on the precipice within seconds. I tip my head back, squeezing my eyes shut, but mourn the loss of this visual and quickly look back down at him.

His eyes meet mine and he smirks, the tip of my dick still resting on his bottom lip. I pant as he unwraps his hands, moving them slowly back to my hips and then slams forward, taking all of me to the back of his warm wet mouth in one go. I blank, mind completely short-circuiting as my hand threads into the hair at the back of his head to hold him against me. I cry out at the same time, hips thrusting forward without my control. My dick bumps against the back of his throat and I start to retreat, but his grip on my hips tightens. His brows furrow in concentration and my eyes widen as he relaxes his throat around me, pushing me further into him, the tightness of it gripping around the tip of my cock. He seems to smirk around my dick, eyes alight with humor at my shock.

"Holy shit," I whimper. I've never had anyone take this

much of me in a blowjob. My hips jerk forward again at the sensation. Bentley grunts below me, nose brushing the smooth skin above the base of my dick. I realize I've closed my eyes and open them to find his hazel gaze lasered in on me. He hums, the vibration making sparks shoot up my spine, my vision blurring.

Holy fucking shit. This is the best blowjob of my life.

I move my hand to the side of his head, placing my other one on the opposite side and he nods slightly, still choking on my dick. I revel in the unspoken communication and trust he's giving me before I grip his head, sliding out of his mouth and slamming back in. My hips move over his face as I fuck into him.

Bentley breathes through his nose, staring up at me the whole time as my rhythm increases before I lose it altogether, chasing my high over the edge and spilling in his mouth before I can even warn him.

He swallows around me making my toes curl and prolonging my orgasm. He continues to lightly suck for a moment as my vision goes white before everything comes slamming back, making my ears ring. I find my hands massaging lightly over the sides of his head, soft hair brushing against the pads of my fingers. His head backs off unhurriedly, my hands falling away and cock slipping from his mouth as it starts to soften. I sag as my breath comes in long deep pulls and he stands up, hands still on my hips, keeping me steady. I watch him, waiting for his next move.

He leans forward, kissing me again, and my eyes flutter closed as his tongue brushes against mine and the taste of our releases mix in between us. He groans, gripping me harder as he steps back, taking me with him. I go willingly, arm wrapping around his waist while my other goes around his shoulders. We break apart for a moment, staring into each other's eyes a few inches apart and the bliss of the moment seems to crescendo.

He suddenly spins us around, surprising me and pushing me down so I fall on his bed, hands leaving his skin to catch my weight behind me. I stare up at him as he stands over me, panting as his hungry eyes rove my face for a long minute, before he follows me down onto the bed, gripping the back of my head and kissing me deeply again. My heart splutters as I grip the back of his head, eyes falling closed.

We keep kissing as we move, shuffling back together and maneuvering ourselves underneath his comforter until our heads land on one of his pillows. Finally settled, he pulls back, leaning over me to turn off the light switch behind us, shrouding the room in moonlight from his uncovered window.

The darkness suddenly sharpens the last twenty minutes in my mind. The rest of the day filters in on a few words. Roommate. Group project. *Janette.*

I have a moment of panic, thinking maybe I should just go back to my room to unravel by myself, but then Bentley lays back down beside me, eyes shining and bright. We stare at each other for a few moments, breath mingling between us.

The idea of crawling out of this bed right now seems stupid.

Questions still filter in through the settling haze. Are we still just friends? Roommates? Fuck buddies?

Janette's face swirls in again. How does she fit into all of this? I saw the way he looked at her tonight, watched over her. Saw the way his eyes roved over her the same way they roved over me. Cold fear laces through me as another question pops up.

Am I just a stand in for her?

My breathing picks up. I need to get out of this bed. My brain swims in confusion, panic setting in and freezing my tongue in place before I can make any excuses.

I lay there on my back still facing Bentley on his side. I watch as he smiles and his arm comes up across my torso, holding me. The weight of it sinks into me and I revel in his warmth, the contact scattering my thoughts for a moment in a good way. My muscles start to unlock.

"Goodnight, Axel," he whispers, eyes fluttering closed. His smile morphs into a smirk, making my chest feel even lighter. "Thanks for helping me out."

My spine stiffens.

He chuckles a little to himself as his breathing evens out.

I keep staring at him, studying the angles of his face. His arm still comforts me, but his words slide around in my head, joining the already mounted fears.

What's a blowjob between friends? No big deal. Thanks for helping me out. Friends. No big deal. Helping me out.

I can see him staring at Janette during the beer pong game, leaving the wall to touch her every now and then. My eyes roam his softened features, my fears giving way to dread slowly over time. My stomach twists as I remember the way she looked back at him.

I don't know how long I stay in his bed, my heartbeat growing louder in my ears as I question if this was a mistake. If I just went to my room when I came home, I wouldn't have had one of the best orgasms of my life. But I also wouldn't have this ache that I just know Bentley doesn't want to fill. Not with me.

Mason clung to me, even after I laid it out that nothing else would ever happen between us.

I don't want to be that person to Bentley. That person he

stresses over having to see. Over having to turn down yet again.

And I promised him this wouldn't make things weird.

I carefully lift Bentley's arm off me, moving it back over to his side. He readjusts, thrusting one of his hands under the pillow and snuggling in. I slide off the bed, grabbing my clothes off his floor and tiptoeing out of the room. At the doorway, I look back at him sleeping, grabbing the knob and swinging it closed silently behind me. Staring at the door, I feel an chasm crack open in my chest, knowing I'll need to take some time to sop up the bleeding edges before I can go back to being around Bentley casually again.

Sighing through a deep breath, I walk over to my room. Closing myself in, I lie down and stare up in the dark, debating if I made the wrong move tonight.

13

BENTLEY

I sling the strap of my bag over my shoulder, sighing as I head out of the suite. Looking over at Axel's closed bedroom door, I shut the one to the suite, something sharp moving in my chest. Walking over to the elevator, I feel the absence of my roommate as I wait by myself in the hall.

Waking up alone yesterday morning, I figured Axel had just gone to the bathroom or was getting dressed for the day in his room. My plan had been to ask him out to breakfast, psyching myself up to tell him how the night before meant more to me than a random one-off hookup between horny friends. The moment I looked down at him on his knees after he made me see stars, I realized just how not casual I felt about us. That's why I reached for him, kissing him as he settled over my lap and wanting to return the favor. I wanted to see where things could go between us, wanted him close to me while we slept.

But after getting dressed and running my hands through my hair over a hundred times, I emerged from my room, looking around and finding no Axel. He didn't have classes till the afternoon on Thursdays and he usually spent a lot of the morning sleeping but checking the bathroom and knocking on his bedroom door had yielded no results as the realization slowly slid over my shoulders and tangled in the center of my chest.

He left.

I don't know if he slept next to me. But as time passed and I paced the length of the living room and then my bedroom in two separate panics, I started to think he escaped as soon as he could. Feeling myself going a little crazy, I forced myself to leave the dorms, going on a walk around Ring Road and feeling the pit in my stomach start to gnaw at me from the inside.

Taking another deep breath, I step off the elevator, walking out to the sidewalk and heading toward the library. Keeping my eyes on the tall cathedral spires in the distance, I remember how the rest of yesterday played out.

Axel came home after class last night and went directly to his room after a grunted, "Hey," to me on the couch. I kept playing video games, trying to keep my eyes from drifting to his closed door too often before completely giving up and going to my own bedroom to stare at the ceiling and try to quiet my rambling thoughts.

It would be one thing if he wanted to write off our hookup as a one-time thing. But his complete avoidance of me had me questioning how big of a mistake we actually made. He'd been the one to tell me we should explore our attraction, the one to offer to start this. But I pulled him into my bed. I tucked us in to go to sleep next to each other. I crossed the line past hookup to something more.

And now Axel has spent the entire day yet again avoiding me. I finally broke down and texted him if we were still meeting Janette to start our research project in the library, just to see if he would respond. Watching the little grey texting bubble made my palms sweat, but the message made my stomach plummet.

AXEL

Yeah, I'll meet you guys there.

Great. I don't know what I expected.

I turn off Ring Road and cross into the shadow of the Gothic cathedral that looms over me. The grey stone façade shrouded in ornate details gives the building a foreboding edge and it mixes with my anxiety for this group meet up. Walking toward the library's stone steps, I run my hand through my hair for the zillionth time and try to stave off the prickly panic making my hands shake. Not only will I have to interact with Axel who will probably avoid talking to me as much as possible, but Janette will probably be back to her usual iciness as well.

She hadn't reached out at all yesterday either, after I basically spent the whole of Mira's party watching after her and carrying her back to West Tower. We'd exchanged numbers when we planned out the schedule for the steps of our project, and the only text I had from her was the one that said her name so I could save her number in my phone.

Crossing under the stained-glass mural above the heavy wood doors, I bristle at the shock of cold AC blasting in the cool foyer, but it helps jolt a bit of the nerves in my system, allowing me to calmly survey the open central room I walk into. High stone archways cover the vaulted ceilings, warm lighting emanating from within them creating a pleasant glow around the area. I count two more floors above, finding balconies lined with dark railings and seeing some people walking around the edge of the room. Shadowy stacks line the walls on all three sides, more taking up the farther half of the room. A large circular information desk sits a few feet in front of me, a dozen circular study tables scattered around behind it and covered in students. Comfy chairs and sofas mingle in between the tables, some occupied and others abandoned. A couple computer stations seem out of place around the edge of the study area, the modern seemingly forced in among the ancient.

My feet echo on the dark marble floor, shoes squeaking a bit as I pass the information desk, looking for Axel or Janette or an open table to snag.

I spot Janette, sitting by herself at a far table with open books already spread out around her, bent over her laptop and typing away. Her hair is in two buns again, like the first time we met, and she wears a white tank top that shows off the smooth skin of her neck and shoulders. I walk through the tables, regretting letting Axel sit us next to her in the first place. We might have had to contend with Cassie for the rest of the semester, but it's only been two days since we got assigned as a group and we've already managed to tangle everything between us up further.

"Hey," I say, pulling the chair out across from her.

She blinks up at me, eyes adjusting after staring at her screen for so long. "Hey." She glances around. "Where's Axel?"

I reach into my bag, pulling out my own laptop and setting it on the table in front of me, ignoring the twinge in my gut at the question. "He's meeting us here."

"Okay." She shuffles some of the books around, closing two and stacking them to make more room on the circular table for when Axel shows up. I type in my password once my laptop lights up, letting it take a minute to connect to the Wi-Fi before I check my email to clear the red badges in the corner of the icon.

"Thank you, by the way," Janette says softly, and I look up, eyes meeting hers over the top of her laptop. "For taking care of me the other night. I remember you carrying me a bit and figure you left the water for me in the morning. You didn't have to do that."

Her quiet voice warms my gut, settling the earlier twinge. I smile, nodding my head before saying, "No problem." She goes back to typing and I linger for a second, eyes roving over her as she works. The image of Christopher's name on her phone rolls through my mind and I look back down, opening my browser to get to the doc where I type up my notes from class.

"Sorry I'm late," Axel mumbles, rushing up to the table and grabbing one of the seats between Janette and me. The legs scrape across the floor, making several people around us glare over as Axel falls loudly into the bucket chair with a thud. He shuffles his bag off, swinging it onto the table on top of some of the books and papers Janette has spread out around her.

"You're good," she says, pulling her stuff out from underneath it. "We haven't started yet."

Axel nods, still not looking at either of us as he pulls out his stuff and tosses his bag to the floor. My hands shake on my keyboard, and I grit my teeth, trying to will myself to calm down. Anger pours over top of the ache that's been growing in my chest, hardening around it and pushing its way through the rest of my body.

"So, Gutenberg," Axel says, picking his head up and looking at each of us with a jovial grin. "Where do we start?"

I stare at the side of his head as Janette starts explaining the plan she thinks will work best, showing him how each of us can split the research and glancing over at me a few times as she rambles. He listens intently, not looking back over at me, but I saw the look on his face when his eyes met mine. Like nothing had happened, like everything is fine and he hadn't spent the last twenty-four hours avoiding the shit out of me.

The anger in my blood boils under my skin, mostly directed at myself for being such an idiot. I wanted to ask him out, wanted to see if we could be more than just roommates who sometimes fuck when we're bored, but clearly, he has already decided we're not even that anymore, barely even friends at this point. Why else would he just show up to this meeting and act like nothing has happened, but avoid me as much as possible when others aren't around?

I turn back to my computer, opening another tab to start researching the sub-topic Janette has assigned me and ignoring the other two sitting at the table. My fingers mash the keys as I type and keyword search the articles and research papers, I find online. Axel merrily does his own research beside me, asking Janette some questions when he hits a wall or gets confused and making me clench my jaw even further each time. His upbeat voice rubs my skin like sandpaper, making me franticly think of an excuse to leave early.

Janette peeks over at me several times as she does her own research, questions playing across her face, though she never vocalizes them. I ignore her concern, feeling like it's more salt in the wound that she notices something off with me while he acts like everything is normal.

Seconds away from just packing up and saying I have other plans I need to get to; another voice cuts in as a shadow falls over our table.

"Hey guys!" Cassie says, voice overly cheerful and matching the beaming excitement on her face. "Starting your project for Howards?" She directs her question to the group, but her eyes find mine quickly, staying there once she has my attention.

Janette looks up at her in confusion and I hear Axel's jaw snap shut beside me. I smile, the anger in my gut singing. "Hey, Cass," I say with a nod. "Yeah, figured we'd get a jump start on it."

"Us too." She points over her shoulder, the three of us looking to see the three others from her group sat around another circular table and talking amongst themselves. Cassie leans her hands on our table. "Can't believe this is worth thirty percent of our grade. We got stuck with Weapons and Armor of the Middle Ages." She rolls her eyes and I see Axel's fist clench on the table next to us. "Which topic did you all pick?" Once again, the question is posed for the whole table, but her eyes never stray from mine. I smile.

"The Impact of Gutenberg's Printing Press," I say, rolling my eyes dramatically.

"Oh, that shouldn't be hard. You guys can get that done super-fast and be done before midterms, probably." She smiles showing off her straight teeth while her cheeks heat. She doesn't seem to notice Axel lean back in his chair away from her and cross his arms over his chest. I feel Janette's eyes on me as well, but I ignore her, keeping my focus on Cassie and the reaction she's helping me get out of Axel.

I decide to skip straight to the kill. "I've been meaning to ask you, Cass, did you want to go out sometime? Maybe we could do dinner sometime next week?" Cassie's mouth pops into an O, eyes lighting up as her excitement intensifies.

"Yeah! Definitely! That would be so much fun!" Her whole body seems to shake as she nods profusely.

I pull my phone out of my pocket, leaning closer to her. "Here, give me your number and we can figure out the details later." She takes the phone from my hand after I unlock it, typing quickly into the new contact profile she pulls up in record time.

I text her quick after she hands it back.

Hi, it's Bentley

Smiling again, I watch her cheeks blush further. "I'll text you after we're done with this." I add a wink, seeing Axel's hand dig into the striped sleeve of his shirt in my periphery.

Cassie giggles, the sound too loud in my ears, and nods a bunch before turning to Axel and Janette. "See you guys in class," she says in a high-pitched voice, waving hastily before rushing back to the table her group sits at.

I watch her until she sits down, feeling both Axel and Janette staring at me before I turn and meet his glare first, a satisfied smile set on my face. I glance over at Janette, and the smile falls.

Janette's furrowed brow and fiery eyes make the satisfaction in my gut spoil. She glares at me, a muscle on the side of her jaw ticking. "I think we're good for today," she spits, breaking our eye contact and standing to gather her stuff rapidly into her bag.

I try to think of something to say, but my brain stays blank as I watch her whip around and stalk out of the library. I swallow, the hard ball of anger melting as the ache returns when I turn to look at Axel. He glares at me, still leaning back in his chair and away from the table.

"You happy with yourself?" he mutters, grabbing his laptop and backpack before getting up out of his chair. His words spark a remnant of anger, wanting to rip into him for the last thirty-six hours, but it quickly goes out as the image of Janette storming away from the table replays in my mind.

Why was she so upset? My anger sparks a bit when I remember Christopher's name on her phone again.

The rapid emotional flux leaves me a bit dizzy as my eyes refocus on Axel's retreating form. He leaves at a more normal pace, but his spine stays ramrod straight as I watch him walk through the foyer and out into a blaze of sunshine, leaving me behind in the shadows.

14

Janette

"Hi, babe," Christopher says, smiling as I meet him at the front doors of West Tower. I lift the sides of my mouth, turning and walking straight back toward the elevator.

My mood has been terrible for the last week, according to Layla. Probably due to the image of Bentley flirting with Cassie two feet from me and Axel. The boys didn't sit near me in class this week, not even sitting next to each other. I know the display had pissed off Axel too, but I couldn't tell if it was a protective thing because he could tell I'm attracted to Bentley or something else. But since he's not answering my texts with more than a few one-word answers, I'm thinking they had their own little fight.

Layla even mentioned how similar our moods have been. She keeps asking if something happened last weekend, but all that happened was Christopher showed up and ate half of my food while complaining again about the cafeteria food. Plus, my mood had soured before Christopher even stepped foot on campus last week.

Leaning against the back of the elevator, Christopher crowds me, putting his hands on my hips and jostling me a little. "Cheer up. *I'm* here!"

I bite my tongue to stop myself from rolling my eyes. The elevator starts moving.

He ducks down a bit, fake pouting. "Why the bad mood?"

I fold my arms between us and try to wipe the frown off my face. "No bad mood." Christopher quirks an eyebrow. "Just hungry," I say quickly to cover.

He leans back, dropping his hands and adjusting the duffle over his shoulder. "Perfect because I was thinking we could go out tonight for dinner." He takes my hand as the doors open and tugs me along to my suite. "I found this hibachi place, Kitsune Grill. It's twenty minutes away, but it looked great."

I look down at the sweats and tank top I haven't changed out of since waking up. "I don't know. I kind of wanted to stay in tonight. We could get takeout." I walk around him and unlock the door, holding it open as he walks in and dumps his bag on the couch.

"Baaaabe," he whines, turning back toward me. "We haven't had a night out in sooooo long and the food here sucks. And they do this volcano thing with the onions that looked so cool online. Please please please please please?" He puts his hands together, pleading and stepping closer to me with each please until he wraps his arms around my waist and pulls me against him on the last one. I fight the urge to push him off and just close my eyes.

"Fine," I say, stepping back when he lets go of me to double fist pump the air. "But I need some time to get ready." He nods, walking around the couch and grabbing the remote.

"Take your time. I'm not super hungry yet." He falls back against the couch, flipping through the streaming apps that appear after he turns on the TV.

I roll my eyes at the back of his head, palms itchy. Layla pushed me to break up with Christopher all week, continuously reminding me it's dumb to stay in a relationship I don't even want to be in. But Mom's reaction keeps the words trapped on my tongue.

I walk into my room, closing the door behind me so I don't have to hear whatever he puts on in the living room. Walking to my vanity, I sit on the little stool in front of it and pull open the drawer with my headband and skin care stuff. Making eye contact with myself in the mirror, I pull my hair back and start unscrewing the top of my face moisturizer. My eyes stray to the room behind me, lingering on the empty bedside tabletop.

Waking up the day after Mira's party, the water bottle had been the first thing my eyes saw after the blurriness of sleep cleared. I knew Bentley put it there, remembering him asking me if I needed any before I fell asleep. After downing most of it, I'd grabbed my phone and opened my messages with him, staring at the one text in our chat. Different things I wanted to say flitted through my head as my thumbs hovered over the keyboard.

Thank you for taking care of me.

Thank you for helping me get home.

I'm so embarrassed.

The last one sat in my brain, spreading through me as I recalled the night before. I'd gotten drunk in under thirty minutes all because of a stupid taunt. I'd danced on top of, and then fallen off of, a kitchen island. I'd passed out against him when he had to carry me home.

He probably didn't want to hear from me. Probably

annoyed that I ruined his night. He spent the whole time looking out for me, probably out of some sense of obligation since he was the one who egged me into drinking in the first place. He didn't get to relax and probably felt like I'd wasted his time.

I stayed in bed most of the day, occasionally opening Bentley's chat again before turning off my phone and stopping myself from sounding even more pathetic than he already thought I was.

But when I saw him on Friday, I realized I needed to thank him. No matter what he thought of me, he'd taken care of me, made sure I didn't get hurt or into any big sort of trouble. And he'd smiled at me when I thanked him. My heart had lurched at the affection I'd seen in his eyes then, all of my fears from the day before washing away.

And then he'd pulled that shit with Cassie, and it all came flooding back in. I felt like an idiot. Still do. Of course, the night before didn't mean the same thing to him. In his eyes, I'm his best friend's bitchy roommate who he had to take care of when she got sloppily drunk on basically a dare. Not to mention he knows I'm with Christopher. I made the attraction between us up completely. We were nothing.

The swirling thoughts in my head had stoked a bonfire in my gut as I watched him get Cassie's number. I couldn't sit there and just go back to researching Gutenberg. I needed to get away from him and maybe scream.

But even rushing back to my room and punching my pillow a few times to extinguish the fire hadn't left me feeling any more settled. Instead, I felt empty afterward. I kept wondering what Bentley was doing, where he would take Cassie on their date, if they would go on more, if I would have to watch them slowly become a couple over the semester while Axel and I were forced to interact with him, so we didn't fail class.

And then there was Axel. I keep feeling like I *should* feel guilty for wanting him just as much as I want Bentley, but I haven't been able to summon even an ounce. For all the time I spent thinking about Bentley, I also thought about Axel. How he looked across the beer pong table, practically devouring me with his eyes as we played. The sly smile when he let me win at Uno in front of Christopher. His intensity when he asked me a question about the project while we'd been researching.

The tension had mounted so high, I'd stripped down and thrown on my running clothes, going for a run for the first time since I got to the Coast.

And now I haven't spoken to either of them for a week. They each separately cancelled our Friday library meet up this morning. Confusion and anger with a touch of despair had been my companion but reading their excuses in text had made all of it flare up again.

Finishing my light makeup, I pull the headband out of my hair and grab a scrunchie to tie it all back. Pulling on some soft leggings and a cropped hoodie, I take a second to try to shake some of my bad mood off before opening my bedroom door.

"Ready?" Christopher says, glancing back at me. "You're going to wear that?" He looks over me before scrunching up his face.

"Is this place fancy or something?" I glance down at my outfit again, rubbing the side of my thigh.

"No," he says, standing and shutting off the TV. "But you might as well have not changed," he says under his breath. I scowl, clenching my fist as I slide on my sneakers.

Christopher blathers on about his week and work and everything mundane going on back in his world in Georgia as he drives us to the restaurant. I nod and murmur mmhmm when I need to, but I spend most of the ride staring out the window at the passing scenery. Layla's words keep filtering through my thoughts. *You don't even like him.*

The car stops and I glance around, clicking the button to my seatbelt and getting out. My feet land in a puddle, the ground still wet from rain that fell for an hour earlier this morning. Grey clouds still crowd the sky, but the air stays dry as we walk toward the brightly adorned building with a flashing neon sign reading Kitsune Grill over the door.

Christopher puts his hand on my back as we walk into the dimly lit restaurant. Noise greets us, the splash of oil on a hot grill, cheers and claps from somewhere behind the hostess stand, light music in the background.

"Hi, hibachi or booth?" a young girl with bright red hair greets us behind the hostess stand as we walk up.

"Two for hibachi," Christopher says, dropping his arm and rubbing his hands together excitedly. The hostess nods, picking up a pencil and scribbling some notes on the seating chart in front of her before grabbing two menus and ushering us to follow her. Christopher leads the way and I follow behind, staring down at my wet feet on the way to the table.

"Oh my god, Janette!" My head snaps up at the sound of my name being called. Cassie sits at the corner of a hibachi table, waving frantically at me. Bentley sits beside her, eyes wide and mouth open as we take each other in. My heart stops as the waitress walks us right over to the pair and places our menus down in the two open seats right next to Cassie and Bentley. We're basically kiddie-cornered next to each other with Cassie to my left.

"Hey, guys." I mumble, keeping my eyes on her.

She jumps in her seat and claps. "What a coincidence you're here! Isn't this place so nice? When Bent told me where we were going, I figured we wouldn't run into anyone from school." She beams, clinging to Bentley's arm as she speaks. I sit down in the chair next to her, Christopher already settled into the other and investigating the menu intensely.

"Seems he might have wanted it that way," I murmur, picking up my menu and feeling bad for the comment the moment I say it. The hostess asks which meat each of us want and we order. She nods after writing it down before rushing off to get our drinks.

"Is this your boyfriend?" Cassie asks, leaning onto her palm on the table.

I go to answer, but Christopher drops his menu and reaches across me, extending his hand to her. "Christopher Phillipe Tonkins." He flashes his teeth as they shake hands, Cassie leaning back. "Nice to meet you."

"You too," she says, a little more subdued than before.

A man in a tall chef's hat walks up to the grill between us, rolling a cart of bowls and sauces into the little cooking area. He smiles at all of us and asks how we're doing before pulling out two large knives and starting to swipe them together. Cassie claps when he squirts a clear liquid across the grill and then lights it on fire, using a large spatula to spread it around. Christopher leans back from the heat, placing his arm around the back of my chair.

The hostess returns with our drinks, and I take a sip from my straw, eyes lingering over to Bentley on accident. He stares ahead, jaw set and eyes hard as he watches the start of the show. I dart my eyes away, looking back as the chef reads off his list and checks that he has the right meat for everyone on the three sides of the table.

Tossing shrimp and chicken onto the hot grill, he places a peeled zucchini down next, chopping it at lightning-fast speeds into equally sized cubes. He nods to the guy on the end of the table across from us, setting a cube on the end of his spatula and slinging it toward him as he moves to catch it in his mouth. The guy succeeds and we all clap, the routine continuing down the line before crossing over to the side of the table Bentley and Cassie sit at.

The two beside them catch their pieces, the woman next to Bentley using her hand under her chin to help as they both laugh.

Bentley's up next and nods to the chef when they make eye contact. The zucchini flies and Bentley doesn't move an inch as it falls in an arch right onto his tongue. He chews it twice before swallowing, my eyes lingering on the bob of his throat before he turns and looks directly at me. I look away, watching Cassie flail to catch her piece, narrowly grabbing it after it hits her nose. She laughs, cheeks heating as she looks over at Bentley.

He chuckles. "You've got a little oil," he says, leaning in to swipe the tip of her nose. She freezes, eyes falling wider as she stares at his hand. He looks over at me before smirking and then staring down at her as he sucks his finger into his mouth and brings it out clean.

Cassie giggles, eyes still locked on him.

My stomach turns, the embers of the fire he stoked in the library flaring back to life.

And then I hear Cassie say, "Holy shit. I still can't believe I'm actually on a date with the *Bentley Marshall*." She squeals and I watch a little bit of the light die in Bentley's eyes. He smiles though before facing forward again.

I turn back toward the chef, realizing it's my turn next. I gulp, nodding after he sets up the cube on his spatula, nerves sparking up my spine. He flicks the cube into the air, and I follow it with my eyes, moving my open mouth to where I think it will land. It bounces off my forehead, falling to the floor and a round of awwws go off around me. The tops of my ears heat at the sound of a low laugh from beside me though.

Christopher holds his stomach, shoulders shaking as I lower my head and glare at him. "Babe, you weren't even close!" He pats my shoulder, still laughing as he turns toward the chef for his turn.

I stare at the side of his face, Layla's words drifting back to me, and feel the nerves from earlier crest and crash into a wave of anger in my chest. I scoot my chair back, three pairs of eyes falling on me as I stand. "I need to go to the bathroom." I fast walk away from the table, fists swinging by my thighs.

I bypass the ladies' room, pushing the black heavy door beside it with NOT AN EXIT written across in white paint. The grey sky greets me, and no alarm goes off as I let the door close behind. A blue dumpster sits on one side of the back parking lot area I find myself in, the brick wall behind it belonging to the part of the restaurant that wraps around to form an L shape.

I fly down the steps and away from the door. Digging my nails into my palms and holding them out in front of me, I grind my teeth, seeing Bentley's smirk as he sucked the oil from his finger for Cassie. Hearing Christopher's laughter ring in my ears. Feeling my mom's looming reach touching even this.

It all bubbles up, every frustration I've ever had coming to a head and pushing to get out. Every shackle I've worn since the day Dad died tightening around me. The burning in my chest moves outward to the very surface of my skin and I open my mouth to try to breathe. A scream escapes my throat, and I lean into it, screaming at the ground and shaking violently. When I can no longer push any more air from my lungs, I gulp in the clean cold air, reeling back and feeling a surge of euphoria. The burning pit is now empty and the space to finally breathe feels amazing.

Panting and smiling, I register the sound of a slow clap behind me.

Swiveling around, I glare at Bentley, the smile dropping off my face. He stands on the top step in front of the now fully closed door. His eyes gleam, a fiery look in their hazel depths.

"Nice show," he drawls, gesturing to me. "I'm surprised you didn't stamp your little foot like a brat."

I drop my hands to my sides, fists re-clenched. Fire licks up my spine at his words, but my chest still feels blissfully free. "Go away," I grit out.

He snorts, eyes studying my face. "Chris seems great. Real winner you got there." He smirks, but there's bite in his eyes with every step he takes down the stairs to reach ground level with me.

"Shut. Up," I hiss, needing him to go away. Needing him not to see me raging in this alley right now.

"No, I think you guys make a great pair. Really," he sneers and steps toward me with every venom laced word. We stand practically chest to chest, glaring at one another, and he leans down closer to me. "Perfectly. Matched." Each word is punctuated by the snap of his jaw. I focus on the movement, feeling heat press in against me.

"Well, I think you and Cassie make an amazing couple," I spit out. "You seem to be loving all the *attention*." I widen my eyes and mimic Cassie's higher voice, batting my eyelashes as I say, "*I still can't believe I'm actually on a date with* the *Bentley Marshall!*" Rolling my eyes, I still catch the flash in Bentley's hazel depths. "Got to love the perks of everyone knowing *Mommy and Daddy.*"

His jaw clenches, every muscle in his neck seeming to harden. "You don't know me."

"And I don't want to," I lie, crossing my arms over my chest to try to hide the way my hands are starting to shake. "I don't know why you followed me out here, but—

His hand shoots out, closing around my upper arm and pulling me up short. I crash against his chest, limbs untangling only to be met with his hard edges.

Tipping my head back, I glare. "What are you—

His lips crash against mine as he pulls me closer still and barely a moment passes before my lips are moving with his. The fire inside me roars at the contact. He walks into me, pushing me back until I feel the brick wall bite into my shoulders, our kiss never breaking. His tongue swipes across the seam of my lips and I gasp, reaching up to grip the back of his head as he takes the opportunity to delve between my lips. He explores every inch of my mouth with savage enthusiasm, my tongue following suit against his. I moan into his mouth crushing myself further against him as he winds his arms around my waist, pulling my lower half against his. I feel him hot and hard against my stomach, the muscles in my core clenching.

His phone buzzes in the pocket of his pants, the vibration jolting through me. I break the kiss, turning my head and gasping. He leans back, and I turn to face him, our eyes locking. Panic plays in his eyes and I imagine the same can be seen in mine. Christopher's laugh echoes in my ears again, but this time the sound feels like a twist in my gut.

Axel's face appears next, winking at me across the beer pong table and I shake out of Bentley's grip, turning us around and backing away from him slowly.

"Janette," he says breathily, hands still held out in front of him in the air where I had just been. His forehead wrinkles as we stare at each other.

I shake my head, turning and running back into the restaurant, slowing down to walk back to the table at a normal pace. My heart thunders in my chest as I sit next to Christopher.

"You missed the saké part, babe. They never carded me, so I got some when he squirted it in everyone's mouths." I lean forward, giving Christopher a closed mouth smile as I reach for my water and gulp it down.

Bentley walks back in a minute later and I pointedly ignore him for the rest of the meal, staring down at my food and murmuring responses to Christopher's random talking while trying to ignore Cassie's multiple attempts to get Bentley into a conversation. I can feel his eyes burning into the side of my skull. He answers her politely every time she asks a question, but things die off after each answer he mumbles.

When it's finally time to leave, I stand, briefly glancing at Bentley as I push my chair back in. He stares up at me, eyes wide and questioning, the same last look he gave me outside. I avert my gaze when Christopher puts his hand on my back, and we walk out of the restaurant together.

Having to step through the puddle again to get back into the car, I stare down at my once again wet shoes the whole ride back to campus. Christopher stays quiet after making one comment about how good the food and show were and I nod, still staring down.

We get out to walk into the building, standing in front of

the elevator when he finally turns to me and asks, "What's going on with you, Jan?"

The doors open and I stare into the empty elevator as I say, "I think we should break up." I step inside, going to the back and turning around to lean against the wall. Christopher stands outside, staring in at me as the doors slowly start to close. He puts his hand out, stopping the doors and rushing inside.

"What? Where is this coming from?" The elevator closes behind him, and I cross my arms, flashing back to a couple hours ago when he showed up.

"I don't think this is working. You should grab your stuff and head back to Georgia, Chris."

"Is this because of that guy at dinner tonight? He kept staring at you after you came back from the bathroom. Did something happen?" His voice slowly rises until he's yelling the accusation as we stand in the stagnant elevator.

I stare up at him, watching his face turn red and fists clench at his sides. "Yes," I say. "And I don't think we should be together."

His nostrils flare as he looks down at me, eyes darting between mine for a moment before he whirls around and jabs the elevator button for my floor. We ride up without saying a word, the sound of his heavy breathing filling the metal box.

When the doors open, he stalks off, stopping next to my door and waiting for me to walk up and unlock it. He walks in, grabbing his duffle from the couch before turning back on me. I stand in my living room, looking at the man I dated for my mother.

"I always knew you were a fucking whore," he says, spitting as he speaks. "But Dad said it'd be good optics for us to be together. We were supposed to be the next step toward creating the new all-American dynasty." I roll my eyes at his hyperbole. "And we still can be, but you'll regret this little setback. I'm sure your mother will be in touch soon." With those final words, a smug smile grows on his face before he walks out of my dorm.

I stare at the closed door for a moment, before shaking my head and muttering to myself, "I'm sure she will."

15

Janette

y head lolls off the end of Layla's bed as I stare at her upside down in her desk chair, typing up an essay on her laptop. She said she had to finish it when I asked to come over, so I made myself comfortable after she opened the door and then went back to her desk thirty minutes ago. I hold one of her plant shaped pillows against my chest, running my palm against the fuzzy material while I wait.

Layla stops typing, grabbing the mouse and aggressively clicking the left button before sliding away from her desk and watching the screen. A blue light spins around in a circle as it loads before a *Congratulations, your paper has been submitted* message pops up and she throws her arms into the air and whoops.

I laugh, saying, "I take it you made the deadline?" as I glance at the time and see it's five minutes to eight.

"With a couple hours to spare!" She spins toward me, leaning back and pulling her legs up to tuck underneath her. "Now tell me how your meet up went!" She grabs a throw pillow off the floor, tucking it onto her lap and then laying her chin in the palms of her hands as she stares me down.

"How many energy drinks have you had in the last 24-hours?"

"I don't know. Three? Doesn't matter. Tell me!"

I sigh, sitting up and taking a second to let the blood drain from my head.

Axel cancelled again on our Friday library meet up last week, not even coming to our classes either, but then he showed up in our Wednesday class, still sitting away from Bentley, but coming right down to my front row seat and sitting down next to me. We didn't speak since he showed up just as Howards walked in, then packed up and left the moment class was over. I wanted to ask what was going on, but he didn't even look at me to give me a chance to try to say something.

Then I showed up to class this morning to find Bentley sitting in the seat on the left of my usual spot. I paused on the stairs, limbs faltering as I remembered our kiss two weeks ago. Shaking off the feeling when someone bumped into me to get to their seat, I walked down to my usual spot with as much bravado as I could summon and sat down.

Bentley looked over at me and I met his eyes as I pulled out my notes for the class. He'd searched my whole face, and I wondered if his thoughts were in the back of Kitsune Grill like mine were. But then he just nodded and faced forward again without a word.

Axel showed up right as Howards did again and it made me wonder if he was hiding in the hallway, waiting to go in at the last possible moment so he didn't have to speak to either of us. He sat down next to me on my right side, avoiding my eyes when I looked over at him. Bentley looked at him too, but I found regret playing across his features when I glanced over at him. He tried to hide it, smiling to me as Dr. Howards started class, but I spent most of the hour thinking about that look and trying not to explode under the tension running in all directions around the three of us.

"Still meeting in the library later?" Axel said when Howards released us to go. His eyes stayed on my face, not sparing Bentley a glance. It had been the most I'd heard him speak since the first time we sat together in the library on the second week.

I turned to look at Bentley who stared up at Axel before nodding and staring down into his bag as he packed up.

"Yeah, see you there," I said as Axel nodded once and walked off.

I remember watching him leave as I sit on his sister's bed and stare into her eyes that almost perfectly match his.

"I didn't tell them," I say, picking at a thread on the pillow in my arms.

"Coward!" Layla yells and I let my head fall back against the wall behind me.

"I know, but things are so weird, not just with me but with them too. What was I supposed to say? 'Hey guys, here's the research I've compiled and oh by the way, I broke up with Christopher so now I'm free and open to date either one of you.' Be fucking for real." I narrow my eyes at her, squeezing the pillow further against my chest.

She leans forward and shoves my foot. "Yes! You need to tell them. They're both operating under the assumption that you're off-limits when you're finally home free!"

"We're barely all talking to each other again. I'm not throwing another wrench in the mix right now. If them thinking I'm still with Christopher helps us all get along, I'm not going to change anything."

"Bentley kissed you while you were still with Christopher," Layla points out, starting to spin back and forth on her chair.

"You need to calm down." I laugh. "Take some melatonin or something, you're way too jittery right now."

Layla shrugs, starting to complain about how she thought her Romantic Period English class would be more Pride and Prejudice and less William Blake poetry, but my brain wanders off as I nod along.

Axel had already been in the library when I showed up at two minutes to five. He sat at the same table I picked out last time, already focused on the screen of his laptop. I picked up my pace, wanting to talk to him before Bentley showed up, but as I came up to the table, I realized he had earbuds in. Not wanting to disturb him if he was actually trying to avoid us, I sat down, pulling out the books I took out last time we were here and my laptop to keep taking notes on the passages I marked with sticky notes.

"Hey, Blue," Axel whispered, pulling my focus back over to him as he took out the earbud on the side closest to me.

"Hi, how have you been?" I turned toward him in my chair, gripping the edges of it to stop myself from reaching out to him. The urge to touch him had apparently only grown in his absence the last couple of weeks.

He sighed, tipping his head back and staring at the ceiling. "I'm sorry I ditched the last few times. I've been feeling off for a bit and just needed to figure some stuff out." He glanced down at me with a small smile. "Forgive me?"

I rolled my eyes. "Nothing to forgive, Axe. We have the whole semester to do this project. Plus, Bentley cancelled once too so it wasn't just you."

Axel deflated a bit, looking much more relaxed as his

smile grew larger. "I was worried you'd be pissed at my flakiness."

I shook my head. "You're good, Axe. Just next time you're feeling off, talk to me or Lay. We were both worried about you."

"I don't think you want to know about what's bothering me," he murmured, playing with the earbud in his hands.

I'd been about to prod him about it more when Bentley walked up, dropping his bag next to the chair across from me and sitting down with a friendly greeting. We spent the next hour in a tense silence, Axel putting his earbud back in once I showed them both the research I already compiled. When we hit the hour mark, he pulled out the headphones, closing his laptop and saying he'd see us in class on Wednesday before leaving quickly.

Bentley sighed, watching after him before looking to me and then ducking his head. We'd packed up quietly, an awkward silence around us before we both stood up and just nodded, heading in different directions at the door.

"Where's your head, babes?" Layla calls, snapping her fingers as I glance up.

"Sorry, got lost in my thoughts." I slump down a bit, picturing Axel's face as he sulked at the library table.

"Heard anything else from Aunt Sandy?" she asks cautiously.

I sag further down. "Yes." I wiggle my phone out of my back pocket without sitting up. "She texted me yesterday." I pull up our chat, reading the long text she sent before I woke up yesterday.

MOM

> Christopher and Paul will be coming to the Alumni event we have tomorrow. I expect you to act civil and salvage this relationship. I spoke with Paul, and he says Chris hasn't moved on yet, so there is still time. Pietro will have your dress delivered Saturday morning.

Layla rolls her eyes. "She's so fucking delusional. Does she really think she can order you to make up with him after the last conversation you guys had?"

Mom called me the morning after Christopher left, immediately lecturing me about how big of a mistake I had made and how much I'm going to have to do to make it up to the Tonkins'. I'd let her speak, waiting for her to get it all out while I sat on my bed, still in my pajamas at nine in the morning. Once she was done, she asked me what I was thinking, and I'd started.

"I don't want to be with him, Mom." It was all I said as she continued to give me reasons we were good together. I had to have said it eight or nine times before she exhaled in frustration and told me I was acting like a child.

"Then maybe I'm not mature enough to be dating right now, Mom." The weight of the conversation had started to take a toll on me, making me feel like I'd gone on a twenty-mile run.

"Please be serious, Janette."

"I am, Mom. I don't want to be with him. I did it for you and it made me miserable. So, I broke up with him for me. You can't ask this of me anymore." I listened to the silence that followed with my heart hammering in my chest.

"We're not done discussing this, Janette," Mom hissed and then hung up on me.

I told Layla the whole conversation, smiling as she paced

my room and angrily complained about how unfair and crazy Mom was acting.

"Clearly she does think that," I say and pull my legs up, squishing the pillow between them and my chest. "It's going to be a fun event with Mom smiling and shooting daggers at me the whole time. Plus, Christopher will be there probably hovering around me and making stupid comments about how lucky I'd be if he took me back." I roll my eyes and sigh, rubbing my shins.

"Oh my god!" Layla jumps up from her chair, clapping her hands and then grabbing her phone and typing into it manically. She squeals when she's done, whispering, "I'm such a genius," to herself.

"What?" I furrow my brows at her, hugging my legs tighter.

"You need to bring a date!" She claps again, jumping a little as well.

I sit up, dropping my legs. "Lay, what did you do?"

A devilish smirk lights up her face as she sits down, leaning back and crossing her legs. "Just wait. He's on his way. It'll be perfect."

I groan, already knowing I'm not going to like this plan. A loud knock on her door startles me and Lay chuckles before getting up to answer it.

"What's the emergency, Lay?" Axel asks, walking in and stopping when his eyes fall on me atop her bed. His eyes flick down to the pillow in my hands before smirking. I smile weakly.

"Take a seat," she says, pointing to the fluffy folding chair in the corner. He walks over, plopping down and folding his arms over his chest as he glares at his twin. "J needs a favor." Layla sits back down facing him with a serious look.

He sits forward, leaning his elbows on his knees. "What's going on?" Axel looks over at me, worry instantly written in the lines that appear along his forehead.

"I have to go to one of my mom's campaign events tomorrow." I try to sound confident but end up wringing my hands in my lap and avoiding his eyes.

"Okay," he says after a long pause. "What's the emergency here?" He looks between me and Layla with raised eyebrows.

"She needs a date," Layla blurts. I glare at her, but her overly excited eyes are locked onto Axel.

He looks directly at me again and I meet his eyes, feeling like a middle schooler asking a boy to the dance again. "Why isn't Chris going with you?"

I squirm. "Um, we sort of broke up." I stare down at Layla's comforter, finding the words so much harder to say than the first time I had to in this room.

Axel sits up further, the motion pulling my focus. "When?" he asks, clearly trying to hold back a smile. The look makes the corners of my mouth tilt up.

"Two weeks ago," I say, and he releases his smile, dispelling the prickly feeling in my chest that told me he'd react like Mom did.

"So, you need someone to hang out with at this thing?" He leans back, crossing his arms again and my eyes track the flex of his biceps under the tight long sleeves of his shirt.

"More like someone to keep him and Aunt Sandy at bay. Think you're up to the task?" Layla mimics his posture, adding a quirked eyebrow as she challenges him.

"Chris is going to be there?" Axel's head swivels between the two of us. I nod, wringing my hands again. "I am so in." His smile turns into a vicious grin and my stomach flips. "What's the dress code?"

Layla smiles too, bouncing in her seat while Axel stares me down. "You don't have to do this, Axe. I can handle them on my own."

"Oh, I know you can, Blue. I'll just be there for my own amusement, don't worry." He winks at me, still smirking and my heart lurches, remembering the kiss with Bentley randomly. "Dress code?"

"I'm pretty sure it's business casual," I whisper, eyes still locked with Axel's. "But my mom's assistant is dropping off a dress for me in the morning, so I don't know what exactly I'm wearing yet."

"You should show up in matching outfits," Layla says, giggling.

I give her a blank stare, shaking my head. "I think just showing up together will be enough to piss Mom off. No need to give her an aneurysm trying to maintain a fake smile while steam comes out her ears."

"Don't worry, Blue. I'll make sure we have a great time." Axel leans back, snuggling further into the fuzzy grey chair, still smirking.

16

Janette

om's alumni event is in a huge ballroom at some fancy hotel an hour away. She offered to send me a car, but Axel said he'd rather drive so I told her I have a ride and she didn't ask any follow-up questions.

Sitting in Axel's car, my hands grip the gauzy skirt of the mint green dress Pietro handed off to me this morning. We park, Axel shutting the car off and letting the noise of the city drift in around us. I sigh.

"Want to make a run for it? There's still time." Axel gives me a toothy grin, reaching across the center to squeeze my exposed knee. I suppress the shudder his touch causes.

"It'd only make things worse." I showed him the text from my mom yesterday, so he knew what we were walking into together, and he clenched his jaw so hard I worried for the structural integrity of his molars.

"It'll be fine, Janette. I won't leave your side the entire time." He squeezes me again and I nod, psyching myself up before opening the door and getting out.

A few people walk in ahead of us, dressed in suits and

nice dresses and we follow. Axel places his hand on my lower back as we walk across the swanky lobby. I can't help but focus on the tingly heat soaking through my dress at the contact, distracting myself from the walk of doom we seem to be on.

We enter the ballroom under a *Welcome Alums!* banner and balloon arch, the room decorated in the Coast's black and white color scheme. Multi-sized star shaped sculptures wrapped in sparkly gold tinsel sit haphazardly throughout the room, creating a walking path through the standing tables that leads to the lacquered dance floor, currently filled with people mingling and sipping champagne. A table covered in baskets and random paraphernalia sits against the wall, serving as the silent auction space where a few people meander, reading the cards on the table. We continue to follow the couple from the lobby into the room, greeted by wait staff with drinks and appetizer trays. I take a flute of sparkling grape juice from the waiter with the nonalcoholic drinks and Axel waves him off when he offers. We walk onto the dance floor, but turn and head to the corner, standing together on our own by the food tables. Axel looks around, hands in his pockets and surprisingly quiet.

I find Mom standing near the front of the room, smiling, and speaking animatedly with a bald man sipping champagne. I watch her look over and notice us, her smile becoming a bit tighter as she takes in and recognizes Axel. She nods to the man a few more times before excusing herself and walking straight toward us.

"Incoming," I whisper, twisting the silver ring on my right hand at the same pace as her steps. I take a sip of my juice, suddenly wishing I grabbed a champagne flute instead.

Axel rubs my back and I lean into him, realizing how much I need him here right now. Christopher walks in with his father at that moment, seeing me and Axel immediately and glaring at the two of us. My eyes toggle between him and Mom, stomach churning as it tries to eat itself.

"Breathe, Blue," Axel whispers as Mom clears the crowd and Christopher and his father start heading toward the dance floor.

"Janette," Mom hisses, a smile still on her face as she waves to someone nearby. "What is he doing here?"

"Good to see you again too, Aunt Sandra," Axel drawls, still rubbing my back lightly.

"You need to leave, Axel." Mom looks over her guests as she speaks. "Why are you trying to embarrass me, Janette?"

Christopher and his father make it to the dance floor, immediately stepping off to the side at a table near the edge only a few feet away from the three of us. "Come say hi to Chris and Paul with me," Mom says, narrowing her eyes ever so slightly at me.

"No, Mom. I think I'll go mingle with Axel. But feel free to pass on my well wishes to the Tonkins." I pull out the smile Pietro had me practice for days leading up to every photo shoot and grab Axel's hand, pulling him into the crowd and away from Chris and his father.

"That was hot," Axel whispers in my ear, his breath on my neck making me shudder, but I keep my fake smile in place. We walk between people, stopping to make small talk with the handful of people who recognize me as The Senator's daughter. They all ask me the same thing, how I'm liking the Coast, and I gush about classes and West Tower, joking about the food not changing since they attended, while Axel stands beside me, still holding my hand.

Finally on our own again, he lets go of my hand,

wrapping his arm around my shoulders and kissing the side of my head. "That was amazing to watch. You're a natural at this."

I snort, grabbing another sparkling grape juice as a waiter passes by. "Hardly. All of that was pre-planned talking points drilled into me by Pietro and Belinda from Mom's team. I'm rarely allowed to have my own thoughts at public events." I down the juice, ignoring the sting of the bubbles in my nose. "If I could drink at these things, they would be so much easier." I place the empty flute onto a nearby table and cross my arms.

"Janette," Christopher says, suddenly appearing out of the crowd and eyeing Axel up and down. The hairs on the back of my neck instantly go up at the angry look in his eyes. He smiles though, keeping up the outward façade everyone here is wearing. "This the reason you decided to end things between us? Or was it the other guy?" He turns toward Axel. "You tell your newest guy why we broke up? Are you aware she hooked up with someone else while we were out on a date together?"

My heart sinks as he hisses the words and I close my eyes, feeling my hands start to shake.

Axel shrugs beside me. "Probably the same guy I hooked up with a few weeks ago," he says, squeezing my shoulder and pulling me closer. I look up at him, eyes popping wide as he waggles his eyebrows at Christopher.

Christopher reels back, face turning red as his façade drops and a look of disgust takes over. Then he shakes his head in disbelief before locking back in on me. "Oh my god, you brought a gay guy as your beard. Could you get any more pathetic, Jan?" He laughs, hand on his stomach.

"I can assure you I am not a beard, though I won't claim to be completely straight." Axel pulls me back, away from

Christopher. "Come on, Blue. I think your mom wants a photo." I glance around, finding Mom deep in discussion with Paul and a few other people, but let Axel take my hand and pull me away as Christopher's angry eyes watch us escape.

Axel continues walking the edge of the dance floor, avoiding everyone and heading straight for the food and drinks area. He grabs an unopened bottle of champagne off the back of the table and then heads toward a door with a sign next to it showing stairs. I glance around, making sure no one is watching and catch Mom's eyes as she watches us disappear.

The stairwell echoes with our footsteps as we enter and close the door behind us. My pulse races as I lean against the wall and watch Axel, waiting for him to say something.

"How the fuck do you get this wire shit off?" He pulls at the cage around the top of the bottle, and I step forward, pushing his hand out of the way and twisting the intertwined wires until they're loose enough to pull off. I can feel Axel watching my face as I do it and ignore him.

I lean back, holding the wire cage, and watch him rip off the foil and place his thumbs under the head of the cork. My hands come flying up to protect my face as he points it away and starts to squeeze it off. A loud pop ricochets off the concrete walls and I laugh as I look back, seeing the foam pouring down the sleeve of his bright blue button down.

"Fuck," he mutters, laughing a little with me. "Thought you might need a little bit of fun and a break from all that, but half of this just went all over me."

My laughter dries up, eyes meeting his as he holds the bottle by the neck and stares at me, dripping wet and totally at ease. "You don't want to ask about what Christopher said?"

He shrugs, taking a sip from the champagne before holding it out to me. "I don't care what you did while you were with that prick. I know who you are, Blue. Nothing someone else tells me would change my mind about you."

I take the champagne bottle from him and gulp down a mouthful before passing it back. "I kissed Bentley." He pauses, the bottle halfway to his lips and blinks, before bringing it the rest of the way to his mouth and chugging a little more than before.

"We slept together," he says, and my mind instantly conjures up the image of Axel and Bentley tangled up together. My mouth goes completely dry at the image and heat flares in my veins. "Well, sort of. I sucked him off and then he let me fuck his face. So, just oral really." The image changes, Bentley on his knees while Axel grips the back of his head and pumps his hips into his mouth. My stomach clenches and I take a shaky breath, trying to keep my reaction off my face.

He watches me for a moment, eyes molten, before passing me the bottle. I take it and pour more champagne down my throat, trying to cool the new fire growing inside me.

"So, you guys hooked up and now you're not speaking?"

He nods.

"Was it bad?"

Axel sits down on the stairs next to me, running his hands through his hair. "No, it was kind of amazing actually. But I think he wanted it to be a one-time hook up." He looks up at me. "And then he did that shit with Cassie like the next day and I just got even more pissed because that night fucking meant something to me, and I don't think it meant anything to him."

I feel the need to soothe him. Letting it lead me, I sit

down beside him, leaning my head on his shoulder and passing him the champagne. He takes it and swigs, wrapping an arm around my back and resting it against my waist on the other side.

My head pops up as what he just said hits me. "Wait, you guys hooked up after Mira's party?"

He nods, looking down at me. I laugh breathlessly, expecting to feel hurt that he tucked me into bed then went to his room and fucked Axel but the only feelings that bubble up are warm. I still can't clear the images of them entangled, suddenly imagining myself in between, and I rub my thighs together to try to alleviate the ache that's started in my core at the thought.

"When did you two kiss?" he asks, starting to rub my side and passing me the champagne.

I wave off the bottle and he sets it down on the step next to him. "Two weeks ago. The night I broke up with Christopher." I peek over at him, but he just stares back with the same heady look as before. "We ended up sitting next to him and Cassie out on their date at a hibachi place and I needed to get away from the table because watching the two of them together while Christopher was annoying me was making my blood boil. So, I went outside to scream out my frustration and he followed me and cornered me, and we argued." I can hear my voice getting hysterical, but Axel just watches me falling apart and keeps rubbing my side. "And then I don't know what happened. We kissed. And I realized I needed to break up with Christopher." I turn away and bury my head in my hands, trying to ignore the comforting feel of Axel's hand moving over me.

"Bentley Marshall really did a number on both of us, huh?" He chuckles humorlessly.

I bleat out a laugh too. "I was really worried that you were going to be mad if you found out."

"To be honest," he says, hand stopping on my waist. "The idea of the two of you together is hot to me." I look up at him, eyes wide again. "Oh, come on Blue. You have to know I'm attracted to you. I've never been described as subtle before."

I laugh, tendrils of sparks unfurling in my chest. "No, I kind of figured that out. But that's why I thought you'd be mad."

"Are you mad I hooked up with Bentley?"

"No," I say instantly, realizing how deeply true the answer is. "To be honest, I find the idea of you two together kind of hot too."

He smirks, fingers digging into the side of my dress. "Interesting," he murmurs, eyes trailing down to my mouth. "I really want to kiss you right now."

"Who's stopping you?" I murmur, leaning forward.

He surges in, lips meeting mine as he pulls me forward. My eyes fall closed as his other hand comes up and cups my jaw, tilting my head to where he wants it. His tongue meets mine and the sparks in my chest blossom into full blown fireworks, fizzling out to my fingertips. I grip the front of his shirt in both hands, pulling him closer as I nip his lower lip. He groans, fingers sliding from my jaw to the back of my head and gripping my hair. I moan when he grabs a handful and tugs lightly, breaking the kiss and staring up at the ceiling. He trails his lips down my throat, biting my pulse point when he reaches it and I cry out, the move drenching my underwear.

Axel chuckles, pulling back and looking into my eyes. "As much as I love where this is going, maybe a stairwell at your mom's campaign event isn't the best place for us to get together?"

I nod, trying to catch my breath as he brings reality back into focus. "You're right," I say a moment later, letting go of his shirt. He loosens his grip, slipping his hand out of my hair and we both turn to sit side by side again on the stairs. He keeps his arm around me, going back to rubbing my side soothingly while I lean my head on his shoulder again and he places his chin atop it.

"While we're admitting truths to each other, I should probably let you know that I hate your mom." He stops rubbing, tensing beneath me as he waits for my response.

I stare ahead, letting his words settle for a minute. "Yeah, she's not the same person she was in Maine." My voice breaks and tears suddenly flood my eyes.

Axel wraps his other arm around me, tucking me in against his chest. "I was pissed when she took you away from Layla...and me." He hugs me tight against him, turning his head so his cheek lays on my scalp. "Mom and Uncle Levi had just died and suddenly you and her were just gone too. But hearing her speak to you like that, seeing who she is now. I hate her. I know Mom wouldn't want me to."

I pull back wiping my eyes and looking into his.

He stares back with a hardness in his eyes. "But I can't help it."

I place my hands on either side of his face, swiping my thumbs across his cheeks as he watches me with trepidation. "I think Aunt Tati would understand." His eyes get misty. "She's not her best friend anymore. She's barely my mom most days. I love her, because I know she's hurting still. She doesn't talk about Dad or Aunt Tati. Doesn't talk about anything from Maine at all. There are no pictures of anyone in our house and she spends most of her time in this world." I gesture at the door beside us. "I think she really needed to escape when she woke up and they both died. She gets drunk on Dad's birthday every year and spends Aunt Tati's out of the house, usually at her office or planning some event so she doesn't have to slow down enough to think. She's my mother and I love her, but I hate her too. For taking me away from Maine, and Layla, and you. For making me miss the funerals and changing so much I don't recognize her anymore." I hiccup as hysteria starts to edge up my throat. "But she's all I had of them for a while. And now I have Layla and you and I'm starting to get better at telling her no. So, thank you for coming and helping me with that. Please don't feel bad for hating who she is now."

Axel leans forward and kisses my forehead. "I'll be there for you anytime, Blue," he whispers as he tucks me back in against him. "I'm sorry we lost so much time."

I laugh. "We were thirteen, Axel. Who knows what would have happened if we had stayed in Maine."

"I do." He resumes his methodical rhythm against my waist. "You would have continued to live across the street and come over all the time to annoy me and hang out with Layla and I would have slowly fallen in love with you. What other choice would I have had?"

I roll my eyes even though he can't see me and smile despite myself. An ache blooms at the picture he paints that I never let myself imagine once we settled in Georgia.

He squeezes me, saying, "We all got back to each other in the end though." I nod and we sit together, the mild warmth from the champagne settling in with the lingering sparks from our kiss.

"Think they've noticed we're gone?" He leans back, nodding toward the door.

"Mom saw us escape so it doesn't really matter." I shrug my shoulders.

"Let's get out of here then." I look over at him and his head tilts to the side. "We drove on our own. We can leave any time you want."

I look at the door, imagining going back in there and having to make small talk with a bunch of random people while Mom tries to get campaign donations and Christopher leers at us from the sidelines. "Yeah, let's get out of here."

He stands up, holding out his hands and I give him both of mine, letting him pull me off the step to stand in front of him.

"How's my makeup look?"

"Messy," he says with a shrug before swiping his thumbs under my eyes. "Not much we can do about it in here."

I nod and purse my lips before taking a deep breath. "Okay, let's do this."

He takes my hand, opening the door with his other and pulling me back into the ballroom behind him. I look up and see a handful of people throwing us scandalized looks and the idea of the two of us emerging from a dark hallway disheveled makes a laugh bark out of my throat. Axel chuckles, leading me across the dance floor. We weave through people, and I see Mom notice us trying to make a hasty exit.

"Janette," she calls, plastic smile in place even as her eyes beam lasers in our direction. She stands in front of someone with their back turned, leaning over the silent auction table Axel and I never went to before our escape to the stairwell. "Come say hello to Judge Marshall and his grandson." She waves us over and Axel pauses, looking down at me.

He lifts a shoulder. "We can tell them we're on our way out."

I nod, squeezing his hand and then heading over to her. Her smile stays in place as she turns away from us, stepping to the side so we can fill in the little circle she's creating. We walk up and I smile and nod to the older man in a grey suit who holds a champagne flute and beams at us with twinkling eyes.

"Hello, Judge Marshall," I say, offering my hand for him to shake. He takes it and the man beside him, who I assume is his grandson whips around, nearly knocking into his grandfather with his speed. I hear Axel's sharp intake of breath before my eyes slide over to find Bentley Marshall staring down at me in horror.

My perfected façade falters as his eyes find Axel, trailing down his wet shirt and then stopping on our hands intertwined between us. His cheeks flush as he stares at the point of contact, seemingly frozen in place.

"Nice to finally meet you, young lady. Your mother was just telling me you're a freshman at The Coast." Bentley's grandfather lets go of my hand, turning toward Bentley and clapping him on the back. "Bentley here just started as well on the pre-law track." He chuckles. "Following in my footsteps, though that was nearly a millennium ago."

Mom laughs, the sound harsh inside my ears. "Oh, Tyson, stop." She waves her hand at him. Bentley finally comes out of his fugue state, eyes finding mine before moving over to Axel and narrowing. "You're not that old," Mom finishes, oblivious to the tension choking me right now.

"We were just on our way out," I blurt, unable to look away from Bentley. I can see Axel standing up to his full height as they stare each other down and feel his grip tighten around my hand.

Mom looks at me, radiating annoyance while Judge Marshall looks a little surprised, but chuckles politely. "Of course, darling. Go have a good rest of your Saturday. You kids are always running off, having something to do. It's a wonder I got Bentley to accompany me at all tonight."

I nod, taking a step back and tugging on Axel's hand. He doesn't move at first and I look between him and Bentley, trying to predict who will lunge first. My heart feels ready to burst through my chest just as Axel finally responds, walking away and breaking the standoff between the two of them. We rush out of the ballroom, people moving out of the way when they see Axel coming. I see Christopher smirking at us, leaning against a wall with a champagne flute in his hand.

Glancing back at Mom, my eyes find Bentley's blazing gaze instead as he watches the two of us leave together, knuckles white around a flute of sparkling grape juice.

17

AXEL

Walking out of the campus coffee shop, the autumn breeze hits me head on, and I grip my warm latte and Janette's hot apple cider a little tighter. The leaves have started changing and the air is getting cooler, but a smile sits on my face as I walk toward Riggs in the early morning light.

Kissing Janette has kept my mood up the last few days even if things ended with Bentley seeing us together. Reading the hurt in his eyes as he stared at our hands made me even more mad at him than I already was. How he could stand there and dare to be hurt by seeing us together, as if he hadn't flaunted how little he cared about either of us when he asked Cassie out in the library, blew my mind. And then he went and kissed Janette while on a date with someone else and after fooling around with me, confusing the hell out of both of us as to what exactly he wants.

I know what I want though.

I nod to the guy who holds the door of Riggs open for me, thanking him as I pass. People move quickly through the hallway around me as I make my way to the stairs, excited to see Blue and ready to ignore Bentley if he tries to sit with us again.

I spent the rest of the weekend in my room, door closed, music on, basically telling him to fuck off without hanging a sign on my door that said so. Janette had been nervous on the car ride home, staring out the window the whole way back and twisting her ring on her finger. I walked her up to her room and kissed her cheek before heading back to my suite, neither of us really saying anything. She called me the next day, apologizing for being so out of it when we left and sounding panicked.

"Don't worry about it, Blue," I said. "We can take our time figuring things out. I don't expect you to process everything instantly."

She sighed on the other end of the line. "Thank you, Axe. You're being way too patient with me."

I laughed, settling back against my headboard and drumming my fingers on my chest. "I think that's the first time I've been accused of being patient." She chuckled and I knew she was rolling her eyes. "Layla used to accuse me of being so impatient, I left her behind in the womb."

She chuckled again and I decided it was my favorite sound. We ended up talking for another half hour, trading stories we each remembered from our childhood.

"Thank you, Axe," she'd eventually said, making my spine tingle as she said my name.

"You need to stop thanking me, Blue. But what exactly is this one for?"

"For letting me talk about Dad." My heart broke for her. We'd both lost a parent that day, but I'd had Dad and Layla and Gwen to help me figure out how to live without Mom. Janette had been all alone, trying to figure out how to live without Uncle Levi and watching her mom abandon her at the same time. "It's been a while since I could talk about him with someone who was there when he was."

I swallowed against the lump in my throat. "Anytime, Blue. You should come back to Maine for Thanksgiving break and see all the photos Dad has all over the place of you and Uncle Levi and Aunt Sandy."

She chuckled, the sound a little broken and I contemplated walking down to her suite so I could comfort her. "Maybe. I think I'll need to face my mom in a few weeks after she's cooled down, but maybe I could take a raincheck and come visit another time."

"I already said anytime, Blue," I said with mock sternness.

She sighed. "I'll probably break down the second I see the street," she whispered.

"Probably. But Lay and I will hold your hand the whole time."

We hung up a few minutes later when she said she had to go to a yoga class with Layla soon, but I told her to text me whenever she needed. We'd ended up texting lightly over the last couple of days, mostly me asking questions about our project or annoying her with pictures of my food. She'd responded and hearted the pictures, but we hadn't seen each other since the alumni event.

And I could not climb these stairs fast enough to get upstairs and see her.

Walking into the seminar room, my eyes fall on the back of her head, bent over her phone in the same seat she sits in every Wednesday and Friday. I shuffle down the stairs, nearly tripping as my giddiness builds. She looks up at my approach, smiling when she sees me coming toward her and the look makes a ball of warmth expand in my chest.

I hold out her cider, standing in front of her finally. She

eyes it, wrapping her hand around the cup and brushing our fingers together. "What is it?"

"Hot apple cider," I say, sitting down beside her and sipping my latte. She smiles, taking a sip and closing her eyes.

"I can't believe you remembered I like these," she says, turning toward me.

I roll my eyes. "How could I forget? The one time you made me try it, I nearly threw up. Never going to forget that day." I take another sip of my latte, shuddering.

"You always were over-dramatic, weren't you?" She laughs, and the sound makes it hard to hold the scowl I throw at her.

Footsteps near us as I watch her eyes flick over my shoulder and her laughter die off. Bentley walks past the two of us, taking a seat on the other side of Janette and rummaging through his bag as per usual. I glare at him for a moment, my anger instantly at the surface again, before looking away and sitting straight forward. Janette follows suit, sitting tensely between the two of us.

"Janette," Bentley says, his tone neutral. I look over at him and so does she, swallowing.

"Bentley." Her voice comes out a little breathless.

His eyes meet mine and his jaw tightens. "Axel." His tone is harsher for me.

Janette's hand reaches out, gripping his arm. "Don't," she whispers.

"It's fine, Blue," I spit out, trying to calm down so I can speak to her. "Don't coddle him."

She flashes me an incredulous look.

"So, you two are together?" Bentley asks, looking between us.

"What do you care?" I say at the same time as Janette

whirls around to face him and says, "No, he was just helping me out!"

The ache in my chest that Bentley created fractures even further at her words. She glances back at me with a stern look, and I feel the embarrassment of my assumptions crash over me. I once again assumed what happened between us meant more to her than it clearly did. I suddenly feel like they've both stranded me at sea, left treading water in the middle of the ocean rather than standing on solid ground.

"Why do I care?" Bentley hisses. "I care if you're being a dick and stringing her along just to get back at me."

My brain rushes, trying to catch up to the conclusion he's somehow drawn. "What?"

"Bentley, no," Janette says, still gripping his arm.

"You've been pissed off and avoiding me ever since—" He glances down at Janette before looking back up at me stonily. "Ever since what happened between us, and now you're using her to get back at me for something, aren't you?" He practically vibrates with indignation, and I stare at him open mouthed not understanding a single thing he's saying.

Dr. Howards walks into the room, shutting the door and making his way to the desk at the front.

"Can we talk about this after class?" Janette hisses, swiveling her head between the two of us.

"No, I don't think we need to," I say, leaning away from the two of them. "I was just helping you out, right? And I'm only interested because I want to get back at him." I shake my head, looking at each of them in turn. "I'm tired of you both ignoring what what's happening with us." I try to gesture between Bentley and I and then Janette and I but end up just making a swirling motion between the three of us.

"You would know all about ignoring someone, wouldn't you?" Bentley spits back, eyes still alight.

"Something you three want to share with the class?" Dr. Howards calls out, glancing between the three of us. We all shake our heads, settling into our seats to face the front of the room. "No? Then if you don't mind, I'm going to start class now." Some people titter at the comment, but I barely hear it over the sound of blood roaring in my ears.

Bentley and I sit rigidly throughout the whole class while Janette spends the hour peeking over at each of us and trying to catch our eye. When Howards finally releases us, I spring up, not even bothering to put my notebook back in my bag as I walk out with it in my hand and my bag over one shoulder. I hear Janette call my name, but keep walking, her words buzzing around in my head like a horde of angry bees.

I stand on the sidewalk outside of Riggs, usually going back to the suite after class, but not wanting to be anywhere near Bentley right now. Knowing they'll both come out of the building soon, I turn and start walking down Ring Road, not even seeing anyone around me as I just keep walking, ribs cracking around the growing ache spreading throughout my whole body.

18

BENTLEY

I sit on the couch in the dark, knee bouncing as I wipe my sweaty palms on my jeans. Axel left class last week and disappeared. He started avoiding the suite again, coming home late at night and leaving in the morning before I even woke up. I tried to catch him before each of our classes, but he managed to arrive just as the profs did and run out the second we were dismissed. I'd been angry when I thought he was going to hurt Janette just to get back at me for Cassie. But seeing his confusion in class made me rethink the whole thing after we all left. If he wasn't using Janette to get back at me and genuinely liked her, then maybe I was getting in the way of them being together?

But then why did Janette kiss me back outside of the restaurant? And why was he so pissed at me for asking out Cassie if he wanted to be with Janette? The questions had swirled around in my brain for days and I tried cornering him to ask them, but he slipped through my grasp every time I thought I had him.

So, here I am, skipping class and sitting in the dark on

the hunch that I might be able to catch him coming back to the suite.

The digital clock under the TV glares at me as I watch the numbers climb slower than they should. I start to think this was another futile attempt when I hear a key jangle in the suite's door. Sitting up straighter, I wait for him to come in and flip on the light, trying to stop my knee from bouncing and giving me away too early.

He closes the door and turns around, eyes landing on me instantly. We both freeze, gazes locked, and my mouth goes dry, all the preplanned speeches flying out of my head now that he's here.

"What are you doing here?" he asks. "You have class."

"I skipped," I say, shrugging and having no idea where this nonchalance is coming from. My chest feels like it's about to explode.

He looks around, both hands going to the straps of his backpack, still slung over his shoulders.

I stand and his eyes find mine again as he takes a step back.

"I wanted to talk," I say, holding my hands up.

"No thanks," he says, starting to walk toward his bedroom.

I step in his way. "I know you're not using Janette to get back at me," I say quickly. He glares at my chest, refusing to look up at my eyes but stops trying to get around me. "I'm sorry I accused you of that. It was stupid and I was hurt."

He snorts, eyes finally coming up to mine again. "And what exactly did you have to be hurt about?" He folds his arms over his chest, leaning away from me. I search for my practiced speeches, coming up empty and just staring at him for far too long. He sighs, shoulders loosening as he pinches the bridge of his nose and closes his eyes. They flash open a moment later, hurt echoing in them as he asks me, "What do you want, Bentley?" He searches my face, adding, "Other than Janette clearly."

"I want both of you," I say, without thinking. He takes a step back, mouth popping open. "I think I always wanted both of you." I think back to the night of the party when I couldn't stop watching both of them play beer pong and spent the whole night rock hard in my jeans. I step back from him, shaking my head. "But I understand if you just want her. I saw the way you guys looked together at that event. It was stupid of me to think us fooling around one time meant anything more. I just wanted to tell you to hopefully clear the air so we could all still work together on the research project."

Axel stands in the same spot, searching my face for a few moments while I grow uncomfortable. Maybe things have gotten too far out of hand. Maybe we can't work together the way I thought we could if I gave them my blessing, heart cracking open at the idea of watching them grow closer while I sit on the sidelines. My eyes start to sting, and I dig my nails into my palms to try to stave off the feeling. "Anyways, that's all I wanted to say. I'm sorry for everything, and I'll get out of the way if that's what you want." I start to walk around him, planning to hide in my bedroom and get myself back under control, but he steps in my path this time.

Anger lies in the lines of his face as he takes off his backpack and throws it across the room. The thud of it hitting the wall next to the TV distracts me for a moment as he points a finger at me, poking me in the chest. "*You* said it didn't mean anything. 'What's a blowjob between friends?' remember? 'No big deal' you said. You're the one who said it didn't mean anything, *not me!*" He shakes with anger, teeth gnashing together when he's done.

I stare at him, remembering the words, but not understanding the context he's given them. "I was psyching myself up," I say finally, looking between each of his beautiful brown eyes. "I didn't know if you were offering a random hook up or a chance to see if it could be more. And then after you were done, and our eyes met, I realized *I* wanted more. That's why I kissed you. That's why I wanted to make you come too. That's why I fucking pulled you into my bed and tried to sleep next to you!" I start yelling at the end, not really angry, but desperate for him to understand that he has it all wrong.

His eyes grow wide as I get every word out.

"And then I woke up and you were gone. And I thought maybe he's just getting dressed or something. I wanted to go to breakfast and figure out where to go from here. I waited in the suite for you for hours. But you're the one who ran away. You're the one who avoided me for weeks after. So, yeah, I got mad, and I stupidly went out with Cassie. I'm sorry about that, but I thought you were cutting me out. And it fucking hurt."

Axel steps back, head shaking as he stares at the ground. Minutes pass, my heart beat the only sound I can hear as I wait for him to say something. And then he starts laughing. My heart squelches in my chest, the pain leaving me breathless for a moment.

"So, we both thought the other didn't care for weeks?" He keeps laughing, leaning back and holding his torso. The hurt leaking out of the hole in my chest starts to reverse itself back into a beating heart as his words take shape in my mind. I chuckle, watching him come down from his mania as I realize that we've both been idiots for a while.

"I'm sorry for avoiding you," he says, stepping toward me. "I thought you were the one who didn't want anything more and didn't want to come off as clingy or annoying. I may have over-corrected." He shrugs, but I can see the sincerity on his face.

"You think?" I raise an eyebrow and he starts to blush. "Maybe this time we communicate a bit more before jumping to conclusions." I take another step forward, standing chest to chest with him now.

"This time?" he asks, eyes lingering on my mouth.

I smile and reach forward, burying my hand in his hair as I pull him forward and crush my mouth against his. He opens immediately with a groan, fisting the front of my shirt and pushing in closer. I wrap my other arm around his back as our tongues move against each other and his taste floods my senses. My hand lands on the small of his back, pushing our lower halves together so that he can feel how hard I am in my sweats. I feel his answering erection against my thigh, and move my hand lower, squeezing his ass through his pants.

"Fuck," he sighs, breaking our kiss and tipping his head back as I pull on the hair at his nape. I trail my lips along his jaw, nipping with my teeth, while he grinds against my thigh, his own leg rubbing against the length of my cock.

I start licking down his throat when he starts shaking his head, panting and breathlessly uttering, "Wait."

I stop, pulling back as he moves his hands to my shoulders.

"Wait," he pants, bringing his head back down to look me in the eyes. "How does Janette fit into this?" He gestures between us, and my lust addled brain adds her short frame in between us, both of us working her over as she moans.

I shake my head, stepping back to give us each some more space. "I don't know, exactly." I run a hand through my hair, calming my breathing as I try to think clearly. "I think we'd need to ask her which of us she wants more. I don't know how she'll feel about the two of us together." I gesture between us, feeling the soaring happiness of a moment ago start to take a nosedive.

"I might have told her we hooked up," Axel says, rubbing the back of his head and looking at me sheepishly. "She told me you two kissed and thought I would be mad, so I offered her some information in return." He shrugs and I wipe my palms on my sweats over my thighs to stop myself from reaching out for him again. "She said she was into the idea of the two of us together."

My brain explodes, all thoughts dying in its wake as I stare at Axel. He chuckles, reading my blank look perfectly. "How do you feel about sharing? The idea of the two of you together turns me on, but I don't think it'll work if you're not also interested."

"Interested in what?" I say, thoughts still not coming in as I hear the words he is saying.

"Think about it, Bent. Does the idea of me and her together turn you on?"

His words conjure up the image of her pressed between the two of us again. This time I imagine Axel leaning down and kissing up the side of her neck as one of his hands inches down toward her center. My dick twitches in my pants and I say, "Yes," before I even realize it.

Axel smiles widely. "I think we need to talk to our girl then," he says. "Let's go see if she's home right now." He turns toward the door, but I reach out and stop him by grabbing his shoulder.

"Janette tends to be skittish," I say remembering the panicked look on her face as she ran away from me after our kiss. "I think we need to come up with a plan of attack before we just bombard her with this."

Axel nods. "What do you have in mind?"

"You said the idea of the two of us together turns her on?" He nods. "And your sister's her best friend?" He nods again, head tilting to the side a little. "Do you think she'd help us out with this?"

Axel snorts. "I think she'd practically hold Janette at gunpoint to get her to do this. She's been bugging me to get Janette with either one of us since the start of the semester." I nod, a plan forming in my head. "Why what are you thinking?"

I smile at him, pulling out my phone and texting Mira and Autumn. "You got a fake ID?"

19

Janette

I slam the empty cup down on the bar, swallowing the last gulp of my second Sex on the Beach. "And now your brother won't speak to me! I've been texting both of them, but we're in another fucking standoff and I don't know what else I should do."

Layla pouts, nursing her first vodka cranberry and glancing toward the door for the tenth time.

"Are you waiting for someone?"

She looks at me wide-eyed, adamantly shaking her head at the accusation. "No, of course not!" She sips her drink, pulling in more through the straw as she stares down at the bar. "I'm just nervous." She laughs and leans in, eyeing the bartender at the other end tending to some giggling customers. "I've never used a fake ID before."

I smile, shaking my head. "We already got through the door. We'll be fine." I pat her knee. "Don't worry, Lay."

"So, the boys are fighting again?" Layla waggles her eyebrows at me, and I push her away by the shoulder, making her cackle. "No, seriously. They're both idiots for acting like this. I already knew my brother was stupid, but it's kind of disappointing to find out Bentley Marshall is too."

I shake my head again. "Stop saying his name like that, Lay," I say and then sigh. "I blew up my life for those idiots." My shoulders fall and I lean a little heavier onto the bar top. "Mom hasn't spoken to me since the alumni event. Not that she really checked in daily, but not even an angry voicemail this time. Just complete silence." The alcohol in my stomach mixes with the flare of panic, churning into a hard ball in my gut and making me nauseous.

Layla pats my hand, pursing her lips. "I'm sure she'll brush it all off like nothing happened in a week or two. Don't worry too much over what Aunt Sandy is going to say. You can always come stay with us for breaks if she gets nasty again."

"Did I make a mistake?" I whisper. Layla's eyes widen and I rush to explain. "Breaking up with Christopher has only made things more complicated with Mom and Axel and Bentley. And now they're fighting over me." Or over themselves? I don't really know anymore, but the thought has kept me up several times after Axel told me they slept together, working myself up thinking about it more than once. I'm not about to tell Layla there's an added layer to all this shit, though, if Axel hasn't told her he likes guys yet.

"J, no. Things might be complicated right now, but you don't deserve to—

The bell over the door rings, cutting her off as we both glance over to see who's walking into the minimally crowded bar. Mira stands just inside the door, looking back as she waits for the people behind her to get ID'd. My stomach drops, the ball of anxiety inside it plummeting too, as I watch Autumn and Aria come in after her, smiling and looking around. I've been meaning to talk to Mira and try to get to know her better, but with classes, and trying to figure out what's going on with her best friend and his roommate, I've barely had the time to try to catch her.

"Hey guys!" Layla calls over, waving at them.

I snatch her hand without thinking, and she turns toward me. "What are you doing? What if Bentley is..." My voice trails off as the fear I was just about to voice comes to life and Bentley walks through the door, following the trio of girls as they head toward us. Then the fear quadruples as Axel steps into the bar and follows behind Bentley. Both guys stare at me over the heads of Mira, Autumn, and Aria, trapping me in their gazes.

"Hi, Layla, Janette," Autumn greets as they reach us, leaning against the bar beside Layla. Mira and Aria stand behind her, looking around rather than at us. I nod to Autumn, ripping my eyes away from the magnetic presence of the men behind her. "What are you guys doing here?"

"Needed to get this one off campus for a bit," Layla says, pointing at me over her shoulder. "She's been stressing hard lately."

I blanch at Layla as Autumn pouts at me, feeling both of the guys still staring at me, listening to every word.

"Yeah, my classes have been getting so much harder lately. I'm freaking out about my midterms next week. Starting to think med school might be a pipe dream if I have to suffer through four more years of this first." Autumn leans into the bar, flagging down the bartender who nods to her and starts wrapping up with the group at the other end. "What are you guys drinking?"

"I had a Sex on the Beach," I say, keeping my eyes on Autumn as Bentley and Axel crowd in with the other girls, getting closer so they can shout their orders when the bartender comes over.

"What's in that?" Aria asks, staring at the chalkboard of drink names behind the bar.

"Vodka, orange juice, and cran, I think." My eyes stray, meeting Axel's over her shoulder and he beams at me, white teeth gleaming. "Maybe some grenadine or something?" I whisper, transfixed on the molten look in Axel's gaze.

Layla giggles next to me, pulling me out of my trance as I look around. Mira gives me a puzzled look before averting her eyes when I glance at her.

Aria shrugs. "That sounds good. Get me one of those, Blossom?" Autumn nods, leaning forward as the bartender walks over.

She orders their two cocktails, Bentley pressing forward and ordering a round of beers for him, Axel, and Mira.

"It'll be good, I promise," he says to her as she scrunches her face up at the beer order. He pokes her in the side, and she bats his hand away, laughing and shaking her head. I watch the interaction with a little smile, fascinated by playful Bentley, before leaning forward and ordering a soda.

"Want to grab a table together before this place fills in?" Layla asks as the girls' cocktails get made in front of us. Autumn nods her head, looking around and pointing out an empty high-top near the middle against the windows. Their drinks get made and Autumn passes her card over to open a tab, my soda coming up next. We take our drinks and walk over to the table. I have to jump up a little to get on the bar stool next to Layla and my feet rest on one of the bars across the legs of the chair, so they don't dangle above the floor like a toddler. Autumn sits across from Layla and Aria grabs the seat next to Autumn, taking a sip of her drink through her black painted lips and surveying the room still.

Mira walks over, Axel and Bentley flanking her with their beers in their hands. She takes the stool at the head of the table, facing the window that looks out on the front street. Multiple people walk by in the setting light of the evening sun. She takes a sip of her beer and grimaces, glaring over her shoulder at Bentley who stands at the corner of the table between Autumn and her. He smirks, downing a third of his in one swig. I watch the way his throat bobs with the movement.

"You don't like it?" Mira shakes her head at Bentley's question but grabs his arm when he turns to go back to the bar. "Let me get you something else. I'll drink that." Axel settles behind Aria and Autumn across from me, one hand in his pocket while he slowly sips his beer and stares out the window. I study his profile, straw sitting in the corner of my mouth while I mindlessly chew on it, only half listening to the conversation around us.

"No, it's fine. I don't want anything else."

"You don't like it, Mir."

Axel glances over at me, catching me staring and holding my gaze as his heats up, smirking at me. Heat blooms underneath the ball of anxiety, flooding my stomach, and I continue staring at him, not caring that he caught me.

"It's fine, Bentley. I want to try getting used to it." She takes another sip. "It's really not that bad on the second try." Autumn laughs and Bentley shrugs.

Layla leans over, saying, "I've never liked beer either. If the drink doesn't at least have juice to cover the alcohol, I usually won't touch it."

"Same!" Autumn says, holding up her plastic cup.

Axel winks at me and I smile, letting the straw fall out of my mouth and turning back toward the group as they start talking about cocktails they all like and then the first drinks we all had. Aria nods to her cup when it gets to her turn, and everyone pauses.

"Well," Axel says, leaning forward with his hand on the back of Autumn's chair. "What do you think of Sex on the Beach?" He smiles mischievously at her as she side eyes him.

"Subtle, dude," Bentley murmurs, sipping his beer to hide his own smile.

Axel laughs, opening his mouth, probably to try to fit his other foot inside it, but Aria beats him to it. "It's good, but I prefer sex in less sandy locations."

Axel bleats a laugh, Autumn and Mira chuckling as well. "Touché," Axel adds, cheers-ing his beer against her cocktail. He makes eye contact with Bentley across the table, and I see the same heat he directed at me in his eyes. I glance between them, watching the way they hold eye contact and feeling the heat in my belly grow.

The group starts trading stories about their hometowns and childhoods, Layla and Axel starting to argue about the events of certain family holidays. But I stay silent, watching Axel and Bentley. They seem relaxed, sharing heated stares every once in a while, and then each turning toward me. Bentley licks beer off his lips at one point, my eyes following the movement while he watches me, and Axel starts telling the story about how he fell off his roof chasing squirrels.

I notice Mira staring down to check her phone every couple of minutes, eyebrows pulled together, and forehead wrinkled in worry. Bentley sees it too and they have a wordless conversation of nods and shrugs before they're both back to paying attention to the group.

Autumn rolls her eyes as Mira, Layla, Aria, and I laugh at Axel's story, culminating in him crumpled on the front yard in a dumbfounded heap. "That was completely your own fault."

"No way!" he insists. "It was the squirrel's! If it hadn't charged me, I wouldn't have fallen." Autumn shakes her head and Bentley tilts his to the side, staring at Axel with a lopsided grin.

I snort, pulling everyone's eyes toward me. "Squirrels don't charge people."

Axel narrows his eyes, putting his hand on the back of Autumn's chair again to lean across the tabletop and say, "Maybe if someone hadn't dared me to go catch one, I wouldn't have fallen, hmm?" His look makes all the air leave my lungs, rendering me unable to respond as I get sucked into their brown depths.

Autumn laughs. "Still your fault, Axel. You were the one stupid enough to climb up there."

He leans back, nodding slightly but still staring me down. "Touché."

"What are you doing here?" The furious voice draws all our attention to the group of men standing at the end of the table. A guy looking very similar to Mira stares down at her, Bentley having moved out of the way to stand behind her as they glare at each other. Another guy, slightly taller and more muscled stands right behind the first, arms crossed over his chest and a slightly lesser look of anger on his face.

I see Tanner over at the bar, ordering with the same bartender who fixed our drinks and notice a sandy haired man in nicely tailored clothes come around to stand behind Layla and me.

The Ravens surround us, all their attention on Mira at the end of the table as she stares up at who I assume to be her brother Ramsey.

"Hanging out. What the hell are you doing here?" She sits up to try to match his height from atop the barstool.

"You're not old enough to hang out in bars, Amiria." Ramsey glances down the table at each of us, skipping over looking at Autumn entirely. "None of you are, actually."

"Don't chastise them! Like you never drank before twenty-one," Mira yells back, face getting red as she looks over at the guy behind Ramsey and glares harder for a second before returning her attention to her brother. "You're being a hypocrite." Bentley reaches out, placing his hand on her shoulder and stepping in closer behind her. He glares at the guy behind Ramsey, body completely tense. The guy's eyes track Bentley's movement, staring down at his hand. Mira shakes it off, and I glance between her and the newcomer then over at Bentley whose jaw is clenched tight.

"That's different. I didn't have anyone there to stop me from making mistakes. You have me, so you're not going to do the same stupid shit I did." I'm certain he's her brother after that remark, silently thanking my parents for not having more kids after me.

Autumn cuts in suddenly, snorting at Ramsey's words. His eyes fly to her, immediately leaning back when he realizes how close they are. She openly glares at him from less than a foot away. "Oh please. Because sitting here in a bar having one drink is really going to ruin her life." Tanner approaches from behind them as Ramsey and Autumn try lighting each other on fire with their minds. He carries three beers easily in his massive hands, passing one off to the guy behind me, then handing another off to the guy behind Ramsey.

"Figured Ramsey would be dragging Mini-Adams home," he murmurs after sipping his own and making eye contact with the guy behind me.

"He will not be!" Mira looks ready to put up a fight and Ramsey turns toward her, matching the energy as they face off.

The guy from behind him steps forward, getting between the two and facing Ramsey. "Drink a beer, dude. Cool down, hang out." He pushes his beer against Ramsey's chest, who grabs it and chugs two-thirds in one go. "School's been stressing you out too much. You're burning out with all your pre-med classes and TAing."

Autumn jumps in her seat, eyes flying to look over at Ramsey beside her, lips pursing but eyes less anger-filled than before.

"I'll take Mira home. The girl I was supposed to meet never showed up anyways. You guys stay and have fun," the guy between Mira and her brother says.

Bentley leans forward, about to intervene with his fists clenched at his side, but Mira grabs the guy's arm, seeming to give up the fight. "Whatever," she says, jumping off her stool and subtly shaking her head at Bentley. He shares a look with her, and she pleads with him with her eyes. I look to the guy next to Mira and see him watching the exchange as well, mouth twisted to the side. What is his deal with Bentley?

Mira storms out, taking her stuff with her and the guy puts his hand on the table, looking around at us as he says, "Sorry guys, have a great night and don't let this one spend the whole-time sulking." He nudges Ramsey who grunts before disappearing after Mira through the front door.

Bentley stares after them and I glance over at Axel. He watches Bentley too, concern etched into the crinkles around his eyes and hard set of his mouth. Tanner comes around to stand behind Layla and me, and I notice Aria playing with the straw of her cup, glancing over my shoulder every now and then.

Ramsey moves behind Autumn, standing beside Axel who glances around at the new guys filling in our table.

"Bent," Axe calls, nodding to the empty seat at the head of the table. "You going to take that seat?"

Bentley rolls his eyes at Axel and sighs. "No, Axe. You want it?" Axel scoots around Ramsey and plops down, smiling at the table as he does so. Bentley shakes his head, but a small smile sits on his face, and I see Layla notice it too, looking between the two of them before turning to look at me with wide eyes.

I look out the window, avoiding her gaze as Ramsey and Bentley start talking about sports and Autumn asks Tanner how the hockey team is doing so far. They get into an argument about the mascot, Aria even laughing along when Axel starts howling at the ceiling, making people look over from other tables in the now busy bar. I watch them all interact, sipping my soda and laughing along.

Until I glance over at my guys and notice Bentley's hand.

It rests on Axel's thigh casually, neither of them looking uncomfortable and enjoying the contact. But my eyes home in on the hand, mind exploding as I remember Bentley accusing Axel of using me to get back at him. And then I remember Axel telling me they slept together. All the looks between the two of them from tonight play through my mind and a twinge goes through the center of my torso.

My breath comes shallow, the noise in the room seeming to dim as the lights suddenly feel too bright and I jump up from the table.

Everyone looks over at me, Layla reaching out to touch my arm. "You okay, J?"

I nod, giving my practiced public smile. "Yeah, just need to get some fresh air quick."

"Want me to come?" She starts getting off her barstool, but I quickly shake my head, avoiding looking at anyone else.

"No, it's fine. I just need a sec."

She nods and everyone goes back to their conversation as I pass between Tanner and the guy beside him, heading for the slightly ajar back door beside the bar.

Stepping into the cold night air, I breathe heavily, pacing the width of the small alleyway I find myself in. Images of Bentley and Axel, real looks passed between them, and things I've imagined of them wrapped together, reel through me, as I try to calm down. My hands go to my head, holding the sides of it and holding back my curls as I stare at the ground, trying to think clearly.

Was I always just in between the two of them, getting in the way when they both thought they couldn't have each other?

Christopher calling me pathetic comes to mind and I feel the lance of the barb sink deep as I question what's happened between them since the last time we were all together. They could hardly look at one another and now they're exchanging charged looks and touching each other in public. Maybe they realized I was the wrench in the system.

The door opens behind me and déjà vu slams into me as I whirl around and find Bentley staring me down. "I've been trying to figure out how to get you alone, but you seem to make it rather easy for me each time," Bentley says, chuckling as he steps into the dim alleyway. "What is with you and back doors?"

I stop pacing, as far from him as I can get in the limited space, and stare at him, hands still in my hair.

The humor leaves his face, and he closes the distance between us quickly. "What's wrong?"

"I'm so stupid," I whimper, staring up at him in the moonlight. "I'm the problem, aren't I?"

His face clouds further, scrunching up as he tries to understand my panicked conclusion.

"The reason you and Axel fight is because of me, right?" I look away from him, going back to pacing, only heading away from him and then back toward as I rant. "I was always sitting between you guys, causing problems the whole time. You both knew you wanted each other, and I threw a grenade in the whole thing, coming in and causing problems by liking both of you, so suddenly you guys were fighting, and it was all because of me. You've both put it together, haven't you?" The fault line fracturing up the center of my being, rumbles as I stop a foot away from him, finally dropping my hands in defeat and meeting his wide-eyed gaze.

His mouth hangs open a little as he stares down at me.

"You've both realized you're better off together rather than one of you trying to get the girl and the other ending up alone. So, I'm the odd one out, right?"

"Sunshine," he says softly, walking up to me and placing his hands on my shoulders. "You've got it all wrong."

I feel my lower lip start to tremble, the back of my throat and bridge of my nose tingling. "It's okay." I sniffle, looking away from him. "I'm not going to plead or anything. I'll bow out graciously, I'm just coming to terms with it right now."

He shakes his head, whispering, "This is not going how I planned."

I step back, but he doesn't let me get far, stepping with me so that we stay chest to chest. I throw my hands up between us, landing on his pecs. "I get it, Bentley. Please just go so I can pull myself together on my own."

"Absolutely not," he says. One of his arms comes up, banding around my waist and pulling me further into him as the other wraps around the back of my neck, long fingers sliding into the back of my hair. Goosebumps erupt across the skin, but I only have a moment to process the feeling before his lips meet mine and we're kissing. It takes even less time than before for me to respond in kind, digging my nails into his chest and feeling the rumble of his answering groan vibrate beneath my palms. He pulls away much quicker this time, only moving back an inch to look down at me, rubbing the tip of his nose against the length of mine as he does so.

"Better, or still confused?"

I narrow my eyes on him, digging my nails in a little further. "This is your way of clarifying the situation?"

He shrugs, releasing my head and reaching into his pocket to pull out his phone, his other arm still squishing me against his chest. "I thought it was enlightening," he mumbles with another shrug.

I roll my eyes and he puts his phone away after sending a text. His free arm joins the other, holding me against him while I drum my fingers against his chest.

"We just going to stand here now?" I ask, not even moving an inch away from him. Warmth radiates from him, oozing into me at every point of contact.

"Give him a moment," he says, reaching his hands down to grip my ass.

Noise from the bar suddenly floods the alleyway for a

moment and Bentley lifts his head, looking over mine. "Getting started without me, I see," Axel drawls from behind me. My spine snaps straight, head turning to look at him as he leans against the closed door and lets his eyes roam over both of us.

"You were taking too long," Bentley says with a smile, squeezing my ass. Axel's eyes jump down, and he licks his bottom lip, watching Bentley's hands flex. "Janette here is under the impression that we've decided to be together without her." Axel's eyes fly up to mine, mouth hanging open. "She thinks we've decided she's a problem and that she's the reason we've been fighting."

"Oh, Blue, no." He steps toward the two of us, and my heart squelches.

Bentley reaches up and snags my chin between his index and thumb, turning my head back toward him to look me in the eyes. "We were going to try to make this a slow seduction, but it seems like we need to clear some things up."

Axel brackets me in from behind and he loops an arm around my waist, sliding it between Bentley and me. He hunches down and his chin lands on my shoulder. He pecks my cheek. "You are not a problem, Blue." He steps in closer, and Bentley moves his hand off my ass to press against my lower back and rest against Axel's stomach. "And you were not the reason we were fighting. I told you I was attracted to you in the stairwell. Do I need to reinforce the point?" He squeezes my middle and I stare into Bentley's eyes, breath stuttering as I stand sandwiched between the two of them.

"Pretty sure my attraction is evident," Bentley says, rubbing his finger along my jaw as he presses his hips into my stomach. The hard length of him rubs against me and my mouth opens at the contact, a moan escaping when Axel starts trailing his lips along the side of my throat. I tip it back, giving Axel more access, and close my eyes. Letting go of my chin and brushing my curls back, Bentley leans forward and nips the shell of me ear on the other side.

Already attuned to each other, they both pull back at the same time and a whine escapes my throat without my permission. I bite my lip, looking back at Bentley, who smiles down at me.

"We were fighting because we're both stupid, not because of you. It was never a jealousy or 'fighting over you' thing, sunshine." Bentley pecks my lips, lingering a bit and nipping my bottom one when I pout.

Axel laughs next to my ear, cuddling closer into me. "I don't think I ever even considered choosing between the two of you, if I'm being honest."

I turn to look at him, rolling my eyes when he can see my face. "Of course, you didn't." He leans forward and captures my lips, slowly teasing them open before rolling his tongue against mine. I moan and he shuffles forward, meeting the brick wall that is Bentley.

Someone whistles at the mouth of the alleyway, and we all break apart instantly. My blood spikes with fear, as I glance around, seeing a laughing group of drunk kids passing by and not the flash of cameras my mind conjured up. The three of us glance between each other, the heat of the moment still present beside the adrenaline of getting caught. I lick my lips and both boys follow my tongue with their eyes.

"Maybe we should take this back to West Tower?" Bentley says, shifting his weight and running a hand through his hair.

"Let's go," Axel says, reaching forward and grabbing my hand before rushing toward the end of the alleyway.

"Wait," I say, pulling him to a stop and grabbing Bentley's hand with my other. "I need to go tell Layla I'm leaving."

"Text her," Axel says, before continuing on his way, pulling the two of us in his wake.

20

AXEL

The door to our suite closes behind Bentley and the tension between the three of us ratchets up to an eleven. I want to reach out and devour each of them, but I don't know which one to start with. My eyes ping pong between them, chest heaving as my breathing becomes shallow. Janette pants as well between us, and Bentley looks over each of us slowly, hand still on the doorknob behind him.

"Bedroom," Bentley says, and we both head toward his room without a second thought. I pull my overshirt off on the way, letting it fall to the floor in his room. Janette wears a striped, blue sweater and tight black jeans and I click my tongue when I turn around, still finding her fully dressed.

"Turn around," I say when all three of us are in the room, pulling my tee shirt over my head. Janette turns to face Bentley, who smirks down at her, before using one hand to pull his burgundy sweater over his head at the back of his neck. His stomach and abs appear first, followed by his broad and tanned chest smattered with hair. I step in behind Janette, placing my hands on her hips and sliding them up slowly under her sweater, trailing my palms against the sides of her waist. She lifts her arms up when I hit the edge of her bra and I whip the sweater away. She leans back against my chest, warm skin meeting mine and making me shudder as my hands land on her jean clad hips again.

Bentley steps up, grabbing her jaw in one of his hands and tipping her head back. "How do you want us, sunshine?"

She opens her mouth, eyes widening as she stares up at him. "How do you want me?" she asks, and he chuckles.

His eyes meet mine and he reaches out with his other hand, grabbing my jaw the same way he holds hers. He pulls me forward, pecking me on the mouth over her head. "I want you to taste her first, before I fuck our girl and then you can call the shots. Good?" I nod as he speaks, my jeans feeling impossibly tight now.

He leans down and kisses her quickly too, before releasing both of us and stepping back. I spin her around, smiling down at the dazed look on her face. She stares up at me through lidded eyes, hands landing on my bare chest. "Hi, Blue," I whisper, moving my hands to pop the button of her jeans and slowly sliding down to my knees as I pull down her zipper at the same pace. "You good with Bentley's plan?" She nods vigorously, following my descent with her head. I grin, grabbing the sides of her jeans and shimmying them down her legs, kissing her skin as I reveal each new inch.

"Words, baby," I murmur.

"Yes," she breathes as she steps out of her pants, and I toss them behind us. She stands before me in her black bra and teal underwear, and I take a moment to let my gaze travel over her, noticing goosebumps appear in its wake.

"Beautiful," I say, still on my knees before her.

She closes her eyes and I stand, placing my hands on her waist and then sliding them down to the backs of her thighs. Her eyes fly open as I part her legs and lift, hoisting her up so that she wraps her legs around my waist, grabbing onto the back of my neck with a yelp. I turn and toss her onto the bed, watching her bounce a couple of times before sitting up and reaching back to rip her bra off.

Her breasts spill out in front of me, and I hear Bentley groan from behind me. I glance back, finding him in just his boxers, hand already moving beneath the waistband. I wink at him before turning back to Janette. "Impatient, Blue?"

"More like internally combusting. Get down here." She reaches forward, popping the button on my jeans and ripping the zipper down in under a second. I start pushing them down my legs, but she reaches into my waistband, straight past my boxers and grips me tight in her soft palm. I grunt, stepping closer as she starts to stroke up and down my cock at a measured pace, staring up at me through her lashes.

My head tips back and I enjoy the feel of her touching me for a moment before I hear a throat clearing behind me. Shaking my head, I look back down at her, grabbing her wrist to stop her movements. "I'm supposed to be taking care of you, Blue. We're following Bentley's instructions, remember?" I pull her hand away, pushing her lightly back down to the bed and following as she crawls back from the edge. Every part of my skin touching hers feels on fire as I lay myself over her. My lips touch her collarbone, and she squirms, hand coming up and gripping my hair. She whines as I kiss and suck my way down her chest, bringing my hands up to cup her tits and massage them against my face.

I pull her nipple into my mouth and nip lightly, pinching her other one in my hands. A hard warm body lies over top of me, a chin nudging my hand away from the nipple I'm playing with. I open my eyes, moving my hand back as Bentley bends over me and sucks Janette's free nipple into his mouth. He side-eyes me before grinding his hips into my back, making my eyes roll back in my head a bit.

Janette cries out, writhing beneath the two of us as she tries to get friction against her covered core. I slide my hand down the center of her sternum, letting it slowly trail down to the edge of her underwear.

Releasing her nipple, I drag in a heavy breath, pushing my fingers past the elastic barrier and across her damp skin.

"You're going to need to get off me, if you want me to get her wet enough for you," I say huskily, watching Bentley suck a hickey into the underside of her breast. I move my hand against her center, finding her clit with my middle finger as I hold her open with my index and thumb. I start to rub slow circles against her, using barely any pressure and Janette cries out, throwing her arm over her eyes and trying to catch her breath.

Bentley continues his assault on her skin, and she unfolds her arm, bringing her hand down to tug at the hair at the back of his head. He closes his eyes blissfully even as my scalp prickles in sympathy pain. Bentley releases her skin, licking over the purply red spot that blooms, his teeth marks stark white around the center. "You can be rougher than that, sunshine," he whispers against her skin, eyes meeting her burning gaze from below. I groan, feeling my dick twitch at the look shared between them, still covered by my boxers against her thigh.

Bentley turns to me, grabbing the back of my head over Janette's hand, now loosely resting there with her fingers weaved into my hair. He holds my head in place as he wraps around me from behind, kissing me soundly before biting the tip of my tongue.

"Hurry up," he mumbles against my lips and pulling back to remove himself from the bed again.

I snort, looking back at him over my shoulder as Janette starts massaging my scalp. "Not going to happen. I'm going to take my time and you're going to wait your turn." His eyes narrow on me before I turn back around, feeling the sting of his palm against my ass, slightly dulled by the boxers protecting my skin.

I grunt and smirk up at Janette as she bites into her bottom lip and rolls her hips against my hand, still moving lazily in her underwear. "I'm team hurry up," she whines, and I press against her clit, making her cry out again.

"You got it, Blue." I kiss down to her stomach, dipping my tongue into her naval and pulling my hand away from her center. I move both hands to the sides of her hips, grabbing the edges of her underwear and rising up to pull them down her legs. She helps, widening her knees once they're free. I kneel on the edge of the bed, looking down at her for a moment, completely naked and panting, skin flushed around her chest and neck. Bentley's mark blooms across her skin and I make a note to leave one of my own somewhere before the night is over.

Placing my hands on her inner thighs and massaging them, I press her wider and scoot down so that my face is level with their apex. Her skin glistens with arousal, and her hands return to the back of my head, trying to push me forward as I start to lick around the edges of her skin. "Patience," I murmur, letting the vibration of the word wash over her skin.

"If you don't do something soon, I'm going to fucking die."

I chuckle, licking up the center of her folds and parting her for me. She mewls and I meet her eyes over the length of her body. "Can't have that," I whisper.

"Quit teasing," Bentley grumbles. Her eyes stray over to him behind us before her head falls back to the bed as I dive in. I start licking and teasing with the stiff end of my tongue, circling her entrance before trailing up to suck on her clit. Her taste floods my mouth, making me moan against her and continue to lap up all that I can get. She rocks against my face, muttering curses as I hold her legs wide, and they flex under my hands.

Janette climbs higher, muscles tensing beneath me before she shatters with a scream, hips spasming as her legs tense further. I drink up her cum, feeling it run down my chin and try to catch as much of it as I can against my tongue, slowly working her through her orgasm and bringing her back down.

She heaves air into her lungs as I sit back up, feeling on top of the world as we stare at each other. Her whole body goes slack against Bentley's comforter, eyes barely open as a lazy smile paints her face.

"Fast enough for you?" I say, palming my crotch to try to ease the need to bury myself inside her. She stretches out beneath me, not bothering to answer as Bentley presses in against my back, chest warm and solid. He snakes his hand down my stomach and into my boxers, batting my own hand out of the way. I groan as he strokes me, spreading the leaking precum from my tip around the head of my cock. My eyes fall closed, and I lean my head back against him.

"Go sit over there and watch me fuck her," he whispers in my ear, taking my earlobe in between his lips and sucking on it. I jolt, and he releases me, pushing me a little toward the corner of the bed. I scramble over Janette's leg, turning to sit with my back against the headboard and watch them together. My hand goes to my straining dick, pushing my boxers down with my other hand to release it and slowly squeeze and pump myself.

Bentley slides into the space I left between her legs, sitting back on his knees and grinning wolfishly down at her. "Did he get you ready enough for me, sunshine?" She sits up on her elbows, muscles a little languid and shaky.

"When do I get to watch you two together?" she asks, trying to sound authoritative, but still breathless. I bark out a laugh, earning a glare over her shoulder.

"Next time," Bentley promises and my stomach contracts at the idea. "Tonight's about reassuring you, remember? How we doing so far?"

Janette falls back against the bed, breasts jiggling with the light impact. "Fabulously," she says, tipping her chin up to look back at me and smile. I wink down at her, feeling my chest expand at her praise.

Bentley taps her thigh. "Good, now flip over." She complies, moving her legs around his body and ending up facing me on her hands and knees, ass aligned with Bentley's boxer covered crotch. She trails her eyes down my naked body, coming back up to watch me stroke myself and lick her lips.

Bentley stands up, dropping his boxers to the floor, and leans over behind her, opening a drawer in his bedside table. He rummages around and Janette looks over her shoulder, watching him pull a condom out and close the drawer.

"Not needed," she whispers, making his head whip up to look down at her. My eyes widen with his as she shakes her head. "I've got an IUD so as long as you boys are clean, we're all good." My brain explodes as my dick jumps in my hand at the idea of fucking her bare.

Bentley picks his jaw up, clearing his throat and flipping the wrapped condom between his fingers. "You sure?" She nods and he tosses the condom onto the table, climbing back in behind her hurriedly. She giggles, turning to look back up at me, pupils blown wide. I lean forward, taking her chin in the hand not currently servicing my cock and kiss her swollen lips, licking along the bottom one before pulling back again.

"I want you in my mouth while he drives into me," she says, staring me down. I groan, looking over her at Bentley who rubs circles into her hips, watching us.

"That work for you?" I ask, silently praying he says yes.

He snorts. "You get to call the shots once I fuck her, remember? If you both want that, no way in hell am I stopping you."

I smile. "Well, get to fucking her then."

He smooths a hand over her back, pushing her knees wider with his own and focusing his attention on her ass. She hums as he lines himself up, running his tip through her folds to spread her moisture onto him. I watch from the side, holding my breath as his hand reaches her shoulder and he notches himself at her entrance. She sucks in a breath sharply, and he presses forward, head dipping in and stretching her out. Her arms give out and her chest falls to the bed as she gives us a little whimper. I squeeze myself, slowly bringing my hand down my length as he rocks into her inch by inch.

"Fuck," he mutters once his hips are flush with her cheeks, one hand moving off her shoulder to rub circles into her back while the other holds her tightly by the hip. "You good?" he checks with her.

She nods against the comforter, mumbling "Mmhmm," before picking her head up and finding my eyes. "Want more."

I clamber to my knees, rushing over to kneel in front of her face as she pushes back up onto her hands. Bentley waits, face pinched with the effort. Once I'm within range, she grabs the base of my dick, licking around the head slowly before sucking it in between her lips. My chest rises and crashes harshly as I gasp and put my hands on either side of her head. She sucks me in farther and Bentley brings his hand from her back to her other hip.

"Ready?" he asks, and she hums, making my eyes roll back in my head. Her tongue laves around my length as he pulls back and then slams forward, making me hit the back of her throat. I pull back a bit as Bentley starts to move, starting with slow measured thrusts that continue to push her forward onto me. She taps my hand, closing her eyes and relaxing her mouth to give me permission to move.

I grip her curls, dragging myself along her tongue before pushing back in at the same time Bentley snaps forward. We move in tandem, quickly matching the others' rhythm. Janette moans around me with each thrust and my mind goes blank in pleasure, hips taking over. Bentley reaches forward, tangling his hand with her hair and one of mine as we start to lose our rhythm, racing toward the building release I can practically taste in the air around us. His other hand winds around her side and disappears. I know the moment he finds her clit because her eyes fly open, and she starts sucking me with renewed fervor.

Groans and panting accompany the sound of her slurping on my cock as we all keep moving, each interlocked. Bentley leans over her, untangling his hand from mine and hooking the back of my neck to pull me forward and plunge his tongue down my throat, mimicking the frantic movement of him inside her. Two more pumps and he grunts into my mouth, drawing back to press our foreheads together as he spills inside her. Janette screams her release, the vibrations making my balls draw up tight. I come across the back of her tongue, crying out as she swallows around me and prolongs my orgasm.

I pull back first, dragging myself from her mouth so she can breathe. We all pant and collapse to the side, falling in a heap on the pillows at the top of Bentley's bed. Janette ends up between the two of us, back pressed against Bentley's chest and nuzzling her face against my neck. Bentley throws an arm across her, reaching my back and holding both of us. I reach down and push the comforter out from underneath us before pulling it up to cover our entangled sated bodies. Janette wedges a leg between both of mine and I throw my arm across both of them, hand landing on Bentley's hip.

"You settled on how we all feel now?" I murmur into Janette's hair.

She mumbles something and I chuckle, squeezing them both a little closer.

"Night, Blue," I say, kissing the top of her head. "That was soul altering so don't be surprised if you wake up with one of us between your legs again."

She chuckles sleepily, eyes staying closed, and Bentley's hand reaches down to squeeze my ass. "Night, Bent," I whisper, leaning across her to kiss his forehead quick. He mumbles something too low to hear as his breathing evens out and I settle back against the pillow, quickly falling asleep too.

21

AXEL

Bentley must wake up first because my brain slowly comes to when I feel his rough hand glide across the skin of my back.

"Wake up," he whispers near my ear before kissing between my shoulder blades.

"What time is it?" I groan, voice still thick with sleep.

"Like nine." He keeps kissing my skin, moving up toward my hairline on the back of my neck. I open my eyes, finding myself staring at the edge of his bed and the rest of his room beyond. We must have all shuffled around in our sleep. I vaguely remember Janette leaving at one point to pee before climbing over both of us to snuggle back in from behind me where I rested my head against Bentley's shoulder.

Flipping my head over, I find Bentley beside me, Janette's mass of light brown curls visible just over his shoulder. Her soft snores float over us, and I smirk at Bentley. "Why is she allowed to sleep in, but not me?"

"She had both of us tire her out last night, and I woke up wanting you." I smile lazily at his words, stretching my arms out underneath the pillow and enjoying the pop of my spine.

I groan and settle back in. "Well, I'm not going anywhere." Bentley smiles, leaning in to kiss me slowly. He takes his time, hand on the back of my head, threading into my hair and massaging my scalp. I open up to him, letting his tongue invade my mouth and rove over my own.

His hand coasts down my back, dipping under the edge of the comforter laying across my lower half. He grips my ass, digging his fingers into my flesh. "I want to fuck you," he whispers against my lips. The words travel through my blood, lighting a trail of fire in me as it all travels south to my already stiff cock pinned beneath me.

I tip my head forward, touching my forehead to Bentley's as he stares into my eyes. "Do it."

He groans, eyes fluttering closed for a moment. Then he sits up quickly, the comforter sliding down to reveal his nakedness. I glance at Janette, finding her on her stomach, head turned away from me still softly snoring.

Bentley pulls the comforter away from me, icy morning air biting my skin. I whine and bury my face in the pillow, Bentley rubbing over my back and legs with a chuckle. "Ass up," he says, tapping my side as he gets off the bed and walks over to rummage around in his dresser. I tuck my knees in underneath me, keeping my face in the pillow and listening to him move around. He stops rummaging and closes the dresser drawer lightly, padding back across the floor to the bed. It creaks a little as he kneels on the edge and moves in behind me. Something lands on the bed beside me, bouncing once on the mattress.

His fingers knead the muscles of my lower back and I hum, smiling into the pillow. "Have you done this before?"

I nod, closing my eyes as I turn my head to the side.

"Yes," I say, watching the sun streaming in through the window above us and fall on the floor of his room. I look back at him, smirking. "You're not my first."

Bentley swats my ass, creating a sting that he rubs in with a returning smirk. "Good. This will be easier then." He runs his hands down the backs of my thighs, pushing my legs wider, before bringing them back up. One slides along my side, grounding me as his other hand slides down to rub over my perineum. My cock twitches beneath me.

He reaches out, still rubbing me with his other hand, dabbling closer to my puckered rim. He grabs the bottle of lube he threw down on the bed beside me and I hear the cap click open as my breathing picks up. His hands leave me for a moment, and I wait in bated anticipation as he squirts some into his hand. My chest tightens at the first slick glide of his finger over my back hole, but I steady my breathing. He takes his time, relaxing every muscle as he spreads the lube around, making sparks shoot up and down my spine.

The first press of his finger past my oiled muscles makes a long groan escape my throat and I push back toward him at the familiar pressure. He sinks in to the first knuckle, turning his finger to the side to stretch me out slowly. "You're tight," Bentley says in a gravelly voice.

"It's been a while," I murmur, fisting my hands in the sheets on either side of me as he presses in further. His other hand smooths over my ass, kneading and pinching as he starts adding a second finger. I sigh when he starts moving them together, stretching and twisting his hand for a while. My mind goes blank when he adds the third, muscles fully relaxed so that it slides in easily. He starts moving his hand faster, plunging his fingers in, and curling them inside. He chuckles when I cry out, fingers finding the right spot to tease.

"Fuck, Bent," I mutter, pushing my hips back to meet the heel of his hand. My cock bounces as I move, straining and starting to leak as the pace increases. I turn my head back into the pillow and Bentley removes his fingers, smoothing his other hand down my back to my shoulder. His back lays over me, lips ghosting over the spots he kissed as I woke up.

When he reaches my ear, he asks, "Do you want me to wear a condom?"

I turn my head to the side, seeking out his mouth with my own. He quickly kisses me before pulling back to look me in the eyes.

"No, I trust you," I whisper.

He stares at me for a moment before kissing me again, warm hands massaging my skin.

I turn my face back into the pillows as he positions himself over me.

The tip of his lube slicked cock prods at my back entrance, and I reach back. Bentley's hand leaves my shoulder, grabbing mine and folding my arm behind my back as our fingers intertwine. He squeezes, asking, "Ready?" I nod, head still buried in the pillow until I turn it to the side.

"Yes," I breathe just as he presses forward, entering me slowly as he did with Janette last night. I moan at the feel of him sliding deep inside me, the muscles of my ass squeezing around his length as I breathe. "Jesus, you're huge."

Bentley chuckles in my ear. "You can take it, baby."

He keeps slowly rocking forward, each new inch making me groan. When his hips finally touch my skin, he pauses, giving me a moment to adjust. I squeeze his hand, whispering, "Please, Bentley."

He chuckles, running his knuckles down my spine. "Please, what?" he whispers, kissing my temple.

I bow, my head turning to the side to meet his shadowy hazel gaze. "Fuck me. *Hard.*"

Leaning back, he pulls out, almost all the way and then slams forward. I groan, biting into the pillow beneath me. He sets a steady slow pace, thrusting into me sharply then pulling out oh so slow.

Unintelligible sound leaves my lips before I'm able to say a single hoarse word, "Faster."

Bentley's skin presses in against mine until his short, labored breaths caress my ear. "Uh, uh. You wanted hard." He punctuates the sentence with another rough thrust. "Let me savor this."

His maddening slowness makes all thought impossible. Combined with the heat of him across my back, the tight grip of his hand in mine, and his harsh breathing in my ear, all I can sense is Bentley. He surrounds me, consuming my mind and body, as his hips start to stutter, and his pace increases ever so slightly.

"Fuck, baby," he murmurs, groaning into the side of my neck. I feel his lips press against the skin before his teeth replace them, biting down on my flesh. My dick twitches, trapped between myself and the mattress and painfully hard.

Groaning as he pulls back, his hand finds my hip, and I suck in a breath, feeling the tension in the room ricochet. Bentley pounds into me, suddenly setting a brutal pace that draws long moans from my lips and bashing any distance between me and the edge of orgasm to pieces. I squeeze my eyes closed, barely able to catch my breath as I leverage myself up on my free hand and grind back, matching his pace happily. He swears behind me, reaching around my waist to grab hold of my dick and starts to furiously stroke in time with his hips. I cry out, mindlessly pumping my hips into his fist as he fucks my ass. We breathe together, racing toward our peaks and I hear him grunt, low and masculine, behind me before feeling his warm cum fill me.

He lets go of my cock, and I cry out, the move pulling me back from the edge I was so close to falling over. Bentley sits up, letting go of my hand and lazily thrusting into me a couple more times before pulling out. His hands move back to my hips, pushing me over so that I land breathless on my back and feel some of his cum slide out underneath me.

I stare up at him through the lusty haze clouding my vision, chest raking in air, and watch as he backs down the bed before leaning forward and taking my hard cock in his mouth. I throw an arm over my eyes as he sucks hard, deep throating me twice before I explode, coming while he swallows around my head.

Swiping my arm upward across my forehead, I shake my head, catching sight of the sage green eyes peering over at us from the other side of the bed. "You two are beautiful together," Janette whispers and I smile as Bentley lays back down between us.

"Good morning, sunshine." He leans over to kiss her shoulder, letting an arm fall over my stomach.

Janette pushes up on her arms, looking down at us as she stretches out her back. "I don't know how I feel about that nickname."

I chuckle, turning on my side to snuggle into Bentley and hitch my leg up over his. "Maybe we should make one for Bentley."

A sly grin creeps onto her face as she lowers herself back down, hiding her chest from view again. "Muffin?" she tests.

"Honeybun?" I counter.

"Beefcake." She chortles and I smile, watching her.

"Why are these all food based?" Bentley grumbles, face stormy as he stares up at the ceiling.

"You're a growing boy," I say, patting his taut stomach.

Janette snorts. "If I'm sunshine, I could call you 'my moon.'" Her sarcastic tone makes her thoughts on that known but does nothing to stop the smile from splitting Bentley's lips.

He tips his head toward her. "I wouldn't be against it."

Her eyes narrow on him. "Not going to happen." He shrugs but continues smiling at her.

"Maybe we should know more about you, Bent. Tell us your life story." I shuffle closer and Janette laughs when his head flips over toward me, looking wary.

She presses in closer to him, tangling her leg with both of ours and wrapping her arm around his chest. "Yeah, spill all your secrets."

"What about you two? Why do I have to share first?" He glances between us, reaching up to brush some haphazard curls off Janette's forehead.

"We grew up together. We already know most of each other's history." She shrugs, and I watch Bentley's face grow pensive, eyes going back to the ceiling above us.

"Does that bother you?" I stroke small circles across his stomach as I ask.

"No," he hums, pulling an arm up and tucking it under his head. "Just going to have to catch up." He shrugs.

"How long have you known you're bi?" Janette asks.

I bark out a laugh, looking over at her curious face. "Into the thick of it then? Not going to start with something easy like favorite color first, Blue?" I wink when she glares over at me.

"It's okay, sunshine. I can already guess yours." Bentley tucks his chin in to look down at Janette on his chest. "I figured it out a couple years ago." We both settle in, staring up at him as he tells his story. "I had only dated or wanted girls for most of high school, but my parents took me on a trip to Rio before my junior year. They usually work on our 'vacations,' so I'm pretty used to being on my own for hours in a new city. This guy was in the lobby of our hotel and saw me looking at a map on my phone to try to figure out where I wanted to go. He offered to show me around and I knew the moment I saw him that I wasn't totally straight. We spent the day just wandering around the tourist sites and hanging out. He knew the city and showed me his favorite food spots. Nothing really happened between us other than having a nice day out, but after that, I branched out, exploring my sexuality more."

Janette nods. "That's sweet that he showed you around for the day. I've never really gone on a vacation with my mom. Usually, she leaves me at home when she travels for her campaigns."

Bentley brings his arm down around her back, hugging her against him. "What about you, Axe? How'd you find out?"

I look past Janette, taking a breath. "I think I've always known I felt the same way about boys as I was supposed to feel about girls. To be honest, I thought everyone did. My first kiss was with a boy on my pop warner football team in middle school. We were sitting in the back of the bus after a game and joking around and he just leaned forward and kissed me." I smile at the memory, remember how much my heart hammered in my chest. "It was nothing special, just pressing his lips against mine, but he pulled back really fast with this terrified look on his face. I smiled before he cocked back and punched me in the face. I was so surprised, I didn't even hit back, even when he stood up and called me the fslur so that all the other boys could hear." I look over at Bentley and Janette who each have frozen, horror-stricken faces. "I never felt ashamed for it after that or anything. He ended up telling the coach I was starting fights when he wasn't around, and a couple of the other kids backed him up. I got kicked off the team, and they spread the rumor that I was gay around school. I never denied it, so I ended up being the first one openly out in our year which kind of sucked in middle school." I shrug, thinking back on it. "But once we got to the high school, most people didn't care anymore and there were enough out people in the grades above ours, so it got a lot easier."

A pause passes once I finish and then Bentley leans down and kisses the top of my head.

"I didn't know that," Janette whispers, green eyes misty across from me.

I shake my head. "It was a few months after you moved."

Her eyes pinch and she reaches for my hand, gripping onto me. I rub my thumb back and forth over the back of her hand, trying to soothe the look in her eyes. She laughs, the sound still a little off kilter. "See," she says looking up at Bentley. "Looks like there's still some secrets about him we can learn together."

Bentley smiles, eyes still a little sad as he looks over at her. "You could probably just ask Mira for some stories from our childhood. She'd probably be more than happy to embarrass me in front of you."

Janette laughs, but it's not quite comfortable, lips tense at the edges.

"Oh, fuck," Bentley says, face going blank before he sits up, jostling the two of us out of the way as he climbs out of the bed.

Janette sits up, letting the comforter fall to her hips as

she watches him grab his phone out of his discarded pants and check his messages. He glances over at us, pausing to drag his eyes over Janette and me.

"What's wrong?" she asks, snapping his attention back up to her face.

"I told Mira last night we are going to grab coffee and talk today. She's been acting weird a lot lately. I'm checking to make sure she hasn't been texting me." His phone buzzes in his hand and he looks down. "She's up and getting ready." He looks at Janette again. "We have like twenty minutes until she's going to show up here."

"Fuck." Janette jumps out of the bed, rushing around the room to grab her clothes and get dressed. Bentley texts Mira back, glancing up at me when he's done.

"You can't be in my bed when she gets here," he says, gesturing at me relaxing under his covers.

I sit up, stretching my arms back behind me. "Why not?" I challenge.

Bentley walks forward, leaning down to kiss me quick. "Because this is way too new for me to be explaining why you're naked in my bed while Janette walks out in her clothes from last night." He kisses me again, pulling the comforter away from me. "Get dressed."

Janette stands by the door, looking around the room in a panic. "I can't find my underwear so if you find it, give it back." She points at Bentley as he walks up to her, still naked.

"Sure, sunshine." He leans down and kisses her too, turning her around when he pulls away and pushing her toward the front door to the suite. "We'll text you later."

He turns back to me as I hear the front door open and close. "I'm going to go shower quick. Please be dressed when Mira gets here."

I waggle my eyebrows, smirking. "Trying to hide the goods, sweetheart?"

He rolls his eyes. "More like trying not to scare my best friend. It'd be easier if she wasn't scarred by you greeting her naked before I tell her we're together." I laugh as he walks out of the room, taking my time to collect my clothes and make my way over to my room to get dressed.

22

BENTLEY

"What'd you get up to last night?" I run my hand through my still damp hair, shoving the other into my pocket so Mira doesn't notice it clench.

"It's a whole thing. I'll tell you all about it when we sit down." Mira nods, looking down at her feet as we walk through campus. She's been fidgety since we left West Tower and I keep biting my tongue. I want to ask her what happened with her and Harley last night after they left the bar, but then I also want to tell her all about the amazing night I had with Axel and Janette and fill her in on the whole thing that has been happening all semester.

When I told her I was paired with them for the history project, she'd said at least I had Axel and at the time, I hadn't corrected her. As things progressed the way they did with the three of us, I never got the chance to tell Mira about any of it since she was going through her own shit with Harley. His fault, in my opinion, but I know Mira doesn't see it that way. When they left together last night, I wanted to stop her, to go toe to toe with Harley and snap some sense into him, but Mira held me off. I'd gone to the bar with a purpose and overstepping in Mira's love life wasn't it. But now I needed to know what the fuck is going on with them, because there's no way I'm letting Mira go through whatever it is without someone to talk to about it.

I hold the door to the coffee shop open for Mira, chewing the inside of my cheek. I don't know which of us should go first when we finally sit down, and I don't know how Mira will feel about me and Janette, not to mention Axel in the mix.

We order our drinks and wait off to the side in silence. They come out together and I grab them, heading over to a free table in the corner of the cramped shop.

"So, what happened with Harley after you left?" I start, needing to just jump into things.

"Guess I'm going first," Mira mumbles, wrapping her hands around her drink and staring down at it. I try to smile at her, feeling my stomach churn as my coffee meets it. "Do me a favor, please? Don't say anything until I'm done." I nod, knowing whatever she says is going to piss me off now. I grip my coffee a little tighter, hoping to mitigate my reaction so I don't upset her, but I can tell she sees right through me when she rushes to explain. "It's just a friends with benefits thing that we started a little bit after he started training me. I got followed home from the birthday party at the Ravens' place and I wanted to learn how to defend myself after. I accidentally ended up at his gym and he offered to train me personally when one of his trainers started hitting on me. We started hooking up a bit after that because it became too hard to be around each other and not have little mishaps after the kissing incidents."

All the new information settles over me, wiping everything else from my mind. I look around the shop, trying to figure out what to pinpoint in all that as the most important thing. Someone followed her home from the party. She'd been in danger because I stayed behind with Janette and let Mira walk home alone. I grit my teeth, knowing that if I had gone with Mira, Janette would have been unsafe with how drunk she was getting. My chest tightens as I try to accept the decision I made.

Mira mistakes my anger at myself for anger toward her. "I wanted to tell you so badly, but you didn't want me going around him anymore after that day I cried at the gym. It was hard though. He came by and apologized, and we started this whole thing. I know it's not going to end well but I can deal with the fallout when that comes. I haven't been able to start anything serious with anyone else so might as well try purging him from my system while I have the opportunity."

I think back to the day I picked Mira up from Harley's gym and found her crying outside. I immediately went inside and yelled at Harley, knowing he was the reason for it. But Ramsey walked up, wanting to know what was going on and I let Mira drag me out with some excuse. Her brother would get pissed if he found out something was going on between them and I'm not sure which of them his anger would land on.

I look back at Mira, finding her watching me nervously. "Say something, Bent."

I sigh, wishing I could go shake Harley. Mira doesn't deserve to be someone's dirty little secret. "I'm not mad you didn't tell me. I get why you didn't. But, Mir, I don't think it's healthy." I lean forward, placing my elbows on the table. "You're not just hiding from me; you're hiding from Ramsey and he's going to find out eventually. And when that happens, Harley will pull back again, the way he did after whatever happened at your birthday."

"I know," she says, leaning back and heaving a sigh. "I know this ends badly, Bent. I'm preparing for that. Harley doesn't want anything more and I have killed any hope that he will." She says it so confidently, but I can see the lie when she twists her hands together in her lap and scrunches up her nose.

So, I try killing her hope, so that she won't have to. "He won't choose you over Ramsey, Mir."

"I know," she whispers.

"And his friendship with Ramsey will be ruined."

She sits up. "We would end it before that could happen."

I shake my head. "You might not have a say in that, Mir. What if he finds out?"

She leans forward, jaw clenches. "He won't find out Bentley."

I hold my hands up, backing off. "Okay, let's say he doesn't. This can't go on forever. It's going to end with him hurting you, Mira." I reach forward, grabbing one of her hands. I need her to understand now so that she doesn't get hurt later. I've already watched her pine over Harley for the last three years and if he leaves her in the same or a worse state this time around, I'll kill him. And I'm pretty sure Ramsey will help. Squeezing her hand, I say, "It doesn't end any other way."

"I know that." She squeezes my hand back. "And when it does, I'll be able to mourn and move on. I couldn't do that before, Bentley. I don't know why but I couldn't. When this ends, I'll finally have closure."

"Closure?" I consider the idea. Maybe she's right. I know she thinks she knows what she's doing, but she's right in that she wasn't getting anywhere close to getting over Harley back home, and I doubt moving to the same town he lives in helped that any. She nods at me across the table, and I let go of her hand to lean back and sip my coffee. "Are you at least exclusive? Herpes is forever, Amiria."

She laughs and I smile, glad she looks more relaxed now that she's told me. I can still see the stress of it around the lines of her face, but she doesn't look as tense as when we walked in here together.

"I don't know," she whispers and looks down and away from me.

I watch her, waiting for her to look up at me again. Once she does, I say, "I'll be there when it ends, Mir. You know that right?"

Her eyes water. She smiles slightly. "I know, Bent. I'm sorry for not telling you earlier." I nod, acknowledging her, but her words bring everything with Janette and Axel swirling back to the forefront. The need to spit it all out stabs the back of my throat, but I hold it back, realizing how fragile it is at this point. We've only just all gotten together. Maybe I should wait before I dump it all on Mira's already overloaded shoulders.

"Harley thinks I should change my major." My eyebrows shoot up as I realize I agree about something with Harley Sanders. Mira surprised me over the summer when she told me her major would be chemistry. My best friend is an artist, just like her mother, and I don't understand why she's killing her spark for something she doesn't even like. "He saw my sketchbook last night and thinks I should switch to art," she adds.

"He's not wrong. I never got why you wanted to do chem." I fiddle with the lid of my coffee.

She sighs, eyes clouding as she looks outside. "My dad suggested it. Thought it would be good for me to go into science and chemistry was my best one at Emerald Grove."

I raise an eyebrow at her when she glances over at me. "I mean sure a B- is better than a C," I say.

She rolls her eyes at me. "My mom overheard, and they started to fight about him trying to influence my choices and I didn't want them to fight so I just told my mom I thought it was a good idea." She shrugs and my mouth falls open when I realize what she did. What she always does.

"Amiria Nicole Adams, you did not choose a college major to try to stop your parents from fighting." She shrugs again, looking out around the room.

"I don't not like chemistry," she says.

"Once more, with feeling, Mir," I drawl. She has always felt like it is her job to keep the peace between her parents, to her own detriment.

"I don't want my mom to get upset and if I switch, she'll know I was unhappy and blame my dad again. Ramsey and I aren't there to keep the peace anymore, Bent. I don't want to be the reason they're fighting." Her eyes plead with me to understand, but I'll never agree with a plan that hurts her in the long run.

"That's convoluted. April will be happy that you are happy and if you think she can't tell that you're not right now, you don't give her enough credit." I drink from my coffee again. "And Ramsey never worried about keeping the peace with your parents. That was the burden you took on, Mir. And their relationship is not on your shoulders." I watch her mull over my words, chewing her bottom lip. "You should switch, Mir," I insist. "Not just because you don't like chem, but you're an amazing artist. You deserve the chance to dive into that more."

She nods, directing a fake smile at me and I sigh, knowing she's not going to listen to my advice. "What was it you wanted to tell me about?" she asks.

I swallow, picturing Axel and Janette and the ball of knots that seemingly untied itself last night. Mira will definitely have an opinion about things, and I know she'd never judge me, but it'll take some lengthy explanation for her to understand everything. I sip my drink, going over it in my mind and realizing she'll be worried for me if I tell her right now.

I shake my head at her as I lower my cup back to the table. I'm not putting anything else on her shoulders right now. Not until this thing with Janette, Axel, and me is solid and there's something to tell her. "Doesn't seem so serious now. I just hooked up with this girl last night and she was awful so now I'm worried about seeing her in class later," I lie, feeling the burn of my hypocrisy in the pit of my stomach.

Mira watches me skeptically, searching my face. I know she can tell when I'm lying so I physically restrain myself from scratching my face. I try to drive her away from asking questions. "Seriously, I can go into detail if you want." She scrunches her nose in disgust as I waggle my eyebrows at her.

"No thanks." She holds up her hands and I laugh. I quickly sip my drink while she stares at the table and then start joking about lines I could use to deflect this fictional girl's attention, thinking about Cassie as I do so. I let her down at the end of our date, saying I had a good time, but I felt like we were better set as friends. She hasn't spoken to me since, even glaring at me in class a few times when we made eye contact. I couldn't feel bad for kissing Janette on our date, but I felt bad for doing it to Cassie when she had been so forward with her interest. The line about her being on a date with *the* Bentley Marshall plays in my ears and a shudder goes down my back.

Mira and I chat and laugh for a little while longer as I try to take her mind off all the shit in her life and forget about some of the shit in mine. She mentions going to the library with Autumn and we get up, tossing our empty cups on the way out of the shop.

I grab her hand when we get outside, making her pause before she heads off. "Don't hold it all in anymore, Mir," I say, looking down at her and feeling my shoulders prickle, knowing I'm doing just that to protect her. "Talk to me whenever you need to." She nods, smiling up at me and squeezing my hand.

"I will. Promise." She lets go of my hand and walks off toward the library. I watch her for a moment, hoping I'm wrong and Harley doesn't hurt my best friend.

23

BENTLEY

Walking back to West Tower, the events of last night cascade in my head, stirring my cock. I smile, pulling out my phone and texting Janette to see if she's free. Maybe we can all go grab lunch together in a bit. Or just stay in the suite for the weekend.

I walk into our dorm, finding Axel on the couch, hunched forward with his eyes trained on the TV as his fingers fly over the Xbox controller in his hands.

"Hey," he grunts, not looking over at me. I smile, slipping my shoes off and throwing my keys onto the closest table. Flopping down on the couch, I bump into him, making him bump me back in annoyance as he continues to play.

"I like you not avoiding me this time," I say, relaxing back and folding my hands behind my head as I watch the screen. "Was thinking we could get Janette, and all go out for lunch in a bit?"

"Doubt it," he says, eyes following his character on the screen. "Looks like it's her turn to be the evasive one."

His words make me sit up, looking over at him. "What do you mean?"

He pauses his game, turning toward me. "She hasn't responded to any of my texts or calls since you left. If I know J, she's freaking out about last night."

"Why are you just sitting here?" I ask, jumping up from the couch.

He joins me, tossing the controller aside. "I was waiting for you to come back. She seems to respond better to a tag team effort." He smirks and I shake my head, already grabbing my keys and walking out with Axel at my heels.

We get down to the sixth floor quickly, flying down the stairs rather than using the elevator. I walk straight up to Mira and Janette's door, banging my fist against it hard as my heard pounds wildly. No way am I losing this without a fight just as it begins.

The door stays closed but we can hear the floorboards inside creak with a repetitive motion. I know Mira's not home, so Janette must be the one freaking out on the other side of the door.

"Come on Blue, open up," Axel calls, knocking again.

A minute passes before we hear the lock twist, and the door opens slowly. Janette stands on the other side, curls in disarray and eyes rimmed in red as she stares up at both of us cautiously.

"Hi," she croaks, throat scratchy with the words. I step in immediately, wrapping my arms around her and pulling her into my chest. Axel follows closely, shutting the door behind us before coming around and wrapping us both in his own arms, squeezing Janette against me from behind her.

Her arms stay at her sides and my breath hitches with the stab to my chest.

"Talk to us, sunshine," I whisper. She has her eyes closed with the side of her face laying against my chest.

With a sigh, she pulls her head back, resting it against

Axel's chest as she looks up at me. "This isn't going to work." My stomach plummets and all the air leaves my lungs. Axel's arms tense around us. The panic in Janette's eyes grows as she starts to ramble. "I don't see how it can! People won't understand and once my mom finds out, she'll do everything she can to ruin it because it won't look good for her career. The press will be brutal and I'm sure it will get even worse with how much your parents are already in the spotlight." She nods her chin at me, and I grit my teeth. "I don't want this to hurt you. Either of you." She twists her neck to look over her shoulder at Axel. "You know how Mom will be. Best case scenario, she cuts me off altogether, but then we'll be defenseless when the public finds out. I don't want all of us to suddenly become some scandalous spectacle." She breathes heavily when she's done, squirming out of our grasps, and taking a few steps away. "We should end it now, so none of us get hurt."

I clench my fists at my sides, gnashing my lips together to keep the anger swirling in my chest from running down my tongue.

"Aunt Sandy's opinion doesn't matter in this right now. Neither does the public's, in my opinion. I don't care if anyone else ever understands it, honestly. I want this and I'm already in too deep to not be hurt right now, Janette." She winces when Axel uses her full first name, pain lancing through his words. He looks over at me. "What about you?"

I unclench my jaw, still staring at Janette. "I don't give a fuck what anyone thinks or if paparazzi try to destroy this. My parents' have never cared about who I'm dating as long as I'm happy and they have a whole PR team for a reason. If, and when, *we* decide we want to be publicly open about this, they will help us if we ask."

"Seriously think about this, guys." She pleads, leaning

toward us a little as she hugs her arms around her torso. Her eyes meet mine. "Neither of us have experienced the real lack of privacy our parents have. My mom can't go anywhere in Georgia without planning it in advance. My school had to get extra security to keep photographers off campus."

The flashes of the cameras at graduation play in my mind, the claustrophobic feeling crowding my throat. I swallow past it, reminding myself and her, "The Coast has a no press policy. We're safe here."

Janette shakes her head, saying, "If they get wind of this, that will change. I know it will. The second we step off campus there'll be photographers and people wanting to make a spectacle of us."

I step toward her. "We're not our parents. People don't care what we're doing." Janette starts shaking her head.

Axel holds up his hands. "Do you want an out?" he asks. "Because it sounds like Bentley and I are prepared to fight for this, but you don't want to do the same."

Her eyes water, a few tears escaping as she stands across from us. "I want this," she whispers. "Please believe me. I do. But I'm scared of what will happen because of it."

Axel reaches her first, placing his hands on either side of her face and swiping her tears away with his thumbs. "We don't have to figure it all out right now, Blue."

I step in behind him, rubbing her upper arm to try to soothe her. "We literally started this less than twenty-four hours ago."

She laughs shakily, watery eyes darting between the two of us as I speak.

"Let's just explore this together for a bit before we go thinking about other people's reactions and going public globally." I roll my eyes a little at the idea, silently grateful I chose not to tell Mira yet now that I can see Janette's panic over the idea.

She sighs, pulling her face out of Axel's hands and swiping her own under her eyes. "I'm sorry I freaked out." She laughs again, the sound shaky and not at all like the one I already love hearing. "I panicked way too early, didn't I?"

Axel shrugs, letting his hands fall to her waist. "I already knew Aunt Sandy's new world view had fucked you up a bit. But you've got both of us here for you, now." She reaches out and squeezes his upper arm. "Please just come talk to us next time you start spiraling, though. That way we can avoid the pain of the last few minutes. We make decisions about this together, got it?"

Janette nods, reaching out to take my hand. I pull our intertwined fingers up to my mouth, kissing her wrist. "And for the record, I am also in too deep to not get hurt at this point," I add.

She smiles more normally than before, eyes still a little misty. "It killed me to think about ending this. I was bluffing when I tried to make it seem like walking away wouldn't affect me."

Axel pulls her closer and I wrap an arm around his waist. "Bentley suggested getting lunch, but I think we should stay in for the afternoon." He looks up at me.

"Mira is with Autumn right now, probably for the rest of the day." She mentioned still avoiding the suite today.

I look over at Janette who worries her bottom lip. "I told her Christopher and I broke up. She caught me coming back in and asked. She knows I'm seeing someone else."

My stomach plummets. Did she know the whole time we were at the café?

"But I didn't tell her who."

Relief floods me. "Okay, sunshine. Want to order a pizza and relax together for a little while?"

"I was thinking more like round two in Blue's bed," Axel says, and I bump his shoulder, nodding toward Janette's tearstained face. "But we could watch a movie and cuddle too."

Janette laughs, grabbing one of his hands off her waist and pulling the two of us over toward the couch. "We'll let you pick the movie, Axe."

24

BENTLEY

xel lays across the couch, feet in my lap while I scroll through social media on my phone. Some crime show plays on the TV on low, Axel's eyes trained on the screen with his arms crossed tensely over his bare chest. The suite has become a very clothes optional area in the last two weeks, not that I've complained. Living with my boyfriend and having our girlfriend come over basically every night has made me start thinking of clothes as pretty pointless, if not just in the way most of the time.

A knock sounds on the suite door and Axel sits up, letting his feet fall from my lap. I get up, pocketing my phone in my sweats and crossing over to open the door. Janette rocks on the balls of her feet on the other side, smiling when she sees me. I move to the side to let her in, closing the door before I turn and wrap my arms around her from behind, leaning down to place my chin on her shoulder and kiss her exposed neck. "Hi," I breathe against her skin.

She laughs, turning to peck my lips before shoving my arms away and walking toward the couch. She takes off her backpack and tosses it at her feet. "Hi," she says to me before sitting down next to Axel who leans over to pull her against him and kiss her as well. I walk over and sit on the other side of the L shaped couch, watching them together with a smile.

"Missed you," Axel murmurs, moving his lips to her jaw.

She pushes him away with another laugh, hands lingering on his chest while his stay loosely wrapped around her. "I saw you both in class this morning." She rolls her eyes, leaning down to open her backpack and start taking things out and putting them on the coffee table.

"Yeah, but we can't touch you in class," I say, winking when she looks up at me with a faux exasperated frown. I can see the desire growing in her bright green eyes.

"And you didn't stay the night last night, so it's been even longer." Axel leans forward, arms still wrapped around her, and kisses her shoulder. Her hair swings behind her in a long ponytail, curls straightened today.

I spread my arms out behind me on the couch, not missing the way both of them trail their eyes over my uncovered biceps. The arm holes of my loose tank are cut wide, leaving most of the sides of my torso exposed. I lean back, watching Janette shake her head and look away while Axel's eyes light up, trailing to the obvious slight bulge forming in my sweats.

"I'm here for us to work," Janette says, pulling out more books and setting them next to her laptop. "We only have five weeks till our presentation is due and we need to get started on the paper."

Axel groans, forehead hitting Janette's shoulder. I get up off the couch, going to my room to grab my laptop. Janette shoulders Axel off before I get back and he sits on the end of the couch by himself, arms folded with a petulant look on his face.

I put my hand on his shoulder over the back of the couch. "She's right, baby. We can play later." I lean down to kiss the spot where his neck meets his shoulder. He shudders beneath me, and I smile as I pull away, heading back to the couch I was on before.

Axel grumbles, getting up and disappearing into his room for a minute. Janette already has her laptop open and types away on the keyboard. She's moved off the couch, settling into a crisscrossed position on the floor in front of the coffee table.

I boot up my laptop, logging in and opening my browser while Axel returns and settles onto the couch again. He sits right up next to Janette, the side of his leg touching hers. I stare at the two of them, mind wandering with ideas of what we could and have done alone in this suite.

I get up, heading to the kitchen to grab a water bottle and distract myself from the two of them. Cracking the seal, I lean back against the counter, remembering last week when I ate out Janette on the edge of it while Axel sucked me off. I close my eyes, trying to discipline my rushing blood. I drink some cold water, letting it chase some of the heat in my chest and head back toward the living room. I find Axel bent over Janette's shoulder, breathing on her neck as she tries to show him something on her screen. She speaks slowly, hand shaking as she points at something and eyes drooping. I see Axel lick his lips, knowing he's one second away from leaning in and running his tongue over her skin.

"We should go back to the library," I blurt. Axel's head whips up, dilated pupils meeting mine, and eyes narrowing.

Janette takes a deep breath, closing her laptop and starting to pack up. "That's a good idea. Get dressed Axel."

Axel huffs, standing quickly and going back to his room to grab a shirt. I whip my tank top off, walking to my own room to change into a sweater. The winter chill has started to creep in across campus and although the buildings have pretty good heating, walking across campus in a tank top is no longer an option. The snow will probably start soon and although Janette grew up mostly in Maine, I'm worried the last few years in Georgia have made her soft in the cold. She's already started complaining about the bitterness.

My eyes sting and I quickly pop my contacts out, grabbing my back up glasses and throwing on some warm socks. Packing my stuff into my bag, I return to the living room, finding a disgruntled Axel standing by the door, already bundled up and no Janette. "She went to get her coat and warmer shoes." He places his hands on the straps of his bag, already slung over his back.

I walk up, placing my hands on his hips. "It's too distracting trying to work here. We need to get some of this project done and then we can come back here, and both Janette and I will be all too happy to take turns fucking you for hours if you want."

"You better," he grumbles, sticking his bottom lip out in a pout. I lean forward, biting the invitation he just threw out, making him wince when I pull his lip away a little before releasing.

"Let's go," I say, smacking his ass after I put my shoes on. He opens the door, heading down the hall and I follow, closing the suite door behind me. We head down the stairs to Janette and Mira's, picking up Janette before all getting into the elevator on her floor.

"We should go get dinner after we're done," Janette says when we step into the lobby after a tension filled ride down.

"You sure you want people to see all of us together?" Axel and I have been cautious around her the last few weeks, holding off on suggesting we go out of the suite to hang out and usually bringing food back with us or ordering out when we knew she would be over. Her initial panic still clawed at us a little and we didn't want to spook her if she wasn't ready to be out yet. We both knew what it was like to be judged for who we were with. We'd talked about it, and both decided to take things at her speed.

She shrugs. "We might have to be careful about too much touching, but I don't think anyone will see us eating together and automatically put together that we're a thing. We already sit together in class and at the library. This will be the same thing, just with food," she reasons.

I nod, tamping down the warmth in my chest at the idea of the three of us going out to do something nonacademic. It's a baby step, but the first one at that. "Food sounds good."

Axel rolls his eyes at me over Janette's head and mouths my words back at me with a disbelieving look.

I shrug, mouthing *What?* back.

That sounded stupid, he mouths.

"You both know I'm right here, right? I can feel you talking over me," Janette says, side eyeing each of us with pursed lips. "I know it's a lame first step, but I do want to leave your suite sometimes and do normal couple things." Her forehead wrinkles. "Or throuple things, I guess?"

Axel flexes his hands around the straps of his backpack, holding himself back from touching her. "I was telling Bentley his response was stupid. Nothing about you, Blue. We'd both love to go get food with you." She smiles up at him before turning the same look over to me. We keep walking down the sidewalk together, Axel joking about calling us The Triple Threats.

"Oh! Or how about Three of a Kind?" He looks at both of us with so much excitement.

"We're not a superhero group," I say, pulling open the heavy wooden door and holding it for both of them to enter first. "We don't need a group name."

Axel pouts and Janette laughs. "I like Triple Threat. Sounds intimidating."

"Don't encourage him." We walk over to our usual table, still vacant though the crowd around here has grown nearly every week as the semester passes.

"But it's so much fun to gang up on you." Axel snorts at her words and I stare at her as we sit down, waiting for the double meaning to sink in. Her eyes widen when she realizes, and she grins at me, licking her lips on purpose. I grunt across the table from her in response.

"Let's get working so that we can leave soon," Axel huffs, already setting up his computer and starting to focus on the screen.

We start working, each of us mostly silent aside from the random questions or comments about the project as we work. My eyes start to tire at the forty-five-minute mark, and I look away, taking off my glasses and rubbing my face. They aren't blue light lenses since I don't wear them often and I instantly feel relief closing my eyes for a moment.

Opening my eyes, I find Janette watching me over the top of her laptop. Her face is blurry without the glasses, and I put them back on and watch her swallow slowly. I raise an eyebrow, but she shakes her head, going back to her work with heat in her cheeks.

I glance over at Axel, but his focus is studiously on the

words he types at a rapid pace. When he gets in the zone, the world around him tends to fall away, so I know he's not paying attention. I look down at my own work, the words blurring on the screen as I slowly extend my leg underneath the table.

Janette jumps a little when my foot slides down her calf, eyes flying back up to me. I bite back my laugh, not looking up and pretending to be working hard. She looks around, realizing what I just did and that no one is paying attention to us and shakes her head. I slide my foot along her leg again and she shakes it out, trying to shake me off. I chuckle lightly, looking up under my lashes, to see her nose wrinkle up and lips purse. She looks adorable.

Still, I back off, not wanting to push her too far. Trying to refocus on my part of the paper, I shake my head a little, rereading the last page I wrote. My hand comes up, playing with my bottom lip as I go over the words.

"Bentley, can you help me find this book?" Janette asks, writing down some info from her computer on a scrap piece of paper. I nod, closing my laptop and standing. I stretch my arms above my head and lengthen my spine. Axel continues typing away, not paying us any attention. Janette jumps up, heading off toward the stacks without looking over at me. I follow after her, grinning.

Janette Iris Davidson has never needed anyone's help finding a book in a library in her life, I'm sure of it.

She rushes down one aisle, turning the corner ahead of me and disappearing again. I rush to catch up, following her further into the shadows of the giant open room that makes up the ground floor. She doesn't look back or check that I'm behind her, knowing I'll catch up as she rushes to whatever destination she has planned. She doesn't even look at the paper in her hands, or glance at the labels on the sides of the stacks saying what letters and DDC numbers are shelved in each row.

We end up in the last row, against the farthest wall where all of the breakout study rooms are located. Their doors have little whiteboards on them with schedules meant for people to sign up and check them out for segmented hours when they want to work in their own area. I try to picture what they could have been when this was an active church. Not confessionals certainly.

Janette checks each of the boards we walk past, stopping outside the fourth one and picking up the dry erase marker tied to a string on the side of the board. She scribbles hastily across the current hour slot before recapping the marker and opening the door. I walk in after her, leaning back against the table inside as she closes the door behind us.

"Did you just check out a room to have sex in?" I ask, crossing my arms over myself and trying not to outright grin. She glances around the room quick, probably looking for cameras before looking me dead in the eye.

"Yes." She comes toward me, grabbing the hem of my sweater and starting to pull it up. "Take off your clothes." I rip the sweater the rest of the way off, complying with her demand. "Leave these on," she says breathily, pointing to the bridge of my nose.

She starts to take off her sweater and I stare, a sly smile sliding across my face. "Do you like me in glasses, sunshine?"

"Yes," she says again, unbuttoning her pants. "You look hot as hell in them, and it's been distracting me this whole time."

I snort, standing up to pull her in against me once she's gotten rid of her pants. "I'll wear them more often then." She's completely bare other than her bra, having started to forgo underwear around Axel and me. We ruined a few pairs in frenzied need for access to her and she got tired of chastising us.

She groans as I start to lick and lightly bite across her shoulder, banding one arm around her lower back and cupping her wet core in my other hand.

"Gotta stay quiet, sunshine," I murmur. My finger slides down her seam, opening her up to me as she widens her stance. "It's a library."

She huffs through her nose. "Make me."

I pull back, grinning down at her and she grins right back. "Your wish, my command," I say, leaning in to peck her lips before spinning us around. I lift her onto the big oak table, and she lays back, baring herself to me with wide parted knees.

"We need to be quick, before Axel comes looking for us." I nod, slotting myself in between her legs and bending down to cover her body with my own. My cock strains against the cotton of my sweats, wanting to be released and inside her, but I ignore it as our lips touch, and my tongue delves into her mouth. Her hands come up around me, one in my hair while the other reaches down over the muscles of my back. Her feet wrap around either side of my hips, trying to push off my sweats with her sneaker clad feet.

I go back to rubbing her, knowing just how to strum and circle her clit so that she's bucking and panting against me. "Bentley," she whines, and I bite her lip in admonishment.

"Shhhh," I murmur as I slide my index finger home inside of her, finding little to no resistance in her slick state. My eyes flutter shut as I add a second finger and start stretching her out. "How long have you been like this? You're fucking soaked."

She just moans underneath me, and I bring my free

hand up to wrap around the lower half of her face, effectively muffling her. Her eyes fly open, wide and lust filled. She clenches around my fingers, and I chuckle.

"Scream all you want, sunshine," I tease, adding a third finger and upping my pace. Her eyes roll back in her head, showing me the whites underneath and I nip at the skin on her neck, holding myself back from marking her like I usually do. I try to do it somewhere out of sight since she doesn't want people to know about us yet, but the need to leave something right there in plain sight always flares when we're like this.

Pulling my hand away, unable to wait any longer, I sit up a little, hand still over her mouth and push my sweats down just enough to free my dick. Lining myself up quickly, I thrust to the hilt in the first go.

My groan echoes off the stone walls around us as she arches her back and screams beneath my hand, the sound making my throat go dry as I start to move in and out of her. It didn't take long for either of us to figure out we both like a little pain mixed in with our pleasure and I grip the side of her waist roughly with my free hand. She snaps her hips wildly, meeting me perfectly as I pound into her. White spots break out across my vision as I stare down at her, holding myself back to make sure she comes first.

It doesn't take long after I release her flesh and press hard circles into her clit, still ramming into her with as much force as I can. She screams again as she comes, tightening around me like a vice. My balls draw up and my vision almost blacks out with the force of my release. I bite my lip to stop my own groans from escaping, tasting blood. We ride out our joined orgasm together, each continuing to move against the other for a few more moments.

When we finally stop, I release her mouth, letting her

haul in deep breaths. I stare down at her through the black rimmed lenses still perched on my nose.

"Definitely going to wear these more," I say breathlessly. Janette sits up, still keeping us connected as we come face to face.

She leans in and licks some of the blood off my lip, making my eyes close and cock twitch inside her. "I like that idea."

"Mmmm," I manage to mumble, and she laughs, tapping my shoulder. I move back, pulling out of her slowly and then watching some of my cum slide out after me. I look around at the room, finding nothing I can clean her up with in the dim study room.

"It's okay, Bent," she says, reading my thoughts. "I can run to the bathroom quick."

I shake my head, going down on my knees. Swiping my tongue over her, I catch the mixture of my cum and hers. The taste of us makes my spent cock start to twitch back to life and I groan around our flavor.

"Bentley!" she squeals, shuddering above me. I swallow us and go in for a few more licks, holding everything I catch in my mouth as I stand up. She stares up at me with shocked eyes and I lean down, pushing my tongue past her lips and feeding her our mixture. She responds instantly, wrapping her own tongue around mine and drinking from me.

"All taken care of," I say, stepping back from her again.

"All you've done is turn me on again, asshole." She jumps down off the table, grabbing her pants and I chuckle.

I pull my own sweats up to cover myself and grab my sweater off the floor. Once we're both dressed, I pull her hair out of the haphazard state of a ponytail and hand her the tie so she can redo it. She swipes it all up quickly, making a sloppy bun with a shrug. I kiss her quick, tasting the two of us on our lips again.

"Don't worry, I've stupidly made things harder for myself too." I lean my forehead against hers, trying to regulate my breathing as it gets shallow again.

"Let's go wrap up and grab Axel then. We can eat quickly and head back to the suite." She grabs my hand, pulling me from the room and erasing our names from the board with the sleeve of her sweater. She keeps our fingers interlocked until we're in the last row of stacks, dropping my hand when the atmosphere gets lighter and people at tables come into view again.

Stepping out of the shadows, we hastily take our seats again, Axel still locked in on his screen.

"Where's the book?" he asks, not looking up or slowing down his typing.

I stumble, looking over at Janette who stares at Axel with an open mouth. "Uh," she stutters.

"Mmhmm, I expect compensation for being left behind to do work." He looks over at both of us with playful vindictiveness lighting his face. "One of you is paying for my dinner and the other is sucking my dick when we get back."

25

Janette

I flick through the menu on the TV, trying to find something to watch as I wait to go meet the boys after their class. After the success of our first dinner out together, and the subsequent apology sex with Axel back at their suite, we've been spending more time out doing normal things the last few weeks. We're supposed to go get sushi after their class, but that leaves me on my own for the next hour now that I'm done with school for the day.

The lock jangles open as Mira comes into the suite, stomping her boots against the little slush rug I got when it started snowing. She leans down to pull off her boots, dropping her bag in the process. I bite my lip, realizing this is the opportunity I've been waiting for to start to mend things between us, but nervous it's already too late. Mira is a huge part of Bentley's life, and I don't want her to hate me since I plan to keep him around for a while.

"Hey," I call out and her head snaps up, looking at me in surprise. I smile, trying to stuff down the flurry of nerves in my gut.

"Hi," she says slowly, looking around as if she might find another person.

"It's just me." My palms start sweating as she takes off her coat and then grabs her bag off the floor. "I was just looking for something to watch before I meet people for lunch. Do you want to watch something with me?"

She freezes on the way to her room, mouth popping open. "Um, yeah, sure," she says, shuffling her bag a bit. "Just give me a minute to change."

I nod, smiling widely. Nerves jump around in my stomach, but I ignore them, tapping my nails against the remote.

Mira disappears into her room, and I continue surfing, trying to find something we can put on together. When she comes back out in a baggy sweatshirt and leggings, I smile again, wondering if I look like a lunatic or as relaxed as I want to be. She comes around the couches, plopping down on the one next to the couch I'm on and drags the fuzzy blanket off the back to drape across her lap.

"What are we watching?" she asks tentatively.

I fiddle with the remote. "Not sure, I haven't been able to find anything interesting yet. There's too many choices."

"What do you usually watch?" Her fingers play with the blanket, twisting it around as she watches me flick through movies and shows on the screen.

I shrug. "A little of everything really. There isn't really one genre I usually lean toward." She nods and I panic a little as things lull. "Unless something has Tony Markell in it. I'll watch anything he's in."

"Ugh, same!" Mira squeals, turning toward me. "Did you watch him in that baseball movie a few years ago?"

I roll my eyes toward the ceiling. "Hell yes. Those pants?" I groan. "Amazing. I genuinely tried watching baseball after that, but the lack of contact made me realize I just liked him in the movie, not the sport." We both laugh, and my nerves start to settle.

She sits back, getting comfortable. "So, is that your type? Like he's hot, but I prefer brunettes over blondes."

"Is Swedish supermodel my type?" I snort. "Yeah, I guess in an ideal world. But I do tend toward brunettes in reality." I picture Axel and Bentley, trying to decide which is more "my type." They both have their differences. Bentley's wavy dark chocolate hair always laying in a casually messy way and curling around his neck versus Axel's unruly straight honey strands that seem to stick out from his head at all different angles but never seeming to look haphazard or styled. Bentley's broad muscular build versus Axel's wiry lean beauty. Cloudy hazel eyes next to deep endless brown. Not to mention their personalities. They are sometimes total opposites and other times exactly the same. All of it appeals to me, not a single comparison coming with a clear winner in my mind.

I tap my thigh. "I think my type is very loosely defined."

"Well, what about Christopher ticked your boxes?" She doesn't ask it maliciously. Her tone is genuinely curious. But I suddenly realize how difficult the answer might be.

I fiddle with the remote again, looking down at my hands in my lap. "I don't know, honestly. I kind of dated him because my mom thought we made a good match." For her career, I add silently in my head. "I'm much more attracted to who I'm seeing now. So far, they tick all my boxes." I stifle a laugh. Layla has been pestering me for details about how things are going with Bentley and Axel, but since I told the boys I didn't want anyone outside of our bubble to know, I've been keeping everything under lock and key. She's not stupid, seeing how happy her brother and I have been lately, and I haven't complained about Bentley in at least a month so I know she can probably put two and two together and get some form of bigger picture from it.

But it's still nice to just brag about the guys to someone.

Mira's nose scrunches up, face souring. "Sorry, I forgot you're seeing someone new now. Not another one of your mom's picks, I hope?"

I laugh, shaking my head. "Definitely not. My mom probably won't approve of who I'm dating now." I bite my lip. We're going to get to a point in this conversation where she asks to see him or asks who it is I'm seeing. Part of me doesn't want to lie to her since that will just bite me in the ass when the three of us eventually tell her. But I don't want to tell her without checking with Bentley that he's okay with it. She is his best friend. If he told Layla about us before I was ready, I would be pissed.

"Why not? Is he scary or something?"

"No." I laugh. "Nothing like that." I bite my lip again, mulling over how much I should tell her. "My mom's just very particular about our family image. She's a politician back home so everything I do reflects onto her. Can't do anything that might impact her career."

Mira nods. "I get that though, not being able to do things without thinking about how it will affect your mom. My parents fight sometimes, and everyone keeps telling me it's not my job to try to keep the peace, but I can't really help it. I don't want to do anything to upset them."

I smile sadly. "We can't always live for them though, right? Layla drills that into me all the time."

Mira laughs. "Bentley's definitely one of the people reminding me of the same thing."

I grin, remembering who I ran into in the hallway the day I tried to sneak back in after sleeping with Bentley and

Axel for the first time. "That guy I saw leaving our suite a few weeks ago one of the other ones?"

Her cheeks turn pink, eyes falling back down to her lap. "Harley is one of them yes, but it's...complicated."

"Hey, it's fine, whatever is going on with you guys." I hold up my hands. "I don't need to know the details."

She scans over my face, fingers digging into the blanket again. "He's my brother's best friend. I know he cares about me, when he tells me stuff like that, but I'm not really sure where things are going." She sighs. "Bentley doesn't approve, and I can't really tell anyone else in our circle since they all know Ramsey."

"I'm dating my best friend's brother," I blurt, stomach churning as I realize what I've just said. "Trust me I get how it can be complicated."

Her eyes grow wide, and she smiles. "You're with Axel?"

I nod. "Yeah, we've been seeing each other for the last month or so. It's still new so we're going slow." Sort of. I already know Axel won't care that I told Mira we're together. He'll probably jump up and down on the spot when I tell him.

She leans forward. "Does Layla know?"

I shake my head. "We haven't exactly told her, but they're twins and she's my best friend. I'm pretty sure she knows and is just waiting for us to tell her." Mira nods, leaning back and looking pensive. "She's tried pushing us together before though. Axel's not really subtle with his affection and she knew he liked me probably before I did." I feel light, being able to talk about him, though the niggling feeling to say something about Bentley too dwells in the background.

Mira laughs. "Yeah, I like Axel. You guys are paired up with Bentley on that big history project, right? How's that working now that you're with Axel?"

I roll my eyes. "Keeping him on task has been a little tricky." I think back to how we had to bribe him to finish his draft for the essay with a tandem blowjob and how quickly he suddenly found the motivation to finish. "But it's working out. They both want to get a good grade and know how much this is important to me since the course counts toward my major."

Mira nods. "Yeah, Bentley takes his grades seriously. But he's a brain so it doesn't take much effort for him." She shakes her head, still smiling all the same.

"I've noticed that," I muse. Glancing at my watch, I realize I need to leave to meet the boys soon.

"Time to head to your lunch plans?" Mira pulls her legs up, loosely circling her arms around her knees.

"Yeah, sorry." I stand up, stretching my limbs.

"No, you're fine. Go." She waves a hand at me, and I pass her the remote before going into my room to put on some socks and grab my side bag. Mira sits in the same spot when I come back out, now starting some show that looks a little familiar. I put on my coat and boots, pulling my fuzzy earmuffs wide to fit them over my curls without crushing them.

Before I leave, I glance back at Mira, smiling. "We should hang out more. This was fun."

She smiles, nodding her head fast. "You know where to find me," she jokes, nodding toward her bedroom.

I nod, feeling warm. "I'll see you later then." I leave the suite, heading down to the lobby, excited to tell the guys I made the first step toward fixing things with Mira.

Janette

I head toward the building the boys and I agreed to meet at, practically skipping down the sidewalk. Seeing my guys standing at the bottom of the front steps, I speed up, heading straight for them. I bounce a little when I'm standing before them, Axel already smiling to match my energy.

I grin. "Hi, babes!"

"Ugh," Axel groans, deflating dramatically. "You sound like Layla. Don't remind me of my sister when I'm thinking about kissing you."

I giggle at Bentley's rolling eyes. "Got it. No babes. Hi, hotties?" I try and Bentley cringes.

"Better," Axel muses. "We'll workshop it later. I'm starving."

"Let's go then." I start to head down the sidewalk toward the closest road leading off campus, but Bentley slides into my path.

"Wrong way, sunshine."

My brows lower. "Aren't we going to get sushi? The place

is that way." I point in the general direction I'm pretty sure the restaurant is in.

"Yes, but our ride is this way." Axel calls, already heading in the other direction.

I turn around, Bentley stepping up beside me as we start walking. "Our ride?"

"You didn't think we'd make you walk that far in the snow, did you?" He looks down at me like it's ridiculous.

"It's not that far." I shrug, but I can already feel the tip of my nose going numb in the biting winter air.

We enter the parking lot beside the building, trudging through the slush around the edges of the cars. "Whose car are we taking?"

"Mine," Bentley says, pulling out his keys and clicking a button. The lights flash on a black Mercedes, completely clear of snow. "I moved it over here earlier so we wouldn't have to go far to get back to it." Axel hops into the back, leaving the passenger side for me.

Bentley gets in behind the wheel, starting the car with the push of a button and cranking the heat in the backseat. I look around, smiling at the sleek interior. "You have a car. How did I not know you have a car?"

He shrugs, backing out of the space and putting his hand on the back of my headrest to look behind the car. "It was a graduation present from my grandfather."

I whistle. "All my mom got me was a gift certificate to her favorite spa." I run my hands over the dashboard. "I've never had a car."

Axel sits forward, head appearing between the front seats. "You have your license?"

I nod. "Yeah, but I never had the time to get an actual job and Mom was too busy to look for a car for me."

"How'd you get around if she was always out?" Bentley asks, watching the road, but side eyeing me for a moment.

"I didn't really." I shrug. "I went running a lot if I needed to get out of the house. And I would ride my bike to the park, but otherwise I took the bus to and from school and Mom had someone to drive me to events if she had to be there before I did." Looking outside, I add, "Christopher would take me out sometimes too so I wasn't just trapped in the house *all* the time."

Axel stares at me from the side and when I look over, I feel overwhelmed by the compassion radiating off him. "There are a million reasons I wish you stayed in Maine."

I laugh. "Layla used to write these really convoluted plans for me to run away and come live with you guys in her emails. She'd probably agree with you."

Bentley reaches over and takes my hand, intertwining our fingers before bringing them up to his mouth to kiss the inside of my wrist. "I'll buy you a car if you want."

I balk at him before pulling my hand back from his. "You are not buying me a car."

"Will you buy me a car?" Axel asks, batting his eyelashes at Bentley in the rearview mirror.

Bentley laughs. "You already have a car."

"Yeah." Axel shrugs. "But I'd be okay with having two."

Bentley rolls his eyes. "What did you do after class?" He places his hand on my thigh as he changes the subject.

"Hung out with Mira, actually." I smile when he turns his head completely over to look at me before snapping his eyes back to the road.

"Really?" He squeezes my leg with a smile. "How did it go?"

"Pretty well actually. We talked about boys," I joke, waggling my eyebrows at Axel.

He laughs, shaking his head. "I hope my name came up then."

Bentley glances in the mirror at him, smile falling.

His reaction sets my nerves off, but I push forward, knowing I need to tell them the juicy part. "Actually, it did." I watch Bentley's reaction as I say, "I told her I'm seeing Axel."

"You did?" Axel's posture shoots up, bright smile lighting up his face. I nod and Bentley continues to stare ahead, but I notice his teeth grind a little bit.

"I thought we weren't telling people anything yet," he mutters. Axel deflates a little at his reaction, looking over at him.

"She knew I was seeing someone, and I accidentally said that it was Layla's brother," I explain.

He nods once, pulling into the sushi place's parking lot and focusing on finding a spot. Once we're parked and the silence from the lack of car engine hum sets in, he turns toward the two of us. "That's probably smart. She won't think it's weird if she catches you at our place now." I nod, feeling relieved that he's okay with it.

Axel sits back, biting the nail of his thumb. We both turn in our seats to look back at him, spread out in the middle of the back row.

"What's wrong, Axe?" I reach out to touch his knee.

He looks up at Bentley, dropping his hand from his mouth. "You don't want to tell Mira about us?"

Bentley glances at me. "We're trying not to tell *anyone* right now, right?"

"Yeah, but it's killing me not to tell Layla about this. The second you both are comfortable with it; I'm going to spill everything to her."

"Everything?" I raise an eyebrow.

"Well, she doesn't need the dirtier details, but yeah,

everything I can." He shrugs one shoulder. "But you don't want to tell your best friend."

Bentley glances over at me again, fear seeping into his features. "We're still figuring things out. Getting solid. Janette wasn't wrong that first day. The media is going to be brutal when this gets out. I just want to live in our little bubble for as long as we can."

"And you think Mira will run to the tabloids?" He crosses his arms over his chest.

"No, of course not!" I place my other hand on Bentley's arm.

"Then telling her wouldn't be a problem, right?" He points at Bentley, eyes narrowing.

Bentley chews the inside of his cheek. "She's got a lot going on right now. I don't want to add to her plate. I know she'll understand and be happy for me, but she's not close with Janette and I don't want her to worry about me and how this works for us right now."

My chest squeezes when he mentions my relationship with Mira. It's my fault he's worried about his best friend's reaction. I've started making progress with Mira today, but I silently vow to put in more effort so that he doesn't need to worry about this anymore.

"I will tell her," Bentley adds, resolve hardening as he stares down Axel. "After Thanksgiving break. I promise."

Axel studies his face, seemingly finding what he needs. "Okay." He nods. The tension lessens, but I can feel it still lying beneath the surface.

I squeeze both of them at our points of contact. "Now that that's settled, let's go eat our weight in raw fish."

Axel slowly smiles, nodding before sliding toward the door to get out.

Bentley watches him get out, taking a deep breath. I

squeeze his arm again and he smiles at me, getting out too. I follow, jumping out of the car and rushing toward the restaurant to get out of the cold.

27

BENTLEY

I place another folded pair of jeans into the open suitcase on my bed, tucking it in and moving things around to try to use as much space as possible. I can hear Axel yelling at the TV a few feet away, playing some online team game with random people while he waits for Layla and Gwen to be ready to leave.

A knock on the door gets him to quit the game and throw the controller down on the couch. I continue packing, figuring it'll be one of his sisters.

"Hey, Blue!" Axel's excited voice stops my movement. "What are you doing here?"

I walk over to the open door of my room, leaning against the frame and taking in Janette, standing all bundled up in the threshold of our suite, an overstuffed duffel bag and brimming tote slung over each of her shoulders.

"I wanted to see you guys again before I leave for Georgia." She bites her lip, and I can see the nerves bubbling up under her surface.

I try to ease her tension. "Packed enough stuff, sunshine? It's only going to be five days." Janette walks into the suite,

Axel closing the door behind her. I push off, coming forward to stand closer to them as she drops her bags and starts wringing her hands.

Janette shrugs. "You never know what the dress code will be with Mom. For all I know, she has the next five days booked up for me to do appearances with her. I packed for relaxation and formal events."

Axel frowns. "I still think you should come to Maine with us."

Janette shakes her head and takes a deep breath. "I'm going to need to face her at some point. The radio silence has been way too eerie. And it's Thanksgiving. I'm not going to intrude on your family holiday."

Axel wraps her up in his arms, leaning the side of his head against hers. "You are family, Blue. Not just to me, but Layla, Gwen, and Dad too. They'd all be so excited to have you home with us." He kisses the side of her head, and she laughs lightly.

She turns in his arms, putting her hands on either side of his face. "I will come back to Maine with you some time. But not this time." She pecks his mouth, Axel deepening the kiss as he presses her closer against him. She moans and he pulls back with a reluctant groan.

Shaking her head, she turns back toward me, one of Axel's arms still loosely around her waist.

I raise one shoulder, the fire in her eyes matching the one roaring in my blood. I don't want to be away from her for five days. "You could come to the Alps with me? I can get another ticket when we get to the airport."

She chuckles nervously. "I'd need a lot more preparation to meet the parents, Bent." I hold up my hands, tilting my head in acquiescence. She bites her lip again, eyes unfocused as she looks away from either of us.

"Hey," I call, walking up to her and putting my hands on the sides of her neck. "It'll be okay. If you need either of us, call. I will pick up any time of day, promise."

"I'm just nervous about what she's going to say." I nod and she looks over her shoulder at Axel's concerned face. "She was really pissed at the alumni thing and was so terrible to you. I don't know what I'm walking into really. She could be totally over it, or she could have been stewing for the last month, planning out some lecture or intervention to get me 'back on track.'"

Axel fishes around in his pocket, pulling out his phone. "I'm telling Layla I'm going home with you. You shouldn't have to walk into that alone."

Janette grabs his hand, stopping him from sending a text. "No, Axe. I'll be okay. I'm not ruining your time off with my family issues. And you need to go home and see your dad." My heart squeezes for her when I think about how much she probably wishes she could do the same. "Go gorge yourself on turkey and Uncle Jack's stuffing. I'll be okay." She turns back to look at me. "I'll call if I need to."

I nod. "I can always cancel my trip. My family doesn't really do the whole turkey and stuffing thing so I wouldn't be missing out."

She shakes her head. "You don't get to see your parents that often. Go be with them. I'll be okay, guys, I swear. I can handle my mom." She glances at her watch, shaking my hands off her shoulders. "I need to get going, my Uber's going to be here in a few minutes." She walks back over to her bags. Axel and I each grab one before she can, helping her shoulder them both.

She leans up on her tip toes, kissing Axel quickly before turning toward me. I lean down and kiss her, holding her head in place as I deepen the peck she tries to get away with.

She opens up to me, tongue tangling with mine before I pull back and wink down at her.

She leans back, looking a little bit dazed. "I love you guys," she whispers, looking between each of us with a small smile.

My heart stops. Axel freezes up next to me, mouth popping open.

Janette chuckles, turning and opening the door and walking out of the suite without another word.

"What the fuck?" Axel exclaims, taking a step toward the door once it closes.

I reach out, grabbing his arm to stop him. "Let her go. She has a flight to catch."

He whirls around on me, eyes wild, and runs a hand through his hair. "You're fine with what just happened? She just dropped that bomb and then left!"

I chuckle, feeling like I've been losing mass ever since she said those words and could just start to float away any second. Shrugging at Axel, I squeeze his arm to ground me. "She said it on her terms. It very much fits with who she is."

Axel shakes his head, shaking my hand off. "She didn't even wait for us to recover. She just said it out of nowhere like it was no big deal." He yells in frustration, starting to pace behind the side of the couch. "And now we have to wait five days to say it back!" His hands take up permanent residence in his hair, and I watch him spiral with a smile on my face.

He stops suddenly, pulling his phone back out. "I'm going to call her. I can't wait that long." He puts the phone to his ear after tapping a few times and I watch him go back to pacing, the ringing on the other end going on for a while.

"She sent me to voicemail!" He pulls the phone away from his face, looking at it like it personally attacked him.

I put my hands in my pockets, still standing by the door. "She's probably freaking out in the back of the Uber. You know she has to settle into these things. Give her a little time."

"Uh-huh," he mutters, pulling the phone back to his ear and listening to the end of her voicemail message. When the record tone goes off, he stands still. "I can't believe you just did that, Janette. I am so pissed off and turned on, and just —ugh—why did you leave like that? You didn't even wait for us to say anything." He shakes his head, looking me in the eyes as he leaves the rambling message. "I'm not going to say it back right now, because I want to do it in person, but ditto, okay? And when we all get back in a few days I'm never going to stop saying it." The mania in his eyes dies down and he swallows. "Call us if you need us. I mean it, Blue. Don't hold it in because you don't want to ruin our vacations. We want to be there for you when you need us. Let us do that." My smile grows, the light feeling expanding through me. "Alright, I'll see you in a few days. Layla's going to try to make Mom's cobbler. I'll bring some back with me. Oh, and start planning how you're going to make this up to me. Later, Blue." He hangs up, a sly smile on his face. "I hope it involves chocolate sauce," he says to me, still looking at his phone as he answers a text, probably from one of his sisters.

"I love you," I say, waiting.

He freezes up again, recovering much more quickly though when his head whips up to stare at me. His mouth opens and closes, and I walk up to him slowly, stopping when we're chest to chest. "I love you," I repeat, grabbing the back of his head and crushing my lips to his. He kisses me back, arms wrapping around my waist. Our tongues tangle and I start to press him forward toward the wall a few feet away when another knock sounds at the door. We both jump apart, breathing heavily. His eyes scan my face, wide and unfocused. I run a hand through my hair, licking my lips before turning and heading back over to the suite door.

Opening it, I find my best friend standing on the other side, eyes alight and smiling. "Hey, just wanted to stop by and say have a great time with your parents! Ramsey's downstairs waiting for me." I nod, leaning in to hug Mira.

"Tell them we said Happy Thanksgiving," she whispers in my ear.

"I will. You guys have fun too. Bring me back some of April's food, Mir." I lean against the door.

"Will do. Bye Axel! Have a great holiday!" She waves at him over my shoulder before heading back to the elevators. I shut the door, turning back around to look at Axel.

He stares at me, the desire from earlier drained from his face. A stony look takes its place. "If you love me," Axel says, voice low. "You'd tell your friends about us."

I rock back a little, seeing the hurt flash in his eyes before he turns and heads into his room, closing the door behind him. I stand in the same spot for a few minutes, debating going in after him, but knowing there's nothing more I can say to make this better. Huffing a breath, I head back to my room to finish packing, ignoring the urge to go to him.

28

Janette

The Uber turns down Mom's street and I feel a weird mix of apprehension and excitement. Everything looks the same, the grand houses we pass, the same trees lining the street, the same roundabout at the end. But it feels different too, familiar, but still not mine. Even more so now. My anxiety over seeing Mom again explodes throughout my body, starting in my stomach and expanding out, making my limbs feel heavy and awkward.

We drive slowly toward the white wall and the driver stops just outside the closed gate. I thank him, getting out and going to wait by the trunk. He hands me my bags, nodding when I thank him again before I turn toward the house. Walking over to the little silver box, I type in my access code, the metal gate starting to swing open slowly. I duck through, putting my code in again on the other side and stopping it from opening all the way as it automatically starts to close again.

Turning and looking up at the huge house, I take a deep breath.

Five days. I can make it five days.

I start to walk up the drive, remembering the voicemail Axel left me right after I told the guys I loved them and then left. I smile. I know it's probably him yelling at me for leaving, but I saved it to listen to after dinner when I already know I'll want to hear his voice. Bentley won't touch down in Switzerland for a few more hours so I'll text him then to let him know I got home safe and check in with how his flight went.

I stop abruptly in the drive, registering the car parked at the top right in front of the garage. Christopher's car. My heart plummets.

I look to the front door, not taking another step toward the house. Mom had to invite him, but I don't know what she thinks him being here will accomplish. Closing my eyes, I breathe in through my nose and out through my mouth a few times, reminding myself that it's only a few days. Then I will be back at the Coast with Bentley, Axel, and Layla. I can do this.

Shuffling my bags on my shoulders and regripping the straps, I open my eyes and walk toward the door, letting my anger take over with each step. Walking into the house, I drop my bags and take off my shoes, leaving them haphazardly on the rug and hearing Mom in the kitchen.

"Hello?" I call out, starting to walk down the hall toward the low voices.

"Janette? We're in the kitchen, honey."

I pause. Mom hasn't called me honey in five years. The sound of it brings back memories of her helping me with homework at the kitchen table, checking in on me and Layla while we played, kissing me goodnight. The images make my throat clog.

Shaking off the nostalgia, I keep walking, seeing Mom first, standing at the stove, stirring a pot. But Christopher sits at the kitchen island, eyes immediately on me when I walk in.

"Hi, honey. How was your flight?" Mom looks over at me quick, voice sickly sweet, but her eyes are hard, mouth pinched on the sides.

"Fine," I say, crossing my arms, my anger mounting with her bastardization of my old nickname. "Why is he here?"

"Janette don't be rude," Mom admonishes in the same gratingly sweet voice. I look over at Christopher who smirks smarmily at me. "He's here to have dinner with us. Go set the table."

"What table?" I ask, looking back at my mother. We've never sat down and had a meal together in this house. Ever. I usually eat at the island or in my room and I don't know when Mom eats. Probably randomly throughout the day whenever she has time.

She looks up at me, rolling her eyes. "The dining room table, obviously. Please go set the table."

"I do not want to have dinner with him." I watch Mom, not even looking over at Christopher. I notice his fist clench on the tabletop in front of him in my periphery, though.

"Janette!" Her voice goes back into its usual annoyed tone, slipping from the sweetness she tried to imbue it with previously. She takes a breath, falling back into her practiced persona. "Christopher is staying for dinner. The two of you have things to work out."

"No, we don't." I stand taller, looking her directly in the eye. "We have said all we need to say to each other."

Mom takes the wooden spoon in her hand out of the sauce and places it on the plate next to her. "Can I speak to you for a minute?"

I nod, turning around and stalking to the foyer. Once I'm around the corner in front of the large staircase, I whirl around, facing my mother who stands two feet in front of me.

"What has gotten into you?" she hisses, speaking low so Christopher won't overhear. "First you break up with Chris out of nowhere. Then you bring Axel to a campaign event? What were you even thinking? What if the press had been there? And now I set up a chance for you to make up with Chris and you walk into my house acting like an ungrateful brat! I don't know who you think you are now, but this behavior is unacceptable."

I step back, arms falling down to my sides as I stare at my mom. Her fiery eyes, the same color as my own, glare at me as she places her hands on her hips, waiting for my response.

I take a breath, looking away for a second before I turn back. "First of all, Mom, I did not break up with Christopher out of nowhere. I never liked Christopher. Not in the way *you* wanted me to. And I was tired of dating him just to make you happy or to keep up the image of me you want to project to the public. And I took Axel to the alumni event because he wanted to come with me since I was nervous about seeing you and the reaction you had when I ended things with Christopher. He came because he wanted to be there for me, like the Clifford's always have." Mom flinches, but I keep going. "And my behavior, that you think is *so* ungrateful, is just me finally making decisions for myself. I'm sorry if you don't like them or if they don't mesh with the preplanned future you mapped out for me, but this is my life. You don't get a say in who I date."

Mom closes her eyes, rocking on her heels and pinching the bridge of her nose. "You need to grow up, Janette. You are acting like a child." She opens her eyes, staring at me incredulously. "Christopher comes from a good family. He is set up to take over his father's company and inherit millions. You're not thinking about this clearly. Let's just go have dinner, you two can talk and—"

"I'm seeing someone," I blurt. Mom freezes, staring at me in disbelief. "And I'm in love with them. Which should be the most important thing to you, not how much money they are set to inherit."

She crosses her arms in front of her. "Who is it? Someone from the Coast? Please tell me it's not Axel Clifford."

My heart stutters in my chest. "You don't care, do you?" I step back again, feeling the need to get away from her. "You don't care that I'm in love. What happened to you? All you care about now is what other people can do for you... including me." I shake my head, feeling my eyes start to sting. "Why didn't you just leave me in Maine with the Clifford's and all your memories of Dad?"

Mom blanches, mouth opening and arms falling to her sides. I step around her, grabbing my bags and slipping my shoes back on. I open the door, pausing to look back at her still standing in the foyer, staring at me. "Have a great dinner with Christopher. Maybe you can convince him to date you since you're so concerned with getting his family's millions."

I slam the door behind me, tears blurring my vision as I rush down the driveway. Escaping through the front gate, I start walking down the sidewalk. I don't know where I'm going to go, just needing to get away from the house right now.

My phone buzzes in my pocket after walking for five minutes. I dig it out, stopping at the corner and glancing down at the screen. Axel's name appears on the message notification, and I open the text.

I go to text him back, thumbs hovering over the keyboard as my mind blanks on what to say. I shake my head and drop the phone to my side. Swiping at my cheeks with my other hand, I glance around, mind racing with what to do now. I can't fly back to the Coast, everyone has to be out of their dorms for break since there won't be any RAs on campus. I'm not going back to Mom's house. Not after the things she just said to me without caring about what I said.

I shake my head. I want to call Bentley or Axel or Lay, but they're all having their own breaks. I shouldn't bother them with my family drama while they're with their own.

I pull up my phone, remembering the voicemail Axel left me and que it up to play.

"*I can't believe you just did that, Janette,*" Axel's voice plays in my ear. I laugh, tears still on my face as I remember the looks on their faces after I said I love them. They both had gone slack jawed, staring down at me, frozen in place and I knew they'd be mad at me for leaving, but I couldn't handle the tension I created, so I just slipped out, figuring I'd call them both sometime over the break.

Axel's message continues. "*I am so pissed off and turned on, and just—ugh—why did you leave like that? You didn't even wait for us to say anything.*"

I kick the pavement with the toe of my shoe, wondering what would have happened if I had stayed. They probably wouldn't have let me leave anytime soon. Maybe I would have missed my flight and had to go with Axel to Maine. Maybe I'd be on my way to Switzerland right now. My chest squeezes at the idea of being with at least one of them right now.

"I'm not going to say it back right now, because I want to do it in person, but ditto, okay?"

My heart stops, whole body freezing up at his words.

"And when we all get back in a few days I'm never going to stop saying it."

Tears well up in my eyes all over again, completely different from the ones I previously shed. I listen to him pause, holding my breath to hear what he has to say next.

"Call us if you need us. I mean it, Blue. Don't hold it in because you don't want to ruin our vacations."

I laugh through my tears at how well he knows me.

"We want to be there for you when you need us. Let us do that."

I sigh, adjusting the tote bag on my left side.

"Alright, I'll see you in a few days. Layla's going to try to make Mom's cobbler. I'll bring some back with me. Oh, and start planning how you're going to make this up to me. Later, Blue."

I laugh again at the end, knowing he probably wants me to start planning some elaborate strip tease or something.

When the voicemail ends, I replay it, just wanting to hear him say it all again. After the second play through, my resolve crumbles, and I know I have to call him. The phone rings twice before he picks up.

"Hey, Blue. Did you make it home okay?" His excited voice makes my stomach gnaw on itself.

"Yeah, I got home okay." I glance around the street when a car goes by, hearing Axel shuffle on the other side of the line.

"What's wrong?" He sounds clearer and I know he must have just taken me off speaker and sat up or something.

"Um," I sigh, dropping the tote bag off my shoulder and

leaning it against my leg. "My mom invited Christopher over for dinner. He was there when I got home. And when I told her I didn't want to have dinner with him, she pulled me into another room and told me I was acting childish for not wanting to be with him for his money." I start crying again, picturing Mom glaring at me and calling me ungrateful.

"Oh, Blue."

"I left the house," I blurt. "I told her I was seeing someone and that I loved them, and she just looked at me like I was stupid and asked me who it was." I leave out the part where she basically insulted Axel.

"Come to Maine, Blue." I hear him moving around on the other end again, probably pacing and running his hands through his hair. "I'll send you some money if you need it for the ticket. Come stay with us for the break. I don't want you alone right now, I want you here with me. Lay will be here for you too. And I already told you Dad and Gwen still think of you as family. Come spend the holiday with us and then we'll drive back to the Coast together."

I laugh through the third wave of tears, picturing their house the last time I saw it. Staring at it as we drove away in the middle of the night. My heart squeezes. "Okay," I whisper.

"Okay? You're coming?" He whoops loudly in my ear, and I laugh again. "I was serious about the money. Do you need any to cover the ticket?"

"No, I've got the cost of the ticket, Axel. I don't know when the next flight will be, but I'll text you when I get to my gate to let you know when I'll be there."

"Okay, awesome. I can't wait to see you. And, Blue?"

I pick up my tote, planning to order an Uber once I'm off the phone. "Yeah?"

"I'm really sorry your mom said that to you. We'll talk

more when you get here, but you don't deserve that. Don't spend the next few hours thinking you do."

I nod again, knowing he can't see. "I love you, Axel."

He laughs, sounding breathless. "Ditto is the best I can do right now, babe. But just wait until you're standing in front of me."

I laugh, smiling for the first time since I touched down in Georgia. "See you in a few hours, Axe."

"See you soon, Blue."

29

AXEL

I hang up the phone, staring at it in my hand for a minute, heart thumping. Then, without thinking much about it, I'm calling Bentley, continuing to pace my bedroom and running a hand through my hair. It rings several times before the generic voicemail audio starts playing. I glance at a clock and realize he won't be touching down in Zurich for at least another two hours.

The record tone goes off in my ear and I take a breath. "Hi, Bent. Hope your flight was good. Also wish you were here right now. Janette's on her way to Maine. Her mom fucking ambushed her with Christopher and then belittled her when Janette tried to stand up for herself." I stop pacing, pressing my nails into my shaking palm. "I'm so fucking pissed right now, Bent. If Blue didn't need me to be here, I would be on the first plane down there and banging down Aunt Sandy's door." I release my fist and run my hand through my hair, pulling it a bit and gritting my teeth.

Taking a deep breath, I let go of all the built-up tension on the long exhale. "But I can't. You would tell me; I need to be here for Blue." I close my eyes. "I really wish you were here. You'd be able to calm both of us down so much better than I can. I'm too mad right now." I stare at the photo of Mom with Dad, Aunt Sandy, and Uncle Levi on the wall. My eyes get stuck on Mom's smiling face. "I'm sorry about what I said before you left. That wasn't fair. I know you want to tell Mira when it's the best time to do so. I shouldn't have ruined that moment."

I bite my lip. "I love you too, Bentley. I should have just said that back in the suite, but I'm not going to make you wait to hear it since you actually waited for my reaction." I chuckle, remembering Janette just walking out of the suite while I tried to restart my brain. "I love you." A smile stretches across my face. "I'm going to tell Blue when she gets here too. I know I sort of said it in my voicemail, but I'm going to say it for real to her face." I sigh. "I still can't believe Aunt Sandy invited that prick over to try to force Blue to talk to him again. You need to call her when you touch down. I don't know what time her flight will touch down here, but I'll text you the details when I have them. I love you. Call me when you get this."

I hang up, checking my messages to see if there's anything from Janette yet.

"You suck at leaving voicemails," Layla says, and my head snaps up to find her standing in my doorway.

My blood starts to race, realizing what she's just overheard. "How much of that did you hear?"

She walks into the room, closing the door behind her and then facing me again. "You need to learn to shut your door if you don't want to be overheard. I've been standing there since about the start of that voicemail. But I heard you talking to Janette before that. My room's right across the hall, remember?" She folds her arms over her chest and leans back against the door. "Are you dating my best friend?"

I drop down to sit on the edge of my bed, looking up at her. "Yes." I flip my phone in my hands. "And I'm dating my roommate." Tension starts to creep into her shoulders, and she purses her lips. I cut in again quickly. "And they're also dating each other."

All the tension leaves her body, arms and shoulders sagging and eyebrows furrowing. "Wait, what?"

I sigh, rubbing the back of my neck. "We're all together. I'm with Bentley and Janette and they're with me. And vice versa...in all directions."

Layla stares at me and I can practically see her brain working to process the information. "She's actually dating both of you?" She laughs a little at the end, swiping her hand across her forehead as she starts to pace the same route I just did. "She told me she was attracted to both of you at the beginning of the semester, but she was so dead set on not ruining your friendship that I assumed she would never act on any of it."

I chuckle. "She kind of didn't. The two of us slipped up and kissed her and both times she reacted by backing off. So, we ended up in this weird limbo for a while where we all knew we liked each other, but not acting on it because we didn't know how the other relationships were going."

She stops, looking back at me. "So how did we get here if you all ended up in a stalemate?"

I smile, feeling a knot unwind in my chest the more I tell Layla about us. "Bentley skipped class and forced me to talk to him. We realized we both wanted to be together, and we both wanted to be with Janette. And both of us were pretty sure she wanted to be with each of us. So, we took a chance, and it ended up working. We've been together since the night we went to that bar Plankton's." I flip my phone in my hand again. "You can ask Blue if you want any more details about it. She's wanted to tell you, but we were all waiting to tell anyone."

Layla comes over and sits down on the bed next to me, shoulder to shoulder. "So, you're dating my best friend and Bentley Marshall. And my best friend is dating my brother and Bentley Marshall."

"Why do you keep calling him *Bentley Marshall*?" I mimic her voice as I say his name.

She throws her hands up. "Because apparently, I'm the only one around here who knows who he is! Who his parents are! His grandfather's a freaking judge for fuck's sake! And you and Janette act like he's just some guy you both happened to have a crush on."

"Oh god." I fall back on the bed, hands falling on my stomach still clutching my phone. "Do you have a crush on my boyfriend?"

Layla laughs, settling down beside me. "No, I just can't get over that three months ago we were just hanging out here, living our random lives, and now you're dating a freaking god *and* goddess." She shakes her head, staring up at the ceiling while I look over at her with skepticism.

"You sure you don't have a crush on my boyfriend? I already know you're in love with my girlfriend, but I feel slightly less threatened by that since I know girls aren't your thing."

She grins, closing her eyes. "Oh, please. I could steal J from you in a second." She snaps her finger in the air. "You do one thing wrong, and I'll be in there like that."

I laugh, settling back to look at the ceiling again. "I don't doubt it. But I'm going to try really fucking hard not to do anything to fuck this up." I pause, drumming my fingers on the top of my phone. "I love them."

Layla's head swivels over to look at me. "Aw, Axe." She wiggles in closer to me, hooking our arms together and resting her cheek on my shoulder. "I can't wait to plan the wedding. Can you even legally marry two people?"

I snort. "Slow down, Lay. I still have to tell them."

She slaps my chest. "You haven't told them yet?"

"Ow," I complain, rubbing the center of my chest. "Janette sort of ran out after telling us she loves us, so I didn't get the chance." I bite the side of my cheek. "I sort of fucked up telling Bentley, but I said it in the voicemail, so he'll know soon."

She groans. "You said it in a voicemail? How did you manage to get two people to be in love with you at the same time."

I smile. "I don't know. Ask your best friend."

Layla shoves my shoulder lightly. We both laugh for a moment, settling back down beside each other. "What did Aunt Sandy do to her that she's coming here already?"

I sigh. "Christopher was at their house when she got there. I think they got into a fight about it. I don't know the full story, but I'm sure she'll tell us both when she gets here."

"We should go tell Dad she's coming. He'll want to make up the guest room for her and go buy that juice she used to drink all the time."

I nod, neither of us moving. "Do you think he'll understand?" I whisper.

"Dad? I think he'll be confused as hell. But he won't be upset. He never cared who you were with, just that you were happy. Same will apply to this." Layla squeezes my shoulder. "Just tell him your girlfriend is coming for Thanksgiving. You can tell him about your boyfriend in the Swiss Alps later." She giggles and I roll my eyes, leaning over to kiss the top of her head.

"Thanks, Lay." She shrugs, and we stay on my bed for a few more minutes.

"I'm going to take a baking class next semester," Layla whispers. I look down at her, not moving my head. "I don't know how to tell Dad. I don't want him to think it'll become anything more, but since I'm just kind of still exploring, I figured it wouldn't hurt to try a culinary class."

I smile, glancing at the photo of Mom and Clifford's Cupcakes again. "I'm sure he'll be excited for you. And you're already a great cook. You always had the most of Mom's touch in the kitchen." Layla nods, chewing her bottom lip. "I can tell him about me being in a triad right after you tell him if you want?" Layla bleats a laugh. My phone buzzes against my stomach.

BLUE

Just got my ticket online. On my way to the airport right now. Be there around 9:30.

I type back.

Okay. I'll pick you up. Call me if you get bored at your gate.

"Blue will be here in about four hours." I sit up. "We should go tell Dad and get everything ready for her. You still going to make Mom's cobbler?"

Layla sits up, running her hands through her hair. "Yeah, Dad got me all the stuff I need so I'll prep it tonight after dinner."

I nod, grabbing her hand. "Come on, I'm going to need you there to tell Dad."

She follows after me, hand squeezing mine as we head down the hall and I start crafting a speech to try to tell our dad about my relationship.

<h1 style="text-align:center">30</h1>

<h1 style="text-align:center">Janette</h1>

I walk out toward baggage claim, following the spread-out mass of people who just disembarked from my flight. My duffel and tote drag my tired shoulders down, feeling like thousand-pound weights. Coupled with the heavy thoughts I've been trapped with the last few hours; I trudge toward the crowd of people waiting to grab their bags and meet up with their loved ones. Scanning for Axel's height and messy hair, I stand still, knowing he will find me faster and growing anxious the longer I don't see him. When my frayed nerves hit their tipping point, I start walking around the large warehouse room, aimlessly, trying to find him in the scattered crowds of people.

The weight of my duffel bag suddenly disappears as someone lifts the strap and I whip around, ready to yell at whoever is touching my stuff, only to find Axel's sad smiling face. I instantly relax seeing him, wrapping my arms around his waist and throwing myself against his chest. He drops my bag at our feet, wrapping me up in his arms and holding me tight. I sniff to try to clear the prickly feeling in my nose and throat, closing my eyes against the slowly pooling tears.

Axel's cheek lands on the top of my head and he rubs a hand up and down my back. "I'm sorry, Blue. I wanted you here for break, but not like this."

I nod, digging my fingers into the back of his shirt.

"I brought something that might help."

I lean back, looking up at him. He swipes his thumbs under my eyes, leaning down to kiss the tip of my nose quickly before pulling back entirely and turning to the side. Layla stands a few feet behind me, smiling.

I laugh, running over to her and hugging her around the waist. She hugs me back, laughing for a second as we sway from the impact. "I can't believe you didn't tell me you're seeing my brother."

I pull back fast, looking at her smiling face for a second before turning my head to look back at Axel.

He stands behind me, duffel now over his shoulder, and shrugs. "She overheard us on the phone. Pretty sure she would have figured it out when I showed up with you at the house."

I turn back to Layla, chewing my lip. "I'm sorry I didn't tell you. It was really new, and we wanted to get more solid before we—"

Layla pulls me back into a hug. "I know, Axel explained. I'm not mad. To be honest, I'm a little jealous you have two boyfriends." She chuckles. "Don't get how my idiot brother fits into things, but I'm happy if you're happy." She pulls back, placing her hands on my shoulders and looking me in the eye. "He told me about your mom and Christopher too. I'm so sorry she did that."

I sniff. "She called me ungrateful. As if I haven't gone along with *everything* she's wanted me to in the last five years. I dated Christopher because she wanted me to!" Layla nods, squeezing my shoulders.

Axel's hand lands on the small of my back. "Let's go get in the car and you can fill us in on everything that happened." I nod, taking his hand as Layla lets go of me and takes my tote bag from me. We walk out together, heading across the street to the pickup lot and get into Axel's sedan.

As we're pulling out of the lot, I start telling them about what happened when I got home. Axel's hand stays on my knee, and I turn in my seat, looking at Layla in the back as I talk. Layla cuts in with disbelieving anger, but Axel just tightens and loosens his hand on my knee, not speaking once through the whole thing.

"And then I left. I just walked out and headed down the street, not really sure where I was going to go until you texted me." I look at Axel and he glances over at me before looking back at the road.

"What a bitch," Layla exclaims, arms crossed over her chest as she leans back against the middle seat disgruntled. "To not even listen to you after you said you were seeing someone else and that you didn't want to be with Christopher. I can't believe that's the same Aunt Sandy who used to let us dress up in her clothes and steal cookies from Mom's baking trays for us before dinner." She shakes her head, and I look outside the car for the first time.

We're still at least ten minutes from the Clifford's house, but already I can recognize the streets around me, even under the dim streetlights. Things have changed, but the old is still there around the new. The road that leads down to my elementary school. The carwash Dad used to take us to every other weekend that had a huge gumball machine. The currently closed ice cream place right next to the park. I stare out the window, seeing it all again after so long. Seeing Dad around me again after so long. Axel's hand starts to rub my knee and I realize tears have spilled down my cheeks again. Layla leans forward and puts her hand on my shoulder.

"I would see her everywhere too. Especially right after the accident. It was like every place we ever went held her ghost. It still hits me sometimes, remembering Mom's laugh at Tina's Diner or how mad she got outside Target that time we jumped into the puddle in our suede boots." I laugh, swiping away more tears as I remember that trip. Mom had calmed her down, laughing at us and reminding Aunt Tati that they had sprayed them with water resistant stuff for precisely this reason.

"I still remember Uncle Levi the most at Tigerland up the road," Axel says, voice thick. "He and Dad would take me mini-golfing and we would play laser tag when you guys had your 'girl's days.'" He smiles, still rubbing my leg.

We turn off the main road, into the residential area that starts my old neighborhood. I grip the door, realizing I'm going to have to come face to face with my old house. In the whole four-hour trip from Georgia to here, I never once thought about what I would feel staying at the Clifford's and looking across the street to where my old life used to be. I thought about what Mom said, what I wish I had said to her, what I wish I had told her all these years, and what it would be like to see Uncle Jack again. If he would get mad at me for showing up out of the blue after five years of radio silence.

Axel turns down the street that his and my old house are on and the first thing I notice is the missing tree on the corner.

"It's gone," I whisper, head turning to look at the clear patch of grass with a stop sign at the corner.

"Yeah, they got rid of it after a big storm while we were in high school. A few branches fell down and blocked the road so after they cleared it up, Mr. Burgen had it removed," Layla says, looking at the spot with me.

"So, kids just stand in the rain when they wait for the bus now?" That tree had sheltered us countless times from a deluge of water coming down in the early morning while we waited for the bus. Not to mention the snow. Mom or Aunt Tati usually would drive us if it was bad enough, but there were a few times I remember being huddled under there together, waiting in the cold dawn.

"I don't think I've ever seen anyone out there when it rains. Parents probably drive them," Axel says with a shrug.

We slow down, getting close to the house and then I see it. And I freeze. My old home. We turn the corner, Axel heading into the driveway, and I stare at it in the side mirror as he pulls up next to a silver van. The car stops and I keep staring, stuck for a moment as I stare at my past in the mirror.

Axel squeezes my knee. I turn to find him looking at me. "You okay?"

I nod, grabbing the door handle and getting out. Layla already has the trunk popped and I head back to help her carry my stuff in. Looking up at the Clifford's house, I smile. Nothing has really changed with the façade. It still has copper red siding, black shutters and trim making it look unique from the white and beige houses lining the street. The same bushes and trees dot the front yard and walkway area, covered in a light dusting of snow. Uncle Jack must still spend his weekend mornings outside keeping everything clean and shoveled.

"Come on, Blue," Axel says, grabbing my hand and pulling me toward the door. He grips my duffel in the other hand and jogs up the steps, not even pausing as he opens the door and walks in. "Dad, we're back."

My heart starts to thump in my chest, feeling like it's attacking my skeleton from the inside. Everything looks exactly the same. We walk in on the top floor, the house being built into a hillside. The open living room expands beyond the door, stairs leading down to the first floor on my left. The same white leather couch and matching loveseat sit in the same pattern around the wall-mounted TV on my right and past that, the sliding glass doors that lead out onto the dark wood second floor deck. I can see the backyard in the distance, sprawling out to meet the tree line of the wooded area behind the house.

And every inch of wall space is filled. Pictures upon pictures upon pictures crowd frames, some singular, some overlapping with multiple photos scrapbooked inside. My young face stands out in several, smiling at various locations with Layla, Axel, and Gwen all around in different patterns. Dad's face hits me next, finding him in a lot of the adult group photos as well. Lastly, my eyes snag on all the photos of Mom and Aunt Tati, arms around each other every time as they take their traditional vacation photo in different locations. A lot have beaches in the background. One shows them both pregnant and laughing, a cabin in the woods the backdrop behind them. My eyes fly over the photos, getting caught up in the way I've seen all of them a million times, but this feels like the first time I've focused on each of them individually.

Layla walks in behind us, kind of shuffling the two of us forward as she shuts the door and toes off her shoes.

"Janette's here?" Uncle Jack's voice comes from downstairs. I hear shuffling and see Gwen jogging up the stairs, a big smile on her face. And then behind her, Uncle Jack appears, looking down at his feet as he races up just as fast.

Axel pulls me to the side, making room for his sister and father as they get to the top. Gwen races forward, snagging me in a tight hug that I return breathlessly. Uncle Jack makes eye contact with me over her shoulder and his eyes start to water behind his thick rimmed glasses.

"Oh, sweetie," he whispers. "You've gotten so beautiful."

Gwen releases me, stepping aside as Uncle Jack comes forward, pulling me against his chest and shaking as he hugs me. I breathe in his scent, burrowing my face in his shoulder as my own tears start up again as well. He always smelled like coffee and wintergreen mint, drinking several cups a day and then trying to throw off the scent by chewing gum.

Suddenly, I'm thirteen, hugging him in the hospital as we waited to find out if Mom would be okay in surgery while he grappled with the loss of his wife and best friend and suddenly becoming a single parent to three kids. While he grappled with being the one to walk away unscathed but changed forever all the same.

"I missed you," I whisper. And then I'm talking too fast. "I'm sorry I couldn't come to the funerals. I'm sorry I wasn't here."

"Shhhhh, it's okay. That wasn't your fault." He runs his hand over the back of my head, holding me tight. "I'm sorry we couldn't be there for you."

I shake my head, pulling back. Gwen stands in my periphery, clutching her hands in front of her mouth and silently crying as she watches us. "How much do you know?" I ask, looking at her and Uncle Jack before turning to glance at Lay and Axel. Axel leans against the back of the couch, smiling warmly at the two of us while Layla leans against his side with a similar expression.

"They told us why you needed to come stay." I turn back

as Uncle Jack speaks. "When Sandra left with you, I figured she just needed time, but to hear that she's still running from who she was..." He shakes his head, taking his glasses off to rub his eyes one handed. "I should have tried reaching out to her more."

I shake my head. "She wouldn't have responded. Probably would have blocked the calls or messages. She doesn't talk about anything Maine, anything Dad. I was surprised she even let me apply to the Coast when I brought up the idea."

He nods, a guilty look behind the smile he flashes. "Are you hungry? I was just prepping for tomorrow, but we have plenty to eat. Come on." He waves me toward the stairs, starting to walk ahead. "Axel put her stuff in the guest room." I look back at Axel, but he nods toward the stairs.

"I'll be down in a sec, go on." He heads toward the hallway leading to the bedrooms, and Layla hooks her arm in mine, towing me toward the stairs.

We eat some cheese and crackers, snacking while Layla preps her cobbler around Uncle Jack who asks me a million questions. Gwen makes mugs of rich hot chocolate and adds a bunch of marshmallows, just like her mom always did and I smile, answering everything asked.

"How are you liking school?"

"It's fine."

"How are you doing in your classes?"

"Good so far. Three As, an A-, and one B on my midterms."

"What's your major?"

"History. I want to go on after my undergrad to the fellowship program and get my master's and then PhD with the six-year track."

"Just like Levi and I did. So, you want to teach at a university someday?"

"Yeah."

"Does your mom know that's what you're going to school for?"

"No, she didn't really ask about school once she paid the application fee."

He nods quietly to that, cutting up some carrots and tossing them into a bowl. "My parents and Tatiana's mom and sister will be coming tomorrow. I hope you don't mind?"

"Of course not," I say quickly, putting my mug down after a fast sip. "I'm the one intruding here. You don't have to make any adjustments to accommodate me."

"You're not intruding," Axel says, squeezing the hand he holds between us on top of the table.

"Axel's right," Uncle Jack says, pointing his knife at me over the countertop. "You are welcome here whenever you need. That invitation will never be rescinded." I smile, my heart warming at the words to match my hot chocolate filled stomach. "So, you and Axel?" He waves the knife at our joined hands before going back to chopping. "Can't say I'm surprised. Axel did always seem to follow you around when you were kids. Always wanted to share his toys with you. And he hated sharing otherwise." Layla snorts at his wording, covering it up with a coughing fit when Axel narrows his eyes at her. Uncle Jack pats her back with the hand not holding the knife.

"Okay, Dad." Axel stands, collecting my empty mug with his. "I think Janette's probably tired from all her travel. We should let her go to sleep, so she's not exhausted for the circus tomorrow."

"Of course. Sorry if we kept you up, sweetie. Go sleep.

We'll talk more tomorrow." He ushers us toward the stairs, taking the mugs from Axel as we walk past.

Axel takes my hand and drags me toward the hall when we make it to the second floor. "Dad was very adamant about you sleeping in the guest room, but since that's right next to my room, I figured I could sneak in later if you want?"

"Axel!" I hiss, whispering, "I am not having sex with you in a room that shares a wall with Uncle Jack's!" We turn into the guest room, and I drop his hand to go to my duffel sitting on the nicely made bed.

Axel's arms come around me from behind. "I just meant so I could hold you while we sleep. I don't want to leave you alone tonight." He kisses the side of my head. "Unless you want to be alone right now?"

I shake my head, pulling out my cotton pajama set. "No, I don't want to be alone. I want you here as long as we don't get in trouble." I turn around in his arms. "Have you heard anything from Bent? I figured I didn't hear anything because I was on the plane, but then nothing came through when I turned my phone back on."

Axel shakes his head, pulling his phone out to check. "No, I haven't heard anything either." He bites his lip before glancing at me and throwing on a fake smile. "I'm sure he just forgot because he's so busy catching up with his parents right now."

My stomach turns and I run a hand through the ends of my hair, picking apart a few curls. "I'm going to look up his flight and make sure it made it okay." He nods, moving to sit down on the edge of the bed beside my bag. "Does your family know about him and us?" I say absentmindedly as I google Bentley's flight information.

"I told Layla after she overheard me on the phone. I

didn't tell Dad or Gwen though. Seemed like too much to try to explain on top of telling them you were on your way here and why."

I nod, finding the information I need.

"His flight got in no problem. You must be right." I toss my phone on the bed. "He's just busy getting settled in," I tell myself.

"He might not be calling because of the time difference? I sort of called him right after you called me and left a voicemail telling him everything you told me." Axel rubs the back of his neck, looking up at me through his lashes guiltily.

I nod, moving in between his legs and letting my hands rest around his neck. "That's okay. It would have been a lot to try to go over everything again, so I don't mind."

Axel nods, leaning forward and wrapping his arms around me. "How are you feeling?"

I shrug. "I think I'm feeling too much to really feel any of it at this point, you know? It's been a long day and I'm just really tired now." As if to prove my point, I yawn above him.

He nods, leaning up to kiss the side of my neck. "I think you should sleep then, and we'll have a great day tomorrow stuffing our faces." He pulls back, moving his hands to either side of my face. "And after that, when you're ready, I think you should call your mom and tell her all the stuff you said in the car with Layla and me." I purse my lips. "You deserve to tell her how you feel. And Lay and I will be right there next to you if you need us." He stares up at me, eyes imploring. "I love you."

I nod between his hands. "You're right. I'll try to call her in a couple days. I love you, too." He pulls me down to kiss him, smiling under my lips.

"Let me get out of your way so you can sleep." He gets

up, moving his hands to my waist and looking down at me. "I'll come back in an hour or so when Dad has gone to bed, but I'll be right next door if you need me, okay?" I nod, yawning a second time. He chuckles and kisses my forehead. "Goodnight, Blue."

"Goodnight," I say as he steps around me and heads out of the room, closing the door behind him with a wink.

I stand there for a minute, holding my PJs to my chest. Exhaustion settles into my bones, and I sluggishly drag my clothes off to change, knowing I'll be asleep long before Axel comes back. Once I'm dressed, I toss my duffel on the ground, pulling back the covers at the same time. I check my phone one more time, opening my messages with Bentley to make sure I didn't miss anything and feel a pang when the same messages I've read stare back at me. I decide to text him, adding a heart at the end before sending it.

> Hope you had a good flight! Made it to Maine without issue. Have a great Thanksgiving 🤍

Shutting off my phone, I turn off the bedside light and lay down, hoping Bentley is just having too much fun to pay attention to his phone right now and ignoring the stab of nerves in my gut.

AXEL

The sound of the doorbell ringing twice jerks me from sleep and up into a sitting position on the bed, jostling Janette from my arms. She groans, sitting up and holding her head beside me. I look around for a minute, disoriented in the dark guest room, but the events of the day before soon come crashing in.

"Who's here?" Janette mumbles, eyes barely open.

"I don't know." I get out of the bed and throw on the pair of jeans I stepped out of only a couple hours ago. The clock on the table blares indigo numbers up at me, reading 4:22, and I shake my head to try to clear some of the sleep from my brain. "I'm going to go down and find out. Stay here?"

"Fat chance," she says, throwing the covers to the side and getting up out of the bed.

I pinch the bridge of my nose but reach out my other hand. She tangles her fingers with mine and I pull her close behind me as we walk out into the hall. Dad stands in the doorway of his room next to us, eyes bleary, in pajama pants and a robe.

"Who the fuck is ringing the doorbell at four am?" I

shrug and he eyes the two of us coming out of the same room. "Seriously, Axel?"

Layla's door opens down the hall, saving me from that conversation and Gwen's door follows a half a second later. My sisters come out into the hall, glancing over at us through sleep addled eyes in disheveled PJs.

"We all going down together?" Layla asks. I nod, heading past them and down the stairs. Dad follows on the heels of Janette behind me, and I can hear the girls at the back in the creak of the floorboards.

I reach the door first, hand on the knob when Dad taps me on the shoulder. I step back, sliding out of the way so that he can get past me and open it, the girls all huddled right behind my back. Janette squeezes my hand, gripping my upper arm tightly as well. Dad flicks on the porch light, unlocks the deadbolt, and pulls open the door to reveal Bentley standing on the other side, suitcase at his feet and hands cupped in front of his mouth as he shivers on our porch. He blinks in the light, looking manic and unkempt as his eyes squint, seeing first my father then me behind him.

Pure relief floods my veins seeing him here in front of us. I didn't want to stress Janette out more last night, but not hearing anything from him at all yesterday made me nervous that something happened. We might know that his flight made it no problem, but something could have happened on the way to the airport or immediately after he got off the plane, and as I held her while she fell asleep, I thought over every possibility and quietly hoped he was okay.

Confusion quickly follows the relief, especially when Bentley starts speaking.

"Axel, I'm sorry," he blurts, and my dad looks back at me with deeply furrowed brows.

I keep staring at Bentley, blood rushing around inside my sleepy body and making me feel lightheaded.

"I love you, and I don't want to hide that. I'll tell anyone you want. I'll call Mira right now and explain everything if that's what you want. I'll put an ad out online, hang a banner from West Tower if you want me to. I just don't want you to think that I don't love you with everything I have."

My heart stops in my chest, all sounds falling away as I stare at him in the doorway.

"When I heard your voice on that message, I knew how stupid I had been, and I needed to apologize to you immediately. I love you Axel, I swear. I'm sorry I ever made you feel differently." He breathes heavily staring at only me when he's done.

My body freezes in place, all thoughts leaving my mind as a building warmth spreads through me, slowly thawing my frozen state. I can feel everyone else looking at me, but the only thing my eyes see is Bentley standing in the snow waiting for me to respond.

I shake my head, closing my eyes for a minute before ripping them open to make sure Bentley is really here. When I find him still in front of me, I smile. "You flew all the way back from Switzerland to apologize for something I already admitted was stupid on my part?" I step forward, Bentley also stepping into the house to meet me, his hands dropping down to grip my hips. "That's absolutely insane." I step into him, gripping the sleeves of his jacket. "I love you, too. I don't need you to tell anyone before you're ready." I pull him closer, pressing my warm lips to his cold ones as he surges forward, moving his arms up to wrap around me and deepen the kiss.

Bentley beams when we pull apart, glancing behind me

as the world around us sets back in. "You weren't the only one I came back for."

I nod, stepping out of the way.

Janette stands in between my two sisters, all three girls misty eyed. Layla's smile looks like it's trying to split her face in half through her watery expression, arms wrapped around herself as she watches Bentley walk up to Janette. Janette's bottom lip trembles, expression just as happy as Layla's and eyes wide as Bentley wraps his arms around her hips and pulls their lower halves together. Gwen's eyebrows shoot up as she looks between the two of them and me. I can see Dad rubbing his forehead across the threshold from me, still holding the front door wide open.

"I love you too, sunshine," Bentley says, pulling everyone's attention back to him. I glance at Gwen when her mouth pops open and eyes light up. "I walked off the plane and immediately booked the next flight back after I heard what happened with your mom. I'm sorry, baby. I wish it hadn't taken me so long to get to you, but I've wanted to tell you I love you since the moment you walked out of our suite yesterday." He shrugs with one shoulder. "Figured doing it in person would be the most helpful right now." He smiles at her, and she chuckles, a couple tears streaming down her rounded cheeks.

She shakes her head, still smiling. "Axel was right. You're completely insane." Bentley bends down and kisses her, arms wrapping tighter around her. They pull back after a few moments and Janette laughs. "I love you, too, crazy," she says breathlessly. "I can't believe you're actually here."

"Can someone explain what's going on? Why is this boy on my porch at four in the morning confessing his love to the two of you?" Dad's hand still rubs at his forehead with his knuckles, glasses off and pinched between his fingers, while he continues to hold the door open with his other hand. Bentley steps back from Janette, facing my father and ending up in between the two of us.

"They're a throuple, Dad," Gwen says with a smile. "Right? You're all in love with each other?"

I nod, Bentley and Janette following suit. Gwen starts fast clapping, smiling widely. Dad looks between the three of us, eyes squinting at each of us before shaking his head. "Okay, I'm still confused but I'm too tired to have any hope of understanding this right now. I take it you're staying here tonight?" He points at Bentley with his glasses.

Bentley shakes his head, walking back out to the porch to grab his carry-on suitcase. "I can get a hotel room, sir. I don't want to impose. I just couldn't wait till tomorrow to come see them."

Dad shakes his head, reaching forward and taking Bentley's luggage from his hand. "Nonsense. It's four in the morning." He passes the suitcase to me, pressing the cold hard shell against my bare chest. I gasp, wrapping my hands around the handles as I take the weight of it. "Axel can take the couch and you can have his room."

Bentley opens his mouth to argue, but Dad holds up a hand, waving him into the house. He nods, stepping back through the door and walking in. Dad closes the door behind him, turning the deadbolt and shutting off the porch light. Moonlight falls through the sliding glass doors across the room, keeping the room visible to all of us.

We all head toward the bedrooms, Janette and I walking hand in hand with Bentley into my room while Layla and Gwen pat my shoulders before going into their rooms. Dad comes to the door of my room, tapping the doorframe to get our attention. "Please don't have sex with anyone under my roof, Axel, Janette." He looks over at Bentley and I say his name so Dad can finish. "Bentley." We all nod, and he taps the wood again. "Alright, you three. Goodnight. See you all in a few hours." He heads to his bedroom, not waiting as we all mumble goodnight back.

"We all sleeping in here?" Bentley asks, glancing at my queen bed with a tired smile. I smile back, setting his suitcase down beside my dresser and nodding.

"I should probably go back to the guest room, so we don't piss off Uncle Jack," Janette says, clicking her nails against each other.

She starts to head toward the door, and I catch her around her middle. "Where are you going?" I pull her back against my chest. "Why do you think he just gave us that warning? He knows we are just going to sneak into one of the rooms and sleep altogether even if he put us all in separate areas."

She glances at the door, starting to worry her lip. "I don't want to make him uncomfortable."

I roll my eyes, looking over at Bentley who has already pulled off his coat and shoes and is working on pulling his shirt over his head. "He'll be fine. We're not going to do anything. But I'm not going to be able to sleep on my own, knowing both of you are just down the hall." I turn my head to look down at her. "What about you, Blue?"

She shakes her head after a moment, and I let her go, walking over to shut the door. Bentley is in his boxers when I turn around, exhaustion setting into his shoulders. I point to the bed, looking at both of them in turn before turning off the light and heading across the room to join them.

We all get comfortable together, Janette cocooned between the two of us, burying her face in Bentley's neck. His arm comes across her, hand falling to the center of my back, holding me against them. I grip each of them as well, kissing Janette's hair and stroking my hand over Bentley's skin.

"I can't believe you flew all the way back here," Janette whispers.

Bentley shrugs, eyes staying closed. "I couldn't wait that long to be here with you guys." I smile, nestling my head against the pillow more. "I'll need to borrow some clothes tomorrow, Axe. Didn't have time to reroute my checked bag and I think I only have one change of clothes in the one I carried."

I snort. "Looks like you're going shirtless then. I'm not giving you one of mine to stretch out."

Janette slaps my arm over her shoulder, and I grunt. "Pretty sure you've already proven you can share, Axel."

I pinch her side, laughing lightly with Bentley. We settle back in, Bentley kissing my forehead and then Janette's. A few quiet beats pass, my body relaxing quickly knowing each of them are next to me.

"I called and told my parents about you two while I was waiting for my flight," Bentley whispers.

Janette's head pops up for a second. "And they just let you fly back here?"

Bentley cracks open an eye, looking up at her with a small laugh. "They were really excited for me. Wanted to pay for my ticket or charter a jet to get me back faster. I've never introduced anyone to them before. Mom made me promise I would bring both of you to see them over winter break."

Janette glances back at me, eyes wide, before settling down again between us. My mind races with the new information, sleep trying to pull me down while my brain fights to overthink every angle.

Bentley chuckles. "I can hear you both panicking. Don't

worry, we can talk about it more in the morning. I just wanted you to know before I fall asleep."

I sigh. "I love you," I say, eyes falling closed against my will.

"Love you," Bentley responds.

"I love both of you," Janette says through a yawn. "Happy Thanksgiving."

I chuckle, snuggling closer into her before falling asleep.

32

Janette

Family surrounds me and I sit quietly in the middle of it all, just taking in the feeling. Uncle Jack sits at the head of the makeshift table, made up of the Cliffords' six-seater dining room table and a long folding table set at the end to extend the seating room. The folding table falls about an inch under the wooden table, leaving a little drop off in the middle underneath the mismatched tablecloths I helped Layla set up this morning to try to make it seem like one joined table. Bowls and trays of food cover every inch of the tables, our plates and glasses crowded in by the salt and pepper shakers, butter platter, gravy bowl, covered bowls filled with way too many Hawaiian rolls, and Axel's hot sauce, which he has put on everything including the mashed potatoes.

I sip my glass of lemonade, hiding a smile in it as I laugh at Layla complaining that Axel cheated when he won the longer piece of the wishbone a few minutes ago. Their grandparents outright laugh across the table from us, and Uncle Jack tries to look stern at the head of the table, suppressing his own smile with a cough. Bentley shakes his head, hand holding mine in his lap as he leans back with another hand on his distended stomach. Gwen throws a roll at her brother when he starts telling Layla that she should have practiced all year like he did. Aunt Tati's sister, Beth, sits beside her, leaning back and holding a glass of red wine.

Beth smiles happily at the twins, and I startle a little at how the fondness on her face reminds me of her sister. When I was younger, I thought she looked nothing like Aunt Tati. With her hair cropped short and dyed blonde as well as her shorter, slight frame, she looks almost like a complete opposite to the dark featured and willowy tall woman I grew up around. But as the day goes on, I've noticed little things that remind me of Aunt Tati. The way she holds the wine glass against her chest. The set of her mouth. The way she brushes her bangs off her forehead every now and then.

Her mother is the spitting image of an older Aunt Tati. I met her a few times when I was a kid, but she lived in Florida then, so they were rare occasions. Layla told me in an early email that she moved up to Maine after Aunt Tati died, wanting to be closer to them and help Uncle Jack. Her demeanor is the major difference between her and Aunt Tati, sitting quietly and only sharing comments here or there rather than feeding the energy of the room like Aunt Tati seemed to always do.

Axel's arm lands across the back of my chair and he leans over to kiss my cheek. His grandmother practically has stars in her eyes, watching the gesture.

The three of us talked about what we were going to do today and if we were going to hide the fact that all of us were together in front of Axel's extended family. No one, not even Axel, was sure what the right move was here, and it was Layla who overheard us and told us all we were being stupid debating it. She said if we were going to all be together there's no point in hiding it now since everyone would find out in the long run and then rolled her eyes and walked out of the room.

So, we just decided to be how we always are. And it has been surprisingly easy to just act on what we naturally feel, sitting together at the table and sharing small touches here and there. And Beth and Axel's grandparents have been nothing but nice to Bentley and me, Axel's grandmother going so far as to tell us we all looked good together and swoon every time she caught a sweet moment between us.

Snow drifts to the ground through the window beyond the table, and the doorbell rings suddenly upstairs. We all turn to look up the staircase set into the middle of the room, the last step marking the separation line of the kitchen and dining room.

Uncle Jack stands up, wiping his hands on a napkin before heading toward the stairs. "This better not be another one of my son's partners."

Axel raises both his hands while we all chuckle. "I don't have any more, I swear."

His grandfather leans across the table to ask Bentley about what his plans are for after college, but I don't hear anything after my ears pick up Uncle Jack's voice.

"Sandra?" he says in disbelief.

"Hi, Jack," my mother's voice responds, sounding off. The tone is almost sheepish, but I can't imagine the woman I lived with in Georgia ever sounding anything other than perfectly poised outside of our house. "Is Janette here?"

I get up, scraping my chair back in the process. Bentley and Axel each turn in their chairs to look up at me, the whole room suddenly quiet. Buzzing rings in my ears and I start to head toward the stairs without realizing I told my feet to move. Two chairs scrape on the floor behind me and I turn, finding both my guys at my back.

I shake my head. "I'll be okay. Promise."

Bentley nods, stepping back, but Axel grits his teeth, eyes on fire. Bentley puts a hand on his shoulder to hold him back and I nod to him, mouthing *if I need you* to him. He nods once, clenching and unclenching his fists.

I walk up the stairs, Mom seeing me past Uncle Jack when I'm halfway up. I hold her gaze, pulling on all the strength I know the guys would give me if I asked them to. She chews her lip, leather gloved hands pulling on the hem of her coat sleeves. I walk up next to Uncle Jack and start to pull my coat off the hanging rack next to the door. Uncle Jack places a hand on my shoulder and I turn toward him.

"You okay?" He looks right at me, my mother watching the two of us. I nod and he searches my face before patting my shoulder and turning back to Mom with a hard look. "Sandra," he says with a single sharp nod before turning around and heading back downstairs.

I slide on a pair of boots, not even sure whose they are, stepping out of the house and onto the porch and shutting the door. Mom steps back to put more room between us, still watching me carefully. Folding my arms to keep myself warm I squint at her in the sunny glare off the piling snow. "What are you doing here, Mom?"

She sighs, wringing her hands together in front of her. "I wanted to come talk to you. I've been thinking a lot about what happened yesterday."

I glance behind her, seeing our old house across the street and feeling a sharp pang in my chest. "Yesterday was a long time coming. Five years in the making really." Mom flinches, looking down at her shoes and nodding.

"I know," she whispers. "I realized that today."

A long pause wanes on between us before she takes a deep breath.

"I wanted to come talk to you, try to explain some things and apologize for others." She glances back at the house, bottom lip starting to tremble. The pang in my chest starts to throb as she continues. "I never meant to cut you out, Janette." Mom looks back at me, eyes shining. "When your dad...when they..." Closing her eyes, she takes another deep breath, shaking out her shoulders.

I squeeze my hands together.

"After the accident, when I woke up in the hospital, and they told me what happened, I fell apart. It felt like I couldn't stop, like I would always be breaking over and over again. And then eventually I went numb."

She closes her eyes, leaning against the porch rail before turning and staring at our old house once again. I turn to face it as well, finally letting myself take in the façade. The paint looks fresh, the blue door I remember replaced by a dark black metal one.

I can barely see it as it is now around the memories flashing across the outside though.

Dad mowing the lawn every Sunday morning. Layla and Axel and I having a snowball fight in the yard while the adults shovel the driveway. Mom making chalk drawings on the sidewalk with me in the summer.

We both stare at the past across the street, trapped in different memories.

"I tried for a few days," she whispers. "I forced myself to get out of bed, make you food, live." She looks over at me again. "But it hurt just doing that. And I got frustrated. Tati always said I was too impatient for my own good." She laughs lightly, tears breaking out over her bottom lashes. "I just wanted to skip to the part where everything felt normal again, but I would break down every morning when I woke up and Dad wasn't there." The tear streams get thicker and her nose crinkles up. She wraps her hands around each of her upper arms, twisting the toe of her shoe into the porch as she looks down.

"Your grandfather called me. He heard about everything. I still don't know how." She laughs looking up at the sky. "He hadn't spoken to me since I introduced him to Levi. He didn't approve." She shakes her head, but I lean back, never knowing why Mom wanted to return to her hometown in Georgia. I never met her parents, and no one ever told me why. Until now.

She looks over at me. "He told me to come home. And it just felt like it would be easier. Levi and Tati were never in Georgia. And he said he had a job lined up for me in the Senator's office. I could take you and leave and never look back. It was cowardice, but it felt like the only way to survive at the time." She tips her head back again and sighs, closing her eyes and tightening her arms around herself.

My memories of those few days are fuzzy, and I try to remember noticing her struggling. But the only thing I remember is struggling myself.

"When I took the job, I just needed something to do every day, some way to make money to support us. Your grandfather offered to pay for us, but he never approved of Levi and I and he didn't even want to meet you." She rolls her eyes, shaking her head and staring out at the street again. "We argued about it, but in the end, I took his job offer and that was it. I got us a place and I started going to work for the first time in years." She looks at me, our eyes meeting. "I spent your whole childhood at home, and I loved it, honey. I really did. But in Georgia, I felt like I needed to get out of the house, needed to be constantly moving. If I sat still, I would think about..." She sighs.

"You have to understand," She says and steps closer to me, reaching out for a moment. Her hand drops though as she shakes her head. "It wasn't to get away from you. I never wanted to leave you behind. I just wanted something to distract me, something to put my focus on so that I didn't have to think." She shakes her head again, folding her arms back over her chest. "The Senator saw my potential, saw an opportunity for me to use my degree since he was stepping down, so I just went with it. And the further I got, the less time I had to think about anything else. I don't know when it started to slip into obsession, but I can see now that it did." She starts rubbing her hands over her arms, trying to keep warm. Her eyes meet mine now, a hollow despondency echoing between us. "I know I changed after Dad and Tatiana died. I thought I needed to. I thought I needed to get rid of everything that reminded me of them. And that included me."

Mom steps toward me, unwrapping her arms to place her hands hesitantly on my shoulders. I flinch a little, cold tears clinging to my cheeks as I blink them out of my eyes. She winces at the reaction, but steps closer to me still. "I never wanted to change toward you, Janette. My career, our address, our life, sure, but I never meant to change us. It's not an excuse, but my grief drove me to become a different person and I'm so sorry it took me this long to realize it."

I stand still in front of her for a few moments. The sound of my breathing rattles around in my head, heart thumping along to the rhythm. "I lost them too," I whisper. "And then it felt like I lost everything else when we moved to Georgia."

"I know, honey. I'm so sorry." She pulls me into a hug and her voice sounds as caring as it did when I skinned my arm after falling off my bike, the memory choking me with the backdrop of our past behind her. A flash of her fake syrupy voice when she called me honey yesterday sounds in my ears.

That wasn't my mom, that was the person she made herself be.

This is my mom.

I hug her back, limbs shaking a bit, and close my eyes.

After a few minutes, we pull back, arms still holding each other. "I want to do better. I'm done running," she says, shaking her head and looking back over at the house. "I've asked Pietro to find me a grief counselor to work with. It's going to take a while to deal with my buried issues and move forward, but I want to try." She looks at me, smiling. "I want to get to know you. I feel like I just woke up to notice everything I've been missing, and I want to catch up."

I nod to her, smiling back as a resounding warmth blankets my ribcage.

"I don't even know what your major is at school. Or who you're in love with!" She shakes me a bit, eyes alight with excitement, but still red and tear rimmed.

"Well, they're both here, so you could come in and meet them." I watch her reaction, wondering if my impulsive words just thrust us out of the pan and into the fire too soon.

But Mom just laughs, shaking her head. "You always were so easy to love," she says, smoothing a hand over my hair. "I would love to meet them, but I think I need to talk to Jack and see if it's okay with everyone else first."

I nod, turning back to the door. We step back inside, the warmth instantly enveloping us as I take off my coat and boots. Uncle Jack comes up the stairs, startling a little when he sees Mom standing there next to me on the welcome mat.

"You okay?" he asks me again.

I nod, touching Mom's shoulder as I head for the stairs. "You guys should talk," I say to Uncle Jack, and he nods once at me before looking over at Mom by the door. I head down, finding Bentley and Axel's eyes as they watch me descend, both leaning against the kitchen island facing the stairs.

I walk up to them, smiling and folding my arms over my chest. "Have you guys been standing here like guard dogs the whole time?"

"Yes," Layla calls from over at the table and Axel glares over at her.

"We just wanted to be ready in case you needed us," Bentley says, placing a hand on my waist. "How are you feeling?"

"Better," I say as I exhale deeply. "Mom apologized and explained why everything changed so much. She wants to go to therapy and deal with Dad and Aunt Tati's death and try to move forward." Bentley nods and Axel crosses his arms. I lean toward him, placing my hands on either side of him on the island. "She wants to meet the men I'm in love with."

Axel searches my eyes, hand coming up to tangle in my hair after pushing it behind my ear. "I'm not done being mad at her," he says carefully.

"I know. You don't have to be. She broke your relationship too. It's on you guys to fix it or not." I shrug. "It won't affect my relationships with you or her."

He nods, shoulders sloping with a release of tension. "Okay, good."

I look over at Bentley too. "You're allowed to be wary toward her too. Everything's not just 'forgive and forget' right now. We'll need to work on things from here on out and she'll need to prove she means it, so it's okay if you don't want to trust her yet either. I'm not fully sure I do one hundred percent, but I'm hopeful."

Bentley nods, running his fingers down my cheek. "That's enough for me, right now. I'll form my own judgement as we go, but I'll take your lead from right here, sunshine."

"I'm still going to be mad at her too," Layla shouts over at us, making Axel roll his eyes and Bentley smile.

Footsteps descend the stairs behind us, and I turn around to find Mom first, Uncle Jack right behind her. "I'll keep that in mind," she says quietly, looking over at the table. Layla goes red, eyes wide as she freezes in her seat. Gwen swallows hard, sitting back and matching Beth's posture beside her which turns rigid.

"I know I owe you each individual apologies, and it might not be possible to repair all of our relationships," Mom says, looking at everyone at the table. Uncle Jack puts a hand on her shoulder, still standing behind her. She takes a deep breath. "But I would like to try."

Aunt Tati's mother stands up, face blank as her chair scrapes against the floor. She comes around the end of the table, standing in front of Mom who seems to cower under her gaze. Only a second passes before Axel's grandmother leans forward and folds Mom into a tight hug. "You've been missed, darling." She pulls back, patting Mom's cheek before looking back at the table. "Tatiana wouldn't want us to hold a grudge against her best friend. Not today."

Layla ducks her head, grabbing a roll and taking a bite. Uncle Jack's parents smile and nod sadly. Beth sips her wine after taking a deep breath and Gwen smiles at Mom. "I've missed you, Aunt Sandy."

Axel's grandmother walks Mom over to the table, pulling out her vacant seat for her and then going to grab one of the extra folding chairs by the wall and setting it up in an open spot by her daughter. Uncle Jack walks back over to the table, tapping Axel on the shoulder as he passes through the kitchen on the way.

I take each of my guys' hands. "Ready?" I ask, looking between each of them.

Bentley nods before looking over at Axel with me. He pauses, breathing slowly for a second, then nods, determined. We walk over to the table, taking our seats again, with Mom now sitting across from Axel. She looks between Axel and Bentley, eyes landing on me with a raised eyebrow and humor in her eyes.

"Mom, you've met each of them, but," I say, squeezing both of their hands tighter before I continue, "these are my guys, Axel and Bentley." I tip my head toward each of them as I introduce them, holding Mom's eyes while my stomach overflows with prickly nerves.

"Hello again both of you," Mom says, smiling at each of them.

"Nice to meet you again," Bentley says politely with a nod.

Axel takes a second, seeming to taste something sour on his tongue. "Hello again, Aunt Sandy," he finally says, immediately reaching over the table to take a sip of his drink afterward.

Conversation starts to flow around the room again, Gwen, Axel, and I helping Uncle Jack clear the table and pack up leftovers while Layla goes to get some games to play before we dig into dessert. Bentley speaks with Mom and Beth about our history project, and I watch them laugh at something together as I scrape one of the plates into the trash.

Axel's arms come around my waist, and a kiss lands on

my shoulder. "Grandma was right. Mom would have liked that she's here now."

I turn and smile at him. He's still been cool to her, but I've seen him smile at a few of her jokes and watching his sisters and dad interact with her again. I kiss his lips quickly, stepping out of his arms and placing the plate next to the sink for Gwen.

"Thank you," I say to him, wrapping my arms around his neck as he returns his around me. "For playing nice for me. I know you wouldn't otherwise, so thank you. And thank you for being there for me."

"Always, Blue." He pecks my lips again quickly, conscious of his family all around us, and then leans his forehead against mine. "Now all we have to do is rock these next two weeks and we can spend the whole break together here."

I laugh. "We'll see. Bentley might want to go back to his hometown for a bit and see his friends and family."

Axel shrugs. "I doubt he'd be against us coming." He pulls back, eyes gleaming. "Plus, his parents already invited us over to meet them."

I swallow, remembering Bentley's words from last night when he blurted that out. Axel laughs, unwinding his arms from around me and using one hand to tip my chin up toward him. "It'll be fine. They probably won't like me out of the two of us." He shrugs.

I push his shoulder, folding my arms after. "Of course, they'll like you. Everybody likes you."

"True," he says over his shoulder with a wink and walking back to the table ahead of me.

33

Janette

The rest of break goes by too fast to notice and suddenly I'm standing in the Cliffords' driveway with Layla, Gwen, and Uncle Jack. Bentley and Axel load our stuff into Axel and Gwen's trunks. Snow falls around us and I tug Axel's beanie a little further down around my ears, letting my curls get crushed underneath.

"You guys don't have to drive back on your own. There's plenty of room in Axel's," I say to Layla for the fiftieth time.

She rolls her eyes at me, and Gwen shakes her head. "No way I'm being crammed in the backseat with any combination of the three of you." Lay points at me and then the guys. "Being in the same house with you three has been enough the last few days. I need the three-hour break." I laugh, looking over at Bentley who stands against the back of the car. One of his hands rests on the top of the open trunk while Axel bends over, the upper half of his body lost in the car as he rearranges things and Bentley clearly ogles his ass. He glances over at me, catching me catching him, and winks with a smile.

We've all been sneaking into Axel's room after everyone

goes to bed to sleep in a pile together, but none of us have felt comfortable going past a slow make out with Axel's whole family sleeping in the connecting rooms. Knowing that when we get back to West Tower all our built-up tension will finally pop, the guys have been giving me light touches and sly smiles all day.

Layla hugs Uncle Jack before turning back toward me. "See you at school, babes." I hug her quick while Gwen hugs her father and then pats my shoulder. Both the girls head over to Gwen's compact SUV, waving to Axel and Bentley as they pass.

"Ready to go?" Axel calls, coming over. I nod, turning toward Uncle Jack who holds out his arms to me a foot away.

I walk into him, hugging him just as tightly as the first night I showed up here again. "Don't be a stranger, kid," he whispers in my ear, and I nod against his shoulder.

"Of course not." We pull back, his hands brushing my shoulders as I smile. "I doubt Axel or Lay would let me, even if I wanted to." He chuckles, nodding to the guys over my shoulder.

I turn to the side and Bentley reaches forward to shake Uncle Jack's hand while Axel slings an arm around my shoulders. "Thank you for everything the last few days," Bentley says and Uncle Jack laughs.

"No problem, son." He looks between Bentley and me. "You both are welcome anytime. Just give an old man a little bit of warning next time." He winks at me, and Bentley's ears go red. I laugh, nodding to Uncle Jack.

Axel squeezes my shoulder, swaying us both a bit. "I called shotgun for you," he says, and Bentley rolls his eyes.

"You can't call shotgun for someone else," he says,

stepping to the side as Axel lets go of me and gives his dad a hug.

"Yes, you can." Axel looks over his shoulder at Bentley while hugging his dad and Uncle Jack laughs.

"Drive safe, son."

Axel turns back to his father, nodding and squeezing him one more time. "Thanks, Dad, but Bentley's driving." He steps back, slinging an arm around Bentley's shoulders. "He lost rock, paper, scissors."

Bentley shrugs him off, looking unamused and I laugh. Axel takes my hand, and we head over to the car. Bentley follows us, getting into the driver's seat while Axel opens my door and waves his arms dramatically.

"Your chariot," he says bowing slightly.

I snort, sliding into the front seat and placing my hands in front of the vents automatically. I wiggle my feet out of my shoes, kicking them to the side and stretching my feet out under the lower vents as I get comfortable.

Axel slides into the back, waving to his father as we pull out of the driveway. I take one more look over my old house, smiling at it finally as we head down the street. Mom and I stood outside and noted all the differences together, getting lost in a few memories and crying a bit more the day after Thanksgiving. She had to get back to Georgia the next day, but she mentioned talking to Uncle Jack about us coming up for Christmas.

I pull Axel's beanie off my head and start tugging at my coat once we get to the highway, the heat cranking up in the car as Bentley drives. I wiggle my feet out of my socks as well, feeling stuffy in their confines. Turning to get more comfortable in my seat, I notice Bentley's furrowed brows and tense shoulders.

I reach over, sliding my hand over his shoulder to

massage the back of his neck. "Mira okay?" I ask. She called Bentley a couple days ago crying and I heard a little bit of their conversation, heart breaking for her as I heard Bentley try to calm her down. I know they spoke again this morning, but too many people were around for me to ask about it back at the house.

Bentley nods, some of the tension leaving him. "Yeah, she's heading back to the Coast in a couple hours and wanted to know if I'd be back yet or not. I'm going to meet her when she gets in. I think she's going to need me." I nod and he shuffles to get himself more comfortable in the seat, eyes never leaving the road.

I look back at Axel, finding him watching my hand on Bentley's neck before he glances at me. He licks his lips, smiling. "Can I get a neck massage too?"

I chuckle, taking my hand off Bentley's neck. Bentley glances at Axel in the rearview mirror, eyebrows no longer furrowed, but peaked.

"If I come back there, I better get a massage out of it as well," I say, folding my arms to appear stern. In actuality, the lingering tension surrounding the three of us the last few days resurfaces, crackling throughout the car.

Axel grins. "You come back here, and my hands will definitely be all over you, Blue." He leans back, spreading his legs in the back seat and placing his hands on his thighs. My stomach clenches as I stare at him, watching his hands move up and down his thighs twice before he pats his lap in invitation.

I glance at Bentley, noticing how white his knuckles are on the wheel. "You going to be okay up here?"

Bentley smirks before glancing over at me with a deadpan expression. "Just go, sunshine. I'll be fine."

I lean over and kiss his temple, unbuckling my seatbelt.

Sitting back, I throw one leg into the back, Axel grabbing my calf and helping to pull me toward him till I straddle the center console, halfway between the front and back. I awkwardly try not to kick Bentley in the head as Axel's hands leave my leg, grabbing me around the waist and tugging me the rest of the way until I'm straddling his lap.

"Hi," I finally say, wrapping my arms around his neck while his arms wrap around my waist. He hums, leaning in to capture my mouth, groaning as my tongue slips past his lips. His hands wander up my back, gripping my shoulders from behind and holding me against him. I shift, needing some friction to match the ferocity of our kiss, my ass rubbing against the growing hardness beneath me.

Axel breaks the kiss, leaning back and staring at me through hazy eyes. His hands land on my hips, mine still playing with the hair at the nape of his neck. We pant for a minute, letting the cascading tension settle a bit. "I believe I promised you a massage," Axel says, breathless.

I chuckle, leaning to rest my back against Bentley's seat. My chest rises and falls between us, matching the pace of his own. "I believe you promised to have your hands all over me." His hands slide up to my waist then back down, resettling on my hips and leaving me covered in goosebumps.

"You're right." He dips forward, lips landing on the side of my neck. I stretch my head to the side giving him more room as he licks and sucks at my skin. My hands dig deeper into his hair, dragging his face back up and connecting my mouth with his. He groans, lips instantly responding with fervent movement. Heat revs throughout my body as his tongue moves with mine, hips starting to grind down against where I can feel him growing hard beneath me. His hands move down to grip my ass through my leggings, helping me keep my rhythm as he bites my bottom lip.

"Fuck, Blue," he moans, as his hips buck up underneath me, hard length pressing into my covered core. Cars fly by us as Bentley drives down the highway, the car's steady rumble adding to the hurried sloppiness of our movements. I lean back, pushing Axel's coat off his shoulders. He helps me remove it and leaves it bunched up behind him as he starts to roll the top of my leggings down my hips. I lift up on my knees, flopping into the seat beside him onto my now bare ass, pulling my leggings the rest of the way off.

Axel's hand on the center of my chest stops me from sitting back up to straddle him again. I raise an eyebrow, and he nods to the window next to me. "Back against the door," he commands. I turn, facing him as he readjusts so that he's on his knees on the seat, back all the way against the other door. Once I'm roughly in the position he wants, he grabs my ankles and places my one foot on the center console, trapping it with the edge of Bentley's seat and forcing my knee to stay bent behind the passenger seat. Taking my other ankle in one hand, he quickly brings it to his lips, kissing the bluebird tattoo I illegally got on a whim at sixteen, and making me shiver before trapping it between the middle headrest, foot pressed against the cold glass of the back window.

I look to the front seat, finding Bentley driving calmly, one hand on the steering wheel, his other in his lap. I wonder idly if he's touching himself but can't see well enough.

"Eyes on me, Blue," Axel says, pulling my attention back to him as he stares down at me. The brown in his eyes has been eaten by his growing pupils and the look makes my throat go dry.

He leans forward, head coming down slowly between my spread legs, holding eye contact with me the whole way. Both of us are cramped in the small space but the bunched position adds to my arousal, feeling like my legs are bound in this position due to the limited space. I gasp when Axel immediately dives in, licking up over my lower lips to part me before sucking my clit into his mouth and lightly biting with his teeth. His eyes close and my hands grab the back of his head, hips trying to rock against his mouth as I fight the position to squirm, unable to move more than an inch.

"Fuck," Bentley says on an exhale, leaning up to glance at us in the rearview mirror. He zones in on Axel's face buried between my widespread legs for a moment before sinking back down and staring ahead again.

Axel hums against me, making me cry out and pull his hair as my head presses against the window behind me and the arm of the door digs into my lower back. The first time Axel tasted and tested me, discovering the different things he could do that unravel me. But now he knows. The stiff tip of his tongue drags slowly down from my clit, circling my entrance as he opens his eyes and looks up at me with a burning smugness. My chest heaves and I stare him down as he flexes his hands on the inside of my thighs and thrusts his tongue inside me. I moan and my eyes close. He continues his fast pace, making my blood boil as I continue to try to move my hips against his face. His nose brushes against my clit as he returns to circling licks and one of his hands slides down my thigh, closer to his mouth. The coil in my stomach tightens further making me pant as he pushes me closer to the edge.

A finger slowly circles the rim of my back hole, making me jump as my eyes fly open. He pulls back a bit. "Too much?" Bentley glances back over his shoulder, concern cutting across his face.

I breathe for a moment before shaking my head. "No, I've just never done anything there."

Bentley turns back to look forward, signaling as he merges into the left lane. He speeds up to get around a slow driver and huffs as he glares out the windshield, checking on us in the mirror a few times.

Axel raises his brow, circling his finger again with a little more pressure as he grins. "Really?" he muses, smiling as he looks back down. He leans forward, tongue meeting my clit again, making me squirm as his finger continues to roam.

The new sensation is odd, but not as uncomfortable as I imagined. "I'm not against it," I whisper.

His eyes meet mine. "Good to know," he hums against me.

Axel starts licking and nipping at me voraciously, making the muscles in my thighs burn as I try to close them around his head but meet the resistance of the headrest and front seat. His finger continues to circle my back hole the entire time and the new feeling overwhelms me quickly. I moan through my release, the orgasm tightening every muscle in my body as it tries to stretch out in the cramped position.

Axel sits up, licking his lips as he hunches against the ceiling of the car. "So pretty," he whispers, hand trailing down the outside of my thigh while his other unbuttons his jeans quickly. "Flip over." He guides my feet out of their holds by my ankles, releasing me so I can follow his command. My knees end up on the middle seat, right cheek laying against the back seat as I stare at the back of the passenger seat. Axel smacks my ass lightly, not having enough room to properly hit me and the light swat makes me giggle.

"Something funny, Blue?" His chest lays down across my back as he kisses the side of my face, lining himself up at the same time. I shake my head, mouth falling open as his tip nudges my entrance before notching. I push back as he slowly enters me, stretching me deliciously as he fills me to the hilt.

Incoherent sounds leave my throat as Axel's lips suck on my earlobe before his teeth press down into the soft flesh. He starts thrusting slowly, making me feel every inch as he drags himself over me. One of his hands grips my hip, the other moving to slide down the back of my thigh between us. He drags it back up slowly. I feel him gathering the wetness from my previous release before his hand starts gliding across my skin again.

"Breathe, Blue," he whispers in my ear as his finger goes back to circling my other hole, spreading my juices like lube around the entrance. I shudder, his cock hitting the right spot inside me as his finger presses into me, slowly sliding to the first knuckle. The feeling there is foreign, but the new pressure somehow makes me feel fuller with Axel filling me so completely. "Good girl," Axel breathes, shallow breaths lingering across my skin. His whole body covers me, the tight backseat area leaving barely any space between us as he rocks into me deep while twisting his finger, slipping it further in. "That's it, baby. Move with me."

I realize I'm slowly rocking with him, my hips meeting the cradle of his as my eyes squeeze closed tightly, and I absorb all the heady sensations around me. His breath fanning my face, coming out harsh and fast. The flex of his fingers on the flesh of my hip as he holds himself back. My own heart pounding against my chest, lungs heaving in air as I gasp.

The buildup is slow, and I can feel how powerful it will be as Axel's rhythm becomes more forceful, until I feel like he's dragging the air in and out of my chest with each push and pull against me. I wiggle my hand out from underneath me, maneuvering it to grasp his on my hip as I cry out, our fingers interlocking as he grunts his release in my ear. His warm cum floods me as I feel my core and ass tighten around his cock and finger, making me feel even fuller. My release explodes through me like a tidal wave crashing, leaving my lungs breathless and limbs jelly beneath us.

Axel kisses the side of my head, pulling an involuntary whine from my lips. "Love you, Blue," he whispers against my hair, pulling his finger slowly out of me. I mumble my response.

I can see Bentley lean over to open the glove box and pass Axel some napkins. "I hope you both enjoyed yourself." Bentley leans forward to look at me in the mirror again. "That was torture and tomorrow you're both making it up to me." His voice holds dark promises and I giggle, brain still in a foggy state.

Axel sits up and cleans each of us off, moving my legs out from underneath me and over his lap. I flip over to lay on my back, humming as he starts to massage my calves and my bare feet press against the cold glass.

"You should sit up," Axel murmurs, reaching over me to grab my leggings and start scrunching them up over the lower half of my legs. I hum, pulling them up my thighs as I wedge the back of my shoulders against the door behind me. We shuffle around, ending up next to each other facing forward again and Axel pulls me against his side, arm slung over my shoulders. I nestle in against him, feeling blissfully pliable as he pulls his seatbelt back on and wedges the middle lap belt over my hips to click between us.

"Thank you for my massage," I whisper.

Axel chuckles, kissing the top of my head. "Anytime, Blue."

My mind starts to drift, eyes already closed, as Axel and Bentley start to playfully argue about new car rules. The next thing I know, Axel shakes my shoulder lightly, whispering my name.

"Yeah," I mumble, opening my eyes blearily. I glance out the window, realizing the car has stopped and we're parked behind West Tower.

"We're here, baby. You need to put on your coat and shoes so we can go inside." I nod, sitting up and letting him move my arms into the coat he holds open for me. Bentley opens the door to my right and passes me my boots, holding out his hand to help me get out of the car once I'm dressed.

Axel kisses my cheek once I'm standing next to him by the trunk in the cold parking lot. "Want to go out to dinner with me?" he whispers.

"What?" My waking mind tries to catch up with the new request. Bentley stands on the other side of me, pretending to ignore us as he leans over to grab luggage.

"I figured Bentley is going to be busy all night with Mira, so we could go somewhere off campus for dinner." Axel shrugs. "We'll go somewhere far from campus if you're worried about people seeing us or something. But somewhere nice if you want." He rubs the back of his neck, cheeks flaming red as the winter air mixes with his sudden shyness.

I smile as I glance over my shoulder, noticing Bentley's warm smile as he watches us.

"We don't have to. It was just an idea."

I quickly step into him, pressing my chest against his. "Of course, I will go on a date with you, Axel."

His eyes fly up to mine, teeth flashing as he smiles. "Really?"

I nod, pulling him closer. "But no hibachi's, alright?"

Bentley groans and taps the top of the trunk, shutting it. All of our stuff sits on the lot at his feet, my duffel bag already over his shoulder.

"Okay," Axel says with a grin. "No hibachi." He and I join Bentley, the boys refusing to let me carry anything else after I swipe my tote before they can grab it. We walk toward the dorm, and I skip ahead a little, feeling bubbly.

"What should I wear?" I say over my shoulder, looking back at them as they grin watching me.

"Whatever you want." Axel shrugs. "You look good in everything."

"Thanks, but I need a little more direction than that," I say, stopping and turning to face them. "Casual or fancy place?"

"Casual," the guys both say as they catch up to me, separating so that I can turn and walk between them. Axel glances down at me. "Wear a dress." His eyes drift down over me. "No tights."

I purse my lips, crossing my arms over my chest to appear stern, even as his words light me on fire. "I'm going to freeze."

Axel laughs, walking into the building when Bentley holds open the door for the two of us. "I'll keep you warm," he says as he turns around, walking backward and facing Bentley and me.

Bentley shakes his head beside me. He looks down at me. "Mira's lucky I love her, because missing the chance to take you out first is killing me a little."

"I'm not planning on going anywhere." We stop in front of the elevator, Axel tapping his foot as he waits for it to arrive. "You'll get your chance. Promise." Bentley smiles, shuffling my duffel on his shoulder. "Or you could always just consider Kitsune Grill our first date." I shrug, biting my lip to hold back a laugh.

Bentley shakes his head, walking onto the elevator behind Axel and me. "I am not considering the time we ended up sitting next to each other on dates with other people our first date."

Axel's eyebrows shoot up and I shrug, smile breaking through. "Suit yourself."

The elevator doors close, Bentley moving to back me up into Axel's chest. "Trust me, sunshine. Our first date will end much better than a stolen kiss in a back alley."

My throat goes dry, and Axel's chest moves at my back, forcing my breathing to match his own.

Bentley meets Axel's eyes over my head. "And ours will be better than a tipsy blowjob."

I suck in air and Axel snorts, hand coming up to palm the back of Bentley's head. "Good luck beating that night." The two meet for a kiss over my shoulder and I rub my thighs together between them.

Bentley steps back when the warning dings for the doors to open, breaking our connection. "But we'll just have to wait for all that."

We step out of the elevator, heading down the hall toward my dorm.

"I plan on telling Mira about us this week," Bentley says once the door of my suite closes behind us.

Axel's head shoots up. "You don't have to."

Bentley nods. "I know." He sets our stuff down, standing back up to face Axel and me. "But I want her and Autumn to know and I promised it would be after Thanksgiving break."

Axel nods and I step toward him, grabbing his hand. "I'll be there when you tell them, if you want?" Mira and I had been hanging out more in the suite before break and I didn't want Bentley to tell her without me there, but I wouldn't force my way in if he wanted to do it alone.

"Me too," Axel says, stepping up and taking his other hand. "We do these things together, right?"

Bentley nods, kissing my forehead then Axel's. "I'll see when they're free for coffee and let you both know." We all nod. "You mind if I stay here to wait for Mira to get back?" I shake my head, releasing his hand and pushing against Axel's chest.

"Out. I need to get ready for our date and I already know you'll try to distract me if you stay here." Axel starts to protest and I tsk, stopping next to the door.

Bentley laughs, settling down on one of my couches.

"Go upstairs and play video games or something. I'll be ready in an hour."

Axel shakes his head, grumbling a little as he leans down to kiss my cheek. "One hour," he says, the serious tone cut by the boyish grin across his face. He looks over my head to Bentley, hand already on the doorknob behind him. "Can't wait for your revenge tomorrow, Bent." He winks and then he's out the door, leaving me to get ready for our first date.

34

BENTLEY

"You ready for this?" Janette asks, blowing on her gloved hands and bouncing on the balls of her feet. I reach over and take her hands in mine, rubbing them to try to generate more warmth. Thick puffs of snowflakes fall around us outside the closed campus cafe, catching on her tight space buns and the little fuzzy hairs of her black earmuffs. She smiles, watching me warm her hands while still shifting her weight around on her feet.

"Yes. I want them to know about us. I want everyone to know about us." Her eyes widen as they slide up to meet mine and I chuckle. "Baby steps, sunshine. Together, right?"

She nods as I bring her hands up to kiss her gloved fingertips. She blushes and puts them in her coat pockets after I release them.

I stare at her for a moment, eyes roving over her face as I take her in while she hops around. "I like this by the way," I say, reaching up and tapping just above her new nose piercing with a grin.

Janette smiles and my chest expands. "Thanks." Her eyes crinkle as she looks up at me again. "I still can't believe

I did it. when I told Axel I always wanted one at dinner, I didn't expect him to take us to a tattoo shop immediately after." She laughs again, the sound airy and making my smile grow. With a shake of her head, she adds, "He's insane sometimes."

"But you love it." I start rubbing her upper arms, wanting to touch her just as much as I want to warm her up.

Janette rolls her eyes. "Like you don't too." She pauses, looking at her hands again. "My mom would never have let me before, and I figured I shouldn't worry about that so much anymore."

I dip down to catch her eyes, holding them as I say, "I'm proud of you, sunshine."

She smiles, bouncing around after a moment to try to stay warm again. I watch her with a smile until she suddenly goes rigid and looks sharply over her shoulder.

My smile drops and I follow her gaze, looking out at the early morning campus. Some people walk through the cleared paths, but most of the school still sleeps or are in their early morning lectures.

"What is it?" I ask and Janette looks back up at me.

"Nothing, I guess." She glances back over the campus behind her. "I just thought I felt someone looking at us." She shakes her head. "I felt it when I was out with Axel the other day too."

My brows furrow and I reach out, rubbing the spot where her neck meets her shoulder. She looks up at me again. "Maybe you just felt people were watching you because you fucked Axel in the bathroom?" I give her a wry smile and she shoves my shoulder. I chuckle. "Did you see anyone watching you?"

She shakes her head. "No, I never saw anyone. I don't think anyone at the restaurant was actually watching us or anything. Maybe I'm just going crazy?" She laughs uncomfortably, looking down again.

I tip her chin up, meeting her eyes. "You're not crazy." She smiles and I drop my hand from her chin. "You're probably just nervous about people finding out about us. I am too. You weren't wrong that publicity will become a problem at some point."

She nods, biting her bottom lip. I pull it from her teeth, rubbing it with my thumb. "We'll handle it though. And we don't have to worry about it right now. The school's security will keep the press off campus."

Janette nods, hugging herself against the cold. "Can I ask you something?"

I squeeze her chin, smiling. "Anything."

"Your parents," she starts, studying my face. "They weren't around a lot when you were growing up?"

I sigh, rubbing my thumb against her skin. "They were around, but no not all the time. They always made an effort though. When they were home and when they were away on shoots. My grandfather was there all the time and I met Mira in elementary school. Her and her mom, April, became my second home. So, I never felt like I was missing anything." She nods and I continue. "I don't resent them or anything. They always made sure I was protected and kept up with everything in my life. I remember one time a photographer got into one of my tee ball games and my dad literally hopped on a jet and came back home to make sure I was okay. Mom wasn't on that shoot, so she was there when it happened. She took a swing at him, and it made national headlines." I shake my head, laughing a little and Janette smiles with me. "Why did you ask?"

She shrugs. "I don't know. I know you didn't resent them, but I wanted to make sure I understood. Being around Axel's family last week was a lot and I wanted to check in that you were okay too."

I hold myself back, telling her, "I really want to kiss you right now. Thank you for checking in with me. I'm okay, promise. I like big family gatherings. Mira's house can get kind of rowdy with all the stray kids April takes in." He chuckles.

We stand in the cold together and I think over her paranoia from earlier.

"If you feel like you're being watched again, let me know. Or Axel. I'm sure he'll be concerned too." Janette nods, looking into the café now. I watch her, looking back the way she suddenly stared and still seeing nothing out of the ordinary.

A worker comes to the glass doors next to us, unlocking the café and changing the closed sign to open. I hold the door for Janette as well as the other few people who were waiting out front with us. Once inside, I nod toward a window booth big enough for four and get in line to buy our drinks.

Janette makes herself comfortable, taking off her gloves and earmuffs, but leaving her coat on as she claims the table I pointed out. I place our order, getting Autumn and Mira's usual drinks as well, before sliding in next to Janette and pulling off my own winter gear.

The bell over the door rings and I look up to see my best friends walk in, stamping their boots on the black mat inside the door. My stomach rolls, and I swallow down the rising uncertainty tainting my gut. Mira will be happy for us. She'll understand.

Mira looks around, spotting us first when I raise my hand and steering Autumn over to our table.

"Sorry we're late, I couldn't find my gloves." Mira says,

smiling at Janette and pulling off her knit hat. The look settles my nerves a bit, warmth spreading through my chest at the idea of them becoming friends. She looks over her shoulder at the menu board above the counter. "Did you guys order already?"

I nod, reaching out to take Autumn's bag so she can take her coat off. "Yeah, I got your peppermint thing and Autumn's tea. Just waiting for them to call the name." Mira turns back, smiling and I hand Autumn her bag back once they've both slid into the booth across from us.

Awkwardness invades my gut as Janette and Mira start chatting about finals. I listen halfheartedly, trying to formulate the right way to ease the conversation toward the topic I want. Janette's hand lands on my knee under the table as she nods along to Autumn. I pat the back of her hand just as my name gets called by a barista. I slide out of the booth, grabbing the drink tray and carrying it over to the little mixing station where I add cinnamon to Autumn's tea and a wooden stirrer to Mira's peppermint mocha.

Walking back, I catch the tail end of the conversation as Janette smiles at me and reaches for her drink.

"I still think you should just switch now." She shrugs her shoulder as she licks the rim of her cup, catching a few fallen drips from the station to table transfer.

Mira holds her mocha with two hands, warming them against the surface. "Classes have already been picked for next semester, so I'll get the duds if I change now. Plus, most majors follow a fall to spring schedule, so starting the classes now will mess up my whole schedule for the next three years."

"Change what?" I ask after burning my tongue on the scalding coffee I ordered. I pull the lid off and rub my thumb against the lip of the cup, feeling the steam against the pad of my finger.

"Change majors. I think I'm going to do it next semester. That way I can get my gen eds done this year and then start all the art courses in the fall like they're set up to be taken." Mira stares at her cup the whole time she speaks, shoulders tense. Autumn rubs her back, half her tea already gone.

I reach across the table, taking one of her hands off the cup, waiting for her eyes to meet mine. "I think that's a great idea, Mir. You deserve to do what you love."

Mira nods, smiling. "Mom said the same thing."

I chuckle, taking back my hand and winking at her. "I knew I loved April for a reason."

"Have you told Harley?" Autumn half mumbles, cup against her lips.

Mira swallows, shaking her head. Her eyes dull a little and I fist my hand in my lap. "We've been weird lately. I don't know if I'm going to tell him right now."

Janette's hand lands back on my knee, squeezing as she sips her drink. I clear my throat, unclenching my fist and sitting forward so my elbows rest on the table. "So, I wanted to meet with you guys today to tell you both something."

"He's speaking formally. Nervous," Autumn murmurs.

Mira nods, sitting up. "Serious. Maybe he crashed the car?"

I roll my eyes, sitting back and trying my coffee again now that it's a little more cooled. Once they start, there's no stopping them until they're done.

"Or he's dropping out?"

"Please tell me he didn't knock someone up."

"A baby? Tyson will be furious."

"Not to mention Heather and Michael."

"Oh, the scandal." Autumn snickers.

I glance at Janette, finding her eyes ping ponging between my best friends, eyebrows slowly inching up her forehead.

"Are you two done?" I ask.

Mira laughs, nodding. "What's up, Bent?"

I take a deep breath, grabbing Janette's hand under the table and bringing our interlocked fingers up. "We're together."

Mira stares at our hands and Autumn's mouth pops open. Janette's head whips toward me, eyes wide at my simple assessment of the situation before she slowly looks back at Autumn and Mira. Mira's eyes lift to mine before crossing to Janette's. She frowns.

"I thought you were dating Axel?" she whispers.

Janette takes a deep breath before smiling. "I am."

Autumn's eyes shoot open wide, sliding over to stare at me. "But you two are also dating?"

"Mhmm," I murmur, watching Mira's reaction. My stomach turns as I psyche myself up to say, "And I'm also with Axel."

Mira's head swivels between the two of us again, but Autumn smiles wide. "Wait, you're all together?"

Janette and I nod in sync. I squeeze her hand, feeling the tremors that start to emerge. "He wanted to be here to tell you both too, but he has an eight a.m. on Tuesdays," Janette says.

"We wanted to tell you both right away after break."

Mira stares at our hands again, still not saying a word. I wait, stomach tying itself in knots.

Autumn glances over, nudging Mira with her shoulder. Mira's head pops up and our gazes meet.

"How long have you guys been together?"

I sigh. "Altogether, about two months. But we've been

making our way toward this since the beginning of term." I wince when she nods, lips thinning.

Janette jumps in, words flying fast. "I was the one who didn't want to tell anyone. I'm not ashamed or anything, but it happened really differently between each of us and then kind of all at once for all three of us and I wasn't sure we were stable enough to let people in yet. Plus, I'm still really nervous about the outside world finding out with my mom's spotlight career and his parents." Janette bumps my shoulder, probably harder than she intends, but I can feel her fidgety energy in charge. "It's my fault Bentley didn't say anything."

I shake my head, pulling Janette's hand closer to me. "No, I was also nervous to tell you. You had so much going on with school stressing you out and the Harley stuff and then your parents. Plus, Janette and you weren't exactly besties at the beginning of the semester. I was worried you would worry about me and didn't want to add to your plate."

Mira laughs. I swallow and Janette and Autumn just stare at her. She chuckles, closing her eyes and shaking her head. "Bentley Kodak Marshall."

I smile, shoulders falling as I hear the playfully stern tone of her voice.

"You didn't tell me you were in a new relationship because you were scared I would worry about you?" Her eyes fly open. "I am not your child! I'm your best friend!" She laughs, shaking her head "You really need to stop trying to shelter me from everything. I already get enough of that from Ramsey and Harley!"

Autumn smiles, going back to finishing her tea.

I nod. "You're not mad?" I check.

"No. I get some of your reasons." She turns to Janette.

"You didn't start hanging out with me just because you're dating my best friend, right?"

Janette shakes her head, letting go of my hand and reaching across the table for Mira's. "No, I wanted to hang out with you, I swear. I started the semester with a bunch of shit from back home and I didn't realize how much it was eating up my focus. I kept doing things for other people and pushed my own stuff to the side. Bentley and Axel kind of figured their own ways in and helped me realize I needed to drop some things and reprioritize myself." She leans forward, Mira doing the same. "I'm really sorry I didn't put in more effort in the beginning of the semester. I was a bitch, and you didn't deserve the effects of my shit."

I wrap my arm around her back, resting my hand on her hip. She smiles over at me.

Mira nods, gripping Janette's hand. "Thank you, but you're not fully to blame. I could have been a bit more understanding."

Janette shakes her head. "You didn't know."

"Still, you weren't a bitch. You were just guarded." She shrugs. "I'm really glad they helped you let down your walls."

Janette beams at me, making my lungs squeeze. "They've both been there for me every time that I've needed them. And I plan on being there for them whenever they need me."

Autumn awes and Janette blushes, taking her hand back from Mira.

Mira turns back to me. "I'm not hurt that you didn't tell me right away. I didn't tell you guys about Harley right away." She glances over at Autumn who nods. "But I know you, Bent. I know you wouldn't waste your time with just anyone. If you had told me you started seeing Janette, I would have been happy for you guys and tried to make more of an effort to get to know her too. And Axel. How does that work exactly?"

I chuckle, running a hand through my hair and glancing at Janette. "We're figuring it out as we go along. So far, that's been pretty easy though since we've been in our own little world."

Autumn finishes the last of her tea, pushing the empty cup toward the middle of the table. "Have you let your parents' PR team know? Or are you just going to blindside them like with the boat incident?"

"What's the boat incident?" Janette sits forward, eyes alight.

"I told my parents over break." I say before Autumn can fill her in. "I don't know if they've told Molly yet, but they were both excited. They want to meet them."

Janette sits back, hands on her disregarded drink.

"Heather and Michael are super sweet. They'll love you," Mira says, smiling at Janette. "What about your grandfather?"

"We've sort of met," Janette says, smirking over at me.

I roll my eyes. "Yeah, I think an actual introduction is still needed."

"Mom will probably want to throw you guys a party." Mira laughs. "I'm sure she'll want to meet you both as well."

"How many meet-the-parents events do we have to go to?" Janette's shoulders slump and I rub her side.

"Well, I already met your and Axel's parents."

"You did?" Mira and Autumn both shoot up, leaning across the table. "How'd it go?"

I rub the bridge of my nose, remembering the tense Thanksgiving dinner. "It's kind of a long story."

Mira settles in, smiling. "We have time. Start about two months ago and go from there."

"Well, we'd probably have to start before the semester started to get all the context in," Janette says before launching into how the three of us came together.

I shake my head, smiling at my best friends while Janette smirks behind her drink each time they gasp or squeal dramatically. Warmth seeps into my chest and I jump in to explain how we spent Thanksgiving break, Janette weaving in the parts about her Mom. Mira and Autumn listen with rapt attention, the snow piling up outside as part of the weight on my shoulders falls away.

After an hour of explanations and betting on who will hug Janette more, April or my mom, I glance at my watch, realizing we're late to meet Axel.

"We have to go finalize our project." I nudge Janette, her spine snapping straight as she glances at the time on her phone. She nods, following me out of the booth.

Autumn and Mira stand as well, gathering their stuff and tossing their empty cups in the trash nearby. "We should get back to West Tower. Looks like the storm is picking up."

We all glance out the window. The light puffs of white have turned into a fast flurry of pelting snow as the wind drifts the tops of the accumulation around to mix with the already falling flakes. I hold out Janette's coat as she puts her arms in, throwing my own on once she starts on the buttons of hers.

Mira smiles at us as I hand Janette her earmuffs and take her empty cup to the trash with mine. I roll my eyes at her soft expression, but my gut twists a bit at the purse of her lips as she looks away.

"We're okay, right?" I whisper, standing between her and Janette as we walk out.

She nods, eyes going wide as she looks up at me. "Of course, Bent. I'm happy for you." She smiles and I sigh. She hugs me just inside the entryway of the café, and I wrap my arms around her as well. "Last week was just a lot and I have a feeling these next few weeks aren't going to be much better."

I nod as we pull apart, still holding her in place once I can see her eyes. "I'm here if you need anything, okay? Anything, Mir."

She nods, Autumn placing a hand on her back and echoing my words.

Janette pipes up after a second as well. "Me too." She steps forward, entering our little huddle and Mira smiles over at her.

"Thanks, you guys," she untangles herself from all of us. "You two need to get going. Tell Axel we said hi!" She nudges us toward the door, and I nod, holding the door open for Janette as we walk out into the storm.

A few feet away from the café, I grab her hand, pulling her closer to me and wrapping an arm around her. "I think that went well."

She smiles up at me, teeth chattering. "It went amazing. I thought they'd be way more pissed."

I chuckle, leaning down to kiss her cheek. She pouts as I pull away and I tilt my head. Janette reaches up and grabs the back of my neck, pulling me back down and kissing me fully. Her lips are cold against mine, but as we get lost in it, warmth spreads between us. I pull back for air a few moments later and Janette laughs breathlessly.

I watch her, mesmerized and lean down to kiss her again

quickly before we continue on our way. The storm churns around us, but my body feels warm and light as we continue down the path toward Axel.

35

AXEL

My foot bounces under our usual table while I wait for Bentley and Janette to show up. I watch the doors to the library, eyeing the random people walking by and making sure no one steals one of the empty chairs. People sit all over, cramming for finals at tables, spread out on the comfy chairs, some even sitting on the floor in the shadows of the stacks since most of the actual seating is taken.

I should have just stopped by the café to see if they were still there. I couldn't focus at all in my eco class, just thinking about Janette and Bentley on their own with Mira and Autumn. What if they were pissed and I left them there to deal with it on their own? Or what if they were confused and me being there would have helped?

I start chewing my thumbnail, leg still bouncing away. My laptop pings with a random email, pulling my attention from the glass doors for a moment before I look up and see Janette and Bentley walk in, both smiling. Everything inside me settles, my leg going back to its normal tempo under the table.

As they walk up, Bentley picks up his pace, leaving Janette behind as she tilts her head at his back. He eats up the space between us, slowly filling in my line of sight until he's standing over me next to my chair. I stare up, completely frozen by the determination in his gaze since the moment he beelined over here. He cups the sides of my face, tilting my head back as he bends down, covering my mouth with his. The kiss starts slow, short circuiting my brain as my body reacts on its own, lips moving with his. He pulls back before I can reach up to tug him closer, but his face makes me pause, reality settling back in.

My eyes flick around the room, seeing a few people openly staring before looking back at their work when my eyes catch theirs. Ice runs down my spine before my eyes return to Bentley's face, still hovering a few inches above my own. The smile on his face creates a heat deep in my chest, washing away any fear that this was a mistake he didn't mean to make. He pecks my lips again quickly before releasing me and taking his seat across the table.

Janette stands a foot behind the table, hands on her mouth as she watches us with shiny eyes. She steps up to the table when our gazes meet, taking her seat and smiling at me before starting to pull her laptop from her bag.

"I take it things went well?" I say, body still turned toward the front door as if it refuses to catch up to the new study vibes.

Janette nods her head emphatically. "They were both fine. Honestly it went way better than I expected. Autumn didn't even bat an eye."

"And Mira?" I ask, looking to Bentley.

He smiles, laptop now open in front of him, though he looks over the top of it at me. "She's happy for us. We had to explain pretty much everything."

"Everything?" I raise an eyebrow, and Janette narrows her eyes at me.

"No, not about us *together*, Axe. They both wanted to hear about our break last week, but otherwise everything went well."

I turn toward the table, nodding my head. "Good." A lightness blooms in my chest and I smile down at my laptop keys. "Step number one out of the way."

"Pretty sure we're at least on like step seven at this point." Janette murmurs, focusing in on the screen of her computer.

"So, is PDA on the table now?" I pull my foot out of my snow boot, running it lightly up the side of Janette's leg. She jumps a little, glaring at me over the top of her screen.

Bentley chuckles. "Nothing excessive. And you might need to go slow with her," he nods to Janette, and she frowns at him.

"I'm right here," she grumbles.

"I know, sunshine." He reaches over to poke her side, but she swats his hand away before he can.

"If I remember correctly, you like slow, Blue." I smirk as she narrows her eyes at me again.

"You two need to focus." She points between the two of us before pointing to her laptop. "We need to finalize the presentation for tomorrow."

I chuckle, pulling up the shared presentation on my own screen. "Fine, but afterward, we're celebrating." I wink at Bentley, and he returns it with a wry smile.

Janette clears her throat, one eyebrow raised when we both turn toward her. "Focus." We each sit up straight, listening to Janette roll through what we need to get done and then quietly working once she's given her orders.

After running through our slides about five more times, I finally slump back, unable to sit still much longer. "Blue, we've gone through it enough. We're ready for tomorrow."

Janette bites her lip, scrolling through the presentation again. "I'm just worried we don't have enough."

"The presentation is already thirty slides long. We have more than enough, sunshine."

Janette nods, still scrolling and reading through the slides again.

I reach out, half closing her laptop to get her attention. "We're going to be okay. The presentation is going to go so smoothly, and Howards is going to love it."

Janette sighs, taking her hands out from her keyboard and stretching in her seat. "You're not going to show up in a suit of armor tomorrow, right?"

I smile, closing my own laptop. "I make no promises."

Bentley rolls his eyes, and we all pack up, forfeiting the table to a rabid group nearby. I hold the door open as we all walk out, pelted by snow the moment we step outside. "Maybe classes will get cancelled tomorrow and we'll have another few days before we have to present," I yell over the wind as we start trekking toward West Tower.

Bentley looks at me sharply over Janette's head as she yells back a little shakily, "Yeah, maybe." He wraps an arm around her shoulder, pulling her against him so she stays warm.

I follow behind, wanting to bracket her in on the other side, but knowing it'd be too forward in our newly growing PDA stage. We trudge altogether to the dorms, banging our snowy boots on the already soaked carpet as we enter.

"It was so nice and fluffy this morning," Janette laments, staring out the windows at the swirling storm.

Bentley nods. "It'll stop later tonight and then it's supposed to be clear tomorrow." We head to the elevator, stripping off gloves and hats.

"I can't wait for a hot shower." I picture the warmth of the water spreading over me and smile, envisioning a couple more people joining me.

"I'm getting in one of your beds when we get upstairs. My toes are frozen."

Bentley's head shoots up at the same moment I yell, "Dibs!" His shoulders fall, eyes narrowing on me.

Janette chuckles. "It's okay, Bent," she says, patting his coat around his stomach. "He's going to go shower so you can just join me." Bentley smirks at her.

I pout. "No fair. I wanted you both in the shower with me." The elevator doors open, the three of us shuffling out and toward the suite.

Janette shrugs. "I don't need a shower right now. I need a warm bed." We walk into the suite, each peeling off our coats and shoes in the little welcome area Bentley's parents created for us at the beginning of the year.

"Fine," I grumble. "My shower can wait."

Janette and Bentley laugh, splitting up as Janette heads toward my room and Bentley walks to the kitchen.

I look between them, following Bentley first. He scrambles around in the fridge, lower half the only thing visible past the door.

"You didn't have to do that," I say quietly, leaning against the side of the kitchen entryway.

Bentley stands up, eyebrows pushed together. "Do what?"

"The big public kiss." I step forward as Bentley shuts the door between us. "I don't want you to feel like you have to keep proving yourself to me or something."

Bentley steps forward, cold hands capturing my face as he comes chest to chest with me. His lips meet mine again, harsher than they had in the library. Their warmth zaps through my limbs, and I wrap my arms around his waist, crushing myself further to him.

He pulls back too quickly again. "I did not kiss you because I feel like I have something to prove. I kissed you because I love you and I can finally do it in public."

I smile, tightening my hold on the back of his shirt.

"Now, let's go fuck our girlfriend before she chews her nails down to the quick." He kisses me again quickly before untangling himself and pulling the fridge open again to grab a water bottle. He tosses one to me and carries another for Janette as we head into my room.

Janette sits against the center of my headboard, duvet tucked in around her hips as she stares forward, biting on her nails. Bentley sets down the water bottles while I jump onto the free side against the wall. Janette looks around as the bed jostles, settling on me and smiling.

"Stop overthinking, Blue. Tomorrow's going to go great." I reach out, rubbing my hand over her covered shin.

"I know," she says while Bentley lowers himself beside her on the other side. "I can't help worrying though. What if classes do get cancelled tomorrow and the new time conflicts with one of my other finals? Or what if the presentation won't load tomorrow? Or we forgot to save our changes and half the slides are gone?"

Bentley leans over, latching onto the side of her neck and making her eyes flutter closed. I slide my hand up over her thigh, shuffling closer to the two of them. "We're going to help you relax, Blue," I murmur, leaning in to kiss down the other side of her neck. She moans above us. "The storm is already slowing down. Class won't get cancelled tomorrow." Kiss. "We emailed a copy of the presentation to Howards, so even if it doesn't load on one of our three laptops, he'll have a copy on his." Kiss. "We saved our changes." Kiss. "And even if we didn't, we only changed a couple of slides so they'll all still be there from the last time we saved it." Bentley's hand slides over her stomach, coming to rest on her side and against my chest. I suck on her collar bone as he nibbles on the shell of her ear. "Relax, Blue."

"Relax," she repeats, eyes still closed. Her shoulders sag as her body follows the command, hands coming up to run over each of us.

We slide the duvet down, revealing her still clothed legs, before moving back in to bracket her completely. Her breathing starts to accelerate, coming in sharp as her chest heaves beneath my lips. I move my hand up, cupping her covered breasts and starting to tease them through the material of her shirt. My jeans have been steadily growing uncomfortable since Bentley kissed me in the kitchen, reawakening the desire he ignited in the middle of the library.

His hand leaves her hip, sliding down my covered stomach to the hem of my shirt. He slides his hand underneath, putting pressure on my crotch. I groan against Janette's chest, hips thrusting toward his touch as I glance up to watch Bentley dominate her mouth with his other hand firmly entangled in her hair. She follows his lead, one hand on the back of my head as she starts to writhe between the two of us.

I pull on the hem of her sweater, Bentley breaking the kiss to lean back and help me take it off her. Once free, the two of them return to their make out, one of her hands now buried in my hair and scratching the back of my head. I lean into the feeling, humming in the back of my throat as my eyes close. I'm not sure I'll ever get enough of this.

Bentley pops the button on my jeans, hand dipping inside once the zipper is down. My eyes fly open, watching him run his teeth along her jaw as his hand bypasses my boxers and grips me roughly.

Janette pants between us, eyes squeezed shut. "I want to try something new," she blurts, opening her eyes when Bentley's mouth pauses on her skin.

He pulls his head back to look at her with a raised brow. "What do you have in mind, sunshine?" We've been together in a lot of different positions, one of my favorite times being when Bentley fucked Janette on the couch while sucking me off at the same time. I practically passed out and barely lasted a few minutes before blowing in his mouth. But the curiosity on Janette's face piques my own.

"I want both of you." Janette looks between us, hands on the back of each of our heads. "At the same time." I swallow, eyes sliding over to Bentley's. He stares at her with a slight smile, eyes dark, and the look makes my cock twitch in his hand. I groan and Bentley responds by squeezing me and making me hiss.

"As much as that idea turns both of us on," Bentley says against the skin of her neck. "Let's slow down a bit. How do you want to do this? Neither of us want to hurt you."

Janette's eyebrows pull together, hand tightening on the back of my head. I lean up and kiss her, smoothing the wrinkle in her forehead with my thumb. "He means do you want us both in one hole or one of us in your ass?"

Her face grows hot, and I kiss the tip of her nose with a chuckle. "I meant anal," she says, glancing between the two of us. "I don't think my vagina could handle both of you at once."

Bentley laughs, releasing both of us and getting up off the bed. He heads over to my closet, both of us staring at his back as he walks. "We can work our way toward that another day." He looks over his shoulder at us. "We'd just need to stretch you out beforehand." Janette and I breathe heavily for a minute, staring at Bentley as he finds the shelf he's looking for and turns back toward us, lube in hand. "Both of you get naked."

We each scramble to follow Bentley's orders, anticipation cutting through the cloud of lusty haze around us. Janette pulls off her leggings while I whip off my shirt and push down my jeans and boxers at once. My dick bobs out, already leaking precum and Janette's hand reaches out and fists around my base. I groan and she giggles, starting to move her hand slowly over me.

"No touching," Bentley bites and Janette's hand disappears immediately. I huff, looking over at a now naked Bentley standing at the side of the bed. I usually love following his commands, knowing what will come is worth it. But sometimes I forget that in the moment. He restores my good mood with his next order though.

"Bra and panties, sunshine."

Janette smirks, removing her bra and making me clench my fists to hold back from touching the newly exposed skin. Her soaked underwear goes next, the little ball of lacy cloth bouncing off Bentley's chest when she tosses them at him.

"Cute." Bentley puts one knee on the bed, dropping the lube on my bedside table. Grabbing Janette's ankle, he pulls her down till her ass meets the edge of the bed, splaying her top half out between us as she loses her balance. "How we deciding this?"

"Deciding what?" Janette says, propping herself up on her elbows.

Bentley stares at me as he answers her. "Which of us gets to be your first."

I smile, kneeling next to Janette's head. "Rock paper scissors?"

He shrugs. "Works for me." We each throw our fists out, bobbing them up and down as he calls out the countdown. On scissors, we each throw, my fingers flattening out to call paper. Bentley smirks, mimicking cutting my hand in half with his index and middle before looking down at Janette. "Looks like it's going to be me. Much better prize than not driving home."

I roll my eyes, sitting back on my knees again and trying to ignore my needy cock at his tone of voice.

He moves his knee off the bed, dropping down to the floor between her spread legs. His eyes find mine over her body. "Help me make her come and then we'll prep her. Hands to yourself, sunshine." With his final command, he buries his face in the apex of her thighs, making her whimper and squirm, his arm banding over her hips to hold her down.

I lean over her shoulder, licking circles across her collarbone as I move down her chest. Taking her right nipple in my mouth, I lightly bite and suck the pebbled peak, rolling the other between my fingers. Janette cries out, head moving from side to side next to my knees. Her hands fist the blanket and sheets haphazardly strewn beneath her and I smile against her skin. My kisses leave goose bumps in their wake as I switch between her breasts and watch Bentley eat her out with his eyes closed. Janette's thighs shake around his head, hips trying to move against his arm before she lets out a long groan, stomach muscles tightening. Bentley's face appears, eyes bright and chin covered in her release. I lean down, grabbing the back of his head and thrusting my tongue into his mouth to taste her. We both moan, the sounds mixing along with our tongues between us.

Bentley lets me kiss him for a few moments before wrenching me back by my hair and smiling. "Lay down on the bed." He nods at the pillows to my right, and I move around Janette. Every time we've all fucked since we got back to the Coast, one of the two of us has played with her ass, prepping her for one of us to eventually take her last virginity. We made it up to three fingers last time, but even that will be smaller than Bentley's cock, especially with mine already filling her.

Bentley helps her sit up so that I can lay down, her movements a little dazed. Once my head meets a pillow, Bentley nudges her toward me. With a single sentence, he has my cock growing impossibly harder. "Sit on his face, sunshine."

She hums, dazed pupils flashing before she crawls up the bed until her knees are on either side of my head, Bentley behind her to reinforce her clumsy movements. I smile, looking up at her and licking my lips. "Sit down, Blue." My hands reach up to grasp her hips, taking a second to revel in the silky smoothness of her skin before I help her come down. She covers my face, my tongue easily finding her soaked clit. She grips my headboard, crying out as I ease her toward another orgasm.

Bentley straddles my hips, his hard cock against mine, making me dig my fingers in against Janette's skin and curse. He leans forward and I hear the pop of the lube cap opening. Janette flinches above me and I feel lube run off her skin and over my neck. I lick down to her entrance, finding Bentley's fingers slowly stretching her a few inches away. I start probing her in rhythm with his fingers, Janette rocking her hips along a moment later. Her thighs tighten to bracket my head more and I smile, massaging my fingers into her hips. Oh, to die between her thighs.

Minutes pass as we work her up together, pulling back each time she gets close to the edge. The sounds of her heavy breathing and Bentley's soaked fingers moving in and out of her create a buzzing contentment in my chest. I lap at her happily, savoring her taste on my tongue. Janette rotates her hips and pants above me, grunting in frustration each time we pause.

"Stop," Bentley suddenly calls, pulling my hands away from her skin. "Axel, sit up a little." He pulls Janette down to straddle my stomach while I grab another pillow and pull us back together. I stare up at Blue and find her eyes almost closed, chest moving quickly to draw her breaths in. My hands come up to cup her breasts, fingers playing with her nipples as Bentley moves in behind her.

"Ready?" he murmurs against her shoulder and her eyes open more, head nodding. He wraps an arm around her middle, lifting her while fisting the base of my dick at the same time. I throw my head back as he positions us, dragging her down over me until I'm fully seated inside her. Her warm walls grip me, replacing the grasp of Bentley's hand and the sensation makes an inarticulate groan rumble from my chest. Blue moans, head lolling back onto Bentley's shoulder, and he chuckles. "Still want both of us?"

She nods, and breathily pleads, "Please."

Bentley groans before pushing her down over me slowly with a hand on the center of her back. Her head lands on my shoulder and she nuzzles into my neck, kissing me at my pulse point and making me shiver. He leans down over her to kiss me for a moment, soft lips commanding mine and scrambling my thoughts to oblivion before he pops back up.

"Don't move yet." I nod, trying to form coherent thoughts and wrapping my arms around Janette. I start rubbing her back. She kisses my throat again, as I watch Bentley line himself up. His hands land on her hips, holding us both still. "Ready, sunshine?"

She nods fervently, nose brushing against me, and he slowly starts to push into her. She tenses and he pauses, one hand joining mine to rub circles into her lower back. "Relax, baby. We'll go slow."

She digs a hand into my hair, holding on to me as he eases another inch into her, rocking his hips slowly. I start to feel him sliding against me, the thin barrier inside her the only thing between us, and almost shut my eyes, breathing through my nose to keep myself from moving along with him. Another inch and Janette moans as he pulls back, trying to move her hips with him and clenching around me. I watch Bentley move, feeling Janette slowly grow more pliable over top of me as she relaxes fully into us. When his hips finally meet her ass, he stares down at me, sweat darkening his hair and lightly lining his shoulder muscles.

"So fucking tight," he whispers, mouth hanging open a little afterward.

"I can feel you," I spit out, barely holding onto any semblance of self-control.

Janette moans, muttering unintelligibly and Bentley leans down to kiss the center of her back and then the back of my hand. "I'm going to move. You both ready?" Janette nods into my neck and I follow suit.

Bentley pulls out almost entirely, the feeling making my hips stutter as I pull back slightly beneath her. And then he's slamming back in, cock gliding against mine and making her clench around me even tighter. I wheeze out a breath, seeing stars.

This right here is heaven.

Janette tips her head back, mouth wide open in a silent scream. We devolve into a messy rhythm panting and cursing around Janette as we each push and pull against her.

"Fuck," Bentley grunts, hand coming up to cover my throat. The pressure makes my balls tighten up and he yells, "Come," just as I explode inside Blue, hips shoving as far into her as I can get from beneath them both. Bentley roars his release as I feel Janette clench around me and scream through her own release.

We fall into a heap of sweaty limbs, still randomly connected as I wait for air to enter my lungs at the right pace and my mind to return. My eyes eventually close and I feel Bentley untangle Janette and carry her out of the bed. I hear the sink running and ease back against the wall, fluffing my pillow and settling in. Bentley returns with Janette, my eyes peaking open to watch her slide under the covers and scooch over to lay against my chest. Bentley follows behind her, the three of us re-tangling ourselves together.

"You two are going to kill me," Janette murmurs.

"Sore?" Bentley asks, rubbing his hand along her side, knuckles brushing over my stomach.

"More exhausted."

"Good." He leans up and kisses her quick. "You'll sleep well then."

Janette hums and I chuckle. "That was your idea, Blue." I kiss her shoulder, hand running over Bentley's hip under the blanket covering us all.

"Next time, one of you is in the middle," she mumbles, turning to tuck herself into me on her side and starting to drift off.

Bentley's eyes meet mine and he grins.

I pull my hand out of the blanket at the same time as him and we wave our fists as he mouths the words. My flat hand covers his fist over Janette's head, and I smile, stomach flipping at the idea of burying myself in him while he's balls deep in her.

Janette

I laugh, rereading Layla's text before typing back a quick thank you. Pulling my skirt on over my fleece-lined tights, I zip the side and smooth the form fitting material down, looking over my pre-planned outfit one more time. My heart hammers in my chest as I mentally go over my introduction for our presentation again before grabbing my fuzzy plum sweater and pulling it over my head. Tucking the hem into my skirt, I nod along, mouthing the words as they scroll through my mind. My reflection stares back at me, as I make little adjustments, before I stop and hear Bentley's phantom voice in my ears. *Take a deep breath.*

Breathing through my nose, I close my eyes, remembering his smile during our lazy afternoon yesterday. We moved to the living room after our nap, ordering Chinese food and playing Mario Party for hours. Axel ended up pouting every time he lost, demanding a rematch three times. Bentley finally shut him down after the fourth game, placating him by sitting for a few selfies that Axel insisted on taking even if we couldn't post them. Of course, Axel had taken more than the negotiated two, making me laugh while watching them wrestle for Axel's phone. I ended up stealing the remote while they were distracted, but Bentley's smile remained the entire time.

My phone goes off again, pulling my eyes open.

AXEL

> Laptops are all set. Grabbed our usual
> seats.

Bentley's name appears next.

BENTLEY

> Presentation is all good. We're the first ones
> here. You owe us coffee.

I smile, starting to text back. They both promised to go to class early for me to make sure their laptops worked with the projector. As much as it soothed my anxiety, I was also just glad they'd be there before me. This way I could just pretend I was walking to meet them and not on my way to speak in front of the whole class.

> I'll show up with two lattes. Promise.

BENTLEY

> Make it a caramel brulée one for A?
> Apparently, he needs the sugar right now.

> Got it!! Leaving soon.

A knock sounds on the suite door, pulling my eyes away from my phone, and I furrow my brow. Calling out for Mira and hearing her responding, "Yeah," from her own bedroom, my confusion grows. I pause my music, tossing my phone down before I head out of my bedroom. Tugging on the sleeve of my sweater, I walk across the living room.

"I thought you guys—" My voice falters as the door moves out of the way and I freeze, ice running down my spine.

Christopher stands in the hallway, a slow smile creeping onto his face.

"Hello, Janette," he sneers, placing his hands on either side of the door frame. I continue to stare at him, trying to figure out why he would be here. "Aren't you going to invite me in?" There's an innocence to his tone that raises my hackles.

"No, I'm not." I say, coming out of my stupor. I cross my arms over my chest, standing firm in the threshold of the suite.

He glowers down at me, eyes narrowing, but just as quickly, another smile falls into place. "I think you're going to want to let me in, babe." He steps forward, pressing into me and forcing me to step out of the way. My stomach turns as he glides past, waltzing into the suite and glancing around.

"Don't call me that," I say, leaving the door open behind me as I turn to watch where he goes.

"Sorry, it's just me, not one of your little boyfriends." He grins as he walks around the living room, looking at everything as if it is the first time he's been here. His eyes fall on the only thing different from the last time he was here, a painting of the moon Mira hung up by the bathroom. He studies it for a moment before turning back toward me. "Do they know about each other?"

I ignore the question and the pit twisting in my stomach.

"What are you doing here Christopher?" I ask, glancing at my bedroom and trying to figure out how to subtly walk toward it and get my phone. I stay standing next to the door though, considering all my options. I could call out for Mira, but I don't know how Christopher would react and I don't want her involved if I can help it.

"I wanted to see your face when the news breaks." He shrugs, leaning against the back of the closest couch to me. "Figured it would feel sweetest seeing your reaction in person."

I shift my weight on my feet, the skin on the back of my neck growing itchy. My hand grips the edge of the door still and I feel my nails dig a little into the wood. "What are you talking about?"

He stands up, pushing off the couch and taking a couple steps toward me. "You really thought you could get away with it, didn't you? Thought they'd never find out. Thought *I'd* never find out." He shakes his head, laughing harshly. His hard eyes meet mine once he's done. "I always knew you were a little slut. The way you always looked at the other guys at my lacrosse games and paraded yourself in front of the cameras at your mom's events." He shakes his head in disgust and my mounting confusion swirls with dread. "I never thought you were this dumb, though, babe. Gotta say you surprised me with this one." He advances toward me with each word, until he's standing over me, hands moving to his pockets as his face grows red.

I freeze again, his words making my forehead wrinkle, as I wonder what the hell he's talking about. But the ominous tone in his voice makes my heart thunder as my limbs lock into place.

"I caught you," he hisses, pulling a hand out of his pocket and running the tip of his finger down my cheek. I turn away from his touch, the feeling cold and unwanted. He laughs, leaning closer anyways. "I figured out you were seeing them both," he whispers, his breath fanning across my skin and making me nauseous. My eyes whip back up to his. "And, I have proof." He pulls his phone out, scrolling through before turning it around. A picture of me kissing Bentley in the snow yesterday glares at me from his phone screen. My stomach drops as he flicks his thumb to the right, displaying a picture of me and Axel kissing over the candlelit dinner table from last week after our drive back to the Coast.

My eyes flick up to his, arms falling limply to my sides. "What did you do?"

He laughs again, the sound cracking through the space between us. "There's the face I wanted to see." He pockets his phone, walking back over to lean against the couch, arms folded in satisfaction this time. "Those pictures should be in the tabloid releases in about," he lifts up his phone, checking the time. "Three minutes. And once the bigger outlets realize that's Heather and Michael Marshall's only son..." He shakes his head, whistling. "You're going to be a trending topic. Can't wait to see what Sandra thinks of your *extracurricular activities*. I'm sure this won't affect her reelection campaign at all." He twirls his hand through the air, cruelty lining every angle of his elated face.

All the air leaves my lungs and my hand comes up to cup the side of my neck. I rip my eyes off his smug face, trying to drag in breath. No air comes in or out and my thoughts crash together like tidal waves. Tabloids. Trending. Reelection.

Fear pounds through my veins, pressing against my skin from the inside.

Christopher continues to prattle on. "I'm sure these two

aren't the only ones. How many more men are there, Janette? Did one of them find out about me and that's why you decided to end things? Couldn't keep stringing them all along when you had such a publicly known boyfriend, huh?"

The sound of footsteps breaks through my rising panic and call my eyes away from the floor. I look past Christopher, watching Mira walk into the living room as she finishes tying her hair up. "Who was at the d—" Seeing Christopher, she pauses, looking over at me. "What is he doing here?"

"Can you text Bentley for me?" I manage to push out, semi-normally. Reaching for my practiced smile, I feel it waver a bit as I say, "Let him know I'm going to be a little late to class." I force the smile to stay in place, feeling like my eyes are pushing against my skull.

Mira glances over at Christopher before nodding. "Sure," she says, walking quickly back into her room with another look at Christopher.

His head swivels back toward me, humor glinting in his eyes. "He won't make it here in time. I'll be leaving right after the news is out anyway. I just wanted to see the look in your eyes as everything comes down around you."

I try to ignore him as a buzzing starts in my ears. Taking a shaky step away from the door, I start to head toward my room, needing to get away from him.

Christopher shuffles his shoulders. "I already warned Dad about pulling funding." My feet stop. "Sandra will probably make you move back home since school has clearly not been a good influence on you." He chuckles, shaking his head and looking at his watch. "One more minute." Standing up straight, he fiddles with his cuffs. "I'm curious, how does it feel to know you're about to be ruined?"

I force myself to continue walking toward my room, the tips of my fingers feeling tingly and numb. "You need to leave," I say, voice surprisingly level.

He laughs behind me. "Don't worry. I'm not sticking around." He walks around the couch, picking up the TV remote. Turning it on, he flicks through channels, the noise making me stop and turn in the doorway of my room. He finds an entertainment news channel, the ribbon on the bottom reading SENATOR'S DAUGHTER TWO TIMING THE MARSHALLS' SON.

The buzzing rachets up to a ringing as I stare at the headline, feeling my stomach drop. I'm still somehow able to hear Christopher's satisfied chuckle. The woman on the screen gleefully reports on my life as the photos Christopher showed me pop up on the screen. I still can't hear what she's saying but my breathing shallows and I stagger against my doorframe, eyes never leaving the screen as I catch myself. Christopher was right. I'm watching all my happiness crash into the ground.

A moment later, Christopher pulls up YouTube and starts searching for Bentley's name. Videos start loading up underneath, most of the titles calling me out by name or calling me "Georgian congresswoman's daughter." My vision swims a little as I feel like I'm going to puke. Christopher's photos of my guys eat up each of the thumbnails. Christopher scrolls through them, a smile growing larger and larger on his face.

"'Janette Davidson cheating on Bentley Marshall with classmate,'" Christopher reads. He looks back over at me. "Let's read the comments, shall we?" He clicks around, pulling up the comments section under a video while I go back to focusing on taking shaky steps toward my phone.

His mocking voice follows me.

"'What a bitch! She thinks she can do better than Bentley Marshall?! Who is this psycho?' 'What a whore.'" He starts laughing gleefully, calling after me louder and louder, the further away from him I get. "'Just another slutty gold-digger, *like her mom*.' These are amazing!" Christopher keeps laughing, reading more and more of the comments as I make it to my desk and finally pick up my phone. It buzzes over and over again, notifications popping up from every social media app I have as I try to get to my texts. Texts start to overlap with the notifications, most from people I haven't spoken to in years, some just asking if we can talk while others spit vitriol through my screen.

I start hyperventilating, the phone seeming to move further and closer away from my eyes as I stare. Dropping it, I let my back slide down the side of my desk and put my head between my knees, closing my eyes and rocking a bit against the wood at my back. It's all over. Flashes of happy moments with Axel and Bentley parade through my bleak thoughts, making my eyes water and chest concave.

It's all over.

"You really thought you could just break up with me and there would be no consequences?" I pick my head up, finding Christopher in my doorway a few feet away. He shakes his head, smile still on his lips. He leans down, getting in my face and baring his teeth. "Good luck with your life, Janette." He spits my name and then chuckles, swiftly standing and turning away from the door to walk out. I hear the TV still playing the YouTube video Christopher turned on as the suite door slams behind him.

My stomach rolls as his words replay over and over in my head, the ringing and buzzing split only by the sound of my phone continuing to ping and vibrate on the floor with more reactions to the first good thing I had in such a long time.

Tears start to blur my vision as I listen to the death of everything we worked to grow and protect. The comments of the video confirm what people will always think of me now. What they will think of me and my guys.

37

BENTLEY

Axel's leg bounces in the seat next to me. I place my hand on it, stopping the motion as I turn to look back at the open doors at the top of the room again. "She'll be here."

He nods, biting his thumbnail and staring at the clock across the room from us. "She's never this late."

"I know," I say, tapping my pen on my laptop again. We'd been here for the last twenty minutes, each of us getting up early to ease Janette's performance anxiety. We'd each texted her asking where she was. Neither of us got a response.

"What if she freaked out? She's been so nervous about this presentation. She's probably still in her dorm having a panic attack." He starts to pack his laptop into his bag.

I put a hand on his shoulder, keeping him in his seat when he tries to get up. Howards closes the doors, walking down the center aisle toward us.

"What are you doing?" Axel hisses. "We need to go find her."

"I don't know why she's not here, but we need to do this presentation for her. She needs this class for her degree."

Howards greets the class, clapping his hands once as he reads out the presenters list for today.

"We'll say she's sick or something and explain it all to Howards after class, but we need to do the presentation."

Axel grits his teeth, nodding once after a moment of searching my face. He shrugs my hand off his shoulder and faces forward again. Howards calls up the first group, and I glance at the back doors again before settling into my seat.

The presentation goes quickly, two of the presenters talking fast while the other keeps a more measured pace. I prop my chin up on my fist, pulling my phone out a bit under my laptop to check if Janette has texted. My hand under my chin falls away as I sit up, pulling the phone out fully when I see a text and three missed phone calls from Mira.

MIRA A.

SOS. Christopher is in our dorm. Get here now.

"We have to go," I say, tapping Axel's chest before I toss my computer into my bag. Axel follows suit, standing with me without question.

"Mr. Marshall, Mr. Clifford. Please sit down. You will present after this group."

"Family emergency," I call over my shoulder as Axel and I head up the aisle to the doors. Bursting out of the room, I turn toward the stairs.

"Where is she?" Axel asks over my shoulder.

"In her dorm." The sound of our shoes on the steps echoes through the empty stairwell. "Mira texted me. Christopher's there."

"*What the fuck?*"

We power walk out of the building doors, the sun momentarily blinding us as it reflects off the snow covering everything in front of us.

"Why the fuck is he even in the state?" Axel exclaims.

"I don't know," I say as we jog down the path toward West Tower. "But I don't want him anywhere near Janette either."

We pass a few people on campus as we rush toward the dorms. Axel pushes up to jog beside me, pulling out his phone and checking it as well. His eyes widen as he reads a notification on the screen and we both slow down.

"What is it?"

"I just got a text from my ex-boyfriend. He said 'tough luck losing out to Bentley Marshall. Let me know if you want to talk about anything' with a winky face." He looks up at me. "I don't know what he's talking about."

I pull out my phone, seeing some random notifications and then a text from my parents' PR manager, Molly. *Call me. We can fix this.* I furrow my brow. "We need to get to Janette. Then we can deal with everything else."

Axel nods and we continue across campus, taking the stairs once we make it into West Tower, rather than waiting for the elevator. Our steps echo again in the stairwell, crashing against my ears as we get closer and closer to Janette and Mira's suite.

Axel pants behind me as I knock on their door, pounding a little harder than I should.

I hear Mira's muffled voice on the other side as her voice comes nearer. "That better be them." The door shoots open, and Mira stands on the other side. "Where have you guys been? I texted you a half hour ago."

I walk past her and Axel rushes toward Janette's room

once he's around Mira. "What happened? Where's Christopher?"

"He left. Right after berating Janette." I head toward her room, heart clenching. Mira's hand lands on my forearm. "He outed you guys, Bentley."

I turn toward her. "What?"

"He had pictures of you with Janette and Axel with her too. He sent them into tabloids. They're saying she's cheating on you."

My hands ball up at my sides as a restlessness whips through me, a need to do something. But too many thoughts pop up and disappear before I can grab one and run with it.

"He read her the comments on a video about it." Mira looks down, releasing my arm. "It was brutal."

I spin and walk straight into Janette's room. She sits on the floor, head between her knees. I notice a tremor in her shoulders and step closer. Axel is sitting beside her, running his hand over her hair while he tries to coax her to look up at us.

"Come on, Blue. Bentley's here now." He looks up at me with worry lines indenting his forehead. "We can deal with this together."

I nod. "Mira told me what Christopher did." Axel sits forward and Janette's eyes peer out timidly over her knees. Tears dampen her face and leak from her red rimmed eyes. She looks up at me with so much fear, making my stomach turn. I kneel in front of her, cupping her cheek and turning her head up further to look at me fully. "This is not your fault."

She tries to shake her head out of my hold, but I bring my other hand up to trap her face between them.

"It is my fault, Bentley!" Her voice comes out dry and off pitch. "Neither of your ex-boyfriends decided to ruin everything." She pulls her face away, tucking it into her knees and tightening her arms around them.

"What did he do?" Axel asks in a low stony voice.

I give him the brief explanation Mira shared with me and his jaw tightens with each sentence.

"I'm going to kill him." He moves to stand, but I reach out and grab his arm, nodding down to Janette when he glares at me. His face falls, arms reaching out to wrap around her. "It's okay, Blue. We can fix this."

"How?" She laughs listlessly, lifting her head again. "Everyone thinks I'm fucking you both behind the other's back. My phone has been going off nonstop since the news dropped. They already know it's Bentley in the one picture. How long do you think it will take for them to figure out who you are?" She looks at Axel with fire in her eyes. "How long until they start berating Layla and Gwen? Uncle Jack? Anyone they can to try to get a quote from that they can use to fan this flame into an inferno. And they'll twist whatever we say to try to fit whatever scandalous narrative they want. Why do you think I did everything my mom wanted me to? This is exactly what I wanted us to avoid!" Fresh tears stream down her cheeks as she huffs at the end of her speech.

"We can fix this, sunshine." Her eyes turn to me, glaring. "Together. Remember?"

"You're both better off walking away now. Save your reputations and leave me to salvage whatever's left of mine."

"We are not leaving you," Axel insists. He looks over at me and I nod, mouth closed as I run through every solution I can think of.

"Christopher ruined everything, Axel." Janette turns, facing him. "If you stay with me, the press will only get worse. They'll start hounding us every time we step off campus, and I refuse to make fools of either of you publicly so unless you want to stay behind closed doors forever, I don't see how this is going to work." Axel's face pinches at her words and my heart falters in my chest.

I grab her chin, pulling her face up to look at me. "Do you want to be with us?"

She gasps, eyes widening. "It's too late, Bentley. People already think—

"I don't care what other people think." I lean in. "Do you want to be with me and Axel?"

"Of course, I do." Her voice breaks and she moves her eyes to the side, trying to look over at Axel too. "I love you." Her eyes meet mine. "Both of you."

"Good." I release her chin, standing up. "Then we're staying together. This will blow over. We just have to wait it out." I cross my arms, contemplating how far Christopher could have gotten and if my Mercedes could catch up to him.

"It's not going to blow over, Bent. The minute any of us are seen together, it will just start up again. Christopher already got a photo of us on campus. How many other students do you think will cash in on a pic of us together? I'm sure your parents aren't going to want to answer questions about your relationship status every time they're interviewed for something."

I shake my head. "Campus has strict rules on paparazzi and exploiting students for tabloid photos. They won't let people take photos of us on campus without legal action. Plus no one around here wants to start that war. I doubt I have the most famous parents here. And I doubt the Coast won't be looking into how that photo got taken." I run a hand through my hair. "I'm going to call Molly and see what we can do."

Axel pulls Janette closer, leaning his head against hers as I pull out my phone. "Don't ever think we won't fight to stay with you, Blue," he whispers. His voice becomes harder with his next sentiment. "And please don't ever give up on us like that again."

She chuckles, more tears falling past her lashes. "I'll try not to, promise. But I don't see a way out of this. Everything outside right now can ruin this."

The sound of my call trying to connect rings in my ear as I frown down at them. "Nothing outside of this right here can ruin it, sunshine. When this is fixed, I'm drilling that into you." She stares up at me with wide eyes while I start to pace.

Molly finally answers my call. "Bentley? I take it you've seen the news?"

"No, actually. But I got a rundown of what's going on. What are our options?"

Axel starts whispering to Janette as she releases her knees, leaning against him. Her phone starts buzzing on the floor near us, and I glance over, seeing a call coming in from her mom.

"Well, depends on the outcome you want." I reach down, picking up Janette's phone.

She sniffles, chin shaking when she notices the name on the screen. "Right when we started making progress," she whispers, and Axel squeezes her shoulders.

"Can you give me a second, Molly?" I pull my phone away without waiting for an answer, swiping Janette's phone to answer the call. "Ms. Davidson? It's Bentley."

"Is she okay? I've been trying to reach her, but she wasn't picking up. We had no idea this was going to run."

"She's panicked. Christopher showed up to rub it in her

face. He's the one who took the photos and sent them in." Janette buries her face against Axel's shoulder.

"Son of a bitch," Sandra murmurs.

"We need a new angle. Hold on I'm going to bring you in on a call with my parent's PR rep." I hang up Janette's phone, pulling my own back up to my ear. "Hang on a second, Molly. I'm going to bring Sandra Davidson into the call." I put the phone on speakerphone, adding Janette's mom to the call.

"I have Pietro here with me," she says once she's connected. "He handles most of my press."

"I was explaining to Bentley that we need to figure out what result we want from this situation. Right now, the media is framing Janette as a cheater, which I'm assuming you're calling to try to change directions on?"

"Of course," Sandra asserts. Janette's head picks up. "My daughter is not getting branded by a ridiculous rumor."

"Molly, have mom and dad filled you in on the actual situation?" I ask, keeping my eyes on Janette.

"Yes, I know you're all together. We can try to spin this, but there's only two options that I can see that might work."

Axel nods. "What are they?"

"Well, we can try to bury the story. Give the press something juicier to latch onto."

"I might have something," Sandra pipes up. "And it would be the perfect way to untangle myself from Christopher and his father during this whole mess."

"But if we do this," Molly warns. "It won't completely get rid of the attention on you three. And it won't restore Janette's reputation. You three would need to be careful in public and wait a few years before you could ever hope to have any sort of normalcy. This would just take the majority of the heat off you."

"What's the other option?" I grit out.

"You three go public." Silence follows her words, the three of us looking between each other as my breathing cuts off.

"I'm thinking a social media campaign. Some posts about how you're all together and whatever else you guys want to share, but the gist being that there is no cheating and you three wish to keep your private lives to yourselves beyond this. We can manage a press release, something encouraging from each of your families and close friends. But you three would do the brunt of it." Axel and I each turn toward Janette. "There'll be even more eyes on you and I'm not saying this will definitely garner support, but it's the only way to kill the infidelity rumors."

I nod and Axel does the same. "What do you want to do, Blue?"

Janette stares at the phone in my hand, clinking her nails against each other. She closes her eyes, taking a deep breath and my hand unclenches.

Her eyes pop open, looking at Axel and me in turn. "We decide together." Her face softens as she smiles at us. "Right?"

Axel beams, hugging her tighter. "Right."

"Right," I finish, feeling the rest of the weight above me start to give.

38

Janette

I fold another pair of socks together, rolling the tops so that the pair doesn't get disconnected in my suitcase. Tossing it in with the rest of my clothes, I turn back to my closet, continuing down my mental packing list.

My phone buzzes on my desk and I glance down to see a text. Rolling my eyes, I drop the shirt in my hands onto my bed and open the notification.

HOTTIE #2

Hurry up. I miss you.

I laugh, texting Axel back about patience and reminding him of the talk we had about changing things in my phone. A picture of his abs pops up on my screen a second later, calling me. I bark a laugh before answering.

"You're two floors away, Axe." I balance the phone between my ear and shoulder, picking up the shirt again. "Why not just come down if you wanted to talk?"

"Blue, you won't get any packing done if I come down there." I roll my eyes while he chuckles. "Remember what happened yesterday when we were left alone in your room?"

I smile, thinking about the slow worshipping Axel decided I needed while Bentley took his Spanish final.

Together, we decided to come out publicly online. Bentley and Axel didn't want to bury the story and wait years to clear the air and I thought the idea would freak me out. But once I weighed the options, I realized I don't want to hide being with them any longer. So once the decision was made, we pulled together a few of the photos Axel took the day before our presentation and wrote out a quick statement that Molly and Pietro approved. And then the joint post went live.

Given the rumors around our relationship, we want to set some things straight. There have been some photos of us leaked recently, without our consent, that started these rumors. They are all false and taken completely out of context.

The three of us are in a committed non-monogamous relationship with each other. No one is cheating and there is nothing scandalous about those photos. Give us whatever label you'd like; we don't really have a name for the three of us other than love. We love each other and though we are making this statement publicly, we want to ask that everyone please respect our privacy.

The photos were cuter than the statement. One of them had me snuggled up to Bentley with Axel's head on my chest as he shot the selfie. Axel kissed my cheek in the next one and Bentley kissed the top of his head in the third, eyes still on the camera as I laughed.

The responses started coming in immediately after we posted it. #loveislove started trending again with mixed results underneath. Bentley showed Axel and I how to curate our notifications, so we stopped getting something every time someone commented or tagged us in posts. We still got some stray texts, Axel's ex Mason being the first to reach out from our high schools to congratulate us. There were some hate comments that made it through, but Molly and Pietro quickly had statements out from Mom and Bentley's parents. Layla and Gwen handled things for Uncle Jack, liking and commenting on the post in support for the three of us.

On campus, the three of us got a few stares, but most things stayed relatively the same. Someone did take a picture of the three of us in class together, making up our missed presentation time in class this morning. Axel went to Howard's office hours right after everything got settled and he let us go last with ten points off for missing our first time slot. I'm sure the photo will end up online and we'll see what the backlash at the Coast is, but at least we'll be able to do it together.

The dean's office did send out an email reminding students of the strict rules against selling photos of classmates and about security being increased due to an uptick in paparazzi trying to get in, so Bentley talked to Mira's brother's friend Royal about getting us extra security when we aren't on campus. I wanted to tell Gwen about it to add to her mafia theory, but Bentley warned me against getting mixed up with the Ravens and her. So, now my new silent friend Lev will be accompanying me on my flight to Georgia and staying with Mom and I until I leave to meet up with the boys in Morocco. Heather and Michael's security will take over after that.

The biggest surprise came from Mom though when she announced that she was stepping down from her position at the end of her term to focus on family and cooperate with the police in their new investigation into SMC Fund

Management. With advice from her lawyer, she came forward with evidence she had on Paul and Christopher for embezzlement and insurance fraud thanks to her close relationship with him as her former backer.

I freaked out and called her when I read the article, but she insisted she wanted to do this, said Christopher doesn't get to fuck over her daughter and get away with it. Her tone reminded me of the mama bear Aunt Tati used to have to hold back whenever someone was mean to Layla or me on the playground. And even though she'll have to change careers, she's a little bit excited to have more time to deal with everything and be present more. Even mentioned that she and Uncle Jack are talking regularly again, and he's mentioned wanting her to meet the woman he's seeing.

The last two days were nothing like I imagined. The world didn't implode, Mom didn't freak out, though her career did end, and even though we got some hate, we ignored the small amount, focusing on the overwhelming positivity not just online but especially from our friends and family.

"Still thinking about how gorgeous my ass is, Blue?" Axel whispers through the phone.

I roll my eyes, dropping the now folded shirt into my bag as I smile. "Eh, it's probably not as hot with my teeth imprints in it right now."

"I would argue, it's even hotter this way."

Walking back to my closet, I take out the last thing on my list and shift the phone to my other ear. "Did you call purely to flirt with me?"

"So, what if I did? I can't randomly call my girlfriend to flirt with her?"

Zipping up the suitcase after I shove my hair ties in the inner pouch, I wait for him to get to the point.

"Are you almost done packing? You're going to have to leave for your flight in an hour and I want to spend the majority of it with you since I won't get to see you or Bentley for ten whole days before Morocco."

I laugh, pulling the bag off my bed and setting the wheels on the ground. "I just finished. I'll be up in a few minutes."

Axel whoops and I hear Bentley's muffled voice in the background. "She's coming in a few," Axel says to him before bringing the phone closer to his face. "We'll see you soon, Blue."

He hangs up and I double check my room, looking for anything I might have forgotten I'll need. My eyes find Dad's photo on my desk, and I smile. "Heading home to see Mom," I tell him. I kiss the tips of my two fingers, pressing them to the glass. "Wish you were here to meet my guys." My heart squelches as I stare at my dad's wide smile and then turn and walk out of the room, shutting the light off as I leave.

I drop my suitcase off by the front door. The bathroom door sits open with the light on, and I can hear the faucet turn on and off after a second. Knocking, I peak my head in when I hear Mira murmur and see her brushing her teeth at the sink.

Heading in, I wrap my arm around her shoulders, squeezing her from the side. "I'm heading out," I say.

Mira smiles at me in the mirror, leaning forward and spitting out her toothpaste. She turns and hugs me back. "I'll see you in a few weeks." I pull back, throat feeling tight as I think about how I'm going to miss seeing her every day. We've hung out a lot more since that first time I told her I was dating Axel. Layla and Autumn have even come over and we had a full-blown sleepover to relax before finals week started. I've gotten used to coming back to the suite and hanging out in the living room together most afternoons.

"Have a really good break, Janette." Mira smiles softly.

"You too, Mir." I smile back. "Text me if you need anything." I wink and Mira chuckles, going back to rewet her toothbrush.

I head back to my suitcase, pulling my coat down and slipping into my boots. Leaving the dorm, I check that I have my key before shutting the door. A few people have their doors open, music playing in the hall. Finals week is over, but we don't have to be out of the dorms for another few days officially. Mira invited me and the boys to a party tonight at her brother's place, but I already had my ticket booked for home.

When I knock on Bentley and Axel's door, only a moment passes before Axel rips it out of the way.

"You took way too long," he complains, grabbing my wrist and pulling me into the suite. Bentley sits back on one of the couches, arms spread wide on either side of him, resting on top of the couch back. He smiles when I regain my balance, dropping my suitcase and coat by the door.

"He's been a nightmare all day. Please make him shut up." Bentley slips an arm around my shoulders when I plop down next to him, pulling me in to kiss the top of my head.

Axel flops down beside me, moving to lay his head in my lap. "We're all going to be apart until Christmas." He wraps an arm around my waist, snuggling into me like a pillow while the lower half of his legs dangled over the arm of the couch. "And even then, the two of us will have to wait another three days until we're with you in Morocco." He reaches over my lap, placing his hand on Bentley's thigh.

Bentley brings his arm off the back of the couch, taking Axel's hand.

"It'll be fine, Axe." I run my fingers through his hair, and he closes his eyes. "Mom wants to spend some time with me, and we did kind of rob Bentley of his family time over Thanksgiving break."

"Yeah, yeah, I guess." Axel squeezes my side. We all sink into the couch, Bentley leaning his chin on my head while he plays with Axel's fingers. Axel pops one eye open, staring up at us. "But we're staying just like this until you have to leave."

I smile, continuing to run my hands through his hair. "Okay, Axe. We'll stay just like this."

EPILOGUE
THREE WEEKS LATER

I flop down onto the four-poster king sized bed, arms splaying out beside me as all the air leaves my body in a long sigh. The plush white duvet contours around me, making me feel like I'm sinking into a cloud. The bed smells like lavender and lemons, probably a freshener spray the maid used after making it this morning. The smell makes me groan and my skin starts to itch with the loss of familiarity I usually get when traveling. The vaulted popcorn ceiling above me fills my vision as I hear Blue and Bent shuffle around on the thick carpet, shutting the door to our room and convening in hushed voices.

"Ideas?"

"I can see if we can get some ice cream sent over?"

"Maybe we should put on that penguin doc he likes?"

"I'd rather just take turns sucking his dick."

I raise up on my elbows, looking at my boyfriend and girlfriend as they stand a foot away, eyes wide. "What do you have against penguins?" I stare Bentley down as he holds his hands up in defense, taking a step back.

"Axel, baby," Blue calls my attention over to her worried face. "What do you need right now?"

I fall back on the bed, another sigh escaping. "A do over."

Bentley comes closer, face invading my line of sight. "It wasn't that bad, Axe."

I move an arm to cover my face, not wanting to see the loving look he and Blue will try giving me the rest of the night. We just spent the last twelve hours traveling from Dad's house to this huge Moroccan mansion to meet Heather and Michael for the first time. And the first thing I did was trip over the entryway. We all laughed it off, but the whole thing just made me feel so off kilter that I hadn't really said a word as they showed us around their vacation rental. Now we were supposed to be freshening up before sitting down for dinner with them, but all I wanted to do was crawl under the covers and hide.

"Seriously, Axel," Janette adds, coming closer. I feel the bed dip on either side of me as they both sit around me. "I doubt they even noticed."

I sit up, arms falling away from my eyes and glare at Blue. "You think they didn't notice me flying through their front door and landing face first in front of them?" I cross my arms, hunching my shoulders.

Bentley leans over, kissing my shoulder and resting his chin on me. "They won't hold it against you, Axe. You tripped. It's not that big of a deal."

I shrug him off. "Your parent's first impression of me is important, Bentley."

Blue starts rubbing my back, shuffling closer to my other side. "They weren't upset or anything, Axel. And we still have the whole week for you to win them over. They're going to love you."

"Easy for you to say." I fall back, laying down again with my arms still crossed over my chest. "They already love you. Heather couldn't stop hugging and fawning over you."

Bentley smirks at her. "I think I'm going to win the bet. Mom will definitely hug you again tonight. April technically only hugged you once. She just never let you go the whole time." He starts laughing and Janette glares at him, making his laughter cut short. "Sorry, right," he says, looking back down at me. "Not the time, my bad."

They both lay down at the same time, cuddling into me and wrapping their arms over me to squish me between them. "They like you, Axe. Grandpa loved you and I'm sure he's told them all about you. It was just an awkward moment." Bentley kisses my shoulder again. "You just need to relax."

Uncrossing my arms, I run my hands over my face. "I just feel like they think I'm an idiot." My throat dries as my eyes start to sting and I squeeze them shut.

"Hey," Bentley calls, sitting up and pulling my hands away from my face. "They do not think you're an idiot. You were excited to meet them. They know that. They are not going to form their entire opinion of you based on a ten-minute interaction." He swipes some wayward strands off my forehead, massaging my scalp as his fingers move through my hair. "I love you and they're going to love you." He leans in, emphasizing his words, "Once they get to know you."

I nod, taking a deep breath. "Okay. I'm sorry, I think all the traveling is messing with me."

"Don't apologize." He lays back down next to me, cheek resting against my shoulder. "You just need to get comfortable. Then you'll be fine."

Blue squeezes me. "What do you need, Axel?" she repeats.

I close my eyes, trying to slow down my racing thoughts. "I feel off kilter. I need to reset," I whisper, dragging my hands over my face again.

"Focus on us. Want us to take your mind off it?" I feel Janette shuffle closer, and her lips start ghosting over my neck.

"I want you to make me feel more in control."

Bentley leans up, and I open my eyes to see him staring at Janette over me. His lips slowly move into a sly smile, heat radiating from his eyes. "I think we can do that." He sits up fully, grabbing the collar of his shirt at the nape of his neck and pulling it over his head.

I sit up on my elbows, staring at his now bare chest. "What are we doing?"

"I don't know," he responds, shrugging as he drops his shirt on the floor. "You're in control."

My eyes widen as I sit up and Janette smirks, lounging back beside me. "I'm in control?" I repeat, testing the words on my tongue.

Janette sits up, rubbing a hand down my back. She leans in, whispering in my ear, "We'll do whatever you want." My head swivels between them, studying their open expressions as I wrestle with what they're giving me. Bentley usually takes on the more dominant role when the three of us are together or if it's even just the two of us. But with Janette one on one, I've gotten to explore my more dominant side and I'd be lying if I said I hadn't thought about getting to be in charge with both of them.

Standing up I turn and face them, both still on the bed looking up at me as they wait for me to say something. Taking off my shirt, I start to unbuckle my pants. "I want to fuck you," I say, looking into Bentley's eyes. He swallows, eyes shuttering as his hand moves to adjust his pants, seeking relief.

"Yes," he hisses, eyes opening to meet mine again. I walk over to my suitcase, unzipping the front pocket and taking out the travel sized bottle of lube I packed for easy access.

Coming back over the two of them, I nod and look over at Janette. "And I want you to fuck him too, at the same time." Bentley curses next to her, but I keep my eyes on Blue, tossing the lube onto the bed behind them. Leaning down, I grip her chin between my fingers, keeping her eyes on me. "I want us working together, me filling his ass while you ride his cock, both of us completely overwhelming him together. You up for that?"

Janette gasps, mouth popping open slightly. Her breath comes in deep and short, and I watch the skin of her décolletage flush.

She nods and I shake my head. "Words, Blue," I warn. Bentley smirks, leaning back on his palms. The movement pulls my attention to the muscles of his stomach, dragging my eyes up across his bare chest.

"Yes, I want that," Janette breathes, pulling my eyes back to her.

"Good." I kiss her lips quickly before releasing her chin. "But I want to make you come first. Take off your dress." I pull my belt out of my pants loops; having forgotten I was working on that in my distracted state.

Janette immediately stands before me, spinning and lifting her hair as she looks over her shoulder at me. "Help me with the zipper, please?" Her eyelashes flutter and I lean forward, kissing her cheek as I slowly pull her zipper down her back. Once down, she shrugs the thin spaghetti straps of the floral dress off her shoulders, still watching me over her shoulder. My hardening cock jumps at her smug little smile, knowing what she's doing to each of us.

Bentley leans forward, placing his hands on her hips, and I step in flush behind her, looking down at him over her shoulder. "No touching." He lifts his hands off her, holding them up defensively as he stares at me with Janette between us. "Good boy," I murmur, moving my hands to her covered waist.

Bentley's pupils dilate as he stares up at me, tongue flicking out to lick his bottom lip. I start revealing Janette's skin inch by inch and Bentley's eyes pop wide as he watches the neckline of her dress lower to reveal her tits.

Her nipples pebble as the air hits them and I leave the dress where it lands, still covering her lower half as it hangs around her hips. Reaching around from behind, I start palming her breasts, making her head fall back against my chest as she arches against my touch. Her skin feels warm and pliable in my hands, making my mouth water. Her eyes close as I play with her, and Bentley's eyes fixate on my hands gripping her six inches from his face.

"Do you want to help, Bentley?" His eyes jump to mine, nodding as his hands clench the duvet at his sides. I pinch Janette's nipples, rolling them between my fingers as she writhes against me, moaning. "Should I let him help, Blue?"

She nods feverishly, curls rubbing against my chest. "Yes," she hisses.

I lean down, continuing to play with Janette's breasts while sucking on the skin below her ear. "No," I say, keeping eye contact with Bentley from behind her. "I want him to watch." Standing back up, I reach out, gripping the back of Bentley's head and pulling him up off the bed. "Pants off."

His hands instantly fall to the button of his jeans, popping the metal and tugging down his zipper. I hold his head back while he moves, our eyes on each other the whole time. He shuffles his jeans down his hips, pulling his boxers with them, but gets stuck, unable to push them down further without making me pull his hair. "Keep going," I whisper. Janette leans against me, an inch of space between her and Bentley as she watches him shudder.

Bentley starts bending slowly, my grip becoming taunt as he rids himself of his clothing. He groans when his hair starts to tug, picking his feet up to get his pants off his calves, but keeping the pressure on his scalp. I smile when he stands back up, naked and hard in front of us.

The power I hold right now makes me feel giddy. "Go lay down against the headboard." I release him and he immediately turns around, making my head spin. My hands move down to Janette's bare waist, gripping her against me while we watch him crawl across the bed. He ends up against the headboard, eyes alight and chest heaving. I love him following my commands, and it looks like he's enjoying the role reversal too. His hand moves toward his hard dick, stroking himself as Janette and I watch and the temperature in the room increases.

"Hands off," I call, making him groan as he releases his cock. Janette shivers against me, a smile lifting her lips. "I want them above your head. You're going to watch me make her come."

"Fuck," Bentley whispers as his head falls back, eyes closing. He slowly reaches his arms over his head and grips the hardwood headboard behind him. He takes a second before his eyes pop open, glaring at the two of us as he waits his turn.

"Good boy," I repeat, smirking when his cock twitches against his stomach. "Keep your hands there." I shuffle Janette to the edge of the bed. Placing a hand on the center of her back, I push her torso down flat against the bed. She moves her face to the side, leaving her hands flat against the duvet on either side of her head and wiggling her ass a little. Her hair splays out around her, curls falling haphazardly across one another.

Stepping up behind her, I smooth my hands over her bare back, grabbing her dress and pulling it over her hips to let it fall at her feet. She giggles when I glide my hands over her ass, a black thong the only material left on her body. I pull the side of it away from her body, letting it snap back against her skin and making her squeak. "Something funny, Blue?"

She shakes her head, eyes wide and mouth open. I roll her thong down over her hips as I slowly kneel behind her. Bringing the underwear down to her ankles, I let it fall to meet the dress. "Look at Bentley, love. I want you both to keep your eyes on one another the whole time." I hear more than see Janette tip her head back to look up at Bentley while I push her legs farther apart with my hands on her inner thighs.

Trusting they'll follow my directions, I lean in, parting her from behind with my tongue. Her legs shake and she inhales sharply as I bury my face into her further, tongue lapping at her soaked folds. Her taste floods me, savory and addicting as I leisurely lick her, wanting to take my time. She wiggles, pressing back for more pressure when I swipe over her clit and I bring my hands up to knead the flesh of her hips.

"Fuck, Axel. More." I pull back, quickly slapping her ass.

The sound of my hand against her skin echoes around the large white room. She moans. "Please," she adds in a whine, stretching up on her toes for a moment.

I dive back in, sucking on her hard and lapping up everything she gives me enthusiastically. She squirms against my face, moving herself over me as I plunge my tongue in and out of her. Her cries spur me on, and I move my hand across her ass, quickly thrusting two fingers into her and pumping while I suck on her clit. She screams when I start curling my fingers inside her, flooding my mouth and clenching around my fingers as she comes. I continue lapping everything up, working her with my fingers still until she's pulling away, small whimpers leaving her lips.

Slipping out from behind her, I stand up, sticking my fingers in my mouth and licking them off while I stare at Bentley.

He glares up at me. "If you both don't fuck me right now, I'm going to explode," he growls, knuckles white behind him, still on the headboard.

"So impatient," I murmur, smiling. I lean over Janette, kissing her cheek again while she catches her breath against the bed. "Ready for the main event, Blue?" She nods lazily, eyes half closed. I help her up, holding her against me as she stands. Bentley watches us, precum leaking from his tip.

"Go lick him clean while I get undressed," I whisper to Janette, nudging her toward our boyfriend. She crawls onto the bed, grabbing his dick and leisurely licking him from root to tip. His hips stutter underneath her, teeth pressing into his bottom lip as he watches her.

I unbutton my pants, watching the show as I remove them. My cock tents in my boxers, and I palm myself for a moment, giving myself a moment of relief before I drop my underwear too. Placing a knee on the edge of the bed, I move across the bed toward Janette and tap the side of her hip. She pops off Bentley's dick, sitting up and looking at me over her shoulder, waiting for my instruction.

"Hands down, Bentley."

He releases the headboard, sighing with the small release.

"Showtime, Blue." I nod toward Bentley, and she moves over his legs, straddling him while I move in behind her as well. Bentley's hands come up to grip her hips, massaging his fingers into her skin.

"You ready, babe?" she asks Bentley, and he nods. Looking over her shoulder, he meets my eyes.

"I want you inside me." His words zap through my heated blood, electrifying my body. He's always been the one in control and moving inside of me. I don't know if he's ever been with anyone like this, but we've done enough ass play together that I know this won't be the first time he's taken something inside him.

Nodding, I place my hands above his on Janette's waist. "Let's get you situated first." I help her maneuver over him until they're lined up, gripping Bentley as she slides herself across his tip. Bentley groans, gripping her tighter while he waits. Pushing her down with one hand, I hold him at the base as I seal them together, watching him disappear into her slowly. Once their hips meet, I sit back, studying Janette's face as she tips her head back, hair spilling down her back and mouth open toward the ceiling.

"I could watch you two together forever," I mutter. Janette smiles, head still tipped back, waiting for permission to move. "Pass me a pillow, Bentley," I call, moving in closer behind Janette. Once I have the pillow in hand, I tap his hip, pushing Janette down against his chest. "Hips up."

Bentley jostles Janette as he lifts his hips, allowing me to slide the pillow underneath him and prop them up for a bit more leverage. Janette places her hands against his chest, settling in against him at the new angle and making his eyes squeeze shut while he waits.

Grabbing the lube from the bed beside us, I pop the cap and pour a generous amount into my palm. "Do you want her to move, or wait until I'm inside you, Bent?"

"Wait," he pants, eyes opening to look between the two of us. "I don't know if I can hold off if she starts moving right now."

I nod and Janette leans down to kiss him. Using the lube to wet my cock and relieve a little more of my own strain, I pour more over the space where they're connected, shutting the bottle and tossing it away again. My already lubed hand leaves my own skin and meets his, sliding around to spread the liquid around his entrance. He moans as I start pressing a finger into him, meeting his muscles resistance for a moment before he relaxes.

"Good boy," I say again, feeling him clench around my finger and smiling. I watch my finger slowly disappear in him, mimicking their connection from moments ago. Stretching and prepping him, I add another finger, sliding them more easily as he grows comfortable with the sensation. Probing with the tips of my fingers, I move them inside, knowing I found his spot when he lets out a long moan, legs shaking around me. I run my other hand down Janette's back, loving the feel of both of them against my hands.

Pulling my fingers out, I move in, holding my cock to line myself up with his slick hole. "Ready?"

Bentley grunts, one hand leaving Janette's hip to run down my arm softly.

"Words, Bent."

"Yes," he spits out. "Hurry, Axel."

"Can't rush this, love," I say, rubbing my tip against him. He grabs onto my arm and Janette grabs his face, leaning her forehead against his as she holds him inside her.

"Breathe, baby," she whispers, and he nods, taking a deep breath. As he inhales, I press into him, his tight ring of muscles gripping my tip and making me groan in the back of my throat. Continuing forward, I slowly seat myself deep inside him, panting as his tight warmth envelops each inch.

"Christ, you're tight." I move my hand to his hip, letting him adjust to the feeling. "Ready to move, Blue?"

She sits up, skin meeting mine as she leans back against me. Her height allows for my chin to rest on top of her head if I lean down a little and she tips her head back, letting me kiss her forehead. My hand comes up, sliding over her sternum until my palm curves around her throat. She sighs, leaning into my touch and I wrap my fingers more securely around her neck, holding her against me with the lightest pressure.

"Together," I say, looking down at Bentley as he fights to stay in control. His eyes stay closed, breathing short and fast.

Janette hums and I pull back, leaving Bentley slowly as she lifts her hips and places her hands on his stomach to balance herself. I thrust back in at the same time she slams down, all three of us moaning together.

"Fuck, fuck, fuck," Bentley breathes, eyes opening to watch as he holds on to each of us. We set a rhythm, moving together and speeding up as all of us chase our highs. Bentley sucks me in, tight muscles clenching around me in time with my thrusts and making me see stars as I tighten my grip a little on Janette's throat. She cries out our names, hips snapping faster and nails digging into Bentley's skin.

"I'm close," Bentley calls from beneath us, hand tightening on my arm and fingers digging in against muscle. He frantically moves his other hand off Janette's hip and rubs her clit, making her thighs start to shake. She screams as she comes, making me feel the vibrations of her throat against my palm. Bentley squeezes me inside him in a vice grip as he spills into her, hips stuttering beneath us.

I lose all rhythm, slamming into Bentley a few more times before I blow deep inside him, leaning against Janette as she continues to ride her release at a languid pace. We all slow, sweat cooling across our skin. Bentley's hand rubs my forearm as he stares up at us with soft eyes.

"I love you both," he whispers, while his other hand rubs against Janette's thigh as well.

I release Janette's throat, staying seated in Bentley as I start to soften. Leaning over her back and pressing her in against his chest, I kiss him slowly, biting his lip lightly and making him smile. "I love you too," I say, pulling back. Janette stays laying against his chest, face nuzzling into the side of his neck. I kiss the center of her back. "And you Blue. I love you too." She hums, eyes closed and breathing deeply. I smile, slipping out of Bentley. He groans at the loss, his eyes closing as I watch my cum run out of him. His own mixture with Janette already seeps down and mixes in.

I get up and walk to the ensuite, wetting a white washcloth and coming back to clean them up. Lifting Janette's hips, I separate them, more cum running down as she rolls to the side, snuggling in against him. I wipe each of us down, bringing the washcloth back to the bathroom before I return to the bed and pull the duvet over us as I lie down on Bentley's other side.

Bentley leans over, kissing my forehead. "Feeling better?"

I hum, entangling our legs under the blanket. "Feeling sore?" I say and chuckle.

He rests his cheek against my forehead. "I feel great," he says.

Janette sits up suddenly. "Do you think your parents heard us?"

Bentley shakes his head, reaching out to run his fingers lightly across her skin. "They're on the other side of the house. They didn't hear anything."

She nods, crawling back to the end of the bed and fishing around on the floor, ass on display for the two of us.

"What are you doing?" Bentley asks as she sits up, crawling back toward us, phone in hand.

"Setting an alarm. We still have another hour and a half till dinner. I'm thinking thirty-minute nap, then I'll need to get up and shower and get ready." She settles back in against Bentley, tucking the covers up under her chin.

He moves to wrap an arm around her, holding her to his side. "Sounds perfect."

A quiet moment goes by, and I settle in, closing my eyes.

"You know," Bentley says quietly, voice lighter as we relax. "The showers here are big enough for three."

Janette and I laugh, Bentley smiling between us. I kiss his chest and burrow my face against his skin, surrounding myself in his heady post-sex scent. "We can have shower sex another day. I want to be able to stand this time when we see your parents again."

Bentley laughs and Janette's hand stretches out across his chest to squeeze my arm.

"I'm good guys. Thank you for that." I smile. "I feel normal again."

"You were normal before, babe. Just nervous." Janette's hand soothes my skin as she speaks. I nod against Bentley's shoulder, feeling their reassurance settle into my chest in a comforting warmth.

We all drift off, spending the next thirty minutes wrapped up together as we decompress. When Janette's alarm goes off and we disentangle, Bentley groans.

"Come on, Bent," I say, pulling him into the bathroom and over to the deep freestanding tub. "Let me teach you about bottom aftercare." I spin the taps, sitting on the edge and testing the water temp as I read the container of bath salts on the side. I check for Epsom salt in the ingredients list, making sure this will soothe him rather than just add fragrance. "And then I'll go impress the fuck out of your parents."

"There's my cocky boyfriend," Janette calls, stepping into the glass walled shower on the other side of the room. "Thought we lost you for a minute there."

"Confident, Blue. I'm confident not cocky." I pour the salt into the bath, spreading it around and watching it make the water fizzle as the tub fills.

Bentley steps in, sliding down the back and wincing a little when he sits. "Whatever you say, Axe."

"That's right." I lean in, kissing him before I lean back, still sitting naked on the edge. "Whatever I say." I wink and Bentley narrows his eyes as Janette laughs behind us.

"We'll see," Bentley mumbles, grabbing my arm and pulling me over the edge of the tub.

Contentment settles into my bones, and I smile, letting myself fall into the water, comforted by the fact that I have both of them. That I love both of them. And feeling how much they love me.

THE END

Next up is the following standalone story in the Imperium Coast series, GREEN LIGHT.

WHAT'S NEXT?

Thank you so much for reading TRUE BLUE!

If you liked it, please leave a review! Your support means everything to me.

Want more Janette, Bentley, and Axel? Check out my website for access to a bonus epilogue.

Curious about what happened between Autumn and Ramsey? Sign up for my newsletter at alaciahalebooks.com for a sneak peek at the next couple in the Imperium Coast series.

GREEN LIGHT is a MF enemies to lovers, he falls first and harder, best friend's brother romance coming Summer 2025. Want to know more? Visit:

AlaciaHaleBooks.com

ACKNOWLEDGMENTS

Thank you so much to you, the reader, for taking a chance on my debut! This book has been the culmination of years of silent, independent rumination and writing, but also an abundance of support. So, I want to take the time to thank the people that helped make this book possible.

Grace, Mitch, Cat, and Alex: thank you forever for your constant friendship and support. Thanks for letting me talk about all my random interests and hyper-fixations and all the people I've made up in my head. And thanks for believing in my overconfidence in being able to do all this myself.

Kayla: thank you immensely for being my alpha reader. Your support kickstarted this whole journey and your excitement for this series is the whole reason True Blue exists. Thank you for letting me bounce ideas off you when I randomly question everything and letting me talk through the crazy jumble in my head so that I can get it down on the page.

Rachel and Kristen: thank you for reading my words and for your encouragement. Your excitement for the little steps I've slowly taken toward this has helped propel me forward each time.

Kristin, Chelsea, Alissa, Christina, Desiree, Madison, Taylor: thank you so much for all of your advice and critique time in Scotland. That trip was a major reset for me creatively, but your care and excitement for story and craft was absolutely awe-inspiring and I will be forever grateful for the time we spent together in that haunted attic 🖤

Thank you again to anyone who has taken the time to read my words. Publishing a book has been a dream since I was a kid and getting True Blue to this point has been a fun, frustrating, crazy process, but I hope you enjoyed the end product!

ABOUT THE AUTHOR

Alacia (pronounced uh-lace-ee-uh) Hale is a contemporary romance writer with a penchant for messy and angst-ridden chaos characters. She loves writing stories filled with devotion, banter, and spice, a mixture that often leads down some intense and twisty paths. When she is not writing, you can find her drawing, travelling, or trying to keep another doomed plant alive. She currently lives in Upstate NY with her best friend, grumpy black cat, crazy orange kitten, and a head full of fictional people.

Want to keep up with everything Lacy and her future releases? Sign up for her newsletter to get regular updates.

ALSO BY ALACIA HALE

<u>The Imperium Coast Series</u>

True Blue: A Why Choose University Romance

Seeing Red: A First Chance University Romance

Green Light: An Academic Bully Romance

Yellow Card: A College Hockey Romance

White Knuckled

Grey Area

Red Duet Part II